A WHOLE NEW BALLGAME

Somewhere on the fortieth toss, the ball I was throwing bounced past the edge of the manicured lawn and down some steps leading to the rocky beach. Tipper bounded after it, racing on her little corgi legs past the thistles, foxtails, and thorn bushes, until she plunged clear out of sight and disappeared.

After a minute or so, I got up to see where Tipper had gone. As I reached the edge of the lawn, I gave a sharp whistle and the dog suddenly came zooming up the stairs. She had a mud-stained white yachting cap in her mouth. When she saw me she stopped, sat, and dropped it at my feet.

"Good girl," I said, just out of habit, then picked up the hat. The back of it, which is where the stain was, felt warm and sticky to the touch. That's when I realized it wasn't mud the hat was stained with.

It was blood.

Praise for the previous Jack Field Mysteries

"The most perfect book . . . beautifully written, fast-paced, and engrossing. What could be better?"
Delia Ephron, screenwriter of *You've Got Mail*

"Not only a great mystery novel, it should also be sold in every pet store in America."
Kevin Behan, author of *Natural Dog Training*

Books by Lee Charles Kelley

To Collar a Killer
Murder Unleashed
A Nose for Murder

TO COLLAR A KILLER

LEE CHARLES
KELLEY

AVON BOOKS
An Imprint of HarperCollinsPublishers

This is a work of fiction. Names, characters, places, and incidents are products of the author's imagination or are used fictitiously and are not to be construed as real. Any resemblance to actual events, locales, organizations, or persons, living or dead, is entirely coincidental.

AVON BOOKS
An Imprint of HarperCollins*Publishers*
10 East 53rd Street
New York, New York 10022-5299

Copyright © 2004 by Lee Charles Kelley
ISBN 0-06-052495-2
www.avonmystery.com

First Avon Books paperback printing: December 2004

Avon Trademark Reg. U.S. Pat. Off. and in Other Countries, Marca Registrada, Hecho en U.S.A.
HarperCollins® is a registered trademark of HarperCollins Publishers Inc.

Printed in the U.S.A.

10 9 8 7 6 5 4 3 2 1

For James and Sue

Acknowledgments

Beaucoup thanks to my brother James and my sister Sue. Their help has been invaluable in completing this book. Their love and familial support have been a godsend.

Thanks to New York's second-best dog trainer, Jason Herman. And huge thanks to Kelly Reilly, the best dog walker in New York. (She also lent me her computer—thanks, Kel.)

Thanks to Melanie Weiss and Frances Kuffel. Melanie makes sure I get my facts straight, Frances makes sure I get my story sold. Thanks too to Erin, my editor, who makes sure I keep coloring between the lines (at least *most* of the time, right Erin?).

As always, a special thanks, and a great big bone, to Fred and all his doggie pals.

Thanks also (in alphabetical order) to Chuck Berry, Raymond Chandler, Dashiell Hammett, Garrison Keillor, Larry McMurtry, Armistead Maupin, Johnny Mercer, Joni Mitchell, J. D. Salinger, William Shakespeare, Mark Twain, Townes Van Zandt, my mother and father (both writers), and to anyone else who has ever inspired me to write.

Thanks too to Tad Danielewski, who taught me how to improve my talent. And to a nineteen-year-old girl named

Tierney, who, years ago (we're both older now), at two in the morning, after a really awful party somewhere in Salt Lake City, put her head on my shoulder and said four simple words that crystallized something important for me:

"Lee," she said, yawning, "tell me a story."

Tell me a story, she said. So I did.

Half an hour later she said, "That was great. Now tell me another one."

"No, Tierney," I said, "I'm *tired*."

"Just one *more*?"

"Tierney, I have to go to *work* in a few hours." (I was a disc jockey at the time and had to be on the air at six A.M.)

"Please?"

"Well, okay. Once upon a time there was this girl who wouldn't go to sleep . . . aren't you tired?"

"Sshhh. Tell me more about the girl who wouldn't go to sleep."

"Well, she was very beautiful but very annoying."

"Un-huh. And then what happened?"

What happened was she went on to become a cover girl in Europe and is now a world-famous photographer. Me? I write detective stories and train people's doggies in Manhattan. We still keep in touch from time to time. She sometimes calls me late at night (New York time) and I tell her stories.

Disclaimer

The following is a work of fiction. There is no such place as Rockland County, and no village named Perseverance, ME. All of the situations and characters are imaginary.

Only the dogs are real.

"You get fond of dogs.
You even like to watch them pee."

Raymond Chandler,
The Little Sister

Prologue

I don't think I ever told you the story of how Jamie and I met. It's kind of charming too, at least the way I tell it:

Shortly after I bought the kennel, my foster son Leon got bit one day accidentally by a rambunctious boxer named Lex. There was a large enough tear in the fleshy part of the hand just below the thumb that I thought it wise to make a trip to the hospital, where it just so happened that Jamie—looking adorable in her blue scrubs—was doing a rotation in the ER.

Once she examined the bite and gave Leon a shot of lidocaine to numb the hand prior to a surgeon coming by to stitch it back together, I took her out of the examination room and into the hall.

"What is it?" she said.

"I need to speak to you about something in private."

I grabbed her elbow and took her into the stairwell, where I suddenly, and inexplicably, kissed her. A nice, sweet kiss—nothing major, but enough of a deal to where she felt it necessary to slap me immediately afterward. Softly.

"What the hell?" she said. "I don't even know your name!"

"It's Jack," I said. "Jack Field."

"Jamie," she introduced herself, then grabbed my T-shirt (it was summertime) and started kissing me back.

We did that for a little while, then I said, "I think I'm going to need your phone number." She gave it to me and I wrote it down on a scrap of paper then gave her my business card.

"What's this for?"

"I'm an idiot," I explained. "Actually, I'm a kind of genius in some ways, but I'm an idiot about most of the practical things in life and, knowing me, I'll probably lose this"—meaning the scrap of paper—"even though the way I feel, these are the seven most important letters in my life."

"Um, those are numbers, Jack."

"See what I mean? And I love how you say my name."

"Jack, Jack, Jack . . ." she said, kissing me some more. "What exactly is going on here, do you know?"

I shrugged. "My feeling is that somewhere in the future we're madly in love, and right now we're just feeling the vibrations rippling backward down the time line."

"I don't think that makes any sense, but I think you're absolutely right. By the way, I'm married."

I took this in for a moment then collapsed on the stairs.

She put her hand on my head. "It's not that serious, Jack. I'm getting a divorce. We're legally separated."

I looked up. "Oh, that's good. Can I see you tonight?"

"Sure, what time?"

I stood up. "Seven? Eight?"

"Eight's fine. We can do more kissing, if you want."

"I really do.'

"But no sex."

I nodded. "I can handle that."

"I just don't want you to think I'm that kind of girl."

"I don't think you're *any* kind of girl."

"What do you think I am?"

"The one and only girl. I mean, don't get me wrong, if you'd said no just now, or kept slapping me, I wouldn't have immediately gone home and hung myself, but I have a feeling I would have never been completely happy for the rest of my life."

She sighed and kissed me again.

Of course, when *Jamie* tells the story, all that happened was I hinted around for a bit then shyly asked for her phone number, and called her a few days later. We went out to dinner the next week. I guess I have a pretty active imagination.

However, the rest of this story is true. Trust me.

1

I was bored out of my skull but couldn't go anywhere until Jamie came back with the boat, so I was sitting in a wooden lawn chair at the far end of Zita Earl's backyard, drinking a Sam Adams, and playing a game of fetch with a red-and-white Welsh Pembroke corgi named Tipper. I didn't hold the dog's name against her; she'd been named by our hostess—Jamie's aunt Zita (I suspect after an invisible childhood friend)—and there was nothing either the dog or I could do about it now.

I *did* blame myself, however, for having no one to relate to but a four-legged critter. Jamie had asked me earlier—after we'd finished our grilled lobster and corn on the cob, and after we'd beat everyone else there at badminton for the sixth time— if I wanted to go with her to pick up her father, Jonas, and his wife, Laurie, so they could come watch the fireworks with us from the comfort of Aunt Zita's private island; supposedly the best spot in the State of Maine to spend the Fourth of July. But I'd gotten myself embroiled—as usual—in a heated discussion about dogs; this time with Dale Summerhays, the crazy old bird who runs the Mid-Coast Animal Rescue League.

"We're sponsoring a mandatory spay/neuter bill in the state legislature again this year, Jack," Dale said, swirling the ice in her gin and tonic. "I hope you'll help get it passed."

I tilted my head and was about tell her what she could do with her damn bill when Jamie read my mind and stopped me.

"Jack?" She put a hand on my knee. "Did I tell you that Aunt Zita has offered to let us get married here? On her island?"

She had a glass of Perrier and lime in one hand. She was wearing white short-shorts—which nicely accented the tan of her legs—and a faded denim cowboy shirt with pearl buttons, over one of my old navy blue NYPD T-shirts. Her long, dark chestnut hair was held back by a turquoise bandeau, which heightened the loveliness of her brown eyes. It also matched her earrings.

"I think it would be a wonderful place for the ceremony." She twirled the Tiffany engagement ring on her finger and gazed out at the harbor and the far-off lighthouse at Pemaquid Point. Then she sighed, looked down, and stabbed at her drink with a plastic straw. "If we ever *do* get married, that is."

I looked at Dale. "We haven't set the date yet." Then I put my hand on the back of Jamie's long, lovely neck and said, "It *would* be wonderful, honey. In the summer. Just perfect. But what if we want to get married in February?"

"In February? Why would we get married in February?"

"I think he means on Valentine's Day," Dale said. "Don't you, Jack?" She brushed a few wisps of gray hair away from her sharp, aquiline face. Her watery blue eyes sparkled.

Jamie *ahhed* and said, "Jack Field, that is so romantic."

I agreed with her; it *was* romantic. "Plus, your divorce was finalized in February and I proposed to you in February. It just seems to me that one year is the perfect amount of time to wait, all things considered." I didn't tell her it would also give me another seven months or so to adjust to the idea of being married. Not just to Jamie, to *any*one.

Dale took a sip of gin and tonic. She wore a beige linen shift and a straw hat with a coral ribbon. She kept her dark glasses on even though the sun had gone behind some clouds, causing the wind to kick up a little. The green canvas umbrella over our table flapped noisily, and the loose folds of my Hawaiian-style summer shirt—decorated with the old red and brown Schlitz beer logo—fluttered around my torso.

Jamie put down her drink and said, "Well, I think I'd better go pick up Dad and Laurie now. Want to come along?"

"Sure," I said.

"At any rate, Jack, about that bill," Dale looked at me, shading her eyes as I stood up, "I hope you'll have everyone who comes to your kennel sign one of our petitions."

"Well, the problem is, I don't actually believe in—"

"Of course he will," Jamie said, putting an arm around my shoulder, *and* a hand over my mouth. She gave me a warning look. "Won't you, Jack?"

I took her hand away. "No, I won't. Frankly, I think the whole practice of spaying and neutering dogs is barbaric and inhumane."

"How can you say that?" Dale was outraged. "Surely, as a dog trainer you know that dogs are much easier to control, not to mention healthier, when they've been—"

"What, castrated? Surgically mutilated?"

"Oh, I see. It's a male macho thing."

"The hell it is." I sat down. "And in my experience—"

"Jack—" Jamie tugged at the back of my shirt.

"—dogs have *fewer* behavioral problems—honey, let me finish—and live happier, healthier, and longer lives—"

"How can you *say* that?" Dale said.

"—when their healthy sex organs are left intact!"

"Jack, we really should get going."

"Nonsense! What about ovarian and prostate cancer?"

"What about cancer of the liver? You want to cut out a dog's liver on the off chance he might get cancer one day?"

Jamie walked a few steps away. "Jack? I'm leaving?"

"Oh, you're impossible. The shelters are full of unwanted animals and all you can think about is your own damn testicles."

"You know, if you're so worried about overpopulation—and who isn't—then why not call for mandatory vasectomies?"

"Vasec—"

"It doesn't interfere with the dog's natural hormonal development and it's much less invasive."

We went on this way, back and forth, like the umbrella, flapping in the wind. By the time we'd finished, Jamie was long gone to her father's house in Christmas Cove, and Dale Summerhays was no longer talking to me.

She was talking *about* me, though; I could tell. I could see her on the screened-in back porch, yakking with her cronies, occasionally casting accusatory looks toward my lawn chair at the other end of the yard. She was also gesturing wildly with her gin and tonic. You'd think I'd know by now: never argue with an "animal rights nut" about anything. Don't get me wrong. I'm totally committed to treating dogs humanely. I just don't think spaying and neutering them qualifies.

So there I was, playing fetch with Tipper. At least *she* was having fun. She would bring the ball to me and take a few steps back, flashing her brown eyes and wiggling her tush—Pembrokes are the brand of corgi born without a tail—and then, when I'd throw the ball, she'd go after it as fast as she could (which was pretty fast for a dog with practically no legs), growling and taking it in her mouth happily in mid-stride.

At one point some of the little kids came over and started climbing in my lap, crawling all over me, and tugging on my beard, begging me to let them play with Tipper.

"Let me throw one!"

"No! Let me!"

"I asked him first!" and so on.

So I let them have a few throws until somebody over by the house shouted something about how the ice cream was ready and they all disappeared like they'd never been there at all.

After they'd gone, Tipper and I went back to our game, and somewhere on about the fortieth toss the ball bounced past the edge of the manicured lawn and down some steps leading to the rocky beach. Tipper bounded after it, racing on her little corgi legs past the thistles, foxtails, and thornbushes, until she plunged clear out of sight and disappeared.

I sat there, waiting for her to come back, swatting at midges and mosquitoes, and trying to tune out the quiet buzz of contempt radiating at me from the back porch.

Then, after a minute or so, I got up to see where Tipper had gone. As I reached the edge of the lawn, I gave a sharp whistle and the dog suddenly came zooming up the stairs. She had a mud-stained white yachting cap in her mouth. When she saw me, she stopped, sat, and dropped it at my feet.

"Good girl," I said, just out of habit, then picked up the hat. The back of it felt warm and sticky to the touch. That's when I realized it wasn't mud the hat was stained with. It was blood.

"Okay, Tipster," I said, wiping my hand on my blue jeans, "show me where you found it."

2

I followed her down the steps—a seemingly random collection of rocks that had actually been put in place quite deliberately to make it easier to get down to the "beach," which wasn't a beach at all, really, but a narrow, crescent-shaped swath of pebbles and rocks (which is what passes for a beach in Maine, pretty much anywhere north of Portland).

Halfway down I had to push aside some branches on a thorn-bush, and one of them bounced back and hit me in the face, scratching my cheek. I put my hand up and felt something wet. I was bleeding slightly. I wiped the blood on my jeans then continued down the steps.

As I did I looked out at the jade water crashing against the iron-and-rust-colored rocks of a neighboring island, and the white sailboats floating off in the sun-dappled distance. I suddenly felt all the stress leave my body; at least for a half a second. Then I sighed, took a long deep breath of salty air and felt another wave of tension wash out to sea. That didn't last either. I knew Jamie was going to be back soon—mad as hell at me for ruining her Fourth of July—and there would be nothing I could do about it until next year, maybe; if I was lucky.

Meanwhile, Tipper had gone ahead, around a big boulder, roughly five feet tall, about ten yards or so from the shoreline. She was still barking, so I followed her voice around the big rock, and that's where I found the body.

I immediately kneeled next to him and put a finger against the carotid artery in his neck. There was no pulse, although he was still warm to the touch.

I stood up and took a look at him. It wasn't my job, and it certainly wasn't any fun—finding a body never is—but *somebody* had to take a look at him, and I was the only one there, so I got elected.

He was a white guy in his late fifties, though it was hard to tell his age for sure since he was lying facedown on the rocks, his left hand and arm under his body, his right arm outstretched northeast of his head, with his hand closed around an object of some sort, maybe a rock. He was wearing canvas deck shoes—navy blue in color—a pair of white shorts and a navy blue cotton piqué polo type shirt. His clothes were all soaking wet, as if he'd swam to shore fully clothed. There was no blood anywhere that I could see.

This presented a number of interesting questions: Who did the hat with the blood on it belong to? And where were they? And why were they bleeding?

There were no knife wounds or bullet holes or any other obvious indications of foul play that I could detect. The guy was just dead.

Tipper was still barking, so I told her to shush. Then I looked out to the bay again, to see if I could spy any sailboats, yachts, launches, runabouts, or cabin cruisers speeding away.

All the vessels I could see seemed very lazy, leisurely, and nonchalant, and not at all intent on fleeing a possible crime scene. A vacationing couple on one of the nearby sailboats was taking turns shooting home videos of one another. The boat had a brightly colored, turquoise and orange striped sail. The only boat that looked even mildly suspicious was a fifty-foot yacht whose stern was facing me, meaning that she was headed away from the island. She was at least a hundred yards off, with hardly any wake that I could see, which indicated that she was in no particular hurry to go anywhere. I couldn't read her name from where I stood.

I didn't have my cell phone with me (I think it's rude to bring your cell phone to a party or any other social gathering, though don't go by me; I didn't exactly flunk etiquette in college, I just got an incomplete), so I knew I'd have to go back up to the house to call Jamie and the police. I didn't relish the idea of telling Aunt Zita and her friends about the party crasher who'd washed up on the beach. Nor did I look forward to telling Jamie what I'd found. She didn't make it a habit of carrying her ME's kit around with her, which meant she'd have to drive clear back to her new apartment in Rockport and root around in the packing boxes to get it. Talk about ruining her Fourth of July.

"Okay, Tipper," I sighed, "let's go call the police."

She ignored me and began barking at the body again.

I took one last look around, to see if I could spot any shell casings, blood spatter, or any other evidence of the crime—if there *was* one—but saw nothing out of the ordinary except some polyurethane ropes that had probably fallen off a boat somewhere out in the harbor and washed up on the island. The Crime Scene Unit was going to have a hell of a time with this, I thought.

There was at least *one* item of curiosity, at least in my mind, if not in Tipper's. I finally figured out what she was barking at: the guy's hand. What was he holding in it?

I knelt down again, and as I did I noticed the bottom half of a tattoo on his upper arm. The rest was hidden under the sleeve of his polo shirt. I could just make out part of an anchor, meaning it was probably a Navy emblem. I didn't bother examining the tattoo, though. I just pulled the man's fingers back to see what he was holding in his hand.

"Well, what do you know?" I said to Tipper.

It was her tennis ball.

3

I went up to the house and called the police, left Tipper inside, then came back down to the beach alone and waited for the cops to arrive. In almost no time there were half a dozen police boats bobbing in the water surrounding the edge of the gunhole where the dead man lay. I gave the bloodstained yachting cap to the first state trooper to come ashore via dinghy. He thanked me and put it into a plastic evidence bag. Then he explained to me what a gunhole is: it's a tiny, semicircular cove, usually too small to navigate with a boat. This unusual geographic forma- tion is not peculiar to the State of Maine, although the nomen- clature apparently is.

Speaking of geography, Aunt Zita's island is shaped more like a rectangle than a circle, but for orientation purposes let's say that the dock—which faces the town of Boothbay Harbor and is a few steps down from the front of the house—is located at twelve o'clock. If so, then the gunhole, where the dead man lay, would be at four-thirty.

Most of the cops and crime scene investigators—at least ten or fifteen of them—came ashore at the main dock, schlepped past the house, ignoring (I imagine) the questions coming from Aunt Zita's party guests, then trudged across the backyard and down the rocky steps to the beach.

I gave my statement twice; once to the first trooper who'd

come ashore via dinghy, and again, several times, to a State Police detective named Sinclair, who'd come the long way 'round.

Sinclair was shortish, in his early fifties, with dishwater hair, moist brown eyes (probably from allergies, I thought), and a dry, laconic manner of speech. He seemed laid back, not at all like a cop; more like a guy who runs a record store.

After the third or fourth time I'd told him what had happened, he cocked his head, as if puzzled or perplexed, and said, "Let me get this straight—you threw a tennis ball down to the beach by accident, the dog went after it, and brought you back a bloody hat instead?"

"That's right."

"And then you decided to come down here to do what? Look for your lost tennis ball?"

"Not exactly. As I said, there was blood on the hat."

"Which you just happened to wipe off on your jeans . . ."

I sighed. "Yes. I got some of the blood on my fingers. And yes, I wiped it off on my pants."

"So that's supposed to explain the stain you have there on your thigh?"

"Detective, it's not supposed to explain anything. It's just what happened."

"Un-huh. And what about that cut on your cheek?"

I put my hand at my face. "Oh, that. I cut it on a thornbush when I came down to the beach."

He shook his head, scratched his chin, and scribbled a few notes on a pocket-sized pad, then handed it to me, along with his pen, and had me write down my name, phone number, and address. Then he excused me, suggesting that I go back up to the yard and wait with Jamie, who'd been instructed in no uncertain terms not to go to the beach. The word had come down quite quickly from the Chief Medical Examiner's Office that the body was off limits to her; it had been found by her fiancé on her aunt's property, so she was to exercise extreme caution to avoid the appearance of favoritism or bias. I had a vague suspicion that this meant I was a suspect, though at the time I had nothing to base it on. Nothing except the fact that no matter how many times I told Detective Sinclair what had happened, he just didn't seem to believe me.

Jamie was very sweet about the whole situation, though. When I finally came up the steps, she was waiting for me, ready to hug me and kiss me and hold my hand. What a woman.

I spent some time fielding questions I had no answers to, mostly coming from Aunt Zita and her guests, though Jamie and her father, Jonas, were also curious about the odd situation.

Dr. Reiner, the Chief ME, showed up around sunset, with a small coterie of bustling assistants. Tall, olive-skinned, with a shock of black hair (probably dyed), he cut quite a figure as he strode through the lengthening shadows that fell quietly on the summer grass. He nodded in passing at Jamie, but didn't stop to say hello or kiss her cheek. Me, he ignored completely. He was still pissed, I think, about the Marti MacKenzie case, and how Jamie had, on her own, reopened an investigation that he'd botched. He got a lot of bad publicity over it and nearly lost his job. Four months later, relations between them were still strained.

It didn't help any that she was engaged to me. I was not a very popular figure with some local Maine law enforcement personnel—this in spite of, or possibly *because* of, the fact that I'm a retired NYPD detective. People in Maine are, for the most part, pretty open and accepting of others. Except when they're not. And when they're not, they're *really* not. Like Yakima Canutt, the stunt man for John Wayne in all those old westerns, Mainers can get up on a high horse with astonishing speed and alacrity. Many had gotten on a high horse with me and I was squarely in the "not" category.

At any rate, once the sun went down Jamie began to get goose bumps, so she went inside to grab a pair of sweat pants. While she was gone, one of the CSIs trekked up from the beach and asked me to hold my hands out in front of me so he could get some fingernail scrapings.

"Am I a suspect?" I said.

He shrugged. "We're just collecting trace evidence."

I sighed, shook my head, then held out my hands, and he

scraped under my nails. When he was done he said he needed a swab of the blood on my jeans and, if I didn't mind, a swab of the blood on my cheek to get my DNA. I said he could do both, but added, "It's not the victim's blood on my jeans. It's from the yachting cap and from the scratch on my cheek."

"Just doing my job," he said, dousing the cotton swab with distilled water then rubbing it gently on the bloodstain in a kind of circular motion until it turned pink. He slid the cap up over the cotton tip and closed it, then got out another and did the same thing to my cheek.

It was at this point that Jonas had had enough. "Now see here, young man," he said, with all the authority of a famous neurosurgeon and professor emeritus at Harvard Medical School, and all the pride of a future father in-law, "this is totally out of line. Do you know who this man is?"

The CSI finished swabbing my cheek and said, "Yes, I do. He's someone who may have contaminated the crime scene."

With that, he left.

"It's all right, Jonas," I said. "It's strictly routine."

Jonas fumed some more until Laurie, his wife, tried to calm him down by reminding him of his heart condition. "It hasn't been that long since your surgery, sweetheart."

"I don't have a heart condition. It was a simple valve re- placement and my new valve works perfectly, thank you."

They argued like this a little until Jamie came back, wearing a pair of faded navy sweat pants over her white shorts. Jonas and Laurie filled her in on what had just taken place. She was less an- gry at the cops than she was sympathetic with me.

"Don't worry," I repeated, "it's just routine."

I have to admit, though, I wasn't all that surprised when De- tective Sinclair, along with two uniforms, came hiking up the steps a few minutes later. This was just shortly after the fire- works had started exploding and falling in cascading colors over the bay. There is no way, I think, to explain the kind of calm that came over me as I saw the looks on their faces. I knew what was coming. And even though what they were about to do was wrong, I accepted it completely.

Sinclair made an apologetic face, lit by the sudden red and

yellow explosion of another burst of fireworks, then asked me to turn around and put my hands behind my back so he could put the handcuffs on.

"What is going on?" Jamie said incredulously.

"Apparently I'm being arrested." I calmly turned around and put my hands behind my back.

As he cuffed me, Sinclair told me I was under arrest on suspicion of murder in the death of one Gordon Beeson and did I know my rights.

Jamie gasped. "My god! *That's* who the victim is?"

I turned to Jamie. "You *know* him?"

Jamie sighed sadly and nodded her head.

"So who is he?" I asked.

To me, Sinclair said, "Oh, like you're going to pretend now that you weren't aware of the fact that he's been stalking your fiancée for the past four months?"

"He didn't know," Jamie said. "I never told him." To me, she said, "He is, or was, Ian Maxwell's helicopter pilot."

Jonas said, "No!"

Ian Maxell was an eccentric billionaire inventor, in business with Jamie's father, Jonas. They were developing a new micro-laser technique for doing brain surgery. Jamie had met the dead man, Beeson, when he'd flown her to Maxwell's private island back in February to pick up some papers that he, Maxwell, wanted Jonas to sign. The fact that Beeson was a helicopter pilot might explain the naval tattoo I'd seen on his upper arm. He'd probably flown choppers for the Navy.

Jamie said to Sinclair, "And he wasn't stalking me. He just called me, like four or five . . . teen times to ask me out."

"Wait," I said. "He called you at the ME's Office?"

She nodded.

"And you told Dr. Reiner about it?"

She got an ah-hah look in her eyes. "That's it! I told Dr. Reiner I was having trouble getting rid of the guy and he must have jumped to the wrong conclusion."

"Well, you're certainly rid of him now," Sinclair said.

I said, "It seems to me that Dr. Reiner is jumping to a lot of wrong conclusions," then resisted an impulse to ask Jamie why she hadn't told me about Beeson before, knowing intuitively that whatever answer she gave would only make matters worse. (Me: "Why didn't you tell me?" Jamie: "I was afraid you might get mad." Sinclair: "See there? Even your girlfriend was afraid of what you might do to him once you found out.") No thanks. I kept my mouth shut.

They started leading me off, and Jamie came around in front of us, blocking the way. "Where are you taking him?"

"I'm going to have to ask you to stand aside, miss."

"What!? *What* did you just call me!?" Oh, you should have seen the glorious fury on her face when she said this. Her face was blazing with indignation. "My *name*," she drew the word out, "is Dr. Cutter. And I am an Assistant State Medical Examiner and the Chief of Pathology at Rockland Memorial Hospital."

"We know who you are, Dr. Cutter. Now stand aside."

She didn't budge. "If you won't tell me where you're taking him, then I'm afraid I'm going to have to go with you."

"No you're not, ma'am. I mean, Dr. Cutter. We've been given explicit instructions from your boss to keep the two of you apart so you can't get your stories straight."

"Can't get our stories straight? Can't get our stories straight?" She was about to have an aneurysm.

"Jamie," I said calmly, "it's going to be okay. I just need you to calm down and do a few things for me, all right?"

She nodded, still glaring at Sinclair.

"Okay, first of all take a nice, long, deep breath."

She did: she breathed in and let it out slowly.

"Okay, good. Now call Flynn and Jill Krempetz and let them know what's going on." (Flynn was the Rockland County sheriff, as well as Jamie's ex-uncle in-law. Jill was my attorney.) "And call the TV station and fill them in, as well." (I had just started doing a regular biweekly segment on the Saturday morning show at one of the stations in Portland, discussing dogs and dog training. I was supposed to do a show the next morning, in fact.) "And call the kennel."

"Okay," she sighed. "And don't worry, Jack. I'm going to bail you out as soon as possible. Tonight, if I can."

Sinclair said, "I'm afraid that's not possible. It's Friday night. He won't be seeing a judge until Monday morning."

She took another deep breath and said, "Can you at least tell me where you plan on taking him?"

"The nearest available lockup, I guess," Sinclair said, and looked at the two uniforms. "I don't know, what's that?"

One of the uniforms said, "Rockland County Jail."

Jamie and I smiled at the same time. That was Sheriff Flynn's jail. Sure, I was going to miss most of the fireworks, but if Jamie was able to get ahold of Flynn, and if he had any say in the matter, which he probably would, I'd be home before midnight. Good old Sheriff Flynn.

They paraded me past Aunt Zita and friends and Jamie's cousins and whatnot, and I thought I heard Jonas say to Laurie, "It's strange. He was supposed to come to the party."

"Who, the murder victim?" Laurie said.

"No, Ian Maxwell. Though, I suppose, since . . ."

And that's all I heard.

As they led me off, I'm glad to say that Dale Summerhays, for all her bad humor about my position on mandatory spaying and neutering, kept her head held high and her eyes locked on mine as if proud of how I was comporting myself in the face of this judicial outrage. Bless her. I almost wished I could go over and take back some of the things I'd said earlier.

Tipper followed us all the way down to the dock, barking at the cops and circling around their legs and nipping at their ankles.

"Will someone do something with this dog?" Sinclair said.

Me? I just laughed.

4

It was a nice jail, as jails go. A bit spartan to my taste—the mattress was only half an inch thick and there was no seat on the brushed-steel toilet—but what are you gonna do? There were four cells in all, and none of them had bars, just iron doors, painted white, with a wide, rectangular slot, waist high (to accommodate meal trays), and another smaller slot higher up, which was basically a peephole.

The place was surprisingly vacant for a Friday night, not to mention for the Fourth of July. My guess was that things would start to pick up after the fireworks, and that by the end of the night the jail would be full of D&Ds, DUIs, and the like.

They took my picture: "Turn to the right. Good. Now turn to the left. Good." Then they took my wallet, my money, my belt, my key chain, my flip-flops, and even the shell necklace Jamie bought me when we were on vacation in the Bahamas back in January. (She'd laughed at me and called me a California surfer dude, which I suppose, being from San Diego, I actually was at one time, so I occasionally wear it to please her.)

Then they took my fingerprints, and when that was done—and I'd wiped my fingers clean on some Baby Wipes—they escorted me to an empty cell and clanged the door shut behind me.

It was already after lights out and the only illumination came from the open peephole and the space at the bottom of the door. I paced the cold floor for a while, getting the mad out of my system, or trying to—my calm act was mostly just that; an act, although the truth of the matter is, once the cops get out the handcuffs? it does you no good to argue, debate, or get mad. Guilty or not, they don't give a shit. In fact, the calmer and more cooperative you are, the better they treat you.

Was I furious? You'd better believe it. But the thing about me is that, sometimes the madder I am, the calmer I get. It drives Jamie crazy. I mean, I rarely get angry, but when I do, Jamie always wants to me "talk about my feelings" and "tell her what's bothering me." And I always decline to do so.

After pacing for ten or twelve minutes, I sat down on the edge of the bottom bunk and began plotting my revenge against Dr. Reiner, who I was sure was the idiot behind all this. I mean, how many MEs tell the lead investigator whom to arrest before they've even determined the manner of death? I'll tell you how many—one, *uno*, *eins*—and his name is Dr. Harold Reiner. (Jamie reminded me later that his name is actually *Howard* Reiner, but I was too pissed off to remember the asshole's right name at the time. All I could think about was getting even.)

I'm not a vindictive person by nature, though, so it didn't take long for me to get tired of my fantasies. Finally, after I'd gotten most, though not all, of them out of my system, I decided to lie down for a bit and close my eyes. After all, there was nothing else to do. I started reflecting on the things that had happened since Jamie and I had solved the Marti MacKenzie case and had made an ass out of Dr. What's-his-name:

Hooch, a Dogue de Bordeaux that Jamie and I had met while breaking into an auto salvage yard near Belfast, as part of our investigation, had become a permanent fixture at my kennel. (I call him Hooch because he looks just like the dog in *Turner and Hooch*.) He actually belonged to the owners of the salvage yard but somehow always seemed to show up at my doorstep, no matter how hard they tried to keep him on their property. The damn dog would escape and trot the thirty miles from Belfast to my kennel (located halfway between the two small mountain villages of Hope and Perseverance), and smile at me and wag his huge tail as I opened the door. His owners would call me from time to time and threaten to come pick up the dog, but he rarely did. By early summer it had become clear that Hooch—whose real name was Jean-Claude—was now *my* dog.

My own dog, Frankie, a seven-year-old black and white Llewellin English setter, had been almost impossible to train. Other than a Welsh terrier named Guinness, a vizsla named Otis, and a few Dalmatians, Frankie was the most difficult dog I've ever worked with. The funny thing is, once I'd got him trained, people would often stop and tell me how "smart" he was. The truth of the matter is he's anything *but* smart. In fact, he's dumb as paint. I just trained the hell out of him.

Hooch, however, was a breeze. I never spent a single moment training him to do anything, and yet he automatically obeyed practically any command I gave him. I had no explanation for this. It was almost as if he were able to read my mind. One of my clients suggested that Hooch simply "grokked" what I wanted him to do and did it (whatever "grokked" means).

The other amazing thing is that, even though neither Frankie nor Hooch had been surgically mutilated—that is to say, they were both intact males—they were also the best of friends. In fact, they had become inseparable. Most people would think it next to impossible for two un-neutered males to get along, let alone be such close buddies.

This is one of the reasons I hadn't taken Frankie with me to the party at Aunt Zita's. I couldn't very well take him along and leave Hooch behind. And I couldn't very well ask Jamie's aunt, and her friends and family, to put up with two dogs, one L and one XXL, running around the property and doing very doglike things such as chasing any puffins or pelicans they might find, digging up the rose beds, or taking turns urinating around the entire perimeter of the property. I find such behaviors charming, yet I know that other people quite often don't.

Leon, my foster son, had been hawking me for months to buy him a car and get him a dog. As far as the car was concerned, since he'd just turned sixteen in June, he was too young. However, the dog was a different matter. During the summer months, the Toland family—who owned a couple of Pomeranians named Scully and Mulder—were spending more time at home and less time on vacation, meaning that Leon's two favorite dogs were spending less time at the kennel. He really loves those dogs and gets kind of lonesome when they're not around. When they *are* around they follow him everywhere and even sleep under the covers with him in the guest cottage, a former carriage house I'd had renovated for his use.

I thought about letting Hooch be his dog, but unfortunately, and again I don't know why this is, Hooch is totally devoted to me and completely indifferent to Leon. Maybe, I thought, I should talk to Dale Summerhays and see if she knows of a shelter dog that would be good for him.

I was quite happy about one thing, Leon-related, though, and that's the fact that the family court had decided to put him into my custody, permanently and legally. There had been some talk of sending him back to Harlem to live with his grandmother and his younger sister, who were essentially all that was left of his family after his mother, father, older brother, and a younger brother (just two years old), had been brutally gunned down in their apartment by a street gang.

Meanwhile, these idiots at the DHS—that's the Division of Human Services—were putting up a stink about Leon staying with me. There was even an argument presented in court that he should be placed with an African-American family, to ensure that he was raised with an appreciation for his cultural heritage. I suppose there's a point to be made there. But me? I tend to think of Leon as a kid first, and an African-American kid either second or third. Or not at all. To me we're all just human beings no matter what color our skin is.

Anyway, things in the courtroom were pretty tense for a while until the judge finally asked Leon what *he* wanted. He stood up and said quite simply that he wanted to stay with me. He acknowledged the fact that I would never replace his real family, but as far as he could tell, I was a pretty close second. Plus he really liked working with the dogs.

My eyes got a little moist when he said that.

I'd found out something interesting about Jamie too. I had always thought that she was a trust fund baby. Her father Jonas was, after all, one of the thirteen richest doctors in the country. And it was true that Jonas had provided a ten-million-dollar trust fund for her, but Jonas told me she wasn't actually able to touch any of the money until she turned thirty-five (she's thirty-two, I'm forty-one), and only if she's married at the time. The reason that *she'd* never told me about this, I guess, is that she wanted to be sure I was marrying her for *her* and not for her *money*. (As if *I* would ever do that.)

I wasn't worried about things at the kennel. I'd hired Farrell Woods to help me run the place. He'd been in the K-9 Corps during Vietnam and was great with dogs. He had ten of his own now, a platoon of beagles. And for as long as I'd owned the place, he'd been trying to hit me up for a job. The reason I'd never given him one is that he also deals and smokes marijuana—or *used* to.

He doesn't anymore, the reason being that he's in love with Tulips—this half-Vietnamese singer he'd met when she came to Maine five years earlier to find her biological father. She is a very bright girl in some ways; according to Woods, she has advanced degrees in both theoretical math and computer logic, but had fallen in with a drug dealer named Eddie Cole, who got her addicted to heroin. Woods has been trying to help her recover from it.

"I can't very well be smokin' the stuff around her while she's trying to get clean, now can I, Jackie boy?" he'd said to me. "And, hey, you always told me if I ever stopped smoking dope you'd hire me in a New York minute."

"I have never in my life used the expression 'a New York minute,'" I'd told him, but added, "So, when can you start?"

He's been my right-hand man ever since.

Then I thought about Gordon Beeson, the dead man I'd found near the gunhole. What was his story? Who was he? Was he there by accident, or had he really been stalking Jamie, and is that how he'd ended up on Aunt Zita's island?

I finally decided that this was one case Jamie wouldn't have to talk me into solving. I couldn't wait to get out of jail and find out who'd killed Beeson, if he *had* been killed, and then cram the truth down Dr. Reiner's throat. In fact, somewhere in the back of my mind I had a fantasy of ousting Reiner from his position as Chief ME and putting Jamie in his place; a real jail-house political coup.

It seemed like only a few minutes after I'd closed my eyes and thought these things that the door to the cell opened and I was treated to the sight of Sheriff Horace Flynn, with his big potbelly and his salt and pepper mustache, along with Jill Krempetz, with her frizzy red hair, pale complexion, and dark bags under the eyes—the latter being a side effect of the chemotherapy she was still undergoing for breast cancer.

Flynn looked me in the eye, twitched his mustache twice, and said, "Just one question Field: Did you croak this guy?"

"Don't answer that, Jack," Jill quickly admonished.

"I *will* answer it. No. I don't even know who he is. That is, I didn't know anything about him until after Sinclair told me he'd supposedly been stalking Jamie."

"Good enough for me," said Flynn. "You're released on your own recognizance."

"Are you sure about that?" I stayed where I was.

"Why? You like it here?"

"Not especially—no offense, Sheriff—but I was thinking that if I spent the weekend in jail, and it got out to the press that I had been wrongfully incarcerated because of the fact that Dr. Reiner is trying to get back at Jamie for showing him up in the Marti MacKenzie case—"

"Wait, wait. You think anybody in the press gives a shit if you're in jail, wrongfully or not? Or what happened back in October with the whatchamacallit case? What are you, some big celebrity all of a sudden?"

I had nothing to say to that. He was probably right.

He went on. "The other thing is, Jamie's waiting out in the parking lot right now. She just gave her statement. Now, I know for certain that she would like nothing more than to take you home as soon as possible."

He was right. And it wasn't just Jamie: I had dogs to get back to as well, so I stepped through the cell door to freedom.

He handed me my belongings and I put on my belt and my flip-flops and my shell necklace and said, "Just one thing, though, Sheriff; what happens when Sinclair decides to track me down and lock me up in another jail cell somewhere in Kennebec, Sagadahoc, or Cumberland Counties?"

He twitched his mustache a few times, thinking it over.

Jill yawned. "I'm tired. There's not much more I can do for you tonight anyway, Jack. If necessary I can ask a judge for an emergency habeas corpus hearing tomorrow."

"That's okay, Jill. You should go home and get some sleep. And thanks a lot for coming."

"Yeah, yeah. I'll send you a bill."

She went to a door with a reinforced glass window at the end of the holding area, pressed a buzzer, and was buzzed out.

Flynn led me to the back door and said, "Here's what I'm thinking: Jamie says you make a pretty good omelet."

I shrugged. "Well, I don't make them light. I actually add an extra yolk, which makes them richer and tastier."

He held the door open for me and rolled his eyes. "Geez, Field, I wasn't asking you for your goddamn recipe secrets."

We went out to the parking lot, where Jamie was pacing next to her green Jaguar sedan. She saw us and came running over to me and hugged me and kissed me.

"Isn't this kind of dangerous?" I said after a few such pleasant moments. "What if someone sees us?"

"Don't worry. The state cops have gone home. All that's left are a few deputies, and they're on Flynn's side. And ours."

Flynn stayed put as we walked back to her car, holding hands. When we got there, she pushed me up against the passenger side and kissed me some more—real hard. Then, with her eyes teasing me, she said, "So, Jack, I hope you didn't start any homosexual relationships while you were in the joint. I'd be jealous if you did."

I laughed and said, "Of course not. I mean, just with Billy Bob. But they're sending him back to Arkansas tomorrow, so I swear, I'll never see him again. Honest." She punched my kidney. "Though he *did* promise to write."

"Get in the car," she said and I did. She got in on the other side. "Did Uncle Horace tell you his plan?"

"Um, I think he was sort of hinting about wanting to come over for breakfast in the morning?"

Flynn, now secure in the idea that all the kissing and such

was over for the time being, walked over and patted the roof of the car. "I'll follow you home," he said.

"Are you spending the night?" I looked over at Jamie.

"I think he should," she said.

I looked up at Flynn. "Okay with me, then."

"I was just suggesting," Flynn explained, "that if you want, I could sleep in the downstairs guest room. You know, as long as you make me some of your famous omelets in the morning. That way if Sinclair tries anything, I'm there to tell him that you're in protective custody and he can frickin' well bug off."

I smiled. "Gee, that would be darn nice of you, Sheriff. I have to warn you, though—breakfast at my place comes pretty early on Saturday mornings. I have to be in Portland and in the makeup chair by eight-thirty."

"Makeup?" he said as if *he'd* never done a TV interview. "A tough guy like you has to wear makeup?"

I laughed. "It's show business, Sheriff. Even John Wayne had to wear makeup."

•

5

So. I was in the hair and makeup room when Lily Chow, my segment producer, came in, frantically looking for me. She was wearing her usual chinos and white sleeveless top, her black hair held back with a plastic clip thingie. She was hugging a clipboard and seemed breathless and rushed, pushing her glasses up on her nose with the back of one hand. But then, she was always like that. I had tried to tell her a couple of times that she ought to get a dog; that it would help lower her blood pressure.

"A dog? Jack, I don't have time to take care of a dog!"

"Get a small dog," I'd said. "Something you can take to work with you and cuddle and pet when you get stressed out."

She'd just shaken her head at me as if I were an idiot.

I now wanted to point out that a dog is much more fun to hug than a clipboard but she interrupted my train of thought:

"Sheila"—that was Sheila Kelly, the news segment producer—"wants you for an interview at the top of the hour."

"What about?"

She gave me a look. "What about? The murder!"

"I didn't know they'd determined the manner of death yet."

She shrugged. "It came over the hot sheet as a murder." She looked at my wardrobe disapprovingly. "I don't know if they'll want you on-camera in jeans and a denim shirt and that—what is that, a safari vest?"

"It's a dog training vest. I keep toys and leashes and shit in it. Anyway, this is what I always wear. You know that." She shrugged. "So. Who's doing the interview?"

"They want Donna." Donna Devon was one of the perky co-hosts of the show.

I sighed. "Can't they get someone with more journalistic credentials than the fact that she has frosted hair?"

Lily gave me a shocked stare. I also got a couple of loud looks from the hair and makeup crew. I wondered briefly if Donna Devon had come into the room behind me. Then they all burst out laughing. Apparently everyone there had been trying to convince Donna to defrost her hair for quite some time.

At any rate, I was pleasantly surprised at how well the interview went. In fact, despite her perkiness and a few other drawbacks—mostly coiffure-related—Donna Devon did a pretty good job of it. They had my bio on file at the station, and she'd read (or at least scanned) it before we sat down under the darkened studio lights and gave the sound crew our microphone checks.

Then, when the commercial break was almost over, the stage manager gave us some hand signals, the lights came back up, and we did our two and a half minutes.

After she explained the basics of the story to the audience and got my bio out of the way, she gave me a perfect opening to get in my first dig at Dr. Reiner:

"Why do you think you were arrested so quickly, Jack?"

"Good question. The only reason I can think of is that the State Medical Examiner, Dr. Reiner, made a premature judgment before he'd properly determined the manner of death."

"Don't you mean the cause of death?"

"No, the cause of death is a medical term, which almost always amounts to heart failure. Whether the decedent died of a bullet wound, a heart attack, suicide, or in an automobile accident, the cause of death is usually written down that way."

"And the manner of death?" (Good, she was keeping up.)

"That's a legal term. In fact, there are four possible manners of death: death by natural causes, accidental death—also called misadventure—then suicide, and homicide."

"I see. So Gordon Beeson's death might not actually be a homicide, and if that hasn't even been determined yet, you shouldn't have been arrested at all, is that right?"

"Right. Even if I were guilty, which I'm not, without a full autopsy, I couldn't be indicted. And by the way, let's say the victim had a bullet hole in him? There have been cases where a victim was shot *after* he'd already died of natural causes. So you have to be very careful."

"Really?"

"That's right. And I'm pretty sure they haven't even *started* the autopsy yet because from what I hear, Dr. Reiner is the kind of dedicated public servant who hates to miss his golf game on the weekends."

"You don't like Dr. Reiner very much, do you?"

I gave her a look. "Would you be terribly fond of a public official who'd used his position of power to have you put in jail as part of a personal vendetta?"

"You think that's what this is?"

I could see the stage manager out of the corner of my eye making a circling motion with one hand, telling us to wind it up. "Well, it sure ain't based on the truth, or on proper procedure. Now, unless you have information that the autopsy has already been completed—"

"Let me check." She glanced at her notes, nodded almost imperceptibly at the stage manager (she was good), then looked at me and smiled. "No, it's scheduled for Monday morning."

"Like I said, who'd want to be stuck inside, doing an autopsy, on a beautiful golf day like today?"

The lights began slowly coming up on the green screen of the weather map located on the other side of the studio.

She laughed. "Our thanks to Jack Field, who'll be back later in this hour for dog training tips. And on that last note, let's turn it over to meteorologist Brantley Parker."

"Thanks, Donna. And you're right, Jack. Dr. Reiner is going to have a great time out on the links today. Though by tomorrow afternoon we should be seeing some pretty heavy thunder bangers." He started talking about a low pressure system, and the lights went down on our part of the studio.

I was about to take my mic off when Donna Devon stopped me with a hand on my knee. Softly, she said, "*I* think that after this? Dr. Reiner is going to reschedule the autopsy for very early this afternoon. That was a great interview, Jack."

"Thanks. You did a pretty good job yourself."

She smiled. "Really? Because I heard that you were making disparaging comments earlier about my interviewing skills, based on the color of my hair."

I smiled good-naturedly. "I guess I should apologize for that crack. I didn't realize how smart you were."

She smiled back. "Oh, I'm smarter than *that*. I don't like the way my hair looks either, but my executive producer *does*."

I nodded. "I guess it must be hard being a woman in the television news business."

"Haven't you heard? It's hard just being a woman. In *any* business. Now, listen, I'd like to do more on this with you at ten. I know you usually leave right after your little dog segment, but—"

"Wait," I whispered, "my 'little dog segment'? Now who's making the disparaging remarks?"

She adjusted an earring. "You think dog training is more important than a big news story like this?"

"Of *course* it is. What you newscasters do, basically, is try to scare the bejebus out of people so you can sell more airtime to advertisers. What *I* do is help people. So which do you think is more important, helping people or scaring the crap out of them?"

She shook her head. "We don't scare people, Jack, we just *inform* them about what's going on in the world."

I almost laughed out loud, but Brantley Parker (if that's his real name) was still twinkling over the weather. "Oh yeah?" I said softly. "Just take a look at all the news teases you've done in the past two years. Every one of them starts off with, 'There's a new health scare today,' or, 'Is your family safe? Tune in at six to find out,' and so on. And my feeling is, if more people owned a dog? and knew how to train it and care for it properly? there would be a whole lot less hard-hitting news stories for you newscasters to scare your audience with because people all over the world would be a lot happier and much less interested in killing and robbing one another."

She put a hand to her earpiece, listening to instructions, I think, from her producer, then said, "You make an interesting point, but we'll have to discuss it later." She stood up. "So does this mean you won't stick around for another interview?"

"No." I shrugged and stood up too. "I'll stick around."

"Good," she smiled. "I think I can get us *three* and a half minutes this time. There's so much I want to ask you."

Poor girl. She never got the chance.

6

They came for me just as I was ending my "little dog segment." The way these things are produced is that I go to a viewer's home with a small camera crew (just three guys and Lily Chow) and spend an hour solving some behavioral problem that can't be solved in the five minutes of airtime I have available. And one that *certainly* can't be solved in the alien and scary environment of a television studio, with its big cameras, bright lights, heavy cables, and crew members lurking in the shadows (at least for a puppy it's scary, if not for Donna Devon). I think it's important for a dog, and especially for a puppy, to learn a new behavior in its own environment. This is why I don't do puppy classes, and why I don't usually do training at the kennel unless the dog has already spent some time there.

Whenever we arrive at an owner's home, I always let the crew go in first and make friends with the dog (by giving her a treat and letting her sniff their equipment). When that's out of the way, they make themselves as unobtrusive as possible. (I like to tell them to become invisible, and they like to tell me they can't.) I also insist that they shoot in natural light, so there's no lighting equipment cluttering up things. They do a hell of a job too. They never know what the dog or I are going to do, so the cameraman and boom operator really have to be on their toes. Some of it comes off looking like a home video, but that's okay. We're actually doing it in someone's home.

My segment started that day, as it always does, with Brianne O'Leary introducing me. Pretty, with short auburn hair, she handles the soft features (this one is part of what's called Maine Life). "We're here with dog training expert, Jack Field." She turned to me and smiled. "What's up this week, Jack?"

"You know, Brianne, I wish you wouldn't call me an expert."

"Why? Are you being modest? How un*like* you."

"No," I laughed, "I just don't like experts. In my opinion, most of them don't know the first thing about dogs."

"Really. So, what would you prefer to be called?"

"Just a dog trainer."

She shook her head. "Well, we've seen the magic you can do with dogs, Jack. So maybe we should call you a magician."

I laughed. I like Brianne. Sure she's perky, but it's a *good* perky. Plus she's funny. "Magician. Yeah, I like that, though in my opinion, it's the *dogs* who are magic, not me."

"Aw, that's nice. So, Kreskin, what's today's problem?"

I laughed, then explained that Buttons, a four-month-old Yorkshire terrier who belonged to David and Christy Washington, a pleasant young couple from Bath, didn't know how to play.

"Is learning how to play that important for a dog?"

"Oh, it's vital. Plus, the first rule of training is, 'Before you teach a dog to obey, teach it how to play.' "

She smiled. "Sounds like good advice to me. Now, let's roll the clip and . . . *watch that old Jack magic.*"

The footage came on the monitor. It started with my arrival at David and Christy's house. As soon as I came in, Buttons came racing up to me, sniffed my shoes, then ran away, in a wiggly sort of fashion. I praised him, "Good boy!" and he wiggled back over to me, then immediately ran away again.

"Of course, you're a stranger," Christy said, leading me into the living room. Then she added glumly, "But he doesn't really play with *us* much either. Can you help?"

"Sure," I said, and immediately lay on my back on the living room carpet. I began making silly noises; a kissing sound, a silly, high-pitched laugh—"*wee-hee-hee!*"—and a lot of praise, "Good boy!" also using the same high-pitched voice. Not as high-pitched as a certain famous trainer, whose name I won't mention. But the reason *he* does it is that he treats dogs so roughly that he has to overcompensate with an *insanely* high falsetto so that the dogs he brutalizes with his harsh leash corrections and his favorite expression—a guttural, "No, bad dog!"—won't fear him completely. Oh, and his second favorite expression? "This isn't hurting the dog."

At any rate, in almost no time Buttons was jumping up on top of my chest and licking my beard.

Now I want to paint a picture of this in your mind because it's an important part of the outcry that happened later, when I was taken back into custody. You see, the image that went out over the airwaves that morning was of a fairly tall guy (I'm six-one), and a fairly *masculine* guy (I have a trim, full beard, a slim yet sturdy physique, and a full head of curly, salt-and-pepper hair). And there I was, lying on my back, letting a three-pound puppy jump all over me.

At any rate, back to the videotape:

Once I got Buttons to play on top of me, I stood up and asked for an old sock and some treats. (No, not for me. For the *dog.*) David went to the kitchen, and Christy went through her sock drawer. They gave me the items I'd asked for, we sat back down, and I started teasing Buttons with the sock.

"Now, watch how I do this," I said. "I try to make it move around like a wounded bird. I also talk to the dog, like so: 'Ooh, get it! You want to grab it! Come on, grab it!'"

After I explained this, I let Buttons grab it and said, "Good boy!" and play-growled at him. Then, as he held on tight, I started to move the sock back and forth, sideways. "Make it move kind of serpentine like this," I explained. "And keep growling at him and praising him. Then let him plant his front paws, let him pull the tug toy taut, then, as he makes a couple of tugs, you 'accidentally' let go so he wins the game. Then praise him very enthusiastically for winning."

I demonstrated this, letting go of the toy, then I said to the dog in a high-pitched, happy voice, "Good boy, Buttons! You *won*! You're the *king* dog!"

Buttons pranced around the room, carrying the stupid sock in his mouth like he'd just won the World Cup or something. Dogs are so funny. We all laughed at his antics.

I cautioned them that when a dog acts like he doesn't know that it's just a game (which can be the case with some rescue dogs), you probably shouldn't play with that dog; he may have other issues. Also, if the dog's teeth tend to stray from the toy and onto your skin, you simply stop playing at that moment and try again later. This will teach him to only grab the tug toy—not your hand—when it's time to play.

"Won't he chew up all our socks now?"

"Probably," I laughed. "If you leave them lying around." Then I explained about the need for puppy proofing their house, and that the ideal tug toy is a bandana, rolled up and knotted in both ends.

"And another thing," I added, "though I sometimes break this rule—don't let the dog play tug-of-war with the leash. And *never* let him play with your clothes. And even though you should always let him win, you need to control when and where the game takes place. When he's old enough to play outside, that's the only place you should do it. Not in the house. He should also be taught to drop the toy on command. Let me show you how to do this."

I praised Buttons some more and he brought the toy back. I held a treat under his nose. He sniffed it, dropped the sock, and the instant he did, I said, "Out!" in a happy voice, and gave him the treat. Then I explained that you have to train the out command without any lag time between the three events: dog drops toy, you say "Out!" in a pleasant voice, then you give the dog a treat: "One—two—three!"

Christy asked, "Why do you say it *after* he drops the toy? Aren't you doing it backwards?"

"Sort of. But there are two reasons to do it that way. First of all, when a dog is learning a new behavior, hearing a command word can sometimes distract him; it interrupts the flow. But when you say it *after* the behavior, he's more able to make an association between the command word and the behavior itself, so he learns to obey. The second thing is, you never want to repeat a command. Repetition dilutes its effectiveness. You want to say it only once, and the best way to guarantee that you don't have to repeat it is to say it after he's already obeyed it. I know it doesn't make any sense, but it really works, trust me."

We went through this entire process three more times on camera. (It doesn't show this on the tape, but in the actual session I had Dave and Christy practice it too, and coached them through it when they weren't doing it quite right.)

Now back to the videotape:

We cut to a shot of me saying, "So, you guys tell me that Buttons doesn't like to play fetch?"

David made a facial shrug.

Christy said, "No, he's not interested in chasing anything. It's like he can't be bothered."

"Okay, watch this."

I rolled the sock up into a ball, then danced it around Buttons's mouth the same way I had before, making him crazy to bite it. Then, when he was positioned in such a way that I could throw it past him, right through his line of sight, I did; a short, low toss about four feet away.

He just stood there staring straight ahead, kind of shocked. Where did it go? Then, like a cartoon character, his head went *boing!*—drawn in the same direction the sock had just gone. Still, he just sat staring at it.

Christy said, "See?"

"Ssshhh. Wait."

In a comic delayed reaction, Buttons finally ran after the sock, pounced on it, grabbed it in his mouth and killed it, shaking his head around to "break its neck." Then he tore off to the kitchen and lay down on his bed and began chewing on it.

"With puppies," I said, "you don't want to throw it too far. That's a mistake a lot of people make. So just toss the ball or toy a few feet at first. Once they get into the fun of it, you can start increasing the distance. Another rule is, always quit playing before the dog loses interest."

"How do you know when he's losing interest?"

"He may start to act a little distracted, or he may seem a little less energetic about chasing the ball, or he may stop bringing it all the way back to you."

"That's great," said Dave, kind of sarcastically. "So how do you get him to bring it back in the *first* place?" (Buttons was still in the kitchen, chewing the sock.)

"Well, I'll show you. I hope."

I made some loud kissing sounds, praised the dog in that silly voice, and he came bouncing back into the living room carrying the sock-ball in his mouth. He came to *me* with it—I was the one praising him—and I said, "Out!" and he dropped it. I praised him again, picked it up and threw it for him to chase, which he did happily and with no delayed reaction this time.

The rest of the footage—about ten seconds worth—showed David and Christy laughing and playing fetch with a very happy and very spunky Buttons. (This is simple stuff, by the way, and comes naturally to most dogs and owners, but some people need to be taught these easy rules of fetch and tug-of-war.)

When the studio lights came back up, there were two extra chairs on the platform. David and Christy were sitting in them, smiling. Buttons was ensconced in Christy's lap.

Brianne smiled and put a hand on my knee. "Well, Jack, it really looks like—what the . . . ? What is going *on* back there?"

A loud crash and some very loud shouting—coming from behind the cameras—had interrupted her. It was hard to see what was happening in the darkness, what with the bright lights in my eyes, but the next thing I heard was Sheila Kelly yelling: "Sir? Sir? You can't just come *in here* like this! We are broadcasting a live *television* show! Security!"

"Stand out of the way, ma'am."

That's when I knew it was Sinclair. I looked at Brianne and she looked at me. We had planned on ending the segment by showing Buttons, not only playing fetch live on camera, but by showing that he would now sit and come on command, using the ball as both an inducement and a reward. We'd also planned to answer a few live phone calls then, introduce the audience to a shelter dog they could adopt. These things were all part of my biweekly spot, but there was no chance to do any of them now.

Sheila was giving the camera crew instructions to show what

Sinclair was doing and how I was reacting. "This is now a live news broadcast, people. Keep those cameras on!"

Sinclair stepped up on the platform, followed by two state troopers. For the life of me, I couldn't tell if they were the same guys from the night before or not. Still, I stood up as one of them came around behind me, holding out the handcuffs. The other one pulled my chair back.

I said, "You know, you can't rearrest me, Sinclair. I was released on my own recognizance by Sheriff Flynn."

He said, "We're not rearresting you, Field. We're just rescinding Flynn's ROR."

I shook my head and turned slightly so the camera could get a better view of what was happening. Meanwhile, the uniform couldn't get the cuffs on because I was still hooked up to my microphone pack. A sound technician rushed up to help and was held back by the other trooper.

"Stay right where you are, sir," he said.

The sound tech said, "What the hell is wrong with you? I need to take his mic off so you can get the handcuffs on!"

Sheila said, "Are you getting this, up in the booth?"

Sinclair said, "Stan, let him come up and take the man's microphone off."

Stan stood aside and let the sound tech come up on the platform and take off my microphone pack.

Brianne turned to David and Christy. They were all still seated. "So, how are you folks enjoying being on television?"

They just kind of shrugged and smiled.

Then Christy hugged Buttons, looked up toward me—as I was being led off the platform—scrunched her face and said to Brianne, "Is he going to be okay?"

"Ya got me, sister," she replied. "Ya got me."

7

The lockup in Portland was far different from the Rockland County Jail. For starters, there were iron bars on all the cells. Also, there were a lot more cells. I counted twelve in all, most of them now full with D&Ds and DUIs. And that was just on my side of the building, which was a drunk tank and a holding area for perps awaiting trial or bail hearings.

I got processed in a little after ten-thirty same deal as before, posing for mug shots, having my fingerprints taken, and then being asked to initialize a list of my personal effects; wallet, shoes, belt, and so forth.

They took me down a long hall, through a set of double doors with reinforced glass windows, and into the drunk tank.

Then—bang!—I was locked up again.

I had a roommate this time; a young muscular college jock with a blond buzz cut. He was wearing a silk-screened T-shirt, proclaiming MAINE—AMERICA'S VACATIONLAND, and a pair of olive drab cargo shorts. He was lying on the bottom bunk, moaning. He'd gotten so drunk the night before he was still a little tipsy. When he heard the cell door clang shut he looked up, stumbled out of bed, and began screaming at the top of his lungs.

"Hey, guard! Get me the fuck out of here!" and words to that effect. He even kicked at the bars with his bare feet, like a little kid pulling a tantrum. He was screaming so loud and hard that his face turned bright red and the veins in his forehead and neck stood out in high relief.

I ignored him and went straight to the toilet. He'd thrown up sometime earlier and had left his vomit just sitting in the bowl, stinking up the place, so I flushed it.

Once the air cleared a little, I shook my head at the kid's screaming act, but figured that, like a puppy pulling a tantrum, he'd get tired of it soon enough, so I went over to the bed and sat on the bottom bunk and waited. He didn't show any signs of tiring, though, so finally, after I'd had my fill, I got up and went over to him and tapped him on the shoulder. He turned and looked me over, his eyes unfocused.

"What the hell do you want?" he said.

"Could you kind of keep it down a little?" I asked.

He stared at me dumbly for a few seconds and then began screaming in my face, treating me to more of the vomit smell.

"Oh, yeah, old man? You want me to KEEP MY VOICE DOWN!?"

He probably could have taken me in a fair fight. So, to save time (and wear-and-tear on my knuckles), I simply grabbed his right hand, digging my thumb deep into the nerve between his thumb and forefinger. Then I twisted his arm behind his back, and he quickly went down to his knees, crying. Actual tears were coming down his cheeks. "Let me up! Let me up!"

The sleeve of his T-shirt had ridden up, revealing a Jesus fish tattoo on his bicep. I deduced that he was the type of Christian fundamentalist who believes in the gospel but has trouble living it, so he has to blow off some steam once in a while and then feels guilty afterward.

Calmly, I said, "This is a jail cell, son. It's not a place for screaming and 'kicking against the pricks.' This is a place for repentance and for the quiet contemplation of your sins."

"My sins? Ow!"

"You heard me. What's your name?"

"Gavin, sir."

"Okay, Gavin—just so you know? Jesus is pissed at you right now and that's why you're being punished."

"Punished for what? Ow! Ow!"

"Don't play dumb. He's pissed about some of the thoughts you've been having."

"What thoughts? Ow! Ow!"

"You know very well what thoughts. The ones about naked girls."

He was amazed that I knew this. "Oh, God. Oh, my God."

"And he's also pissed at you for the way you've been fooling around with that girl."

Again he was stunned at my depth of knowledge. "Darcy? How do you know about Darcy? Ow! Ow!"

"Now, He's willing to forgive you. In fact, He *wants* to forgive you. You know how He is."

He nodded, smiling and crying at the same time. "He's filled with light and love and mercy."

"That's right. But you're going to have to pray long and hard to get your soul free from the perils of hell."

I was actually having too much fun with this, if the truth were known. Of course, I could have cared less about this sorry-ass kid and the fate of his pygmy soul. I just wanted some peace and quiet. Was that too much to ask?

He started exhorting the Lord: "Oh, dear sweet Jesus, please forgive me of my many—ow! Ow!"

"Not out loud! Don't you know those who pray publicly, in a loud voice, are an abomination in the sight of God?"

"Sorry, sir."

"Pray silently to yourself." He nodded and his lips began to move. "Okay, good. Now, I'm going to let you up, and when I do I want you to crawl into the bottom bunk and—"

"You're giving me the bottom bunk?"

I sighed. "Think of it as a sign that Jesus still loves you even though you're a terrible sinner." It had nothing to do with being a sign, of course. It was just that if he had to throw up again, I didn't want to be lying in the bottom bunk and have him spewing his mess on top of me.

"A sign," he exulted. "He's giving me a sign." It kills me how these people are all the time looking for and putting their faith in signs when the Bible clearly states that only a "wicked and adulterous generation seeks after signs." I know this because I spent a few years in Catholic school, until one day, when I was about thirteen, one of the priests got frisky with his hands. Without thinking, I kicked him in the groin as hard as I could, and I was immediately expelled—thank God.

"That's right," I lied. "It's a sign from above. So go lie down. Start your silent prayers. But remember, if the Lord hears you praying out loud, you'll be punished even more." With that I finally let him up off his knees.

"Thank you, sir," he said, and meekly went to the bottom bunk, climbed in, and assumed a fetal position with his hands clasped fervently in front of his face.

My job was done. It was quiet and peaceful once again.

I climbed into the top bunk—all the while trying to keep from laughing—and felt around for a pillow. There wasn't one.

"Do you have a pillow down there?" I asked.

"Yes, sir?"

I reached down. "Jesus wants you to give it to me."

He quickly handed it up.

I got comfortable and a few minutes passed. Finally, he said, "Sir? Can I ask you something?"

"What is it?"

"You're an angel of the Lord, aren't you? I mean, how else could you have known about me and Darcy?"

I stifled another laugh and said, "Son, you know I'm not allowed to divulge that information. Now keep praying."

"Sorry, sir," he said, then under his breath I heard him say, "I *knew* it!" This was going to be a great story for him to tell his Christian brothers and sisters one day, about how he'd once had a visitation from an angel in the drunk tank at the Cumberland County Jail in Portland, Maine.

I eventually fell asleep and took a nap, which lasted a few hours. Then I heard the cell door open and a guard said, "Jack Field?"

I sat up. "That's me."

"You've got a phone call."

8

It was Kelso.

"Where are you?" I asked.

"I'm at the Portland airport," he groused. "Your attorney is apparently unavailable so Jamie asked me to fly up from New York to represent you."

"Since when are you licensed to practice in the State of Maine?"

"Since I passed the multistate, years ago. I'm licensed in New York, New Jersey, Florida, Pennsylvania, and all of New England."

Lou Kelso and I first met while working together on a murder case. I was the lead detective and he was a prosecutor for the Manhattan DA. One of our witnesses, a young woman who knew the victim, was also murdered before she could testify. The two police officers guarding her hotel room were also killed. Someone in the DA's office was on the take and had set up her murder. A few years later Kelso quit prosecuting, hung out a shingle as a P.I., but kept his license to practice law. (He tells this story better than I do, so I'll just go on with what happened while I was in jail:)

"Anyway," he went on, "I just got in from LaGuardia."

"Are your arms tired?"

He failed to laugh. "That's not even the right way to tell that old joke. What is *wrong* with you?"

"I'm in jail. Unjustly accused, unfairly incarcerated."

"Yeah, yeah. So, anyway, listen: I wrote a writ of habeas corpus on the plane. I'm going to rent a car and check into a hotel, then, as soon as I can, I'm going to find a judge and try to get an emergency hearing, then I'm coming to see you."

"Don't rent a hotel room. You can stay at my place. And what's wrong with Jill?"

"Who's Jill?"

"My attorney."

"Oh. I don't know. Jamie told me she had to go to the hospital."

"Jesus, I hope she's all right. But seriously, don't rent a hotel room. You're staying in the guest bedroom."

"Fine, whatever. I'll get there as soon as I can. Just hang in there. It's not as bad as it seems."

He should know. He'd been in jail a few times himself, and had even done a stretch in prison on an obstruction of justice charge when he'd supposedly hindered an investigation into the murder of sixties art icon Sebastian Video. (His conviction was eventually overturned on appeal, but that's another story.)

We said our good-byes in our usual terse fashion then I was led back to my cell and my born-again roommate.

I missed Jamie's press conference, which was held around noon. The reason I missed it, obviously, is that I was in jail, though I watched the whole thing on videotape a few days later. She announced that she was resigning from the ME's office due to—well, I think you can imagine most of the things that this was due to—and that she was going to conduct an independent forensic investigation into Gordon Beeson's death, along with help from noted criminalist Dr. Sidney Liu. She also demanded to be allowed to observe the autopsy on behalf of her client—namely me, and my attorney, Lou Kelso.

Jamie's was not the only press conference held that afternoon. Dr. Reiner—who'd rescheduled the autopsy for two o'clock (thanks to Donna Devon and me)—made a brief appearance in front of the cameras on his way to the morgue. He denied any involvement in the State Police's decision to arrest me.

"This is a murder case, pure and simple," he'd said. "The preliminary report shows more than ample evidence to support

•

my ruling of homicide. Neither I, nor anyone else in this office, have any opinion on the guilt or innocence of anyone in police custody. Our job is to determine the cause and manner of death, not to track down suspects. That is for the State Police and the District Attorney's Office to determine, and it's a course of action they are free to pursue. Now, if you'll excuse me—"

There were questions shouted about Jamie's resignation.

"Please! Ladies and gentlemen, I have work to do."

With that he strode toward the front entrance of the State Morgue Building.

Someone shouted behind him, "So, Dr. Reiner, what'd you shoot today?" (I think this was a golf reference.)

Reiner ignored the comment and kept moving toward the front door, where Jamie suddenly appeared and stood waiting for him. There was just a moment's hesitation in his gait. On the videotape (which I reviewed in slow motion at the TV station) you could even see it from behind, in the way his neck twitched and his shoulders sagged slightly. He really didn't want her there. Still, he shook it off, got to the door, opened it, stood aside and held it open for her in a magnanimous, if completely phony, gesture, then followed her into the building.

The District Attorney—Morgan Lieberman—held his own press conference, as did a spokesperson for the State Police. They both claimed to have sufficient evidence (Lieberman called it "a sufficiency of the evidence") to support my arrest on the murder rap.

Kelso gave me a précis of these events when he came to visit, around six-thirty. (They wouldn't let Jamie come, but he was my attorney.) I was waiting for him in the visitor's room, sitting in a metal chair in front of a metal desk, singing, "I'll Be Seeing You" to myself, and trying to think who wrote it. Kelso would know, I thought. He knows everything about old songs. I got to the line, "In a small café, the park across the way, the children's . . . ," when they buzzed him in.

A few inches taller than I, and a little beefier, he stood in the entrance, kind of wrapped gracefully around the door, looking down at me, with his reading glasses perched on the end of his pug nose. "What are you? Bing Crosby now?"

"It gets boring in here without no radio, man."

He shook his head and came in, somewhat tiredly, it seemed to me. Even his Brooks Brothers suit looked a bit droopy. He came to the desk, dropped his leather briefcase on it, carefully put his laptop computer down, and then plopped a huge book in front of me. It landed with a thud. I looked at the cover. It was Stephen Wolfram's *A New Kind of Science*.

"You think I'll be in here that *long*?" I said.

"You can always skip the hard parts." He sat down and opened his briefcase. "Anyway, Jamie thought you might like to have something to read. That was on your nightstand." He looked me over. "Are you wearing make-up?"

"Shut up. I was on TV when they arrested me, remember?" I pulled the book toward me. "Yeah, this helps me drift off to sleep at night. Hey, who wrote that song?"

"What song?"

" 'I'll Be Seeing You.' "

He pulled some papers from his case. "Sammy Fain and Irving Kahal. I want to go over a few things with you."

"Really? I thought Sammy Cahn wrote it."

"Are you kidding me?" he scoffed. "Sammy Cahn never wrote anything that good." He thought it over. "Though come to think of it, neither did Sammy Fain and Irving Kahal. That was their only really great song."

"I'll take your word for it." (I told you he was an expert on old songs.) "And just so you know?" I pointed to the book. "They're all hard parts. That's what makes it such a good soporific." (Kelso also has a passion for recondite words.) "Hey," I said, "is recondite a word?"

He looked down his nose at me again. "It is."

"What does it mean exactly? I forget."

"Obtuse or difficult to comprehend. Now can we talk about your case?" He went on to tell me about all the press conferences, and the fact that the TV station I worked for was running the tape of me with Buttons jumping on my chest at the top of each hour, giving people the impression that I was anything but a killer. When he was finished he said, "Is there anything you'd like to tell me about what happened?"

"Nah, I'd rather talk about this book." I pointed to *A New Kind of Science*. "Do you know what it's about?"

He shook his head, then took his reading glasses off and tossed them down on the table in an easy gesture. He got out a pack of cigarettes. "Let me guess, some new kind of science?"

"Exactly. Now, I'm not sure if this guy Wolfram's really on to something or if he's just nuts, but listen to this—"

He nodded. "Jamie told me you might be like this."

I stopped cold. "I might be like what?"

"So angry you're totally calm. Hey, if you go up for twenty years, do you mind if I console her for you?"

"No, you may not."

"'Cause she's pretty hot, you know." He lit the cigarette and waved the match around till it went out.

"Forget it, Kelso. Anyway, you're not the type."

He took a puff and waved the smoke away from me and my virgin lungs. "Yeah? What type is that?"

"The type of guy to sustain a long-lasting relationship."

"Who said anything about a long-lasting relationship? One night's all I need." Then he took another puff, waited for my re-action, which I didn't give him. Then he grunted and said, "And so," he shrugged, "what? You *are*?"

"Am I what?"

"The type of guy to, you know, the rest of it."

"Maybe not in general, but with Jamie I am. So, no way— she's totally off limits to you and your smooth charm."

He gave me his smoothest grin. "She have a sister?"

I smiled. "No, but her mother is pretty good-looking. In fact she's a knockout." (This is true. Laura Cutter is one of the most beautiful women I've ever met.) "Now, stop trying to make me lose my temper and listen to what I want to tell you about this book . . ."

He looked at his watch. "No thanks," he said, and put the papers back inside his briefcase. "I've got a habeas corpus hear-ing to get to. Your pal Jill gave Jamie the name of a judge who's willing to listen." He put his reading glasses back on.

"Yeah? How *is* Jill?"

He took another puff. "According to Jamie, not too good. She has to have more surgery tomorrow. Sorry."

"Oh, man."

He stubbed out his cigarette. "If all goes well, I'll have you out of here by eight o'clock and we can go get drunk."

"Okay, cool. Mind if I play with the dogs first?"

"No, that's fine." He got up, went to the door and said, "Ah, shit!" He turned back to me. "See? That's what I should have done to get you riled up. I should have told you that someone's been trying to mess with your dogs. Shit!"

"Wait. Who's been trying to mess with my dogs?"

"Nobody. But see how emotional you are right now? That's the way you should be feeling about this trumped-up murder charge, you asshole! Instead of singing Bing Crosby songs."

"No," I shook my head, "this makes it bearable. If I *thought* about things, I'd go nuts." I took a deep breath. "What was it you once told me? When what's-her-name got iced?"

"You mean Colleen? Our witness in the mob hit?"

"That's her. I was ready to go ballistic and you told me to chill out. 'Take a Zen attitude,' you said. Remember? You said that every murder case is like a Zen hologram."

"Yeah, I remember. I was full of crap back then."

"No, you weren't. We got the guy, didn't we? That mobbed-up Assistant DA who had her killed? We got him good."

He smiled. "Yeah, we got him. Or *you* did. As I recall, I was too drunk or pissed off to be of much use."

"Yeah, I know. You lied to me about the Zen hologram. But you were right. You were right then and you're right now. So I'm going to go back to my cell and sing my Bing Crosby songs and read this book to see if I can find the secret binary code that'll help me unravel the mystery of all canine behavior. I think I can do it. If I can just come up with a few algorithms that could be programmed into a computer, I could prove the whole alpha theory wrong, mathematically."

"What the hell do you know about math or computers?"

I threw my hands in the air. "Okay. So I need someone to help me with it. Someone who knows about both."

"I think you're nuts. You *and* this Wolfram guy."

It suddenly hit me. "Wait a minute! Tulips!"

"Tulips?"

"Yeah, she has a Ph.D. in theoretical math and computer logic. One in each, actually. I just wonder if she's still clean or if she's gotten herself hooked on heroin again."

Something happened in Kelso's eyes when I said this, and I suddenly remembered Tracy Foster, another woman from his past. In fact, I think she was the only woman he'd ever really loved, and she died of a heroin overdose. I could see now that her death still haunted him. I think it was the reason he drank so much. Or at least it was a big part of it.

Shamed, I said, "Hey, look, I'm sorry, Lou."

"Forget it. I'm down to only thinking about her twice a day now anyway. So," he shrugged, "big deal—this was today's second time, so who gives a shit?" He turned his back, pressed the red button, and a second later the door buzzed and he opened it. "I'll see you at eight o'clock," he said over his shoulder.

"Hey," I said, "are you *sure* it wasn't Sammy Cahn?"

"*Please* . . ." he said just before the door clicked shut.

9

At my habeas corpus hearing Kelso argued that I shouldn't have been put into custody and that I shouldn't continue to be *kept* in custody unless and until an indictment was handed down by a grand jury, *and* that a grand jury should not be convened until the final autopsy results were in, or until a coroner's inquest was held. The judge wholeheartedly agreed.

He came to pick me up, and when we got outside—through the side exit—we were met by a crush of reporters, photographers, and camera crews. It was a few notches short of pure bedlam. Kelso, for some reason, scanned the parking lot, as if looking for someone or something. I looked around too, and thought I saw a familiar face—Eddie Cole—through the window of a parked car, out on the street. But then the car took off.

There were a lot of questions being shouted at us, so Kelso raised his hands in the air and said, "Ladies and gentlemen, please! I have a prepared statement." He didn't have any notes, though. He just rattled off the whole speech, right off the top of his head. "Despite the fervid, storm cloud adumbrations coming from various quarters in state government, principally the Chief Medical Examiner's Office, the State's Attorney's Office, and their autonomic lackeys in the State Police, despite their offensive, vituperative echoes beat, beat, beating in our ears like Gene Krupa with a bad case of tintinnus, despite the tacit compliance of those in the news media, intent on perpetuating these stultifyingly contemptible prevarications, innuendoes, and out-right lies . . ." He paused for effect, then really rammed the next bit home. ". . . I have presented the evidence against my client to a fair and impartial judge, and that judge has determined that Jack Field is totally innocent of all charges and should be im-mediately released from custody. And he *has* been."

There was a roar of shouts and murmurs from the crowd.

Kelso raised his hand and quieted them down. "Mr. Field has cooperated fully with the authorities, he has given his statement numerous times, and he never once invoked his right to counsel until after he was unjustly incarcerated." There was some more noise. Kelso raised his hand again. "*Res ipsi loquitor,* people. Jack Field is clearly an innocent man. *Res ipsi loquitor.*"

"What is that, Latin?" someone asked.

"Mr. Field, Mr. Field, do you have a statement?"

"My client has no comment at this time."

"Yes, I do." I stepped forward. "Four months ago, Dr. Jamie Cutter and I reopened a case that Dr. Reiner botched due to laziness or ineptitude. He nearly lost his job over it, and this bo-gus murder charge against me now is his feeble attempt to get revenge."

"Are you planning to sue Dr. Reiner?"

Kelso stepped in and said, "It's too soon to comment on that, but let me just say that when the truth about this matter finally comes to light, I fully expect Dr. Reiner to not only lose his job, but his license to practice medicine as well. And I wouldn't be at all surprised if he didn't spend a few years behind bars on an obstruction of justice charge."

With that we got in Kelso's rental car and tried to drive away. We were surrounded by screaming reporters, though, so it was slow going. Otis Barnes, sixties, tall and lanky, with hair the color of French bread, trotted beside the car and knocked on my window. He's the editor of the *Camden Herald* and a good friend of mine, so I rolled the window down slightly.

"'*Res ipsi loquitor*'? The thing speaks for itself?"

Kelso smiled at him.

I said, "I guess you learned a little Latin in your day."

"That I did." To Kelso, he said, "Nice speech, counselor. A little over the top, though, don't you think?"

Kelso was still trying to get out of the parking lot. I said, "Why don't you hop in, Otis. I'll give you an exclusive interview." I unlocked the back door.

"I thought you'd never ask." He hopped in, though he had to wrestle the door shut.

We finally got out of the parking lot and on the main road. Kelso said, "It was mostly flash powder, meant to confuse the hell out of them. All but the five seconds I designed specifically to be tonight's sound byte. I didn't see any satellite hookups in the parking lot, so I knew that none of the news crews were on live with this. All that verbose, sesquipedalian bullshit? That was just there to dull their brains so that when I finally got to the good stuff, they'd all wake up and remember it."

"You actually thought all that out?" Otis asked, amazed.

"Oh, sure," Kelso said. "What road do I take?" We told him. "You have to know how these people think. They're not there to actually learn anything about the case or to report the truth. They're just there to get a dynamic mixture of audio and video to make the home viewer sit up and go, 'Wow!' "

Otis shook his head, then with his hand he sort of combed the hair out of his eyes. "So, I guess you two have had some experience with this sort of thing back in New York?"

I said, "You've done your homework, Otis."

"Don't I always? You know, I keep telling you, Jack, that there are some of us in journalism who actually know what we're doing." To Kelso, he said, "That bit about nailing Dr. Reiner on an obstruction of justice charge, you've had some personal experience with that, haven't you? What was it you did, five years?"

Kelso sighed. "Okay, here we go. And I served three."

"Don't worry," Otis said, "I don't think it's pertinent."

"Well, that's a relief. Plus, if you were to get your facts straight, you'd know that my case was overturned on appeal."

"Sorry, I didn't know that." He switched on a handheld recorder. "Okay, Jack, you want to tell me what happened?"

"Sure," I said, and told him everything I knew.

We dropped Otis off at the gas station in Perseverance. He said he'd get a ride into Camden from a friend. I promised to give him some more information before his paper's weekly deadline on Wednesday.

We finally got back to the house around ten. Jamie and Frankie were waiting for me in the gravel driveway. Kelso headed straight inside for the liquor cabinet. I headed straight for Jamie. We hugged and kissed and how-are-youed and all the rest.

Frankie, meanwhile, was jumping all over us, trying to get in on the action. Finally, I turned my attention to him and let him jump up and lick my face.

"Did you miss me? My poor little doodle." While Frankie was kissing me, I said to Jamie, "So, how'd the autopsy go?" Then back to Frankie, "Poor little doodle." And he's jumping all over me and wagging his tail and doing his snake dance.

"Well," Jamie frowned, "we need to talk about that. Let's go inside and sit down."

We went up to the porch. Just then, though, Farrell Woods— tall, rail-thin, with long, reddish-brown hair—came out of the kennel—a former barn, located about fifty yards down from my Victorian three-story—and ambled over to us, wearing his usual attire: an old Boston Braves baseball cap (mostly to cover his bald spot) and his Army fatigues.

"There's our jailbird." He smiled.

"Hey, Farrell, thanks for helping out."

"No sweat." He came up the steps. "Okay if I take off?"

"Sure. What? Is there something else?" He was just standing there, looking like he wanted to ask me something but was too embarrassed to do so in front of Jamie.

He tilted his head and walked to the other end of the porch. I looked at Jamie, shrugged, and followed him.

In an apologetic near-whisper he said, "Can you front me a couple of bucks, man? Till payday."

"Sure. How much do you need?" He told me, and I got my wallet out, counted out some money, and gave it to him.

"Thanks, man."

I looked over at the kennel. "Are the dogs all asleep?"

"Yeah, man. They crashed a couple of hours ago."

"Even Hooch?" I said, hoping he was still awake.

He laughed. "You're kidding, right?" (At bedtime Hooch is the sleepiest dog on the planet.)

I sighed. "I guess there's no point in me trying to wake him up and say hello then, is there?"

"Not if you expect a response. But, hey, that's your call. Let me know if you get arrested again."

He went back to the kennel to collect his things and I went back to Jamie. "Gee, sweetheart," I said, "that's a serious look on your face. Have any pesky reporters been by?"

She said, "No, but the phone's been ringing off the hook. Let's go inside and sit down. I need to talk to you."

We went inside and found that Kelso had already poured himself a tall glass of scotch. It was probably his second because he seemed very relaxed and happy.

Jamie sat me down on the sofa, droped herself sideways next to me and said, "There's a problem with your story."

"I beg your pardon? No, Frankie, off." He jumped down. "Go to place." He just stared at me. He wanted to climb in my lap so bad that I gave in, saying, "Ah, poor little doodle."

"Jack, will you knock it off with the poor little doodle. We have serious problems."

"First things first, honey." To Frankie, I said, "Come here, you." He wagged his tail and put his front paws and legs into my lap. I stroked his head for a few seconds, praised him, and then said, "Okay, go to place." By this time he'd had enough contact with me that he was okay with going to his bed by the stone fireplace and settling down. I turned to Jamie. "What do you mean there's a problem with my story? I don't have a story. I just told the truth about what happened."

The phone rang; I picked it up and listened for a second. It was another reporter, asking for a comment on the case, so I hung up and unplugged the phone.

"But see, that's just the problem, Jack." She held my hand. "Your story—sorry, your version of the truth—doesn't match the evidence."

I was stunned. "Is this *your* opinion, or Dr. Reiner's?"

"Come on, that's not fair and you know it."

I pulled away. "And calling me a liar is fair?"

"I didn't say you were lying. Jack, I just said that—"

"Okay, maybe you'd better start from the beginning. What did the autopsy show?"

10

Jamie took a deep breath. "Gordon Beeson died of a subdural hemotoma caused by a small radiating fracture to the temporal bone. There was no external blood loss."

I said, "So he was cracked hard on the forehead."

"Right between the eyes, actually."

"Maybe he tripped and fell on a rock."

"Maybe. But he also had a deep cut on his right hand. And his blood was found on the tennis ball."

"A cut? Like a defensive wound?"

She nodded. "Possibly. There were also ligature marks on his wrists and ankles."

"Well, that would explain the ropes I saw on the beach." I thought it over. "Was there any internal bleeding?"

"Well no, just swelling. But see, that's just the thing. The blow to the forehead knocked him out, and then the swelling cut off the blood flow to the brain." We sat there for a long moment. "There are two ways the body expires: lack of oxygen to the heart or lack of oxygen to the brain. In Beeson's case it was the latter. The swelling caused internal pressure on the brain, which impeded the blood flow. But he couldn't have died in the amount of the time you said he did."

I thought it over. "Then something else killed him. Maybe he died of a heart attack. Who knows?"

"No, Jack, because if he'd gone into cardiac arrest,, there

would've been no swelling. All blood flow would've stopped immediately. Besides, there's another problem."

"Which is?"

"How can an unconscious man grab hold of a tennis ball?"

I let out a hot breath. "Maybe somebody planted it there, how do I know? I'm telling you the autopsy is wrong. Either that or you've missed something."

We sat there for another long moment, then I said, "I can't believe you don't believe me."

She patted my arm. "It's not that I don't believe you, sweetheart, it's just that I *know* you. When there are dogs around you tend to get distracted."

"Okay," I laughed. "I know what you're saying. But trust me, when I find a dead man lying on the beach, everything else becomes secondary. I become extremely focused. I am a highly skilled, well-trained, and very experienced detective."

"You mean you *were*." She shook her head, then looked over at Kelso. "What do you think? You've worked cases with him."

He shrugged. "I was a prosecutor with the DA's office. We only worked together once a case was already set for trial. My job was to know the salient points we wanted to put in front of the jury. Jack's job was to nail down the details of witness testimony, to make sure we weren't sandbagged by the defense." He took a sip of scotch and got this faraway look in his eye. "There was this legendary case once, though—"

"Oh, no," I sighed, "don't tell her that story."

"Why not? She doubts your veracity, or at least your legendary acumen at a crime scene. She should know about it."

"Okay, fine," I said. "Just don't make too much of it."

Jamie said, "What is it?"

Kelso took another sip of scotch.

"Well?" Jamie said impatiently.

Kelso waved her off. He likes to take his time when telling a story. "I'm just trying to remember the details as I was told them. I wasn't there, you see. But I remember it like this: there was a suicide in Gramercy Park. A pretty young woman had thrown herself off her balcony and landed on the sidewalk. In short order the place was, as they say, crawling with cops. Several detectives were there, the Crime Scene Unit was there, even the coroner's investigator was there. By the time Jack shows up, everyone has pretty well decided that it was, in fact, a suicide. It was a secure doorman building. There was no way anyone could have gotten inside her apartment and thrown her off the balcony. It had to be a suicide.

"So, then Jack rolls up in a cab, gets out, takes one look at the body—just the merest glance, mind you—and says, 'This woman didn't kill herself.' And everyone is shocked and they all try to convince him that he's wrong, just as you're doing now with this guy on the beach. And he insists that no way is this a suicide. The woman was murdered." He looked at me. "Do you want to tell her what you saw that night?"

I shook my head. "It was nothing. I just happened to notice something, that's all."

"Yeah," he laughed. "You just happened to notice something while getting out of a cab that nobody else noticed while spending an entire hour examining the body."

Jamie said, "Enough already. What was it?"

Kelso said, "The woman had eyeliner on only one eye." He took another sip of scotch, as if pronouncing the story over.

Jamie sat there a moment and suddenly got it. "That's brilliant. A pretty woman with eyeliner on only one eye—of *course* she didn't commit suicide. She would have finished doing her eyes, not stopped in the middle to kill herself."

"It was nothing," I shrugged. "It turns out that her boyfriend did it. She'd given him her keys. Anyway, I was already skeptical before I got there. Women who want to kill themselves do not generally throw themselves off balconies."

"Really? How *do* they kill themselves?"

"Pills," I said. "Why put yourself through the terror of falling ten stories when you can just go peacefully to sleep?" (That's how my mother had done it.)

She thought it over. "Okay. But back at Aunt Zita's, maybe you miscalculated the amount of time it took from when you threw the tennis ball to when Tipper brought back the bloody yachting cap. I mean you don't even own a watch."

I laughed. "Of course I own a watch; two, in fact. A Tag Heuer and an antique Hamilton with a black lizard strap."

Kelso told her, "Jack can tell the time without a watch. Go ahead, Jack. Tell Jamie what time it is right now."

"Knock it off."

"No," he said. "She should know this about you."

"Okay then, since we're bragging on each other, why don't we tell her about what a great jazz pianist you are?"

"Is that true?" Jamie asked. "You play jazz piano?"

"I'm not that good."

"He's pretty good."

"I'd love to hear you play sometime," Jamie said.

"Can we get back to this thing about Jack telling time?"

"It's nothing," I said. "It's just a trick. Anyone can—"

Jamie said, "I want to hear it. It might be important to the case."

Kelso said, "Go on, Jacko, tell her what time it is."

I sighed. "Okay, it's—I don't know—it's about 10:27?"

Jamie looked at her watch, then looked back up at me, her eyes wide. "You were only a minute off."

Kelso said, "I'm telling you, if he was a minute off, you should probably reset your timepiece."

Jamie said, "How in the world did you *do* that?"

"It's just a trick. I taught myself to do it when I was in high school."

"But how?"

I shrugged. "It was a matter of necessity. Me and my buddies used to go surfing before school every morning. I couldn't afford a waterproof watch and I didn't want to be late for first period, so I taught myself to tell time by using my subconscious mind."

"And it worked?"

"I never missed first period." I smiled at her. "Turns out I never really became a very good surfer, though."

There was a quiet moment while Jamie absorbed all this. A mosquito buzzed somewhere. Jamie pushed a damp lock of hair behind one ear. Finally, Kelso said, "I think I'll let you two hash the rest of this out. Mind if I take the bottle?"

"Okay, yeah, fine," I huffed. "But take the Dewar's not the Glenmorangie."

"Spoilsport." He got up on two unsteady feet. Frankie lifted his head and looked over at him.

I said, "In fact, for the kind of drinking you're doing, you might just as well take the Jim Beam."

"Cheapskate." He went to the liquor cabinet, selected the bourbon, and went off to the guest bedroom. Frankie got up and followed him. "Silas Marner," Kelso muttered, then went inside and closed the door. Frankie sniffed at it for a moment, wagged his tail, then went back to his bed.

Jamie laughed. "What was that last thing he said?"

"Silas Marner. It refers to a fictional character who was famous for being a miser."

"I see."

"Steve Martin made a movie out of that book, believe it or not. I forget the name of it—the movie, I mean. The novel is actually called *Silas Marner*."

"Was *she* in it?" She was teasing me a little.

"Who?"

"Laura What's-her-name, from the dog run in New York. You know, your favorite actress?"

"You mean Laura Linney?" I chuckled. "She *was* in it, now that you mention it. And I just remembered the title: *A Simple Twist of Fate*. And she's *not* my favorite actress."

We were just chattering; mostly to keep from talking about what we *should* have been talking about, what we were *dreading* talking about: the terrible possibility that life or circumstances might somehow separate us.

"Okay, so who *is* your favorite actress?"

"Well, I don't know if you could call her an actress, exactly, but she starred in two of my favorite movies of the last ten years or so—*Michael* and *Groundhog Day*."

She was surprised. "You mean Andie MacDowell? It's funny," she shook her head, "but it always seems to me as if she can barely remember her lines, let alone *act*."

"I didn't say she was a *good* actress, I just said she was one of my favorites. She's one of those lucky types, like Gary Cooper, where the camera does all the acting for you."

"But why those two movies? *Michael* got some pretty bad reviews, as I recall. Although there *was* a dog in it."

I shook my head. "It wasn't just the dog, although I always cry during that scene. It's just a really great movie, I think. And as for the critics, they're all the time complaining about too many explosions and special effects, and here's this little film with a clever premise, that's also witty and full of unexpected nuance, and they rake it over the coals. I don't get it. Besides, I'd watch it again just because two of my favorite songs are on the soundtrack."

"Okay, I'll bite. What are they?"

"A Frank Sinatra song called 'I Took a Trip on a Train,' and a Van Morrison song, from his *Troubadour* album, called 'The Bright Side of the Road.'"

"I like that Frank Sinatra song."

"Yeah, me too. I wish I could remember who wrote it, though. I bet Kelso would know." I called out, "Hey, Kelso! Yo, Kelso, are you still up in there?"

After a moment the door opened a crack and a red-faced Kelso poked his head through the door. "What is it?"

"Who wrote that Sinatra song, 'I Took a Trip on a Train'?"

"You mean, 'I Thought About You'? Johnny Mercer wrote the lyric and Jimmy van Heusen wrote the music. It's a nice song. Is that all?"

"That's all. Thanks."

"Good. Can I go lie down and pass out now?"

"Yes, you may."

"Thank you *so* much."

He closed the door. We sat there for a moment, all out of clever dialogue. Then, before either of us could say anything more, Frankie jumped up off his bed, growling. The hair on his back was standing up. Then he began barking furiously at the front door. I got up and went over, with Frankie at my heels. "Stay here," I told Jamie.

The dog and I went out to the front lawn. He was still barking like crazy. "What is it, Frankie?" I said as if I were Timmy talking to Lassie (silly me).

He went straight to my car (the dark blue Suburban, not the woody). I followed him but didn't see anyone or anything. He got down on his front paws and looked under the vehicle. I got on my knees too, but there was no one under there. There was an odd, musky odor, though, that I couldn't identify; as if some wild animal had been crawling around down there.

I got up off my knees and looked around the property, but saw nothing, so I went back to the house, called Frankie, and we went inside. Jamie was waiting for us at the screen door.

"What was it?"

"I don't know; a wild animal in heat or something. I didn't see anything, there was just this weird, offal smell."

"That's odd."

"Well," I said, shutting the front door and leading her back to the couch, "there's a lot of wildlife around here. I live on the side of a mountain, after all. Frankie, leave it!" He was standing at the front door, still growling. "Frankie, come!" He slowly turned and came over to the couch. "Good boy, now go to place." He went to his bed by the fireplace, lay down quickly, but kept his head held up. He kept staring at the front door and growling softly.

Jamie said, "Boy, Frankie really doesn't like whatever it was that was out there."

"I know. It must've been some kind of wildcat, I guess." To the dog, I said, "Frankie, leave it. Just lie down."

He put his head down but kept growling quietly.

We sat there for a while, not saying anything until finally I said, "So anyway, I'm telling you, if the evidence contradicts my version of events, then the evidence is flat wrong."

"Jack."

"Or else it's incomplete."

"Jack."

"You have to trust me."

"I *do* trust you."

"You do?"

"Yes. That is, I do *now*. I think you're right—something *must* be missing. I just wish I knew what it was."

I patted her knee. "Well, maybe Dr. Liu will have some ideas. When are you meeting with him? Though, to tell you the truth, I don't know how I'm going to pay for all this. First Kelso and now this world famous criminalist."

"We have a web conference scheduled for tomorrow at three. And you're not paying for it, I am."

"I guess I could take another mortgage out on the house."

"I'm paying for it, Jack."

"Let's not talk about it tonight. You look tired—"

"I'm exhausted."

"—and I desperately need a shower and a nightcap, if there's any liquor left, so—"

"Can I join you?"

"What?"

"In the shower?"

I chuckled. "Like you ever have to ask?"

She smiled and suddenly stopped being an ME and became my girlfriend—or I should say my fiancée—once again. She twisted her hips the other way and fell over backward into my arms, wanting, needing, to be held.

So I held her.

We stayed like that for a while, me holding her with one arm and softly stroking her head with my other hand, she lying there with her face pressed up hard against my chest.

After a bit I said, "You really didn't have to quit your job over this, you know."

She pulled away just enough to look up at me. "What do you mean? Of *course* I did."

"But you might not ever get it back, sweetheart."

She pressed herself against me again. "That doesn't matter. All that matters is that we're together, that nothing ever keeps us apart."

I said some tender things and she replied in kind and then we kissed a little and then went upstairs for that shower. But we were both so tired that it was just that, just a shower.

11

"I'm worried about your friend Lou, Jack."

"Who isn't?"

"I mean it. He seems so sad."

"He *is* sad. Now can we go to sleep, honey, please? Let me just read a few more pages till my eyes get tired, then—"

"But I want to *talk* to you about this."

I sighed and put the Wolfram down on my right side; Jamie was on my left, smelling of soap and moisturizer. Frankie was lying at our feet. (Hooch has to sleep in the kennel because he snores.) The air conditioner in the window was keeping the room nice and cool. "Tomorrow's Sunday. We can talk about it then. Now, come on, we've both had a long day."

She said, "Poor baby," and started kissing my shoulders and chest. (I guess the shower had energized her.)

"Damn right," I said, "I've been in jail twice in the last twenty-four hours, you know."

"I *know*." The covers rustled as she moved closer to me, kissing my chest some more. "You've been locked away with all those other burly men, missing the touch of a woman. Needing a release."

"Um, just let me put this book down and turn out the light." She said that was okay and I did those things.

"Poor little doodle," she said, laughing soft and deep.

"That's me," I said. "I'm just a poor little doodle."

Frankie was so tired he didn't even look up and open his eyes. He just wagged his tail in his sleep.

"I know you are, you poor little doodle." Then she said something else, but I couldn't make out what it was because her mouth was busy doing other things.

12

I'd set my internal alarm clock for six-thirty so I wouldn't wake Jamie when I got up. It went off right on schedule. I was having a nice dream too. I don't remember what it was; I just know that it was nice. But right smack dab in the middle of it, I opened my eyes and immediately looked over at the clock on the nightstand. It showed 6:29.

I got out of bed carefully so as not to disturb my still slumbering sweetie, took care of a few things in the bathroom, went downstairs and did some stretching and a few calisthenics. Then Frankie and I went out to the kennel, where I roused the twelve doggies who were spending the Fourth with us. (There were eleven actually, but with Hooch, it made twelve.) They all got up, stretched, then shook themselves when they saw us.

There was Otis the vizsla (his owner, Kate Hughes, named him after her old friend Otis Barnes), Scarlet the Löwchen (the breed sort of looks like a silvery Maltese), Cassie the miniature schnauzer, Satchmo (Dorianne Elliot's German shepherd), Susie Q (an actual Maltese), Saki the black and white Akita, Coco (a chocolate lab/pit bull mix), Scout (another chocolate lab mix), Jackpot (a Jack Russell terrier), Bia (a tiny shi-tzu), Amanda (a West Highland white terrier), and of course, Hooch, my Dogue de Bordeaux. They all began yipping and barking happily. "Let us out! Let us out!"

They were old hands at the daily routine so I didn't bother

putting any of their leashes on, I just draped all twelve around my neck, opened the doors to their individual kennels, each one decorated with some sort of Maine motif—lobsters and sailboats and pine trees and moose and the like—and the dogs immediately ran to the front door. I knew that once I opened it, they would head straight for the play yard, a grassy, fenced-in spot (roughly the size of the infield at Fenway Park), just down the hill from the kennel.

And that's exactly what they did. By the time I got to the gate they were already there ahead of me, running around in circles, or pawing at the chain-link, or barking, or doing all three. I unlatched the gate and held it open for them and they all rushed inside. Some began sniffing around for a place to pee or poop. Others began playing right away.

After they'd gotten their elimination needs out of the way they paired up, each one choosing a favorite play partner: there was Amanda and Scarlet, Cassie and Bia, Satch and Scout, Otis and Frankie, Jackpot and Coco, Saki and Hooch, which left little Susie Q to frantically run from group to group before settling in with Scarlet and Amanda, surreptitiously biting each one on the ass whenever either one of them had their backs turned, the little rascal.

It was a glorious morning—cool and clear with no humidity and few mosquitoes out yet to pester anybody: just thirteen rough-and-tumble doggies, enjoying the hell out of each other, and me enjoying the hell out of watching them play.

I also entertained myself by trying to figure out which one in the group was the alpha dog. I don't think there is any such thing, of course; at least not in the mind of a dog, and in my view, not in the mind of anyone with any sense.

For instance, that morning the only dog who seemed intent on being the boss was Cassie, the miniature schnauzer, who at one point even barked Hooch into a corner! Yet she was the least alphalike of all the dogs there; she's just anxious and a little spoiled. But, as anyone who lives in a multiple dog household knows, it's usually a small, spoiled female (like Cassie) who runs things, not a big "alpha male" like Hooch.

As I was thinking this over, another idea was scratching at

my brain, wanting to be let in. It seemed to be saying something about dogs and lasers, which made no sense. Then I thought of Kelso's theory that a murder case is like a Zen hologram—that everything's connected on some level. Maybe my brain was trying to tell me something.

Then I realized that Gordon Beeson, our victim, worked for Ian Maxwell, who was designing a new kind of laser for use in brain surgery. Maybe lasers really *did* have something to do with the case. But how did that relate to my ruminations on dogs? *Are* dogs like lasers? It seemed unlikely. But if so, how? I mean, since I don't believe that canines understand concepts like rank, status, and who *is* or *isn't* alpha—even though, to all outward appearances, they *seem* to—what *do* they understand?

I suddenly realized that what canines *really* understand is how to align their individual needs with the needs of the pack as a whole. It's that simple. And when they *do* this—particularly when hunting—the results are amazing. They become galvanized *emotionally* the same way that photons in a laser are galvanized *physically*.

This is *phase transition*, a defining feature of an emergent system. During this transformation, a dramatic shift takes place in the underlying structure of a system (in this case, the pack), realigning it in the same way that the light in a laser is reconfigured from scattered waves into coherent light. There is still no pack leader, though, because in a self-emergent system—which is what the pack is—the system *itself* is always the leader.

This is why Frankie and all the other dogs I've trained listen and obey me. Not because they recognize my rank or status (a dog's thought process is too visceral and concrete for such abstractions), but because I know how to galvanize their emotions and put them in phase with me. It's probably the same with most really good dog trainers, though they're probably unaware of it.

I remembered reading somewhere that over half of all American dogs who go to a trainer, a puppy class, or a behaviorist end up not being trained, and *some* end up worse off than they were before. Over *half* of all our dogs! If pet dog trainers would learn to train dogs the way search-and-rescue dogs are trained—using their prey drive, instead of using constant food rewards or the threat of punishment—we wouldn't be having this problem. *All* our dogs would be totally happy, perfectly trained, and well-behaved. It's a shame that more people don't know this.

After an hour of such deliberations I called my beautiful little charges to me and was about to hook them up to their leashes but stopped and did something silly. I got down on my hands and knees and growled at them and did a play bow, the way dogs do, then rolled over on my back and cried, "Oh, no! You *got* me! You're the king doggies!"

They immediately jumped on top of me, all thirteen of them (except Hooch, who didn't quite know what to do with himself—he's so cumbersome). They leapt around and barked and nipped happily and excitedly at my beard and my hands and my clothes.

"Oh, you're the alpha dogs!" I cried as they piled on top of me. "You're *killing* me! You're *killing* me!" (This is what a papa wolf does with his pups, by the way—only without the talking part.) They *loved* this game! And even though they were all nipping at me, and I wouldn't recommend that just *anyone* try it, it was just harmless play and didn't hurt. In fact, their little love bites felt quite bracing and delicious in a wild and primal sort of way.

Then I jumped to my feet, opened the gate, and led them running up the hill, occasionally throwing in a stutter step to make them work harder at staying with me. Other times I would just stop dead cold, and they would all sit instantly and automatically; totally in sync, just like the photons in a laser. Apparently my "submissive" act had got them so tuned in to me, and so galvanized, they were ready to follow me anywhere and do anything I asked them to.

Oh, how I love my little photon doggies.

13

We got to the kennel and I squared them away, put down their food and water, took care of a few things in the office—checking which dogs needed to go home, whether they had to be dropped off or the owners would come by, how many grooming appointments we had, and so on. Plus, I erased the messages left on the office answering machine by pesky reporters. (I don't have a machine for my home phone.)

Then Frankie and Hooch and I went back up to the kitchen, where I put down their morning's provender, in two separate bowls in two separate parts of the room (they try to steal each other's food if I don't do this). Then I washed and dried my hands and began making breakfast.

First I put the coffee on. Then, since it was Sunday, I made lox and bagels, with cream cheese and vine-ripened tomato and Bermuda onion slices. (It's a New York thing.) I also made oatmeal with blueberries and walnuts—all heart-healthy items (except the cream cheese). Jamie came downstairs in her bathrobe just as I was setting the table.

"Mmmm, the coffee smells great," she said, sitting down.

After breakfast it was just the two of us. Kelso was sleeping it off, and Leon, being a teenager, was sleeping in (he does that a lot). So Jamie and I sat in the living room and had a long conversation, most of which is not applicable to the case at hand. There was one thing she said, though, which, I have to admit, was kind of disquieting to me. She said that she thought Kelso and I were like brothers, and that he, being nearly ten years older, was the big brother and that I looked up to him in some way. I hated to admit it but she was kind of right. Then she said something else that I didn't quite get at first. She said that Kelso—and remember, she'd been spending a lot of time with him during the last twenty-four hours—in a way, looked up to me as being smarter than he is.

"Well, that makes no sense. I mean he's brilliant."

"No, it does."

We were drinking what was left of the coffee. Frankie and Hooch were sleeping by the hearth, Hooch snoring loudly, as usual. It was a little before nine, and we were waiting for the footage of Buttons jumping on me to come on again at the top of the hour. (They play these things to death.)

"You see you, Jack, my darling, are a natural born genius."

"Oh, please."

"You are. While Kelso—and he admitted this to me yesterday—is someone who has simply worked hard all his life to make himself *seem* smarter than other people by memorizing words out of the dictionary, for instance, or knowing the names of old-time songwriters. Plus—and again, this is coming from him—you have been genius enough to fall in love with me, which is what keeps you from becoming, in his words, a complete loser like he is."

"Well, *that's* true," I said, then shook my head. "I can't believe he said all of this to you. I can barely get a complete sentence out of the guy—just wisecracks."

"Sounds like someone else I know," she said, then picked up the remote and started clicking around, pretending to look for something to watch, but it was all an act.

"I see. You've been reading between the lines again."

"I have not."

"It's okay. I know it's just your nature. You want to peer into the darkness of my soul and discover some magic secrets about me that will—"

"Oh, shut up." She handed me the remote.

I flipped back to my station, and the Buttons footage came on and we watched it for a few seconds, then I turned off the TV and did the dishes while Jamie took a shower.

When she was done and all dressed and smelling fresh and clean, I tried to get a little something going, but she wasn't in the mood. She was too busy, she said. She had to go to her new apartment in Rockport and do some unpacking, then to the hospital, and then back up to Augusta for her Web consult with Dr. Liu.

I told her, "It's Sunday. Visiting hours for Jill probably won't start until noon. Let's lie down for a while." I pointed to the bed, which was now occupied by Frankie and Hooch.

"I can't. I have too much to do. And so should you. Isn't there some detecting you should be doing, Columbo?"

"There's no point doing anything until we know more about how this fellow actually died, is there? Have the tissue sections been examined yet?"

"No."

"Has the DNA report come back yet?"

"Of course not."

"How about the toxicology report?"

"Nope."

"The blood gas?"

"All due in on Monday at the earliest," she sighed.

"See? And by the way, if you're going to keep calling me Columbo, or Sherlock, both of which you've been doing for about six months now, I think I'll start calling you Quincy. How does that grab you?"

She nearly doubled over. "How long did it take you to come up with that one?"

Chagrined, I said, "About six months. It doesn't quite work, does it?"

"No, not quite." She began looking around the room.

"It's downstairs," I said.

"What is?"

"Your purse."

"How did you know . . . ?" She came over and kissed me. "That's exactly what I was looking for."

We went to the door and began going down the stairs. The two dogs jumped off the bed, shook themselves in unison and followed us. "I guess," I said, "I *could* look into Beeson's background."

"Funny you should mention it. His fingerprints aren't in the system."

"You're kidding me. They ran them through AFIS?"

"Yes, and BCI and every other file system there is. Nothing, nada, zippo."

"Well, that doesn't make any sense."

"Why not?"

"Did you happen to notice the tattoo on his right arm? It was a Navy insignia."

"That's right. Someone in the autopsy room recognized it and pointed it out to me."

"And what is the first thing the military does when you enlist? They take your fingerprints."

"I hadn't thought of that. But, let me get this straight," she began, looking around the living room.

"It's on the coffee table."

She went over and picked up her purse. "You're amazing."

"It's nothing. It's just that every part of you, whether it's your purse, or your shoes, or whatever, is somehow part of me. I mean, we have this ineluctable connection—"

"Ineluctable? You've been hanging out with Kelso too long. And are you sure its not just your anal retentiveness about keeping your house in order?" She kissed me. "Ineluctable. What does that even mean?"

"I'm not sure. It kind of means, I don't know, magical or indescribably delicious or something like that. I don't know. Anyway, the thing about this tattoo—"

"But here's what I don't get. I know that the Navy uses fighter pilots, you know, on aircraft carriers, but since when do they train helicopter pilots?" She looked at the phone. "And how come no one's called here this morning? I would think your phone would be ringing off the hook."

"Don't you remember? I unplugged it last night."

She was shocked. "And you haven't plugged it back in? Jack, what if someone needs to get in touch with you?"

"Then they'll keep calling until I finally plug it back in. And the Navy trains helicopter pilots for lots of things, including covert operations; you know, by the Navy SEALs."

"Oh, wow. The Navy SEALs?"

"Yeah. Now look, before you go, let's sit down a minute and go over the fact that I'm paying for my own defense. Don't roll your eyes at me. We need to discuss it."

"Fine." She plopped her purse back on the coffee table then plopped herself onto the sofa. "But I'm paying for it. It's my fault this whole thing happened in the first place."

I sat next to her. "How is it your fault?"

She looked away. "Remember I told you about my helicopter ride to Ian Maxwell's private island?"

"Yes; back in February. I also remember that you called Beeson a 'handsome helicopter pilot.' "

"Did I?" She looked back at me. "That's just the thing, Jack. I may have flirted with him a little on the ride over. I mean, not deliberately . . ."

"Of course not." I patted her knee.

"The thing is, being up in the air like that, it was so scary, and kind of exciting at the same time, like a carnival ride—you know? I'd never been in a helicopter before so I may have been a bit more talkative and girlish than usual."

I laughed and kissed her cheek. "You know what, Jamie? I like you. I really do."

She was taken aback. "You *like* me? I thought you were supposed to love me."

"Oh, I do love you. But I really like you too."

"You do?"

"Yes. I like the fact that you get talkative and girlish on a helicopter ride with a handsome helicopter pilot."

She smiled. "You mean you're not mad at me?"

"Mad at you? Honey—I find it very appealing. I think you should get talkative and girlish any time you feel like it with anyone you please: maharajahs, intrepid African explorers, the crowned heads of Europe. Anybody."

"Really?" she laughed. "How about that guy at the gym?"

"Who? The one with the big muscles who always wears a tank top?" She nodded. "No, him I draw the line at. Besides, he's gay."

"Guess again, Columbo. He tries hitting on me every time I see him."

"Really? This is news. And does he make you feel talkative and girlish when he does that?"

She shrugged. "Come to think of it, no. He actually nauseates me a little."

"That's my girl."

She kissed me, grabbed her purse, sat back again and said, "I have to go, Jack. And I'm paying for Kelso and Dr. Liu—"

"Kelso won't take money for this."

"—and whatever else needs to be paid for."

"And besides," I said, "you can't afford it. Especially now that you quit your job."

"Wait a minute. What makes you think I can't afford it?"

"Because Jonas told me about your trust fund and how you can't touch any of the money until you're thirty-five."

She smiled a superior smirk. "That's just the principal. I actually receive quarterly dividends on the interest."

I whistled. "Interest on ten mil, that's a lot of dough."

"Exactly. *Now* will you let me pay for it?"

"Be my guest." I looked up at the ceiling.

"Now what are you doing?"

"I'm trying to do the math on the quarterly interest on ten million dollars."

"It's fifteen thousand per quarter, or sixty thousand a year," she said, getting up. "But I don't spend all of it. I usually reinvest most of the money."

"Smart girl." I got up too. So did Frankie and Hooch, who'd been lying on the carpet while we talked.

We went out the front door, followed by the dogs, who were knocking into each other and play biting. I said, "You know, there could be another reason for Gordon Beeson's prints not being on file." We walked out to her car.

"Such as?" She clicked her key ring to unlock the doors.

"Such as the witness protection program," I said.

She got an ah-ha look in her eyes. "Oh, now I know why Beeson had reconstructive surgery done on his face."

"Oh, really? He'd had plastic surgery?"

"Yep. He had cheek implants, a nose job, chin reduction, and a face-lift."

"Well, there you go."

She nodded, got in the car and started it up, but just sat there, chuckling to herself. " 'Quincy,' " she said, and shook her head at me. "Oh, by the way," she added at the last minute so I couldn't argue with her, "I've invited some people over tonight for a 'Jack's Out of Jail' party. I hope you don't mind."

"Well, yes I *do* mind."

"Don't worry, honey, it's just a few people. You'll survive." Then she put the car in gear and drove away.

"Hey! I don't want a party," I shouted after her, but she was gone. "I hate parties," I said, to Frankie and Hooch.

They just wagged their tails and looked yearningly over at the play yard.

14

I called the hospital to find out when visiting hours started, but they said Jill wouldn't be allowed any visitors for the next day or two—just immediate family. They wouldn't even tell me what she was in for, but I figured that Jamie—being on staff—would be able to find out.

At some point, around eleven, Kelso came out of his cave, kind of groaning and moaning the way he does, or the way a bear might do, if a bear happened to have spent the night in my guest bedroom with a bottle of bourbon. He then kind of shuffled his way over to the guest bathroom.

I was in the middle of a fairly long conversation with Jonas Cutter, which, although quite pleasing and enjoyable in many ways, was also pointless, as far as the object of the call was concerned. Basically I wanted to find out certain things about Ian Maxwell, the nature of their laser research for one thing, and whether Maxwell was working on any secret government projects involving the Navy. Jonas either did or didn't know, but told me that even if he *did*, he couldn't tell me about them, due to a secrecy agreement he had with Maxwell.

"It's one of the things I admire about the man," he said. "He runs a tight ship."

"Tight ship, huh? That's a nautical term. Was Maxwell ever in the Navy?"

"Yes, he was. Plus he has a fleet of yachts. But that's the second time you mentioned the Navy. Is it important?"

"Well, that's one of the things about detective work. You never know what is or isn't important until the pieces come together. By the way, didn't I hear you tell Laurie that you'd invited Ian Maxwell to the party at Aunt Zita's?"

"Yes," he said, guardedly. "What about it?"

"I don't know. It's just an odd coincidence that his chopper pilot was found dead on her beach, that's all."

"Oh, I'm sure Maxwell is not involved. He couldn't be. After all, the man has been through countless security checks for his work with the government."

"Yeah, you're probably right. Thanks, Jonas."

"You're welcome. If you need any more information, you can call me in Boston. I'll be there till Friday morning."

We hung up just as Kelso came out of the bathroom and sat heavily on the easy chair across from the big leather sofa where I was sitting. He grunted a little and wiped his brow. Frankie went over and put his head in Kelso's lap. Kelso stroked him absentmindedly. He said, "So, what's on the agenda today, Jack?"

"Do you feel up to breaking into a few data banks?"

"Well, I don't know. The laptop doesn't have the whole hacking program that the computer back in my office does, although it *does* have a mother of a motherboard." He stopped petting Frankie and the dog nudged him. He began petting him again. "Just what are we talking about here?"

I explained about the fingerprints and the Navy emblem. Also that Beeson had had reconstructive plastic surgery done.

"You think I can hack into the computers at the FBI and the Navy? I'm good, but I'm not that good. Anyway, even if I *could*, I wouldn't. They have tracing programs, and it wouldn't be long before some men in suits and Ray-Bans, or a couple of frogmen, showed up. And *frogmen* don't bring a warrant."

"There are other ways to approach the problem."

"Such as?"

"First of all we need to find out when Beeson first started working for Maxwell."

He shook his head. "From what I understand, Maxwell's computer files are more impenetrable than the CIA's."

"But even Maxwell has to fill out W-2s, right?"

"Oh, the IRS." He smiled. "That's a piece of cake. Yeah, I could do that, I guess."

"Do you want some breakfast before you get started?"

"Not especially. Let me just sit here for a minute till I get my legs back." He stroked Frankie some more.

"Something to drink? Some coffee?"

He smacked his lips. "Yeah, you got any Gatorade?"

I got him some Gatorade and he took it to the guest room. Frankie went with him. About twenty minutes later the two of them came back out.

"Okay." He sat down across from me at the kitchen table.

I was having a little light snack, some jalapeño-flavored potato chips and a tall glass of ice cold lemonade. I said, "Do you want anything?" Frankie cocked his ears and wagged his tail. (He always does that when I say the words "Do you want . . . ?") I suggested, "Maybe a sandwich or some lemonade?"

Kelso said, "Yeah, lemonade sounds good."

I poured him some lemonade and handed it to him.

"Okay," he said, taking a sip, "our vic started working for Maxwell in 'eighty-four. Which means that he probably went into witness protection, if he actually *did*—we don't know that for sure yet, that's just a guess on our part—at around the same time, or after his face healed from surgery. He probably wasn't moved around a lot, probably just landed in Maine and stuck."

"Okay, good work. So, now we need to check any trials that took place shortly before that. Trials that involved a helicopter pilot who testified against some mobsters."

He sat back in his chair and sipped his lemonade. Frankie put his head in Kelso's lap again. He scratched the dog's ears. "Are you thinking what I'm thinking?"

"What?"

"Drugs. What better way to smuggle them across the border

than in a helicopter? San Diego is a Navy town. And it's close enough to Mexico that it would be a cinch."

I nodded and smiled. "San Diego *is* a Navy town. But then so is Pensacola."

"Yeah, but San Diego is a better fit. I think I'll fool around with that idea a little and see where it leads me. Mind if I take this?" He indicated the glass of lemonade.

"Take the whole pitcher if you want."

He did, taking Frankie with him, and came back out again in fifteen minutes. I was in the living room, flipping around, looking for something interesting to watch, besides the news. Even *Clifford* if necessary. I know it's a kid's show, but I like the way the dogs talk to each other. Plus, I get a kick out of seeing this huge red dog who is also extremely loving and gentle.

Kelso sat across from me again, smiling. "Okay, Gordon Beeson is actually Hugh Gardner, who testified in San Diego against some drug dealers, just like I thought."

"Wow, that's convenient."

"What's that mean?" Frankie lay down next to his chair.

"I mean, you thought he might be from San Diego and that's exactly what you found out? That quick?"

"It's just a matter of putting together all the elements, Jack. Witness protection for a chopper pilot trained by the Navy; it all adds up to drug smuggling, either in San Diego or, like you said, Pensacola. So I got lucky with Dago."

"It's San Diego, not 'Dago,' " I said, annoyed like a true San Diegan. "So, did you check for news articles and that's how you found out that Beeson was actually Hugh Gardner?"

"Geez, Jack. You don't know much about computers and the Internet, do you?"

I thought it over. "Oh, right, WestLaw."

"Exactly. I looked up the trial transcripts by cross-referencing drug dealers, San Diego, and helicopter pilots."

"And the trial took place in 'eighty-three?"

"Well, that's another thing I cross-referenced—the rough time frame of the trial." He sat looking at me for a second or so. "You're *from* San Diego, aren't you?"

"Sort of. I grew up in a small suburb north of town called Lemon Grove."

"Well, I don't know if this information about Hugh Gardner is going to help us, then. The prosecution could argue—"

"Oh, please. I haven't been back there since my mother's funeral." I suddenly realized something and sighed.

"What?" he asked.

"Her funeral was in 1983."

"That's not good, Jack. I mean, from a prosecutorial point of view, they're gonna salivate when they hear about this."

"All right, well, there's nothing we can do about it now. Can you get me some news reports on the trial from the San Diego papers and print up the transcript of Gardner's testimony?"

"If I had a printer. And if the San Diego papers have transferred the articles in their morgue to their Web site."

I thought it over. "Well, it's after twelve so it's about time I rousted Leon out of bed anyway. He's got a printer. And I should probably call my dad. He was still on the job in San Diego back in 'eighty-three. He might know something."

"Is it compatible with a Mac Power Book?"

"What, Leon's printer? How the hell would I know? He's got an iMac. I bought it for him to help him with his homework. I even got him hooked up to the Internet."

Kelso stood up. Frankie looked at him and did the same, then shook himself. Kelso said, "Well, what are we waiting for? Let's get that bad boy out of bed."

15

After Leon got up and had breakfast, I sent him out to the play yard to clean up after the dogs (it's part of his job) and spray the area with water and enzyme cleaner, which we do once a week or so to keep the place smelling fresh.

While he did that, Kelso went to work finding me the information I needed on Hugh Gardner. Meanwhile, I called my father to see if he remembered anything about the case. It was a long shot: he never made detective; he'd been a patrolman all his life, but he might have heard something.

"Hey, Dad, it's me."

"Hey, Jackie. Is everything all right?"

"Well, yes and no, I guess. How are things at the marina?"

"It's like stealing money, that job. All I do all day is sit on my can and work on my tan."

After my mother died, he'd sold our old house on Central Avenue and moved into a retirement condo just north of Ocean Beach. He'd gotten a job as a security guard at the boat slips in Coronado, a chi-chi, palm-fringed spit of land just across the water, surrounded by the Pacific Ocean, Glorietta Bay, and San Diego Harbor, and connected to the mainland by the Coronado bridge and a narrow strip of land called the Silver Strand. A third of the peninsula hosts the naval base; the rest is a golf course, a Spanish-style resort hotel, and some high-priced waterfront homes. My dad's job is to watch the gate at the Coronado Cays, check ID then buzz the rich, sailboat and yachting crowd through to enjoy their long, leisure hours out on the salty water. I imagined him, from time to time, standing on a pier with a long fishing pole, like an older version of Jim Rockford. He's not a saltwater fisherman, though, my dad. He's a trout man, through and through.

There are four or five things that define him: Irish Catholic, honest cop, Dodger fan (although he flirted with the Padres for a while after the idiots in L.A. traded Garvey to San Diego), faithful Chevy owner, and dyed-in-the-wool trout fisherman. Getting him to fish off a pier would be like trying to get him to buy a Ford or like sending the Mormon missionaries over. You'd get nowhere fast. (He grew up in Idaho, the only Catholic kid in a town full of Mormons, so he hates the Mormon Church.)

You'll notice that nowhere on that list is there any mention of him being a proud father and a good husband. It's not that Jack, Sr. ever had any ongoing affairs, at least none that I knew about—maybe a night in the sack with a barmaid once in a blue moon when he'd had too much to drink. It's just that my definition of a good husband and father is someone who comes home to dinner with the wife and kids every night instead of always hanging out in a bar with his buddies, then stumbling home drunk at two in the morning.

"So, Jackie, I haven't heard from you in a while. How long has it been?"

"I don't know. Two years?"

I'd called my dad when I first moved to Maine and bought the kennel, just to give him my new address and phone number. Other than that, I had no reason to call and chat. I knew that our conversations would inevitably turn, as they always did, to my mother's mental illness and eventual suicide, and how it was all his fault. He always seemed to use our conversations for emotional bloodletting. It's ironic too, since when I was eight years old he told me that her condition was *my* fault; that she'd been happy and carefree until I was born and that's when she first started "acting crazy." It was a terrible thing to say to a child, and I carried it around with me like a dark cloud for a long time. A good therapist might suggest it's the reason I got a master's degree in psychology from NYU, and why I went on to Harvard Medical School, intent on becoming a psychiatrist. They might be right to do so because when my mother died, in my second year at Harvard, I came home for the funeral and never went back to school. By that time I had learned enough about postpartum depression and brain chemistry to realize that it *wasn't* my fault, nor was "curing her" my responsibility. I was finally able to put the blame where it belonged: on the doctors and on American culture in general. Like Donna Devon said, "It's hard being a woman." Well, it was much harder back in my mother's day.

At any rate, I didn't want to give him an opportunity to vent his Catholic guilt, so I did my best to stick to the subject at hand; what he knew or had heard about Hugh Gardner and his working relationship with the drug lords of San Diego.

"Not much," he said after I'd told him what was going on. "It was handled by the Feebs; you know, the Feeble-Brained Idiots." (That's how he always referred to the FBI.)

"Nobody on the force even had a hand in it?"

"Not that I'm aware of. I could ask around, though. Hey—I was just thinking—maybe I could fly out there and help you with the case. I've got two weeks off starting tomorrow."

"I don't think so, Dad."

"Come on. It's almost twenty years since I've seen you. I'm not getting any younger."

"Yeah, I know, but—"

"And neither are you. I'd hate for the next time you see your old dad to be at my funeral."

Jesus. He was going to guilt me into letting him fly to Maine. Then again, there was also Jamie to consider. A part of her soul yearned to meet my family. I couldn't very well say no to my father without saying no to her as well.

"What the hell," I said. "There are a couple of pretty decent trout streams near here. Plus, it'll give you a chance to meet my fiancée."

"You're engaged?"

"Since February."

"Well, hell, son, why didn't you tell me? I suppose you weren't even going to invite me to the wedding either."

I told him all about Jamie, and he said he couldn't wait to meet her and that he'd make the travel arrangements right away and call me back with his flight information so I could come pick him up at the Portland airport. I asked him if he needed me to send him any money for the trip.

"Are you kidding, Jackie boy? What with my pension and this cushy job—if you could even call it that—I've got more money these days than I know what to do with."

We said our good-byes and hung up and I thought, Great, I've just given myself another headache to deal with.

Still, he might prove useful. He'd been trained in the arts of canvass and interrogation. Plus, I knew it would make him feel good to be back on the job again. And I knew Jamie would be pleased. That was the main thing.

Another news story about the murder came on, so I turned the sound up in time to see a report on Beeson's girlfriend, a hippie artist named Sherry Maughn, who also happened to be one of my dog training clients. She had two dogs, a German short-haired pointer named Lucy, and a yellow Lab named Lotte. A local reporter was doing a live interview with her at the carnival and arts fair being held in Boothbay Harbor. She was a painter, and a pretty good one at that, and had a booth set up in the shade of the Ferris wheel, where she was hawking her wares.

"I know Jack Field," she was saying "And I know for a fact that he wanted to kill Gordon."

"What the hell?" I said.

She was lying, but why? I got a bright idea, but before I could take action on it, the phone rang. I had forgotten to unplug it after I'd finished talking to Jack, Sr.

"Hello?"

"Is this Jack Field?"

"Yes it is. Who's calling?"

"This is Michelle Merriweather from Channel Two News."

"Sorry, no comment."

"But if I could just ask you—"

Click.

I quickly dialed Carl Staub, a detective with the Camden PD who'd helped me on a couple of cases before. I asked him if he could get Sherry Maughn's phone records for me, ASAP. "She lives in Rockport," I told him, and gave him her number. He said he'd see what he could do.

Then I called Dale Summerhays and asked her if the animal shelter in Boothbay was open on Sundays.

"Yes, until five. Why do you ask? And are you okay? Do I need to start putting together a legal defense team for you, Jack?" (Dale is one of the richest women in Maine.)

"That's very kind of you, but no, not yet."

Then I told her about Leon wanting a dog of his own and that I was thinking of taking a drive down that afternoon.

"Well," she huffed somewhat good-naturedly (and somewhat not), "all of our animals are either spayed or neutered so I don't know if you'll approve of them."

I sighed. "What's done is done. And let's not argue about that now, shall we? Leon just needs a dog."

She said okay, then told me about a wheaten terrier mix named Magee she thought would be perfect for Leon, and asked if she could meet us at the shelter. I said I didn't know when exactly we would get there. She said she didn't mind— she had some other things to do there anyway, so I said fine and we hung up and I unplugged the phone again.

D'Linda, Mrs. Murtaugh's assistant groomer—a plump, florid-faced girl with straw hair—showed up a few minutes later, around one. She came in through the kitchen door and told me she had a couple of dogs scheduled, and one cat. Frankie woke up, ran over to her, and danced around her and wagged his tail. He gets a bath from her every Monday morning as part of the requirements of being a therapy dog at the pediatric ward. He really likes the way she shampoos him, I guess. Hooch is also a therapy dog, but has no special attachment to D'Linda. But he does like to follow Frankie wherever he goes, so he ran over too, wagging his big, orange tail and giving D'Linda his biggest mastiff smile.

She said hello to the doggies and pet their heads.

She was on the schedule to work till six but I told her about our plans to go to the carnival and asked her if she wouldn't mind sticking around till eight, in case we didn't get back from Boothbay Harbor sooner.

She said that was fine. "Besides, Jack, I'm coming to your party anyway. It *starts* at eight, remember?"

I had forgotten about Jamie's party for me but didn't want to seem ungracious, so I made some vaguely agreeable-sounding comments and she smiled and went out to the kennel.

The dogs came back to the living room and played with each other a little until I said, "Playing is for outside. You guys go lie down." So they circled around and finally curled up next to each other on the carpet, but kept gently batting at one another with their paws and softly baring their teeth.

By this time Kelso had finished printing up all the pertinent material on Hugh Gardner and his relationship with the drug lords of San Diego. Then Leon came back from the kennel looking for something to eat and I said, "We can eat down at the carnival in Boothbay Harbor. Besides, Dale Summerhays says she's got the perfect dog for you, if you still want one."

"Do I?" (I took that as a yes.)

"All right, then. Let's hop in the car and go."

I let Frankie and Hooch go out to the kennel to keep D'Linda company, left her in charge of things, and then we all piled into the Suburban and drove down the mountain. And yes, the Suburban is a Chevy. And yes, I do take after my father in some ways, though I grew up learning to dislike the Catholic Church and to admire most of the Mormons I've met. Still, I spent fifteen years working as an honest cop in New York City, just like my dad did in San Diego. And I have my own trout fishing gear (a carbon fishing rod, a wicker creel, and a pair of rubber hip waders, all stuck in the back of my downstairs closet). And, yes, I admit that I do check the sports pages from time to time just to see how the Dodgers are doing. So I guess, for better or for worse, I *am* my father's son and probably always will be.

16

We drove down the mountain to the town of Perseverance—which consisted of a gas station, a church, and a grange hall—then turned west on 17. As we did, a nondescript blue minivan pulled out of the gas station and began following us. Maybe they were going to the carnival, just like we were.

We took 17 to 131, with the minivan still behind us, though quite a ways back, then drove south to U.S. 1 and headed down the coast. The blue van was still popping up from time to time in my rearview mirror.

At any rate, while I drove, Kelso read details from the trial transcript and the local papers. As he did, the following story began to take shape:

Hugh Gardner—a.k.a. Gordon Beeson—had been quite a striking figure. Even Jamie had described him as a "handsome helicopter pilot." When he retired from the Navy as a lieutenant commander at the age of thirty-eight, he began working in the San Diego area, flying charters for tourists and out-of-town business executives. He was making a good bit of money, and fell in with a fast and wealthy crowd. He also fell in love with, and married, a former debutante named Kathy Greif, whose financial needs, unfortunately, exceeded his income by at least half.

It was the early eighties and cocaine was readily available, and in fact quite plentiful, among his new circle of friends, which put another drain on his income. It wasn't too long before he owed a lot of nasty people a lot of money.

So some "friends of friends" came around one day and offered him a way to get out from under his obligations. They offered to buy him his own charter business, chopper and all. All he had to do in return was fly a couple of scuba divers (with a dozen scuba tanks) to Baja once a week, then a day or two later fly them back across the border. There was just one little hitch. On the flight back to San Diego there would be a slight detour, an extra stop along the way that was not to be listed on the flight plan. Once he got across the border, he was to lose altitude until he was cruising just above ground level, then fly due east to an arroyo just wide enough to accommodate the chopper blades. Then he was to fly north, through the arroyo to a makeshift helipad somewhere in the California desert, and set down next to a dirt road. There would be three men, waiting in a Jeep; a nameless Mexican man, small, dapper, always dressed in a suit; and two Maori bodyguards by the names of Moana T'anke and Ngati Kong, both former defensive linemen for UCSD.

"Maori football players?" I whistled after Kelso read off their names. "Those guys are tough customers."

"The toughest."

"Yo," Leon said, "What's a Maori?"

"They're a Polynesian tribe from New Zealand."

Kelso said, "They're Melanesians, actually."

"Well," I said to Leon, "they're sort of like Hawaiians."

"Hah," Kelso laughed, "tell that to a Maori sometime then call me from the hospital. I'm telling you, these guys will go chthonic on your ass."

"What's thonik mean?" Leon asked.

"Don't ask me," I said. I had no idea.

"It's like *pre*-prehistoric. It comes from Greek myths. It refers to underworld deities who came before time. In fact, the legends say that the Maoris are descendants of a race who could fight the T. rex barehanded and win."

"Whoa," said Leon, "I'd like to be one of them."

"Yeah, me too," said Kelso. "Legends also say they used to ride whales across the ocean, the way we'd ride a horse."

"Let's get back to Hugh Gardner," I said. "The last part of the story was that he made a drop in the desert, right?"

Kelso nodded and went on with his narrative. Gardner's passengers would then debark briefly and exchange the dozen scuba tanks for almost identical tanks provided by the Maoris, T'anke and Kong. Then he was to fly back, at altitude, to Brown Field in San Diego and drop off his passengers, and their scuba gear, to be examined at the local customs office.

Gardner knew immediately what was going on, but he was into these people for a lot of money, and his wife's spending habits showed no signs of slowing down. In short, he desperately needed the cash, so he agreed to the plan.

It was at this point in the story that Kelso caught me flicking my eyes up to the rearview mirror for the twentieth time or so. He gave me a look and was about to say something but I shook my head and gave just the merest tilt of my neck toward Leon in the back seat. Kelso nodded imperceptibly. He got that I didn't want to worry the kid.

I used the power switch to adjust the passenger sideview mirror so Kelso could see what I saw. "A blue minivan," I said softly, and he nodded.

He casually glanced out the window, and when the mirror was in perfect position he said, "That's good, right there." He looked for a while then said softly, "How long?"

"Since Perseverance. He pulled out of the gas station."

"Could be a coincidence."

"Could be."

"Maybe the police?"

"Maybe."

"Reporters?"

I shook my head. "They'd drive a news van. And the funny thing is, I could have sworn I lost him earlier."

"What do you want to do?"

"Let's just keep on our toes."

"Yo," Leon said, "what are you two talkin' about up there?"

"Nothing," I said, and took the exit north of Waldoboro, hoping to lose the tail. I drove through the lovely little town slowly then got back on U.S. 1. The blue minivan was nowhere to be seen.

"Nice work," Kelso said.

"Yo," Leon said, "what about the story? What happened?"

Kelso went on with the tale: the scuba tanks that were loaded on the chopper in San Diego for the trip down to Mexico were the real thing, filled with compressed air. The Mexican customs officials were very careful about their examination. They would even switch the valve open and let some of the air out to make sure the tanks were genuine.

At some point, though, they were exchanged for identical tanks filled with raw heroin. At the drop site in the desert, these were exchanged for real tanks either empty or low on oxygen, as if they'd been used for diving.

Gardner was trained by the Navy SEALs, so from the outset, just in case he ever got caught, he began making notations in his private flight book, done in code in case any of the bad guys got wise and tried to read it. He wrote down the license plate of the Jeep, for instance, and of the Lincoln Town Car that dropped off the "divers" each week. He also wrote down any names he overheard the bad guys call each other, and anything else he could think of for when the Feds caught on.

It took two years before an FAA official at Brown Field got suspicious about these weekly flights and planted a transponder on Gardner's chopper late one night. The Feds followed his movements for a month before making the bust.

Gardner, who had been a fairly decent and honorable sort of guy most of his life, immediately agreed to testify in exchange for witness protection. His wife immediately sued for divorce.

I asked, "What kind of helicopter was it?"

Kelso looked in his notes. "A Sikorsky S-76C+, Executive Model. It seats twelve passengers, two crew members, and has thirty-eight cubic feet of cargo space. Oh, and it has a minibar."

"Sweet." I thought of something. "Who was his copilot? I don't think the FAA will let you leave the airport in a rig like that without two men in the cockpit."

"No, you're right. One of the bad guys doctored up a pilot's license and masqueraded as his copilot, even though he couldn't actually fly."

I nodded. "So, they found a hole in the center radar blanket and that's how they escaped detection."

"That's right," Kelso said.

Leon said, "Yo, two things: What's a center radar blanket, and what's a transponder?"

I looked at Kelso and said, "You want to cover that?"

"You seem to know more on the subject than I do."

"Well," I shrugged, "I took a couple of flying lessons a few years ago at Teterboro." To Leon, I said, "A transponder is sort of like a radio transmitter."

"Then why not just say 'radio transmitter'?"

"Because it doesn't transmit normal radio waves, you know like a radio station. It sends out a specific kind of signal. I don't know what it is or how it works exactly, but it allows the FAA to keep tabs on suspicious aircraft. Transponders are also used in Global Positioning systems, to time sporting events, even to keep track of lost doggies.

"Anyway, as for your other question, there are two types of radar used by the FAA—that's the Federal Aviation Administration. There's terminal radar, which is located at the airport at just a little bit above ground level so you can't fly under it."

"What does 'fly under it' mean?"

I explained that radar is a directional system that sends out radio waves that bounce off objects in the sky. "If you fly above the radar dish, you show up as a blip on a radar screen. If you fly under it, there's no blip."

"Oh, yeah. I seen that in movies and shit."

I went on to explain that terminal radar has a range of about thirty to fifty miles, which is why the bad guys had to have a drop site out in the desert, far away from the airport. I then explained that center radar blankets the rest of the country, using radar dishes, usually located at the highest nearby elevation, and pointed upward. Back in the eighties it was possible to find spots where you could fly a helicopter or even a small plane below these radar dishes and escape detection. Nowadays, you can't do that because the INS and the DEA have radar planes patrolling the border. "And that's also why they had Gardner fly through the arroyo."

"See, that's another thing. What's an arroyo?"

I explained that it was like a much smaller version of the Grand Canyon, made by erosion from small streams or rivulets. Before he could ask what a rivulet was, I told him, "A rivulet is the smallest type of stream, smaller than a brook. And while some rivers may dry up in hot weather, a rivulet usually only exists during or just after a thunderstorm, or during spring runoff."

Then I had to explain what spring runoff is.

Leon sat back in his seat. "I don't know why I has to go to school for. I could get a complete education just listening to the two of you bullshit. So, Mr. Kelso," he went on, "you're from New York. Who do you like, the Mets or the Yankees?"

"Neither," he said. "The Mets have a crappy team and the Yankees don't even *play* baseball."

"They don't play *base*ball? What you talkin' about?"

Kelso shrugged. "They're an American League team and no team in the American League plays actual, real baseball anymore. They all play sissy-ball."

"Sissy-ball? Aw, *hell* no."

"Hell *yes*," he scowled. "What else would you call it when your pitcher is too chicken to stand in the batter's box every third inning and take his hacks at the plate? No," he said in a sarcastic tone, "*he* can't take an at-bat—he's too chicken. He has to have a big strong man come out of the dugout and hit *for* him. Except that the big strong hitter is also a sissy because he's too scared to go out on the diamond and try to field the ball like everybody else."

I laughed.

Leon said, "You're wack, you know that?"

Kelso said, "If we'd tried that shit back at the sandlot, we would have been called cheaters and gotten beaten up by the older kids, I'm telling you."

"He has a point," I said to Leon. "A baseball line-up is supposed to consist of nine players, not ten."

Then Kelso went on to talk about Babe Ruth, and how before he became a batting champion he was a pretty good pitcher, and that if they'd had the designated hitter in his day, no one would have ever known what a great home-run hitter he really was.

Leon said, "Aw, he's not so great. Barry Bonds is better."

Kelso said, "Bonds is on steroids. That's cheating too."

"He is not," Leon said.

I said, "Come on, Kelso. There isn't any proof that Bonds is on steroids and you know it."

"Sure there is. Look at the before-and-after photos. Bonds, McGwire, Sosa, they all display classic signs of steroid use. And of course there's no real proof because the player's union won't allow mandatory drug testing." (Kelso is fond of spouting possibly slanderous ideas like this.)

Leon said, "I think you're wrong. Besides, I seen movies of Babe Ruth and he's always bouncin' around, real jerky and funny-like."

Kelso sighed. "That's because during the silent era, they shot movies at sixteen or eighteen frames per second, not twenty-four like they do now. The Babe was actually quite graceful. He even stole a lot of bases and was a great outfielder."

Then he had to explain what the "silent era" was, and what frames per second meant, and even what persistence of vision means. He said, "Haven't you ever seen a silent movie?"

"Nah. They's all in black and white and has wack music."

I made a mental note to rent some Buster Keaton films for him. He would love the way Keaton races around and does all these acrobatic stunts without ever changing the expression on his face. Leon, I thought, would identify with someone who could do all that amazing stuff and never reveal his feelings.

As if on cue, Leon tuned us out, put his headphones on, and began listening to his portable CD player.

We turned onto 27 at North Edgecomb and drove down the peninsula. The road was like Fifth Avenue during rush hour, but without the buses and taxicabs. In fact, it was pretty much wall-to-wall SUVs. All except for a certain blue minivan that popped up in my rearview mirror again.

17

We got to the animal shelter in Boothbay at about two-thirty. Dale Summerhays had saved us a parking space, so we parked, left Leon to check out the dogs (I gave him ten bucks to buy a burger or something and told him we'd be back in a couple of hours, at the latest), then Kelso and I started hoofing it the rest of the five miles to Boothbay Harbor.

The day had turned hot and humid and Kelso had a hard time keeping up. His face was red and puffy and he was sweating and breathing hard. And we were just walking at a normal pace.

While we walked I told him about Eddie Cole, and how at first I thought that he was the one who'd been tailing us. (Cole had once threatened to kill Jamie and had been arrested back in February for raping Tulips and kidnapping Jamie, but had escaped from custody shortly afterward.)

Kelso said, "He'd have to have a huge set of cojones to show his face around Maine again, don't you think?"

"Yeah, you're right. It was probably someone else."

Then I told him about Frankie's barking episode the night before and the strange, feral smell that I'd detected underneath the Suburban.

"Well, that's why you couldn't shake this guy. He probably planted a homing device on your chassis last night."

"You mean a transponder?"

Kelso laughed. "That's right, bucko. And you know what that means . . ."

"What?"

"It means that he's someone with experience and background in running covert operations."

"Like a Navy SEAL."

"Maybe. And since you run a kennel, and have a dozen or so dogs on your property, I don't know, he probably figured that the best way to disguise his scent was to cover it up with the scent of an animal the dogs would be frightened of—like a moose or a bear."

I thought it over. "I'm not sure that makes any sense, but I guess that *could* be it."

We walked on in silence for a while, then, after we'd gone a couple more miles and Kelso was having more and more trouble keeping up, I looked at him disapprovingly and said, "You know, maybe it's time you thought about quitting."

"What? You mean drinking or walking? Or smoking?"

I laughed. "Drinking, you moron. *And* smoking."

"Yeah, the trouble is, every time I think about getting sober I get this irresistible urge to go out and have one last major binge, which isn't very healthy."

I told him about Jamie's friend, Annie Deloit, and how she'd gone into rehab and had been sober since February, hoping it might sway him to do the same. "You need to quit."

"Like I don't *know* that?"

I stopped and confronted him. "Well, then *do* it. You're no good to me like this. You're no good to yourself. We've got someone tailing us and you can barely walk."

He looked me over. "Maybe you should go on without me."

"Yeah, maybe I should." I stood there for a long moment, watching him sweat. "Do you know your way back to the car?"

He shook his head at me like I was an idiot. "Of course. It's just back up the road a ways. You think I can't—"

"Okay." I cut him off. "I'll meet you back there when I'm done talking to Gardner's girlfriend."

He nodded, found a grassy spot under a sycamore tree, and

sat down. "Go on ahead. I'll be all right. And by the way, what are you going to do about Leon?"

"What do you mean? He's picking out a dog. He'll be fine."

He shook his head. "I mean if you get indicted for murder, you idiot. You realize that the child welfare people are going to come around and try to take him away from you."

I said, "The Division of Human Services."

"What?"

"In the State of Maine child welfare situations are handled by the Division of Human Services."

"Whatever. You need to start thinking about what to do."

I *hadn't* thought about it, actually, and didn't want to think about it now. All I wanted to do was to find out why Sherry Maughn was lying about Gordon Beeson's death, and why she was implicating me in the bargain. If Jill Krempetz weren't sick, she'd be able to handle the whole thing with Leon and DHS for me and I wouldn't have to worry about it. But she *was* sick, and Kelso didn't know the Maine family court system or the genealogy of my case like she did.

I said, "I guess I'll just have to cross that bridge when I come to it."

"Well," he said, "I have a few ideas, but we can talk about them later. For now, just leave me here for a bit."

I hesitated. "Are you going to be all right?"

"I'm fine. Just go, okay? But here." He held out a pack of Marlboro cigarettes. "Take this with you."

"I don't smoke."

"Me neither. At least not these; I like frog butts."

"Frog butts?"

"French cigarettes." He held out the pack again. "This isn't a real pack. There's a tape recorder hidden inside."

"Not a bad idea," I said, taking it from him.

"There's a little switch sticking up through the O. You flip it up when you want to start recording."

"Thanks," I said. "See you back at the car."

I got about fifty yards or so down the road and felt bad that I'd treated him like some toothless wino—he was my best friend, after all—so I turned around, but he'd disappeared. Probably off taking a whiz, I thought. Or maybe he'd found a bar I hadn't noticed earlier. So I turned back down the road.

Once I got closer to Boothbay Harbor, finding the carnival was a snap. I just headed for the Ferris wheel, which was the tallest thing on the horizon. That and the smell of popcorn led me right where I needed to go.

There was an admissions booth where I paid my five dollars and got my hand stamped. I went through the wooden turnstile with the rest of the "rubes" and began looking around for Sherry Maughn's booth.

First I went down a row with the usual carnival games: the ring toss, the coin throw into the goldfish bowls, the shooting gallery, the stacked metal milk bottles with the oddly weighted softball so you can't win the game, and so on.

Then, as I got closer to the rides, I passed the popcorn and the cotton candy booths, the hot dog stand and the barbecue pit with hamburgers, spareribs, sweet corn, and freshly caught Maine lobster.

I passed the tilt-a-whirl, the Ferris wheel, and the other rides, and saw the row of artists' booths on the other side of the Porta Potties located just east of the rides.

These booths were basically just canvas tents held up by aluminum poles. They featured tie-dyed clothing, hand-carved wooden furniture, macramé plant holders, and the like.

Finally, I got to Sherry Maughn's booth, which exhibited her oil paintings of angels, Tolkien-type creatures, and mystical landscapes. Sherry was a pretty good artist in her own right— her technique was flawless, though her imagery was uninspired. Still, she was afflicted with the vain belief that she was on a par with the great painters of all time. It must have really galled her that she had no customers, even though a line had formed at the pottery booth directly across from hers. Oddly, the center pole in her booth was much wider in diameter than the center poles in the other booths. I briefly wondered why, but didn't think about it again until a few days later.

Late forties, tall, handsome, big-hipped yet small-breasted, with henna hair tied back in pigtails and large green eyes,

Sherry was sitting in a folding aluminum beach chair, with a pair of sunglasses perched on top of her head, holding a lit cigarette and flipping the ash sideways, off to her right. She had on white, house painter's overalls over an orange, red, and brown tie-dyed T-shirt and was listening to an oldies station. They were playing "Little Red Riding Hood" by Sam the Sham and the Pharaohs. She saw me, dropped the butt, stood up, dropped her sunglasses down to her nose and said, "What do you want?"

I reached into my shirt pocket, found the switch on the minirecorder and flipped it up.

"Hey, Sherry, you've got some nice paintings here."

"Get lost, Jack. I know you killed Gordon."

"You mean, Hugh Gardner?" I couldn't see her eyes because of the sunglasses, but there was just the tiniest intake of breath when I said Gordon Beeson's real name. She obviously knew about his past in San Diego. "And you know very well that I didn't kill him. If he *was* murdered, it probably had something to do with his smuggling days back in California, or maybe it had to do with his job working for Ian Maxwell. So, why have you been lying to the police and the media about this?"

"Just get out of here before I call security."

"Go ahead. Meanwhile, how are Lucy and Lotte doing?"

The sky had darkened with clouds by this time. The mercury was dropping too. A storm was on its way. A gust of wind shook her booth a little. She looked up at the sky, rubbed her arms, then reached under the counter and grabbed a Levi's jacket. She put it on and just stood there a moment, staring at me. Then she pushed her sunglasses on top of her head.

"The dogs are fine, Jack," she sighed. "And listen, I'm sorry you're the scapegoat in all this. You did a wonderful job training my two girls. And yes, I lied to the cops. But I can't say anything about what's really going on, okay? It's too dangerous. And if you persist, I'll deny we ever had this conversation." She picked up a cell phone, pressed some digits, waited, and said, "Security? This is Sherry Maughn on Artist's Row. There's a man here who's threatened to kill me. His name is Jack Field." She paused. "That's right. He killed Gordon Beeson on Friday, now he's threatening to kill *me*."

I shook my head, sighed, and said, "Whatever's going on, you must be in pretty deep. Is Eddie Cole involved?"

She pushed the off button and said, "Who's Eddie Cole?"

Just then a red dot of light appeared on her forehead. She saw something behind me, over my shoulder, and said, "Jesus," then hit the dirt.

I whirled around in time to see a fairly tall man, probably in his early forties, dressed in khaki coveralls, wearing a nylon stocking mask, standing behind the pottery booth on the left side, aiming a Glock 9mm pistol with a noise suppresser and a laser sighting device right at me. In fact, he had just fired, but because Sherry had ducked and I had turned at the exact same moment he'd pulled the trigger, the bullet missed both of us and got one of her paintings instead. (One of her angels got it right through the heart.)

The guy threw down the Glock and took a snub-nosed Colt .32 (traditionally a woman's gun) from one of his big pockets. He aimed it at me, but before I could do anything or say anything, and before he could squeeze off a bullet, Kelso came out of nowhere and tackled him, ramming him into the wall of the booth, knocking it down. They landed on a shelf full of pots, breaking most of them.

18

"Stay down!" I told Sherry over my shoulder, then started running toward the pottery booth where Kelso was now wrestling with the guy in khaki. Before I made it halfway there, the guy twisted around and turned over on his back. He threw his legs up in the air, grabbed Kelso's head between his ankles in a scissors hold, and flipped him over. Then, in one motion, almost defying gravity, from flat on his back he jumped to his feet and ran off, taking his mask off and stuffing it into his pocket as he ran. He did all of this so fast that I couldn't even get a glimpse of his face, only his totally bald—or clean-shaven—head.

I ran after him with a quick "Thanks, you okay?" to Kelso as I went past.

"Yeah, get him," he coughed. "I got his guns."

I came around the back and got a faint whiff of the same musky odor I'd detected the night before; the one that had gotten Frankie's back up. I looked down the back "alley" behind the row of artists' booths and found that my would-be assassin (or Sherry's assassin, I still wasn't clear on who he'd been trying to shoot—me or her, or both) had disappeared. I ran on anyway, looking into the spaces between booths as I passed by. Then it occurred to me that maybe he'd hidden inside one of them, so I ran back to the main pathway asking all the vendors,

"Did you see a tall bald guy wearing khaki coveralls run past here?"

Impossibly, nobody had.

There was only one way out of the fair that I knew of, and that was back at the main gate, so I ran in that direction, going as fast as I could without knocking over anybody's tub of popcorn or tripping over and possibly mangling some young mother's baby stroller. It was slow, or at least, careful going.

Still, I plunged into the cacophony—moving quickly past the taped, jingling calliope music, the half-frightened, half-delighted screams of the children, and the brash practiced barking of the barkers: "Get your popcorn! Get your popcorn, right here!" and "Cotton candy! Who wants cotton candy?"

It wasn't just the noise. All my senses were inundated with impressions—sounds, smells, images. They grabbed and clutched at my mind as I tried to push past him, training my focus on one specific set of images: a fairly tall bald man in khaki coveralls trying to blend in with the crowd, but still making some sort of movement the other carnival goers weren't. He could be standing at the ring toss but not really focusing on the game. Instead he might be very casually and smoothly scanning the crowd, his body language showing nonchalance, perhaps even boredom, but his eyes would reveal intense focus and concentration. He would also be alone, where the rest of the crowd was parsed into units of two or three or more—boyfriend and girlfriend, Mom and Dad and the kids. And he wouldn't be talking or relating to anyone else there either, knowing that such interactions would cause someone to remember him and perhaps be able to describe him later to the police.

As I was moving through the crowd, searching for these telltale signs, I was also thinking it out: he'd brought two guns with him; at least two. He'd aimed the Glock's laser on Sherry, then—when he'd missed her and she'd ducked out of sight—he dropped it and aimed the woman's gun, the .32, at me.

Had the first gun jammed, or was his intention to shoot us both and make it look like we'd shot each other? Either way, it meant that he'd planned things out in advance. He'd spent some time mapping the fairgrounds, planning his escape, and preparing himself for any possible eventuality.

I ran past the tilt-a-whirl and the Ferris wheel and the other rides asking over and over, "Did anybody see a tall bald guy in khaki coveralls run by here?" Nobody had. It was like he was a cipher, or a ghost.

Or as Kelso had suggested, a Navy SEAL.

Maybe, I thought, he's in one of the Porta Potties. That would be a pretty good place to hide out—stinky but private. So I angled my way over there through the crowd. It didn't look likely, though, because when I got there I saw that the lines were too long. It was doubtful that he'd just stand around, waiting. And cutting in would get him noticed and remembered. Still, I shouted out my by now futile question: "Did anybody see a tall bald guy wearing khaki coveralls run past here?"

A fat guy in a white T-shirt, one size too small, pointed to a trash can. "You mean like those?"

There was a pair of khaki coveralls sitting on top of the wax paper cups, the empty popcorn bags, the barbecue-sauce-stained paper napkins, and all the rest of the debris of a day at the fair. The assassin could be wearing anything by now—most likely khaki shorts and a "Maine" T-shirt to blend in with the crowd. There was no point in still trying to find him—not unless I could get up fairly high, above everything. I thought of the Ferris wheel but that would take too long.

Then I saw the ladder; not a painter's ladder—the kind that forms an A when you set it up and has a little shelf that sticks out to hold the paint can. This was the one-piece kind that you lean up against a building. It was lying on its side behind the first Porta Potti in the row, with the top (or bottom) of it sticking out just enough for me to notice it.

I went over, picked it up, and set it against the side of the john, made sure it was steady and secure, then climbed it to the roof. I crawled off on my hands and knees then stood up, testing the strength of the surface. It gave slightly as I put my weight on it. (Whoever was inside must have been wondering what the hell was going on up there!) The roof held, but the structure itself started to sway back and forth slightly and I had an image of it toppling over onto the next one in the row, starting a domino effect, so that all the toilets got knocked over on their sides. Luckily, that was just a momentary fantasy of mine and didn't actually happen.

I started my search by looking toward the main gate, off to the west, then made a complete circle, scanning as much of the crowd as I could from ten feet up. I was looking for a bald man making any kind of unusual, hurried movement, possibly toward the perimeter of the area. I ended up facing south toward the docks and the lobster pounds, and that's when I saw him; him and his clean-shaven head.

Just like I'd thought, he was wearing khaki shorts and a T-shirt. He'd just climbed over the chain-link fence and was about to jump down. He let go of the fence, twisted sideways, jumped down, landed on his feet, and began running—all in one smooth, uninterrupted motion.

Jesus, he was good. Much better than me.

I wondered, for the first time, how the hell Kelso had managed to tail him to the pottery booth in the first place. Not to mention how he'd managed to keep him from killing either me or Sherry Maughn, or both of us.

Well, I thought, there's no way I'm going to be able to catch up with him now, so I climbed down, put the ladder back where I'd found it, then went to the trash can to retrieve the coveralls. They were evidence.

"Did anybody see who was wearing this?"

Again, nobody had. This guy was *really* good.

I went back to check on Kelso, but when I got to "Artist's Row," as Sherry Maughn had called it, I could see a security guard giving him a hard time. I did my best to blend in with the crowd, which also gave me a chance to do a little eavesdropping. I heard someone say that Sherry Maughn had run off, leaving her booth and her paintings behind. Someone else said that a man had tried to kill her.

"Oh, I know," said someone else. "It was that dog trainer from TV. You know, the one they arrested for killing that helicopter pilot? I saw the whole thing myself."

"You know, I heard the pilot was Sherry's boyfriend. I guess that crazy dog trainer wants to kill them both."

"Why can't the police do anything? I thought they put the evil bastard in jail already."

"He's not evil. Didn't you see him on TV with that cute little puppy?"

It seemed that no one besides Sherry, Kelso, and I (the crazy evil dog-training bastard from TV) had actually seen the shooter. Plus, the guard had been told (by Sherry) that someone had threatened to kill her, so he was determined to take that someone into custody. Kelso had the guy's guns, so he was first on the list.

I caught Kelso's eye from a few booths up the path and he shook his head at me then looked away, nonchalantly. He was telling me to get the hell out of there. He was also holding his left arm, as if it were sprained or broken. I shook my head back at him and continued forward. He shook his head again—a little more forcefully. I had no idea what kind of story he was spinning with the guard and if my presence was going to make things better or worse for him, or for me, so I started to make my way slowly back toward the main gate, passing some paramedics along the way. They were rolling a gurney toward Artist's Row.

I took one last look back and wondered if it was going to be my turn to get *Kelso* out of jail—or maybe to smuggle him out of the hospital. It wasn't until then that I remembered the tape recorder, still hidden inside the pack of Marlboros.

19

I played the tape for the (by now) three security guards. They listened politely several times until they finally got the picture of what had actually happened.

The paramedics, meanwhile, were attending to Kelso. They put a splint on his left arm and were attempting to load him onto the gurney but he kept refusing to get on.

"My friend's fiancée is a doctor," he said. "I'll just have her take a look at it when I get home."

They finally gave up and left. Kelso immediately went into Sherry Maughn's booth, got her beach chair, brought it out to the dirt pathway and sat down in it.

It was about then that Quentin Peck—short and wiry, with tobacco hair and a nicotine smile—along with another Rockland County deputy, showed up and started dispersing the crowd.

"Hey, Jack," Quentin said after he'd chased most of the onlookers away. "Sorry I missed you the other night."

"Don't sweat it. I'm just glad I wasn't in jail long enough to renew any old acquaintances."

He introduced me to the other deputy: Mike deSpain, who was a little taller and had clipped curly black hair, dark skin dotted with moles, and black eyes.

"So, Jack," Quentin went on after the niceties were over, "what kind of trouble are you in now?"

I retold the story then gave him and deSpain the khaki coveralls I'd found in the garbage bin.

I said, "You can have the state crime lab check the right sleeve for GSR," then explained to their blank faces that GSR stands for gunshot residue. The first security guard gave Quent the two guns he'd confiscated from Kelso. Then Quent called the State Police and we had to wait around for Sinclair to show up and (probably) bust my chops again.

It was getting late. The mercury had dropped by fifteen degrees in the last half hour, and off to the west, across the Kennebec River, Brantley Parker's "thunder bangers" were announcing their imminent arrival in our vicinity.

It was close to four-thirty, so I borrowed Quent's cell phone and called Dale Summerhays at the animal shelter. I told her what had happened. She commiserated with me and immediately volunteered to take Leon home. Leon *and* Magee, that is.

"So he liked Magee, huh?"

"That, my dear boy, is an understatement. Here, let me put him on the phone."

Leon came on, all hyped up and excited. "Yo, Jack, you should see this dog. He is the coolest thing."

"He's da bomb, huh?"

"He's off da hook. I can't wait to show you! I already taught him to sit and give a paw. And he follows me everywhere, yo, and when I sit down somewhere he jumps all over me and licks my face and shit!"

I laughed then said, "Listen, I'm going to be tied up for a while with some police business. Dale's going to have to give you a ride home. I'll meet the dog later tonight, okay?"

"Aw, man. They puttin' you in jail again?"

I laughed. "I don't think so. Not this time."

"I hope not. But I can have him, right?"

"Who, Magee?"

"Yeah. He's just the dopest dog."

"Yeah, you can have him. He sounds great." We said goodbye and I hung up then called Jamie's cell phone and explained the situation to her. "I'm sorry, honey, I just don't know how late I'm going to be with this."

She laughed a sour laugh. "You're just doing this to avoid coming to your own party."

I laughed at *her*. "It's not my party, it's *yours*. And I'm doing this to avoid getting killed or put back in jail."

"Sorry," she said meekly. "Are you all right?"

"Yes. And by the way, who's taking care of the food and drinks for this little shindig of yours?"

"My mom, who else?"

That was good news. Not only is Laura Cutter beautiful, she's a great cook. And she loves putting together canapés and finger food for parties. I could imagine her in her kitchen, hard at work, enjoying every moment of it.

"Well, that's one point in your favor. How'd the Web consult with Dr. Liu go?"

I could almost hear her smile. "Great! He says it's entirely possible for someone with a subdural hemotoma to have swum ashore from a boat and then died. Remember? You said Beeson's clothes were all wet. Oh, and he also has some great ideas and he wants to do another autopsy—just me and him. We're doing it tomorrow afternoon."

"That's great. Listen, I called the hospital and they wouldn't tell me anything about Jill. I don't suppose you could find out what's wrong with her for me, could you?"

"I know exactly what's wrong with her; I'm the Chief of Pathology. But I can't tell you about it because of doctor-client privilege."

"But it's just me, honey."

"Sorry. I can't tell you anything, Jack."

"But is she going to be all right?"

"Jack, if I could tell you anything, I would. Now, are you coming to your party or not?"

"Frankly? I'd rather be arrested again. But since your mom is making the food, I guess I'll be there." I was about to say something else when the walkie-talkie on the belt of one of the security guards filled with static. So did Quent's cell phone. Jamie and I overheard the following:

"Clark, come in? We've got a situation."

Clark unhitched his walkie-talkie.

"What?" said Jamie. "Jack, what was that?"

Clark said, "This is Clark."

"Hang on a sec," I told Jamie.

The voice said, "We've got a severe thunderstorm moving in. We need to get everyone off the Ferris wheel forthwith."

"Roger."

"And we need to clear the area around the main gate. There's going to be a mass exodus when it hits."

Clark 10-4ed, then reholstered his walkie-talkie. He explained the situation to the other guards, and while he was doing this I said to Jamie, "Sorry. There was some interference from a walkie-talkie."

"It sounds serious. Are you going to be all right?"

"Yeah. It's just a thunderstorm."

"Well, don't get hit by lightning."

I laughed. "I think they'll all probably hit the Ferris wheel, if they hit anything. By the way, my dad's coming to town for a visit. He'll probably arrive sometime tomorrow."

"Really? That's great. I can't wait to meet him."

"Yeah, well, we'll see you how you feel about that after he gets here and you spend some time with him."

"Jack, he can't be that bad. After all, he *is* your father. And listen, don't forget your party."

"I told you I'm coming even though I don't like parties."

"Jack," she said, exasperated, "I'm supposed to be the one with social anxiety about parties, not you."

"No. You get anxious about *coming* to a party. Once you get there, you're fine. Me—I have no problem *going* to a party as long as there's an escape route available. But if the party is being held at my house—"

"—then there's nowhere to go. I get you. But you *have* to come. I've invited everybody. Plus my mom is making some great hors d'oeuvres."

"Yeah, you said that already. Look, I gotta go."

"Okay. I love you."

I replied in kind, then we hung up. The security guards left.

The carnies got everyone off the Ferris wheel and then began closing down the other rides, waterproofing the game booths, and putting into effect all the other contingencies that come with an outdoor event. The artisans and vendors placed plastic sheets over their wares and unrolled the canvas closures for their booths, tying them down with the attached rayon ribbons. Most of them stayed inside their booths, drinking coffee, listening to the radio, or maybe just counting their money—who knows? They had become invisible.

Once the rain started—a shirt-soaking downpour—the umbrellas and ponchos began sprouting in the field of carnival-goers, and they all headed for the exit. In short order the place was deserted.

It's a strange thing to be left in an abandoned carnival in a sudden thunderstorm. And what a storm it was: streams and rivulets formed on the roofs of the canvas tents, pouring down to the edges, creating small waterfalls that cascaded in liquid sheets to the ground below. Puddles appeared and grew larger all along the dirt pathway, which by now had turned to mud. The raindrops were so big and hit the ground so hard that the mud splashed up around our ankles, spattering our shoes and socks.

It was just the four of us now: Quentin Peck, Mike deSpain, Lou Kelso, and me. Four morons getting soaked in the rain, although the two deputies were smart enough to have brought along some plastic ponchos, which they'd quickly put on.

"Nice work saving my life, by the way," I said finally to Kelso.

"Yeah, my pleasure," he scowled.

"So, was that a drunk act, earlier?"

"Nah. But after you split I saw that the minivan was still following you and, I don't know, I guess I just sucked it up, did a Zen thing in my head, and followed *him*." He looked at the others. "I don't know about the rest of you bozos," he said, tired of waiting for the state cops to show, "but I'm not sitting out here in the rain all day." He picked up the beach chair and took it back inside Sherry's booth.

Just then the first lightning bolt hit the Ferris wheel. I tried to count it out, like you do—one Mississippi, two Mississippi, and so on. In this case I wasn't able to get through the first Mississippi before—*blam!*—we heard, or rather heard *and* felt, down to our fillings, the enormous thunderclap.

In a comical knee-jerk reaction, deSpain actually drew his weapon and aimed it at the Ferris wheel before he realized what he was doing.

I stifled a laugh and said, "Look, I know it's a crime scene, but let's join Kelso inside the booth. Do you guys mind?"

They said they didn't, so we all got in out of the storm and just stood around inside, watching it rain and waiting for the next lightning bolt to hit.

20

Half an hour later Sinclair and his partner (whom I hadn't met) arrived. A matching pair of Feebs and a small CSU team accompanied them. They drove right up Artists' Alley and parked in the mud: Sinclair and his partner in a blue State Police cruiser, the FBI guys in a gray, shapeless Ford sedan with federal plates, and the CSU team in a CSU van.

The CSIs, three guys and one woman, began setting up for their investigation. As they did, some of the artisans and vendors peeked through the cracks in their booths to see what was going on. Meanwhile, inside Sherry Maughn's abandoned booth, more introductions were made. I found out that Sinclair's partner, whose name was Al Ferguson, was Mike de-Spain's brother-in-law, though it wasn't clear to me which one of them was married to the other one's sister, or what.

Ferguson was of medium height and build and had wavy carrot-colored hair. His face was hard and angular and his topaz eyes seemed always on the verge of flashing angrily at something or someone. He and Sinclair wore plastic ponchos over their street clothes, which in both cases was simple jeans and a polo shirt.

The two FBI agents, Bruce Baker and Myles Kuwahara, were both in their late twenties, both of medium height and build (though Baker had a few inches on Kuwahara), and both wore light blue summer-weight cotton suits under transparent plastic slickers. Kuwahara also wore Woody Allen glasses and a Jerry Garcia tie; Baker's tie came from Wal-Mart.

I told this latest law enforcement team what had happened, as seen from my perspective, then Kelso told it from his. Kelso played the tape (again), turning up the volume so they could hear it over the sound of the raindrops. When it got to the part where I mentioned Hugh Gardner's name, Baker and Kuwahara gave each other meaningful looks. Then, when I told Sherry about his smuggling days in California, they went to the back of the booth for a confidential confab.

Meanwhile, Detective Sinclair wanted to appropriate the tape, but Kelso said no, he'd have to make him a copy.

"How do I know it's legit?" Sinclair asked.

Kelso laughed at him. "If you see any high-tech editing equipment anywhere around this carnival, you let me know."

Baker and Kuwahara came over from their discussion and demanded that Kelso hand over the tape to them, *tout-suite*.

"Not without a subpoena." He smiled.

Without a moment's hesitation, Kuwahara flipped open a cell phone and said, "Fine. I'll have to ask you to stay here until it arrives, though." He pressed a few numbers.

"Look," I said, "we know why you're here. Your guy Gardner was in witness protection, okay? Big deal. He's dead, so he doesn't need any more protection. Can we go now?"

"That tape is still a security breech," said Baker. "It could put the whole program in jeopardy."

It was about then that Sinclair told the two deputies, Peck and deSpain, to canvass the artisans, vendors, and even the carnival workers to find out what they had seen, if anything.

Kuwahara was on hold, and while he was waiting, he and Baker had another quick word together. When they were done, Baker told Sinclair and Ferguson to join the canvass.

Sinclair's back went up. "Look, wise guy, I don't take orders from you. This is *my* case."

Almost bored, Baker said, "Not anymore it isn't. If you don't believe me, just put a call in to your captain."

Sinclair did just that. Once he got his superior officer on the line, there was some arguing, until finally the word, "Suspended?" came out of his mouth. His demeanor changed. "And you'd really suspend me if I don't?" He listened for a bit, shook his head, and said, "Fine. You're the boss," and hung up. He looked at Ferguson. "We're off the case."

Baker said, "That's not exactly right. As far as the media is concerned, you're still the lead detectives. That's the only reason I'm letting you do the canvass. Anything else, you clear it through the Bureau first, okay? Or better yet, don't do anything at all unless we tell you to. You got it?"

I was starting to sympathize with my dad's perspective on the FBI; Kuwahara and Baker really *were* Feebs.

Sinclair huffed a little but said nothing.

Baker stared at him. "I said: 'You got it,' Detective?"

"Yeah, yeah, I got it."

I gave Sinclair a sympathetic look and tsked at him. "Poor Sinclair. First it's Dr. Reiner telling you what to do, now it's these . . ." I paused and looked at Kelso. ". . . what's another phrase for know-nothing greenhorns, such as these two?"

Kelso said, "Feckless fools? Jejune upstarts?"

I nodded and looked back at Sinclair. "Now it's these two jejune upstarts giving you orders."

"Can it, you two," said Baker. Then to Sinclair, he said, "And send your CSIs home. We've got our own people coming."

"Whatever you say," Sinclair sighed. He sent the CSU home and then he and Ferguson left to help with the canvass.

Kuwahara got off the phone and said, "A subpoena is on its way." He adjusted his glasses and gave me a hard stare. "Now, maybe you'd like to tell us how you learned that . . ." He paused, trying to think of the right, or the safest, way to put it. ". . . that is, maybe you can tell us how you came to the conclusion that Beeson and Gardner are the same person."

"Elementary, my dear Kuwahara; it was simply a matter of deductive reasoning." I ticked off the pertinent facts; the lack of fingerprint records, the reconstructive surgery, and so on. (I left Kelso's hacking expertise out of the equation, for good reason.)

"You know," I went on, "the mistake you boys in Washington made is giving Gardner a whole new identity while allowing him to keep the same old job, flying whirly-birds."

Kuwahara said, "That decision was made by the U.S. Marshals, not by the Bureau."

Kelso looked at me, then said, "You know, I've been wondering about that myself." He looked at the agents. "Why not arrange to get Gardner a job as a landscaper or a bank teller? That's the kind of thing you usually do, isn't it?"

I added, "And why have him work for such a high-profile boss? Unless Maxwell is involved in some heavy-duty military secrets and you needed someone in his employ to keep an eye on him. Was that part of Gardner's deal with the Feds? Spying on the new boss for Uncle Sam?"

Baker said, "You creeps ask a lot of questions."

"Yeah, and you two jejune upstarts are making a ton of rookie mistakes here." They looked squarely at me. "Instead of bulldozing your way in, pushing people around, and generally drawing attention to yourselves, what you should have done is taken a back seat, let Sinclair run the investigation on his own, and waited in the wings to see what developed."

"Not very smart," Kelso said. "You only made matters worse for yourselves."

Baker said, "When I want your opinion—"

"I know," Kelso groused, "you'll give it to me."

"Give them the damn tape," I said, "and let's get the hell out of here before the Secret Service, the NSA, the CIA, the Army, the Navy, and the Joint Chiefs of Staff all show up, wanting a piece of me."

Kelso shook his head. "Not until I see that subpoena. I want to establish a definite paper trail with this."

I sighed. The rain had stopped by this time but had left a light mist behind. It was almost pretty. A few minutes later three more Ford sedans, a black Lincoln Town Car (full of Federal Marshals), and a large panel truck showed up. In no time flat the place was, as they say, crawling with Feds.

We were given a subpoena, so we handed over the tape and skedaddled; but not before Kuwahara warned me to watch out for myself: "The guy who tried to kill you is probably a maverick SEAL. And there's nothing more dangerous than that."

"Nothing," I agreed, "except maybe a dumbass Feeb like you."

On our way out we ran into Sinclair again. He had just finished interviewing the tie-dye lady, whose name tag said, CINDY BRIMHALL. I knew her slightly. She has two dogs that she claims are toy terrier/Pomeranian mixes, though they look exactly like Chihuahuas to me. They're both girls and their names are Manapua and Lele Wombat. (She spends a lot of time in Hawaii). They were inside her booth, bundled up in a large beach towel, shivering.

"Hello, girls," I said. They looked at me with their big eyes and got all wiggly. Sinclair made a sour face.

The tie-dye lady said to him, "Now, *this* guy I saw. He was running around like a nut, looking for somebody. I don't know anything about the other guy. Look, am I finished here?"

"Yeah, thanks."

She went over to the dogs, picked them up and hugged them. "Poor little babies," she cooed, "all shivery!"

"You know," Sinclair said to me, "I could've done without some of your wisecracks earlier."

"What's the matter? The truth hurt, Detective? And listen, how 'bout giving us a ride to our car? It's up in Boothbay, at the animal shelter."

He reluctantly agreed, and we got in his car and drove out of the carnival. When we got to the main road, Sinclair shook his head at me and said, "Okay, I admit it. You've got a good reason for being pissed off. And you're going to have an even better one tomorrow when the District Attorney convenes a grand jury and indicts you for Beeson's murder."

"That's funny, I haven't even gotten a subpoena yet."

"I know. It's a silent grand jury. They want to roast you in absentia."

Kelso chuckled. "So the dumb cop knows some Latin."

He said, "Very funny. And just so you know I have a bachelor's degree in law enforcement."

"Law enforcement?" I said. "What is that again, exactly? Isn't that where you go after the bad guys and put them in jail? Or wait a minute—no it's not. It's when you're a patsy for a vindictive ME and a stooge for some Feebs from D.C."

"Hey, when the captain says back off, I back off!"

Kelso shrugged. "There *are* ways around such obstacles."

I said, "Yeah, but it's not something they teach you in Good Cop, Bad Cop 101."

Sinclair laughed. "I hate to admit it, but I'm starting to like you, Field. I knew you had some kind of moxie when I saw the way you let us cuff you. Both times. Very cool."

"It's called the Zen of Bing," Kelso explained.

"The Zen of *being*?" Sinclair asked.

"No, the Zen of Bing. As in Bing Crosby."

"Never mind him," I said. "He's into the Zen of scotch. Besides, you seem to have your own Zen thing going."

"I do?"

"Yeah. You seem like you should be working at a little record shop somewhere in California; Santa Barbara maybe."

He shrugged and said, "You think you guys could teach me how to overcome these obstacles of which you speak?"

I smiled. "That depends. Do you want to nail the bad guys? Including Beeson's killer—if he *was* killed, that is." I looked at Kelso. "Although after this afternoon's excitement I'm starting to lean pretty heavily in that direction."

"Yeah, me too," Kelso said, then added, "And let's not forget Dr. Reiner, plus our maverick Navy SEAL, and our two jejune upstarts from the marbled halls of our nation's capital. Those guys are just begging for their comeuppance."

"Comeuppance?" I smiled at Kelso. "How *Magnificent Ambersons* of you."

"Okay," said Sinclair. "Knock off all the clever talk. Just tell me where to sign up."

"If you'd like, you can come by my place later," I said. "There's a party going on."

We got to the parking lot at the animal shelter, got out of the car, and Kelso immediately got down on his hands and knees, I thought to puke. But then he rolled over on his back and shimmied underneath the Suburban like an auto mechanic.

"What's he doing?" Sinclair asked through his window.

I had no idea and said as much.

Kelso fussed around under there for a bit, then shimmied back out, carefully holding an electronic device by its wire antenna. "There's your transponder, Jack."

"Nice work, Lou." I got a bandanna (or tug rag, depending on how you use it) out of my vest and carefully placed the "tracking device" in it. "We'll have Flynn check it for fingerprints." I turned to Sinclair. "This is how our Navy SEAL was able to follow us here."

"Interesting," he said. "So, where's this party again?"

I told him where I lived.

"You're kidding. Halfway between Hope and Perseverance? Is that an actual spot on the map or just a metaphor?"

"Hey—you really *did* go to college."

21

I was sitting on the roof smoking a cigarette when Jamie poked her head through the window.

"What are you doing out here?"

"Smoking a frog butt."

She laughed. "Since when do you smoke? And what the hell is a frog butt?"

"Since it seemed like the only way to avoid your party. And it's what Kelso calls these French cigarettes of his."

"It's not *my* party, it's *yours*," she said for the twelfth time. "And do you know how long I've been looking for you?" She began climbing through the window.

"Don't come out here. It's too dangerous."

"If it's too dangerous, then—"

"It's too dangerous for you."

"What? Because I'm a woman?" She crawled over crabwise and sat next to me.

"I didn't mean it like that."

"Yes you did. And it's not like I'm wearing a ball gown or anything." (It was true. She was dressed in jeans and a T-shirt.)

"How did you find me, by the way?"

"Because someone named Detective Sinclair just drove in and saw you sitting up here. Mind if I have a puff?"

"Yes. I'm already feeling a little loopy. I don't want us both falling off the roof. How's Kelso doing?"

She shrugged. "It's just a sprain. I think. He said he'd have it X-rayed tomorrow. As for now, he's downstairs, happily self-medicating and engaging in what he might call a brilliant series of drunken soliloquies."

I stubbed out the frog butt. "Maybe I should get down there and do something about that."

"Maybe you should. Mom is not very happy with you right now. Among others." There was a pause. "Jack, are we really going to get married or are you starting to get cold—"

"Sweetheart! Why would you even think—"

"Because you've been very distant lately and I don't—"

"That's just because there's a lot going on right now. I have other things to think about, you know? But if it'll make you feel any better, let's set a date."

"Right now? Right up here, on the roof?"

I looked around. Most of the clouds had cleared and there were a few stars shining through the branches of the oak tree to our left. There was a lull in the music coming from the party. Down in the ravine, past the play yard, an owl hooted softly.

"Why not now? Besides, who just signed a lease on her own apartment? What does that say?"

She sighed and shook her head. "It says that I'm tired of living at my mother's and tired of sleeping over at my fiancé's kennel, and that I need my own space."

I took her hand. "I guess we should finally get around to talking about this, huh?"

"Jack, I've been trying to talk about it and you always change the subject or just outright ignore me."

"I know," I sighed. "It's just that you tend to get so excited about ideas for window treatments and where you want to put the throw pillows. It makes me nervous."

"You silly, what's there to be nervous about?"

"I don't know. Everything. I just like the place the way it is, I guess."

"Well, I don't. Not totally, anyway. It *does* have potential. And if it's going to be our house once we get married, then it should be ours, not just yours."

"I can't argue with that." I thought it over and said, "Okay.

You can decorate the house any way that you want—carte blanche."

"Really?" She was very happy.

"Yes, really."

"Good, because I was thinking that in the kitchen—"

"Wait, wait. Just do me one little favor first, though, okay? Don't tell me about your ideas, don't ask for my input, don't show me carpet swatches, paint samples, or furniture catalogues, and don't ask me to choose things you can't decide on for yourself."

She laughed. "And that's your small favor?"

"What can I tell you? I'm a guy. And guys don't decorate, we just accumulate."

"You're impossible."

"Except for Kelso. He's really into that kind of shit, though he sticks pretty much to one look."

"Which is?"

"Mission oak."

"Oh, I love mission oak. Though I think it's too dark and bulky for the living room. That's why I've been thinking we should get rid of that leather couch."

"I *love* that couch. And it's not a couch, it's a sofa."

"Whatever. And the thing is, Jack, the living room needs to be lighter and more open. We could move the sofa into your new den."

"I'm going to have a den?"

"Mm-hmm. Instead of having two offices, one in the kennel and one in the house, I think you should have a den. Now, maybe if we put some sconces in the living room—"

"Enough, okay? You're going to sconce me to death, here."

"But Jack—"

"This is what I'm talking about. If you want sconces, let there be sconces. Sconce yourself silly if you like. But please, honey, *please*—don't *talk* to me about it. Just *do* it."

Her face turned red. She let out a hot breath. "Okay, that's it. I'm not going to marry you."

"What?"

"You heard me. The wedding's off."

I laughed. "Don't be ridiculous."

Oops—wrong thing to say.

"Ridiculous! Jack, I need to talk to you about this."

"Yes, and I need for you to *not* talk to me about this."

"Then we're hopelessly incompatible and our marriage is doomed to end in disaster. I just know it."

"No, it's not. Look, you don't like it when I talk about my theories on dogs, right?"

She hesitated then said, "Well—no, I don't like it when you do that. I find it boring, repetitious, and dull."

I laughed. "Good. That's honest. But I have been better about it, haven't I?"

"You've been trying. Though if I hear you talk one more time about this ridiculous binary code of yours—"

"It's not ridiculous. It's Ockham's razor. Everything can be boiled down to the simplest levels of attraction and resistance, fear and desire."

"Jack."

"These binary choices, which take place too fast for the human eye to perceive and interpret—"

"Jack."

"—create repeatable, congruent patterns of behavior within the pack, which are then misinterpreted—"

"—as a dominance hierarchy, where none exists. I know! I've heard it a million times!"

"I'm just making a point." I took her hand again. "You know that movie, *Michael*? We were talking about it last night." She said she did. "Well, they're always asking John Travolta about this or that aspect of life or asking him to do things as an archangel, and what does he always say?"

"I don't know, I *think* he says, 'It's not my area.'"

"That's right. Well, canine behavior is not your area. Redecorating is not *mine*. It doesn't mean that we have to break up. It just means that we have to respect each other's areas and let things be what they are for the other person."

She thought it over and nodded. "That makes sense, I guess. I want you to help me decorate, but it's not your area. Meanwhile, you have to promise not to talk to me about your theories on canine behavior and Ockham's razor and the Wolfram book, and any other crazy thing that comes into your head about dogs. Okay?"

"I can't talk to you about it, ever?"

"That's the deal. In fact, instead of talking to me, why don't you just *write* about it."

"What do you mean? Like, write a book?"

"Would that be so difficult? You have a master's degree in psychology. You've written a thesis."

"But that was . . . that was just to graduate."

"So? All I'm saying is, you already know how to write. Why not write a book? If you do, I'll stop pestering you with decorating ideas. Although, if you don't like what I pick out, I'm not going to be responsible."

"That doesn't matter. If I don't like it at first, it won't be long before I don't even notice it."

"Then why am I going through all the effort?"

"Because it'll make you happy? And how does October fifteenth sound?"

"October fifteenth? What about it?"

"For the wedding."

"You mean next *year*?"

"No, not next year; October of *this* year. It'll be perfect. The leaves will be at their—"

"Are you in*sane*? That only gives us three months to plan everything!"

"What's wrong with that?"

"Don't you know anything? It takes at least six months to plan a proper wedding. What is *wrong* with you?"

"So then we'll do it on Valentine's Day, like Dale said. I mean we can't do it in November because of Thanksgiving. We can't do it in December because of Christmas. And we can't do it in January because it's too depressing."

"Well," she said, mostly to herself, "if I can get my mom to help out—"

"Of course she'll help out. So will I."

"Shut up, Jack. I'm thinking." She thought it over for a moment, then smiled and said, "Okay!" She shook her head and took a deep breath. "I guess we're getting married in October!" She smiled and kissed me. "Now you *have* to come to the party because we have to tell everybody!"

"Ah, honey, do we have to tell them to*night*?"

She fumed and formed a fist. "I am going to kill you, Jack, you know that?"

I put my hands in the air. "I was just kidding."

"Well, *stop* it." She grabbed my hand. "Now let's *go*."

"Yes, Mommy," I said, and meant it.

22

The party seemed to be doing just fine without me. Kelso had put himself in charge of the music: one of my NRBQ records was on the stereo. The boys were singing "I Like That Girl," which seemed appropriate because I suddenly realized that Jamie hadn't thrown me a "Jack's Out of Jail" party, but a "Let's *Keep* Jack Out of Jail" party. (Yeah, I like that girl.)

"So, Jack," Kelso waved a glass of scotch, "you finally decided to join the shivaree." Frankie, who seemed to have adopted Kelso, was lying next to his chair, wagging his tail.

"Looks like it." I was happy to see that Kelso wasn't as drunk as usual. (If he *had* been, I never would have let him near my record collection, let alone my state-of-the-art Macintosh vacuum tube tuner and turntable.)

I looked around. Everyone who might be helpful in keeping me out of jail—except Dr. Liu (and maybe my dad) was there. The list included Carl Staub, Sheriff Flynn, Quentin Peck, Detective Sinclair (and his partner whose name I couldn't remember), and of course Kelso and Jamie.

There were others there too: Farrell Woods and Tulips, D'Linda, Darryl and Annie Deloit (Annie still not drinking after four months of sobriety), Otis Barnes from the *Camden Herald*, Dorianne Elliot my dog training client, along with Jamie's former assistant at the ME's office (whose face I recognized but whose name I'd forgotten). Even Eve Arden were there. Their names are actually Evelyn and Ardyth, but since I can never tell them apart, I always lump them together as Eve Arden. They glared at me (as usual) when they saw me come in. I had an urge to remind them that the booze in the iced cocktails that they were so decorously clutching in their dainty little hands came from my liquor cabinet, but didn't.

Of course, Jamie's mom, Laura, was also there. She was bustling around, making sure that everyone was supplied with shrimp quesadilla triangles, mini lobster rolls, and smoked Maine salmon croquettes topped with a sour cream and dill sauce. She had also made various chips and dips, but as they had been put out earlier, they were mostly gone by this point. She had even taken some food out to the carriage house, where Leon was happily getting to know his new dog, Magee.

Jamie asked for quiet and made the announcement about our wedding date. There were congratulations, a smattering of applause, and the usual cupped-hand, gallows humor about the loss of the single life and the old ball-and-chain and other such idiotic male conventions that usually follow such news.

At one point I took Tulips aside and asked her what she knew about Stephen Wolfram, systems dynamics, and emergence theory, and if she thought they might go together to create a new and better understanding of pack behavior. She said she'd have to think about it, which was good, I suppose, because it would give her something else to think about besides her drug addiction and how to once and for all be done with it.

There was some more music (Kelso found my Marc Jacobs album, *Street Life*, which is a pretty good party record), more laughter, a lot of casual drinking, some bright conversation (and some not so bright, mostly having to do with the Red Sox' chances), and then that gradual dwindling down of bonhomie which signals the coming end of the merriment.

As people started to leave I told a few of them—either by word or by eye contact—to stick around. Then I told Laura not to worry about the clean-up.

"Jamie and I will take care of it later."

"I will? But, Jack, I'm so tired and my feet are kill—"

"Hey, the party was *your* idea."

She huffed and shook her head at me.

By evening's end—when you could just barely pick up the evaporating scent of Laura's cooking in the air yet still feel the warmth of its effects lingering inside your belly—all that was left was a living room full of six tough lawmen (and *ex*-lawmen), and one tough (though tired) lady. The group included Flynn, Carl Staub, Quentin Peck, Sinclair (his partner had to leave), Kelso, Jamie, and me.

Most of the men were sitting on kitchen chairs that had been brought into the living room for the shindig. Kelso had dragged my office chair in. Frankie was lying next to him, fast asleep. There weren't enough seats, so Quentin Peck sat on the floor, his back against a bookcase, one leg stretched straight out on the floor, the other cocked like a jackknife. I'd never noticed before how much he resembled an elf.

Jamie and I were on the leather sofa. I was sitting on the left. She was stretched out with her stockinged feet in my lap, her eyes closed, moaning softly. I was giving her a foot massage.

"I'm sorry, everybody," she said. "I'm just wiped out. And my feet are—ooh, Jack, that feels so good."

"That's okay," said Flynn, embarrassed. "We don't need you. Maybe you should just go up to bed."

Oops—wrong thing to say.

"No!" She tried to sit up. "I'm a part of this. I want to be involved."

I said, "You *did* your part, honey. Yesterday with your news conference and then later at the morgue, and today with your Web consult with Dr. Liu."

"That's true." She relaxed. "But if anything happens where you need my opinion," she said to the others, "be sure to wake me up. Okay? Jack can pinch my big toe."

"I've done it before and I'll do it again if I have to."

She laughed, softly pleased. "You make me *laugh*," she said, almost in her sleep. She opened her eyes again. "Hey, did I tell everybody? We're getting married in October."

"Yes, you told them that, honey."

"Good." She closed her eyes again. "And you're all invited. And you'd better all *come*."

While this was taking place, the most recent album on the turntable clicked off and Kelso got up and went to turn it over. Frankie opened one eye, watched him and snuffled a bit.

"I think we've had enough music tonight," I said.

"Don't you like Jim Hall?"

"Of course. It's *my* album." (One of my favorites, too—*Concierto*, with Paul Desmond, Chet Baker, and Ron Carter.) Kelso tilted his chin toward Jamie, as if saying, "It'll help her drift off," which was true, the second side of the album is very relaxing, so I said, "Okay, but keep it down."

"So," said Flynn, a little annoyed at us, "what are we going to do about this situation of yours, Jack?"

23

We talked strategy while Jamie slept.

Carl told us that he'd checked Sherry Maughn's phone records, as I'd asked him to, and found that she made a lot of calls to Beeson (or Gardner), quite a few to Maxwell's island, and five long distance calls; two made to San Diego from room 601 at a hotel in Boston, both charged to her home number, and three made directly to the same number in San Diego.

Kelso and I exchanged glances.

To Carl, I said, "Did you happen to find out who that number in San Diego belonged to?"

" 'Whom,' " said Kelso.

"What?"

" 'Whom' the number belonged to."

"Fine. Did you find out 'whom' the number belonged to?"

Flynn shook his head at us.

Carl said, "Yes, it's registered to La Fortuna, a Mexican restaurant, which I found out from sources on the SDPD is—"

"—a front for an organized crime operation, probably dealing drugs," I said, finishing his sentence.

"Yeah, how did you—"

I interrupted him by putting a finger in the air. "Okay, check the airports for any flights originating in San Diego after the day of Sherry's first phone call. Cross-reference with anyone flying in on business for La Fortuna and possibly using the company credit card for tickets and hotel rooms."

Kelso said, "They could have other fronts besides the restaurant. They could—"

I shook my head. "That's too much work. Let's take the first tack, and if we have to explore other angles, we will."

"You're right," he said, then muttered, "I wonder if they sent the Maori boys out."

"The Maori boys?" asked Flynn. "Don't you mean the 'Bowery Boys'?"

I explained about T'anke and Kong, though I couldn't remember their first names. I even repeated the joke Kelso had made about me saying that they resembled Hawaiians.

Quent came alive. His other leg jackknifed and he sat up straight, clutching his knees. "Did you say 'Hawaiians'?"

I told him I had.

He looked at the sheriff. "You wouldn't know this, Sheriff, on account of you bein' up in Buffalo this weekend, but we got a report on Saturday of a couple from Ohio who were assaulted at the carnival in Boothbay Harbor by what they described as two very large Hawaiian gentlemen."

"What day was this?" I said.

"Well, like I said," Quent seemed puzzled by the question, "they came in to file a report on Saturday."

"Yes, but what day did the *assault* take place?"

"Oh." He grinned an apology. "Fourth of July."

The same day Gardner was killed.

Quent described how the couple was taking a photograph at one of the lobster ponds. The so-called Hawaiians were in the background of the shot. They noticed this, came over to the couple and demanded their film. The couple refused, so the "Hawaiians" grabbed the camera and broke it in two.

Flynn nodded. "One of those cheap, disposable jobs."

"Uh, no, Sheriff." Quent shook his head. "It was a metal Nikon. Very expensive, so the wife said. This one guy, he just twisted it in two. We've still got the pieces down in an evidence locker."

"Maybe we can get their prints off it," said Flynn. "If so, I'll check them against AFIS and fax a copy to the SDPD to see if these are the same guys as your Donkey Kong Samoans."

I was about to correct Flynn, by saying that they were two Maoris, not "Samoans," and that their names were T'anke and Kong, not "Donkey Kong," but I found his mistake so amusing that I just let it go.

"Too bad they ruined the film," said Kelso.

I thought about that for a second then said, "Oh, shit!"

"What is it?"

I told them about the couple I'd seen videotaping each other on the sailboat in Boothbay Harbor when I'd gone down to the beach and found the body. "I can't believe I didn't remember this before."

Kelso said, "Don't beat yourself up over it, Jack. That's why we used to go back and reinterview our witnesses, remember? Most of whom got royally pissed off at having to answer the same questions over and over."

"Okay," said Flynn, twitching his mustache, "if it's a Rockland County boat, that's my beat. Trouble is, they could be sailing up and down the coast. They could be anywhere from Orchard Beach to Jonesport at this point."

"And if *that's* the case," said Sinclair, "it's *my* beat."

"Well," I said, "we can try to find the boat, but let's not get our hopes up. It's a crapshoot as to whether or not these people actually caught the murder on tape."

"Life is a crapshoot," said Kelso, yawning. "What's so funny, Jack?"

"Nothing," I chuckled. "I just thought that would make a great epitaph for your tombstone—'Life Is a Crapshoot.' Sorry, I didn't mean anything by it, it just popped into my head."

Kelso found it amusing. "I've always liked W.C. Fields's choice for an epitaph." He did a W.C. Fields impression: "Frankly, I'd rather be in Phila*delph*ia."

I laughed, though nobody else did.

Sinclair reminded me that he had to testify in front of the silent grand jury in the morning. I suggested he try to get the tape of Sherry Maughn "confessing" on the record. If the members of the grand jury wanted to hear it, the FBI couldn't refuse to turn it over on grounds that it was secret, since grand jury proceedings are kept secret anyway. He said he'd try.

"The only other two things to look at are Ian Maxwell—" I looked over at Kelso.

"Don't look at me."

"—and Sherry Maughn. Maybe Beeson was up to his old tricks, smuggling drugs."

Flynn shook his head and reminded me that the usual method for smuggling along the Maine coast involved an airplane that dropped bales of drugs into the ocean, attached to small buoys, one of which usually had a transponder on it, with a specific signal. Then some boys in boats would ride out and harvest the goods. There were no helicopters involved.

"Still," I said, "maybe Carl or you could subpoena her bank records."

"Not without probable cause, which we don't have."

"She was just the victim in an attempted murder."

Flynn shook his head. "That's being handled by the FBI. Local agencies have been told to butt out." He scratched his chin. I looked around. Everyone in the room looked tired and spent. Flynn said, "I don't see why we don't go after these Samoans of yours. They make pretty good suspects."

"Not really," I said. "If Beeson was whacked, it was a finesse job. And finesse doesn't seem to be their forte." I pronounced the word the way most people do: "for-tay."

Kelso corrected me. "It's actually pronounced 'fort,' not 'for-tay.' Not many people know that."

I had to admit that *I* didn't know that. Nor did I care. "Why pronounce something correctly if no one but a lexicographer understands what you're saying?"

"Because," Kelso said, "language should be used properly."

"Language is always evolving," I said. "If enough people pronounce it wrong, then that's the correct pronunciation."

"No, it's not. Language should evolve toward more intelligence, not less."

"I've had about enough of this frickin' conversation," said Flynn. "How's that for using language properly?"

I said, "Nice use of the vernacular, Sheriff," then said, "Okay, where were we?"

Flynn said, "I think we were all just about to go home and go to bed. If you think Sherry Maughn was into something off the books, you should check it out. You take care of her dogs from time to time, don't you?"

"Yeah." In fact, Lucy and Lotte were on the day-care schedule for the next morning. And I was supposed to go pick them up at her place, though I was half expecting her to call at any minute to cancel. (The other half was expecting her *not* to call, since that's her usual M.O.)

"All right," I said, bringing the meeting to a close, "let's stay in touch."

Everyone got up, yawned and stretched, and got ready to leave: all except Jamie and Kelso. Kelso went into the bathroom. Jamie slumbered on.

After they left, I cleaned up the living room, letting Jamie sleep, and letting Kelso shamble off to bed.

Once I had the living room squared away to my liking, I looked at Jamie, softly snoring, and realized this was my opportunity to do something I'd been dying to do for a long time. In fact, I'd been doing extra push-ups every morning for months just to get in shape for it. I crouched next to the sofa, like a sumo wrestler. I put my left arm under Jamie's back and the right one under her knees, and then lifted her up, using my legs, not my back muscles.

What do you know? I was carrying her! (Remember, she's not overweight—in fact she's quite slender—but she *is* nearly as tall as I am.)

She woke up and looked around sleepily. "Jack, what are you doing?"

"I'm carrying you up to bed."

"You can't," she yawned, "I'm too heavy."

"Yes, I can. I've been practicing."

"Practicing on who?"

"You mean on 'whom'?"

"Okay," she sighed, "on whom?"

"On Kelso," I lied.

She laughed, curled her arm around my neck, kissed my ear and said, "Okay, honey." She yawned and said, "I should call my father and tell him we've set the date."

"It's too late to call him now." I got her all the way to the stairs. "You can call him—*unh!*—in the morning."

"Jack, are you sure you can do this?"

"That was just the first step. I'm okay now."

"Okay, but promise you won't drop me."

"I won't. Just as long as you don't talk to me about sconces."

24

The next morning started out overcast and humid, with temperatures in the low seventies. But the weather guy—the regular one, not Brantley Parker—said the sun should burn off the clouds by ten, which might bring an afternoon thunderstorm.

Jamie left early, with no time even for a quick omelet. She just grabbed a blueberry muffin and a can of Diet Coke. She did give me a lot of minty fresh toothpaste kisses before she took off, though—one of the perks of having set the date.

After she was gone I got the dogs exercised and fed and put back in their kennels. Then I checked the daily roster to see what other dogs, if any, I had to pick up that morning. There were three: Lucy and Lotte (Sherry Maughn's dogs), and Roark, a boxer belonging to Ron and Beth Stevens.

I was just thinking about getting ready to leave when the phone rang. It was my dad, giving me his travel schedule; he was arriving in Portland around four. I said I'd drive down and meet him, hung up, then sat there wondering if I should call Sherry to see if she still wanted her dogs picked up after what happened yesterday, or just drive over to her place in Rockport.

Depending on how many dogs are on the schedule, the pickup time is usually from about eight to ten-thirty. Some clients will drop the dogs off; others pay the extra ten bucks for pickup. Sometimes Farrell Woods does the morning run. Sometimes I let Leon drive the Suburban (though no one touches the woody but me). But Leon had summer school that morning, trying to make up for the two semesters he'd missed when I was helping him hide out from the Manhattan DA's office.

Normally, when a dog is on the schedule, you don't call first, you just drive over to the owner's house, pick up the dog, and drive back to the kennel, also picking up any other dogs you might need to along the way. You might have a key to the house, the front door might be left unlocked, or the dog might be tethered up in the backyard. You rarely call the owner first. You just drive over.

Sherry Maughn was no exception, though she *should* have been. She sometimes leaves her dogs with her four brothers, who live just up the road from her. They own a mussel farm in Penobscot Bay, west of North Haven Island. Sherry is a silent partner. Sometimes, on harvest days—once or twice a month, depending on the time of year—they might even take the dogs with them on the boat. Then, once the hold is full of blue-black shells, they chug toward the packing plant in Rockland.

So there *had* been times in the past when I'd come over to pick up the dogs and they weren't there. There had been other times when I'd called Sherry first, gotten no answer, but drove over anyway, to find the dogs waiting for me. There had *also* been times when the dogs weren't at her house *or* with her brothers. She gets charged either way, which isn't the point. The point is—should I call first or just drive over?

I think you know the answer.

I pulled the woody to a stop in front of the lane that leads from Wild Cherry Road down to Sherry's house and noticed a black Lincoln Town Car parked across the street. I got the impression that the front door had just slammed shut, though I didn't actually see this happen.

I switched off the engine and got out of the car, trying to get a look at the license plates. They were federal government issue—probably a U.S. Marshal, assigned to witness protection. I started to cross toward the Lincoln. The sun had burned off the clouds and there was a streak of sunlight reflecting off the windshield, almost blinding me.

The front window—made of smoked glass, so no one could see in—rolled down a crack, a pale hand held an official-looking badge through the opening, and I heard a male voice say, "This is U.S. Marshal Rondo Kondolean. There's no one home at the residence. I suggest you move along, sir."

I stood in the middle of the street. "I'm sorry. I have to pick up the dogs for day care."

"There are no dogs inside, sir."

The window rolled back up.

"Well, I think I'll just check on that for myself."

There was no answer from the car.

I walked the rest of the way over to the vehicle, shielding my eyes from the glare on the chrome and the windshield. He didn't roll the window down again so I rapped on it. He still ignored me, so I said, "I hope you don't mind, but I'm just going to go inside and see for myself. Okay?"

There was no answer.

This is odd, I thought, then said, "Look, can I see your badge again?"

The window rolled down a crack, the badge reappeared, I looked at it, and it immediately disappeared. From what I could tell at just a glance, it seemed like the genuine article. The window rolled back up. A voice came from inside. "This is official government business. I'm going to have to ask you again to move along, sir."

"Not until I check on those dogs."

"Suit yourself, sir."

Goddamn feds and their superior attitude—it was like trying to have a conversation with your refrigerator.

I shook my head, went back across the street, took a deep breath, and walked down the lane, which was a narrow dirt path with stumble stones, enclosed on both sides by overgrown vegetation. The reason I took a deep breath is because it was the perfect place for a maverick Navy SEAL to lie in wait; willing himself not to breathe, willing himself not to sweat, willing himself not to swat at the mosquitoes eating him alive; waiting there with another pistol, or a spear gun, or, who knows, a length of piano wire. Waiting to do me in.

It would've been nice, I thought, to have Kelso along to watch my back, or just to give the guy more than one target.

That's a crummy thing to say, I thought. After all, he *had* saved my life the day before. I imagined him showing up now, out of nowhere, like he'd done at the carnival, but I knew it was just a fantasy. He was home, sleeping it off.

I made it safely to the front porch and breathed a sigh of relief, hoping that I would soon find two impatient doggies waiting inside an otherwise empty house.

That's not what I found.

The door creaked slowly open.

So what? I thought. It needs oil, that's all. Any door will creak if the hinges need enough oil. Big deal.

Still, it was awfully quiet once I got inside. No thumping tails, no paws happily clattering across the linoleum or the parquet, no welcoming barks or sounds of excited panting. Nothing but deadly silence, a car ignition from up the hill, and the distant chattering of birds.

Good, I thought stupidly. No dogs, no Sherry; this will give me a chance to do what I wanted to do in the first place—to look around a bit—not long enough to make the marshal suspicious, just long enough to see if I could find any evidence pointing to what Sherry and Beeson were up to.

Wait a second, hold it. What's that other sound? I could just barely make it out. Nope, now it's gone. Wait, there it is again. It seems at once so strange and yet so familiar. What the hell *is* it?

Oh, yeah. That's the sound of me talking to myself.

Get a grip, Jack. All you have to do is walk around the place a little, go into the back, into Sherry's studio, and look for anything out of the ordinary, like a bulge in the carpet, a place where the floorboards don't quite meet, or the telltale sign of new plaster behind a painting.

So I went to the back of the house, and that's where I found something *really* out of the ordinary; unless you're used to having a dead body stretched out on your floor.

I raced back outside and up the lane to tell the U.S Marshal what I'd found.

The Lincoln car was gone.

I just stood there, dumbly, in the middle of the street.

He wasn't a U.S. Marshal at all. He was a murderer. In fact he'd probably just killed Sherry Maughn. That's why he'd acted so strange. Not because he had that superior attitude the feds have, but because he didn't want me recognizing him.

Shit! He'd gotten away too.

I wondered briefly how he'd glommed onto those federal plates, then got into the woody, drove up the block and around the corner and parked. I got out of the car and walked carefully and cautiously back to Wild Cherry Road and down the lane again to Sherry's house.

25

It's a weathered shingle structure that probably started life as a boathouse or a fishing shack. It's built right next to the water on the southernmost edge of Rockport Harbor. (Rockport is a small fishing village and art colony about twenty miles north of the city of Rockland, the seat of Rockland County.) It's just one story tall, with no yard, but with an architectural extension built on the far side, facing the harbor, with full-length windows, giving that famous north light that artists love. There's also a skylight on the roof, with an adjustable blind inside—on the ceiling—so she can control the amount of light that comes in from above.

That's her studio. And that's where the body was still lying, waiting for me to come take a second look.

I'd been to the house dozens of times before and had started taking for granted all the fragmented little impressions that at first seemed so new. All these forgotten sensory details came back to me now in high relief: the scent of the hot sun shining on lush green vegetation mixed with the smell of salt air from the harbor, the way the one plank right in front of the door always squeaks when you step on it, the silvery web in one corner of the porch overhang, with a fat little nut-brown spider waiting nonchalantly—with all eight arms crossed—for an unsuspecting fly to come buzzing by and get tangled up in his web.

I hesitated outside the door, feeling a little tangled up myself.

I had three options (four if you count going to pieces): I could just walk back to the car and drive home (after picking up Roark first); I could go inside and immediately call the police, then take my lumps; or I could go inside and search the place and *then* call the police and take my lumps. I chose the latter.

I went inside again and started in the back, in the studio, which was tough on my nerves—doing an illegal search with a dead body in the room. I tried not to look, but couldn't stop myself even though it gave me a queasy feeling. Besides, I had to know how she'd been killed.

I knelt down next to her and put two fingers to her carotid artery. The body was still warm but there was no pulse. There was a small entry wound in the back of her head—probably from a .22. There was no exit wound, just a small amount of fresh blood that had pooled around her head.

I stood up and looked down at her. She was dressed in the same overalls she'd worn to the fair. And she was lying face-down in the exact same pose as her late boyfriend—her left arm tucked underneath her body and her right arm stretched out with the fingers closed around something. I didn't even have to guess what it was or pry her fingers back to get a better look. Her hands weren't as big as Beeson's, so the yellow-green fuzz of the tennis ball was quite visible between her right thumb and index finger. Apparently I was on my way to becoming quite an artistic and prolific killer. I wondered who was next on my list of victims, halfway hoping it might be Dr. Reiner.

Then I began looking around.

To the left of the full-length windows—one of which had been left open—was a rough plywood counter with a hot plate and an old battered pot on top. From the smell of it, it seemed to be used for making glue. To the left of the counter was a large double sink for cleanup. To the right of the windows was a small desk with a telephone and some scattered papers on top. Farther over were two large white cabinets with different size drawers—narrow ones on top, wider ones on the bottom. In the center of the room was a worktable, with all the usual accoutrements of an artist's studio: brushes, half-used tubes of paint, a can of linseed oil, some dirty rags, makeshift bowls made from old Clorox bottles cut in half, a couple of sketchbooks (one left open with a rough sketch and a title; *Conchobar with Meis Geghra's Ball,* which Kelso told me later was a story from Celtic mythology), a staple gun, some pieces of lath used for making frames, and a lot of accidental Jackson Pollock type paint smears, all dried.

Next to the entryway—which was just an open door frame—there was a sort of closet with tie-dyed curtains instead of a door. To the left of that was a rack of paintings, blank canvases, and some large cardboard mailing tubes.

I started my search with the desk.

I went through all the drawers and found her check register and her bank statements. There were no unusually large deposits or withdrawals. I searched the rest of the desk and found no lockbox crammed full of cash.

I moved on to the cabinets, where I found fresh tubes of paint, brand new brushes, but nothing out of the ordinary until I reached one of the bottom drawers. Inside was a mortar and pestle along with some small brown paper sacks, each containing some sort of natural pigment—some were mineral and some vegetable. I didn't know enough about painting to be sure, but it seemed to me that Sherry Maughn may have been mixing her own oil paints, just like they used to do back in Vermeer's time. This suggested the possibility that she'd been forging old paintings, not just copying them. I didn't know enough about art to be sure, though. I'd have to check with Kelso. He knew more about the subject than I did.

Before I had time to think this through I heard that board on the front porch squeak, followed by the sound of the door creaking open, then some muffled voices. They were not the voices of cops arriving at a crime scene, but had that half-whispered, surreptitious sound of co-conspirators or perps.

I hid in the closet.

More boards creaked.

A moment later two men entered the room. They spoke with New Zealand accents. Through a crack in the curtains I could see that they were very large individuals, well over six feet tall, and each weighing at least three hundred pounds. They both had curly black dreadlocks, very long and ragged-looking. They had dark skin and were dressed in polo shirts—one yellow and one red. They also wore cargo shorts—one wore khaki, one olive drab—and both had on the kind of sandals that are made not just for the beach but for hiking as well.

"Hey, bro," the one in yellow said, looking down at the body, "someone beat us to it again, eh?"

"Too right, eh?" the one in red said, coming over to get a better look. He kicked her softly to see if she'd move. She didn't. "So, what do you reckon?"

"Dunno," said the other one, looking around. "Maybe we should look for that painting the boss wants." He went over to the desk and sat in the chair. He began to swivel around in circles. "Still, someone's been doin' our job for us, eh?"

"Stop messin' around. We should call Señor Ortiz."

"No way, bro. He's only gonna yell at us 'cause we screwed up." He kept swiveling around in his chair. "You know what *I'd* like to do. I'd like to go back to the carnival and get on some of those rides again."

"Yeah, but I hate Maine, you know?"

"I know. Me too, bro." He swiveled around some more.

"Nothin' to smoke here but lousy grass."

"Too right. I miss that good rock the boss gives us."

"Yeah, bro. And there's no hookers around here, either."

"How come the boss don't know any coke dealers or pimps around these parts, eh?" He stopped swiveling for a moment.

"There's Eddie Cole, but he's disappeared. He had some good hookers too."

"Yeah, bro. Oh, mannnn. I need to get back home and get me some more of that." He started swiveling around again.

"Too right. Hey, you ever screw that Lorelei girl?"

The one in yellow stopped swiveling. "Are you shittin' me, bro?" He laughed. "I had a go at her before you did."

"No you didn't, bro."

"Yes I did, bro."

"You're lying, bro. I was her first trick."

"No, you weren't, bro."

"Yes, I was."

"Hey—screw you, bro."

"No, screw *you*, bro."

The one in yellow got up and started shoving his partner. The one in red shoved him back. They started shoving each other, wrestling, shouting how the other one was a liar, and arguing over who was the first to sleep with Lorelei. It gradually came out that Lorelei had told each of them that they were her first trick. Once they realized that she had played them *both*, they stopped, apologized, then cupped hands around each other's necks, rubbed their noses together, and sniffed each other—a Maori thing, I guess.

"She pulled a good one on us, eh?" said the one in red.

"Yeah, I bet the boss told her to say that," said the one in yellow. "He's always messin' with our heads like that." They laughed some more.

"Speakin' of the boss—we oughta find that painting, bro."

"Yeah. It's gotta be around here somewhere, eh?"

"Hold up! You know what else I miss? Mexican food."

"Too right, eh? There's no Taco Bells around here."

"Yeah, I really miss Taco Bell."

I wanted to tell them there was a Taco Bell in Glen Cove but kept my mouth shut.

"Anyway, let's find that painting."

"Good idea."

They looked around the room then stopped looking when their eyes rested on the closet.

"Hey, let's have a go at that closet."

"Yeah, good idea, bro."

They started toward where I was hiding, and I wondered, quickly, if I were to jump out now, would I be able to outrun them? Probably so, but once I got to the woody and began fumbling with the keys, they might catch up and turn me into pulp. Still, what other choice did I have?

I was about to make a break for it when the sound of police sirens became audible in the distance. I guess the phony U.S. Marshal had called the cops.

The two Samoans—as Flynn had called them—looked at one

another. The one in red said, "Let's nick off, eh? We can always come back later if we get a chance."

"Good idea, bro."

So they left, in a hurry.

After they were gone I started breathing again, came out of the closet, went to the phone and dialed the Camden PD.

The sirens were getting louder.

"This is Jack Field," I said to the switchboard girl. "Can I speak to Carl Staub?"

The sirens got closer.

"I'm sorry, sir. He's not in at the moment. Can you tell me what this is in reference to?"

"Yes, I'm at Sherry Maughn's house in Rockport. Just down from Wild Cherry Road? She's just been murdered."

The sirens got even closer.

There was an intake of breath. "You're currently at the residence, sir?"

"Yes, I am."

The sirens stopped, just up the hill.

"Stay right where you are. Some officers will be there momentarily."

"Thanks, but I think they're already here."

26

Not only was Sherry Maughn dead, but telling my story to the cops killed most of my morning as well. Luckily, Carl Staub showed up, not too long into the ordeal, and I took him aside and explained things to him in private—and I mean *every*thing. He nodded, shook his head, then let me go.

I finally picked up Roark around eleven and got back to the kennel in time to take Frankie and Hooch—fresh from their baths—to the pediatric ward for canine therapy with the kids.

On our way out to the woody, Mrs. Murtaugh told me that Kelso had gone into Camden, hoping to check into a motel or a bed and breakfast. "I didn't know he was in show business," she said as I got the dogs into the back of the wagon.

"Show business?" I said, coming around the front.

"Yes. He said to tell you that living up here was cramping his style, and that he wanted to stay someplace closer to town so he could sample the local talent."

I laughed but didn't explain the reference.

We got to the hospital at noon, and Frankie and Hooch fooled around with the kids for a while. Some of the tykes—the ones not hooked up to IV stands—love to ride Hooch. The staff allows this as long as there's a nurse or volunteer to keep one hand on the little buckaroos. Hooch doesn't seem to mind playing "horsie," either. In fact, I would say that he actually enjoys it, as long as they don't grab his ears too hard. When we were through I took the dogs up to the cancer wing, hoping to visit Jill Krempetz, but we got turned away. She was still in recovery from Sunday's surgery, a nurse said, though she wouldn't tell me what kind of surgery it was or when I could see her.

We were about to leave when I heard her voice coming from a nearby room. "Who's that? Is that you, Jack?"

The nurse tried to stop me, but the dogs and I brushed past her into Jill's private room.

"Sir," said the nurse, coming around in front of me again, "you can't be in here, especially not with those dogs. She needs her rest."

"They're therapy dogs," I said.

"Let them come," Jill said, with as much force as she could muster. "I want to talk to him."

The nurse shook her head and said, "I'm going to have to call the doctor about this," then left the room.

I told the dogs to lie down, then sat in a chair next to the bed. "How's it going?"

"How do you think?" She laughed sourly. "I just got my other tit chopped off. I'm starting to feel like I did back when I was the flattest girl in junior high." She tried to laugh again but couldn't quite pull it off.

She put her hand out for me to hold. I held it. Frankie and Hooch got up and came over to comfort her. I let them.

"It's going to be okay," I said. "You're going to make it through this."

She pet the dogs then let out a deep sigh. "I hope so. I feel so weak. They say it's . . . oh, what's the word?"

"I don't know. They say it's normal? It's natural?"

"No, I mean . . ." She stopped to take another breath. "They say the surgery is more difficult, that it's more difficult to recover from it when you've been on chemo and radiation."

"Do you want me to get you some pot? Would that help? I could sneak it past the nurse."

She smiled, patted my hand. "That's very nice of you, Jack, but I've got a morphine drip. Besides, what I really need now is rest. Thanks for coming to see me, though. And thanks for bringing the dogs."

"No problem."

"If I get better—"

"You mean, *when* you get better."

She smiled. "Okay. When I get better, maybe you'll help me pick out a dog? I think I'd like to have a dog."

"Sure I will," I said, trying not to cry.

"A corgi would be nice, don't you think? Or a beagle?"

"Don't get a beagle. Not until you're a hundred percent. In the meantime, I think a corgi would be perfect for you."

"Good. Then that's what I'll get."

"I'll even train it for you, free of charge."

"The hell you will." Her eyes blazed at me.

"No, I just meant that—"

"I know what you meant. Have I ever done anything for you as your attorney and not asked you to pay me for it?"

"No."

"Exactly. Why would you think I'd let you do anything for *me* for free, then? Because I'm sick? Is that it?"

"I'm sorry."

"You *should* be."

"All right, then. I'll charge you full price."

"Good. That's all I ask." She closed her eyes.

"And I'll start looking for a corgi right away."

She said nothing.

"Jill?" I said. She had fallen asleep.

I got up and stood there for a moment looking at her, so weak and helpless, and there was nothing I could do about it. Nothing but help her find a dog, if that's what she wanted.

"Okay, kids," I sighed finally, "let's go home and let her get some sleep." I went to the door. Frankie followed me, but Hooch stayed a moment longer to lick her hand.

"Aw, good doggie, Hooch."

He turned his head to me and smiled.

27

I drove home under a dark cloud, though the sun was still shining as brightly as before. When we got back to the kennel, Leon was back from summer school and was out in the play yard starting his first training session with Magee. It wasn't going well, apparently.

"Yo, Jack," he shouted as I let Frankie and Hooch out of the woody, "I don't get this dog."

Frankie and Hooch shook themselves in unison. "What's the matter?" I said, walking down the hill, the two dogs now loping ahead of me. I got to the gate where Magee was waiting to meet his two new buddies. I let them inside.

They cantered to the middle of the space, nipping and play biting and the like. Frankie quickly lost interest in such activities, though, and began patrolling the fence, looking for any spot that needed a little dab of his urine to brighten the decor. Meanwhile, Magee was determined to make Hooch play with him. Hooch, though, wasn't too sure. Magee barked and lunged at the big dog, who just stood there, occasionally barking back in his low Hooch voice. Each of Magee's lunges turned into a play bow, but there was still no response from Hooch, so the skinny terrier came in and grabbed hold of the wattle under Hooch's chin and started pulling on it like it was a tug toy. This pissed Hooch off and he batted at Magee with a front paw. Magee held on with all his might, though, and tugged and tugged. Finally Hooch, in all his lumbering orange glory, lunged at him. Magee immediately took off running, looking over his shoulder to make sure Hooch was chasing him, which is what he'd wanted all along.

"So what's the problem, Leon?"

"Look at this dog. He totally ignores me out here. It's like I'm a ghost. I'm gonna take him back."

I laughed. "Shut up."

"I am."

"No, you're not."

"But he's like two different dogs. Inside my room he can't get enough of me. Out here, I'm Casper."

I laughed again. "Haven't I explained to you the difference between den behaviors and outdoor behaviors?"

"Yeah?" he said uncertainly. "But maybe you better explain it to me again."

I reminded him that when a dog leaves the den (or in Magee's case, the carriage house), his hunting instincts start to kick in. This may manifest as a lot of sniffing of the ground, or scanning the horizon for movement, or scavenging, or just looking for other dogs to hunt or play with. "Until you've activated his drive and plugged it into you, he's pretty much programmed by nature to ignore you outdoors."

Of course, not *all* dogs are that way. There *are* some who seem to automatically focus their drive on whoever they're with; allowing or needing that person to be their access to prey. Magee, however, being a terrier, was definitely *not* of that ilk. He was too independent.

"Look," I said, "I'm going to take Frankie and Hooch up to the house. While I'm gone, try to get Magee to chase you around. Get down on your hands and knees if you have to, roll over on your back, let him jump all over you. Get him to bat his paws at you like he's doing with Hooch, then jump up and run away. Zigzag, and make him crazy to catch up with you."

"Get on my hands and knees? Roll over on my back? Nah, I don't think so. I got on my school clothes."

I shook my head. "Then go up and change. But leave Magee

here when you do. If you leave him alone for a while, he'll be happy to see you when you come back."

He thought it over. "I could do that, I guess."

"In fact, you *should* do that. If the roughhousing and the game of tag don't work, playing hide-and-seek *will*. Have you taught him to jump up on you?"

"Nah, I'm sayin'—he won't do nothin' I ask him to. He hates me."

The bell over the kennel door rang.

I laughed. "He doesn't hate you, Leon. You just haven't made yourself important to his drive yet." The bell rang again. "Jumping up on command is one of the first things you should teach a dog. How many times have I told you that?"

The bell rang again then stopped.

"I don't know, about a million, I guess."

"Okay. When you leave, tie Magee to the fence, go up and change, wait a while, then come back down, and I guarantee you, the first thing Magee is going to do when you come through that gate is jump up on you."

"Jack!" It was Mrs. Murtaugh, calling from the kennel door. "There's a Detective Sinclair on the phone."

"I'll be right there." To Leon, I said, "Once you get him to jump up on you, the rest is gravy."

"Yeah? What if I don't like gravy?"

I laughed again. "Just shut up and do what I told you."

He shook his head like he was doomed to failure. "Whatever you say, boss man."

I whistled Frankie and Hooch over and we went up to the kennel. We came inside; I gave them each a rawhide, came around the reception counter, sat at my desk and picked up the phone. "What's up?" I said.

"Well," said Sinclair, "grand jury proceedings are supposed to be kept secret but I *can* tell you this: over protests made by the DA, the foreman of the grand jury has requested that a certain audio tape, currently in possession of the FBI, be brought into evidence."

"Good job," I said.

"Thanks. Now I'm going to get started on finding that sailboat of yours. Anything else I should know about?"

I told him about Sherry Maughn, the second tennis ball, the phony U.S. Marshal, and T'anke and Kong.

"Sounds like someone is trying to frame you, Jack."

"Yeah, no kidding. Maybe you should put a hold on the sailboat thing, locate these two Samoans and bust them for assaulting that vacationing couple and breaking their camera. And try to keep them out of commission for a while."

I could hear him thinking it over. "If we can get someone to ID them or if their prints match the ones on the camera, then yeah, I could do that."

"Good." We hung up. I called Otis Barnes and told him what was going on, then called Sheila Kelly at the TV station.

"Can you come down here," she said, "so I can get you on camera with this for the evening news?"

I looked at the clock. "Well, I can't talk about what happened in the grand jury room, but I can sure as hell talk about that tape and what the FBI is up to."

"That would be . . ." I could almost feel her tingling with excitement. ". . . so great!"

"Just one thing . . ." I told her about my father's impending arrival and asked if she could send a car to pick him up at the airport and drive him to the TV station.

"Consider it done." I gave her the flight information, and she said, "Lily wants to speak to you."

She put Lily Chow on.

"Jack, are we taping a segment for next week's show or not? I've got the whole crew on standby."

"Just run an old tape. I think I'm going to be too busy this week to—" Something occurred to me. "Yeah, you know, what the hell. Bring the crew out here and tape my foster son Leon. He adopted a cute little wheaten terrier mix yesterday and has just started training him."

"I don't know."

"Trust me, it'll be great. Hang on a sec." I went to the door. Leon had changed clothes and was coming back from the carriage house. "Hey, Leon, you want to be on TV?"

"What?" He had just reached the gate. Magee, meanwhile, was going nuts; whining and leaping up in the air, desperate to reconnect with his new owner.

"It's for my TV thing next Saturday." I shouted. "They want to feature you and Magee."

"No shit?" He seemed happy.

"Yeah, but watch your language. You'll be on TV."

He laughed. "Don't worry. I'll be good."

"Okay. They're coming out this afternoon. I have to go into Portland for a while, but you can handle things until Farrell gets back though, right?"

"I guess so." He went inside the play yard, closed the gate, and walked over to where Magee was tied up. The dog jumped up on him and grabbed his wrist with his teeth. "Yo, Jack, now he's *bitin'* me!"

"No, he's not," I shouted to him. "He's *gripping* you. That means he likes you and wants to play. Grab a tug toy from the rack, untie him, and run away."

He did as I told him, and soon he and the dog were running around like crazy. Magee was now totally focused on Leon.

What was it Brianne O'Leary had called it? Oh, yeah—"that old Jack magic."

It works every time.

28

I had taped my sound byte for the evening news and was in one of the editing bays reviewing the videos of Saturday's various press conferences when my dad walked in; silver, suntan, looking lean and fit as ever. In fact, *more* so.

"So, big shot," he says, his white eyebrows frowning at me, "you're too busy to meet your old man at the airport?"

"Old? You look younger than *I* do."

"Clean living and salt air," he says, smiling now and looking around. "So, you're on television these days?"

"That I am, Dad." I pulled a chair out for him to sit on. "Where's your luggage?"

"It's still in the limo. Hey, did you know they have a minibar in the back seat? Very fancy. Not that I had any."

"Still on the wagon, huh?"

The patient parent, he shook his head, sat down and said, "Son, I told you this, years ago when your mother died, that I was through with all that." He yawned.

"Jet lag?"

"I guess so, a little."

While we spoke I was carefully scrolling through the footage shot outside the Cumberland County Jail when Kelso and I made our exit through the crowd of reporters. I saw something interesting, pressed pause, then called Sheila Kelly and asked her to come in right away. "This could be a big news story," I told her. She said she'd be right there.

"What is it, Jackie?"

"Nothing, Dad; just a face in the crowd. Would you like to see a tape of my dog-training segment from Saturday? It's pretty exciting. I got arrested, live on camera."

"You didn't tell me you got arrested."

"Yes, I did, Dad. Remember? On the phone?"

"Oh, yeah."

Sheila came in and I introduced them. I asked her if she could set my dad up with the tape from Saturday in another editing bay, then come back in and look at something with me.

"Wait," my father says, "first you're too busy to meet me at the airport and now you're shoveling me off into a room somewhere to watch videos?"

"I thought you wanted to see me on TV."

"Frankly, I'd rather just go back to your place so I can take my shoes off. Is that too much to ask?"

I laughed. "Not at all, Dad. In fact, you can take them off in the car if you want. I just need to show Sheila something and then we'll go. We can take the tape of me with us and watch it back at the house."

"So Jack," Sheila said, checking her watch, "what is it?"

I pointed to the monitor. "You see that car, there in the background?" I played the tape in slow motion. A window rolled down and you could see a man's face, though his features were barely discernible because of the distance from the camera. I pressed pause, pointed. "That's Eddie Cole!"

"Jack, are you sure?"

"Who's Eddie Cole?"

"He's a bad guy, Dad. He's an escaped prisoner and he might be the person behind these murders."

"Murders? I thought there was just one."

I told him about Sherry Maughn, then asked Sheila if the tech department could enhance the shot of Cole in the car.

She said she'd see what she could do.

Dad and I went outside. The parking lot was wet from a thunderstorm that had come and gone while I was inside. We put Dad's luggage in the back of the woody then got in the front, where Dad immediately took off his shoes and farted.

I opened the windows. "Jesus, Dad!"

"Sorry, son," he says. "I been holdin' that one in."

I made no mention about how bad his feet smelled too.

When we got back to the kennel the camera crew was standing around, looking lost and helpless. Lily Chow was crying. Leon and Magee were nowhere to be seen.

"What happened?" I said, getting out of the car. My dad put on his shoes and followed suit, then went around back for his bags. "Where's Leon and Magee?"

Lily couldn't talk so Brent Robison, the camera guy, said, "The damn dog ran off. Lily thought we should get a shot of the two of them over by the kennel, you know, with the Dog Hill Kennel sign in the background? So Leon opened the gate down there," he pointed to the play yard, "and the dog just booked."

I started to laugh. Lily stared at me.

Brent said, "What's so funny?"

"Dogs," I said. "Sometimes they just crack me up." I shook my head. "He just took off?"

"Jack?" says my dad, "Can you help me with this bag?"

"Sure, Dad." I went around to the back of the wagon, followed by Brent, Lily, and the rest of the crew. I chuckled again to think of Magee running off. I got my dad's bags out.

Brent said, "Yeah. He just ran up the hill, there, behind the kennel building."

The team's audio recordist, Jaime Gonzalves, said, "We got the whole thing on tape if you want to see it."

"No thanks. Was he after a squirrel or anything?"

"No, he just ran away as fast as he could."

I shook my head and chuckled some more. "So, he just decided to see the world, huh? Dad, leave those for now. I'll bring them in for you in a minute."

Through her tears Lily said, "Jack, this is serious. Something terrible is going to happen to him, I just know it."

"Well, don't worry. Hopefully we can find him before he gets into too much trouble."

"Leon is out looking for him now. He's so upset."

"He *should* be. Dad, leave it for a minute, would you please?" I thought of something and said, jokingly, to Lily, "You know what we need? A helicopter. We could fly low over the mountain and find him hanging out at someone's backyard barbecue, you know, begging for—hey, what are you doing?"

Lily had popped open her cell phone. She speed-dialed a number, and began speaking to someone at the station about getting a news chopper to fly up to the kennel. I started to say something and, she held a finger in the air, telling me to keep quiet.

"Lily, I was only kidding."

The finger again. She said, "Yes, I'll pay for it out of *my* budget—the gas, the pilot, the overtime, the works." She listened for a bit then said, "Great, thanks," closed the phone, smiled at me, wiped away her tears and said, "The chopper will be here in twenty minutes."

I shook my head and laughed. "You know, I was just kidding when I suggested that."

"Well, I got you one anyway. It's my fault the dog is missing. Besides, maybe we can turn this fiasco into a segment about dogs who run off or something."

"That's good thinking." I turned to my father and put a hand on his shoulder. "Well, Dad, it looks like we've got just enough time for the two dollar tour."

"I don't care about that," he says. "Just show me the way to the bathroom."

29

Once the two of us got airborne, the pilot—whose name was Mike Brooks—just wanted to talk about the murder case. He'd known Beeson slightly, had drinks with him, traded stories, shared flying tips—just a casual acquaintanceship among members of the brotherhood of chopper pilots.

"I saw you on the news tonight," he shouted into the mouthpiece. His voice crackled in my headphones. "I was really surprised to hear that Beeson used to fly drugs up from Mexico. You know, that whole witness protection thing."

"Yeah? Why is that?"

"I don't know. He just always struck me as a real straight arrow, you know? So who do you think killed him? I mean, it really wasn't you, was it?"

"No," I laughed, "it wasn't me. Can you get us a little lower? There are some vacation cabins up this way."

He took us down to a hundred feet above the treetops. It was starting to come on sundown, and at this point I wasn't looking for Magee per se, but for smoke coming from a backyard barbecue. I just had a feeling that that's where I'd find the dog; that his nose had led him toward the smell of food.

He said, "The other thing is, I could never figure out why Maxwell needed a helicopter pilot in the first place."

I said, "What do you mean?"

"He's as experienced as any of us."

"Ian Maxwell has a pilot's license?"

"Yep. He's been flyin' these babies for years."

I thought it over. "Well, he's rich," I said. "Most rich people can drive but they pay someone else to do it for them. I guess Beeson was his air chauffeur."

He nodded. "So what's your theory of the case?"

"My 'theory of the case'?" I shouted back. "You've been watching too much Court TV." He shrugged. "I'm not sure. It could be payback for his testimony against the drug lords of San Diego. It could be that he and his girlfriend were up to something illegal here in Maine and that's what got them both killed. It's too early to tell. You see that smoke over here on the right?" He said he did. "Well, let's go buzz that barbecue and see what we find."

"Listen," he said as we banked hard to the right, putting a strain on my seat belt and some butterflies in my stomach, "I didn't know him that well, but I'd be really surprised if he was doing something illegal."

"I know what you're saying." We came over the source of the smoke. (It was, indeed, a backyard barbecue.) "But I worked Homicide in New York. Nothing surprises *me*."

"Holy crap!" he shouted, looking down. "Is that him? Is that the dog?"

It certainly was. Magee was happily wandering through someone's backyard—back and forth from picnic table to lawn chair, begging for, and getting, scraps of food; an uninvited yet seemingly welcome party guest. "That's him," I said.

Mike Brooks switched on the external camera and began taping the scene the way he would a pile-up on the turnpike.

"Can you take us down?"

He said he could—out on the dirt road—and he did. We set down, I undraped Magee's leash from around my neck, got out and shouted through the open door, "I'll be right back."

I ran, hunched over beneath the whirling blades, got to the back fence of the house, opened the gate and joined the party. Magee saw me and came running over. I guess he associated me with Leon, or with Frankie and Hooch, his two new pack-mates.

As for the people? There were some introductions, some apologies (for Magee's intrusion and the noise from the chopper), and some explanations made. I borrowed a cell phone, called Lily Chow and told her the good news.

She was very relieved. Leon had apparently already come back, dejected and depressed, but when she'd told him about the chopper he brightened up, then became disappointed that he hadn't been able to go for a ride with us.

I hooked Magee to his leash (using some barbecued chicken as bait), then took him out to the chopper, got in and held him on my lap for the ride home.

When we got back to the kennel, everyone there (except my father, who was inside the house) applauded Mike Brooks as he set down. He waved politely through the bubble window. I was about to take the headphones off and open the door when he touched my arm and said, "I'm telling you, Jack, this guy Beeson—or whatever his name was—he was a good guy. He wouldn't have been mixed up in—"

"Thanks," I said, "I'll keep that in mind." I shook his hand. "Thanks for your help."

"No problem. Anytime you need me . . ."

"I may take you up on that," I said, laughing.

Magee and I got out and ran under the chopper blades to where Leon, Lily Chow, Mrs. Murtaugh, and the others were standing. Leon crouched down and Magee jumped up and licked his face. The chopper took off. Brent Robison and the crew, I now noticed, were taping the return of the prodigal dog.

Lily shrugged at me. "Hey, now the cost of hiring the helicopter can be justified as part of the shooting budget."

"I think it'll make a great segment." I put a hand on Leon's shoulder. "Especially once we get Magee trained not to run off and to come when called. That'll be the kicker."

He stood up, holding the dog's leash tight. "Yo, Jack, I really screwed up. I know." Magee was jumping up on him.

I put my hand behind his neck and shook him a little. "I just hope you learned something, Leon. Never—"

"—let a dog off the leash until he's trained to come back, I know. The thing is, I see you doin' it with Frankie and Hooch, and also when you take the dogs down to the—"

"Those dogs have all been trained. Plus, when I take them down to the play yard, I know exactly where their focus is at all times. I rarely bring them back up to the kennel without first putting their leashes on. Sometimes I do that, but only when I get their drive totally plugged into me first."

"Can we get him a transponder?"

"What?"

"You said they can be used to track lost dogs."

"Sure," I laughed, "but don't worry, we'll have that little guy trained in no time. He won't run off again."

"But just in case?"

"Okay, just in case." Lily Chow and the crew left. Mrs. Murtaugh went back to the kennel. I walked Leon and Magee up to the carriage house.

"Are you hungry at all, or did you already eat?"

"Nah, I could eat, I guess. You're not mad at me?"

"I think you're probably mad enough at yourself for both of us right now, Leon. Anyway, I'll make us some dinner. Did you meet my dad? He's probably hungry too."

"Nah, he ate all the leftovers from the party. Now he's in Mr. Kelso's room, taking a nap."

"Yeah," I laughed, "he's a little jet-lagged. I'll let you know when dinner's ready."

I got up to the house, where Frankie was happy to see me, though Hooch was nowhere to be seen. I went to the guest room and heard snoring from inside. I opened the door and found my father and Hooch taking a nap together. Dad had one arm draped around the big dog's neck. They were both snoring.

I went to the kitchen and started dinner—grilled sea bass with a pan sauce of butter, shallots, onions, cilantro-infused olive oil, garlic, lemon pepper, a little shredded ginger and slivered almonds, served with steamed broccoli, and a baby spinach and watercress salad tossed with chopped tangerines and walnuts and coated with a raspberry/ginger vinaigrette.

I called Leon on the intercom and was just setting the table when Jamie got through to me on my cell phone.

"Hi, honey," she said. "You've got your home phone unplugged again, don't you?"

"Yeah. Too many reporters keep calling."

"Ah, I'm sorry. Besides that, how was your day?"

"A little eventful to say the least. Where *are* you?"

"Dr. Liu and I are just finishing up at the morgue. And I have some great news!"

"Good, I could use some. Are you coming for dinner?"

"I'd love to, sweetheart, but I can't. I've got too much work to do back at the hospital. Things are really piling up in the lab." She sighed. "I'll be working pretty late, then I'm going to crash at my new apartment."

"You mean I won't see you tonight? My dad really wants to meet you."

Leon came in, carrying some strings of firecrackers. I pointed him to a plate on the table. He sat down and made a face at the food. "It's sea bass, Leon," I said, cupping my hand over the phone. "It's really good."

"It's *fish*."

"We'll have chicken tomorrow, maybe."

"Oh, honey," Jamie said, "I want to meet him too, but I'll probably be working till two in the morning."

I laughed. "You know what? I just realized; Dad's kind of jet-lagged so tonight's probably not good for him either. In fact, he and Hooch are taking a nap together right now."

"They *are*?" She laughed. "I would love to see that."

"Yeah, it's kind of sweet. I'll miss you."

"You will?"

"Yes, terribly. What's your great news?"

"The second autopsy rules you out completely as a suspect. There's no way you could have done it."

"*I* know that, remember? I actually *didn't* do it. So what did you find out, exactly?"

"I don't have time for all the details right now. I'll tell you everything in the morning. Dr. Liu and I are going out to Aunt Zita's before sunup. Can you join us?"

"I can come later. Why are you going so early?"

"He wants to use luminol on the rocks and—"

"I know. Luminol only shows up under black light."

She said, "Anyway, just come when you can. Oh, and bring Kelso along, if he's sober."

"Hah. Maybe I'll bring him anyway."

"And your dad too. I can't wait to meet him."

"Okay. I'll see you tomorrow."

"I miss you. I love you."

"Me too, honey." I hung up.

"Yo, Jack, what's this curly stuff in my salad?"

"It's watercress. You don't have to eat it if you don't like it." I sat down and pulled my plate toward me.

"Good. 'Cause I'm not gonna. It tastes like *weeds*."

I picked up the firecrackers. "What are you doing with these? They're illegal."

"I got 'em from a friend at school. I was gonna shoot 'em off but then I thought it might scare Magee and make him run away again. I figured you'd know what to do with 'em."

"Yeah? That's good, Leon." I got up and put them in a drawer next to the sink. "So, how's the fish?"

"Not too bad," he smiled, his mouth full of sea bass.

30

We got a late start the next morning. There were a number of reasons for this: Kelso's hangover, the reluctance of a certain female acquaintance of his to vacate his bed at the motel he'd found in Lincolnville (her reason, I found out later, was that she was one half of Eve Arden and was too embarrassed to come out from under the covers while I was there), and the fact that Farrell Woods called in sick, which left Mrs. Murtaugh and D'Linda in charge of the kennel. There was some debate about whether my dad should stay to help out or if Leon should take a day off from summer school and do it.

"Leon knows the drill around here, Dad. Besides, I need to have your years of experience with me at the crime scene."

"My years of experience? Like what? Keeping reporters away? Canvassing the neighborhood?"

"Dad."

"What neighborhood?" he went on. "It's an island."

I think he just didn't want to leave the house because he'd become attached to the guest bedroom and its proximity to the bathroom, the refrigerator, and the remote control. I finally talked him into coming. I did it by holding out the carrot that he would finally get to meet Jamie.

On the trip to Boothbay Harbor, Kelso casually mentioned that he'd spent a little time at the motel working on his computer, checking out Ian Maxwell and his company.

Maxwell was, by all reports, a multibillionaire, and rightly so. He'd invented dozens of medical gadgets used in hospitals around the world. And, as if the royalties on his patents weren't enough, he'd also formed his own manufacturing company to produce his inventions, which had increased his income tenfold. However, his lavish spending habits—buying his own private island, purchasing a museum's worth of fine art, owning a fleet of boats, employing a full-time staff, and building a huge mansion on an island with no previously established infrastructure (no electricity, no fresh water supply, no sewage facilities, etc.)—put a bit of a strain on his pocketbook. He'd also built new production facilities in Rockland, Belize, and Taiwan, with enormous start-up costs. Plus, Kelso said, he'd recently settled more than a dozen lawsuits for undisclosed amounts.

"Are you saying he's got money problems?"

"Could be. It's hard to know for sure. I'm not a forensic accountant, and even if I *were*, it would take a team of experts at least a couple of years to untangle all his financial records, if you could even get ahold of them."

"So, what's the upshot?" says Dad.

Kelso shrugged. "He might have a bit of a cash crunch, at least temporarily. Did I mention that the finish carpenter on his house quit work because he hasn't been paid?"

"Moon MacKenzie?" I said.

"That's him. How did you . . . ? Oh, yeah. That's the guy whose daughter got killed last year. You had me look up some stuff about her on the Net."

We drove for a bit, listening to the oldies station. They were playing "She's Not There," by The Zombies.

"You said he has an art collection?"

"That's right."

"Sherry Maughn may have been forging paintings." I told him about the mortar and pestle and the bags of pigment.

"That's something to think about. Maybe she and Beeson were stealing his paintings and replacing them with forged copies. Is that what you're thinking?"

"Not exactly. I imagine that that would be pretty hard to do, with the kind of security staff he's got."

"Maybe one of them was in on it."

"Maybe," I said. "Or maybe *Maxwell* was in on it."

Kelso laughed. "I hadn't thought about that, but if he really *does* have a cash flow problem . . ."

"Yeah. The only thing I can't figure out is the San Diego connection." I remembered that the two Samoans, as Flynn had called them, had talked about finding a painting for their boss, a Señor Ortiz. I told my dad and Kelso about it.

"I think I know who he is," Dad says. "Miguel Ortiz. He's the head honcho in the drug trade back in San Diego."

"Really? That might connect him to Beeson and Maxwell."

My father knew quite a *bit* about Ortiz, actually. As we drove toward Boothbay Harbor he painted a picture of the man. A picture he'd garnered from conversations on patrol, hanging around the police locker room, or at McGinty's after hours:

Miguel Ortiz was—in a twisted sort of way—an American success story. He started out as a teenager, a small, slim wetback with no money, very little physical presence, and few valuable skills. Even so, he slowly and carefully worked his way up through the lower echelons of the drug trade.

How had he done it? Apparently he was quite the charmer, for one thing. For another he was smart and willing to wait however long it took for opportunity to present itself. He read a lot. He loved Shakespeare—the tragedies and histories—though he never attended the theater. He memorized *The Art of War*, Machiavelli's *The Prince*, and even Donald Trump's *The Art of the Deal*. Being small in stature, he surrounded himself with muscle (like the two Samoans), which made him feel bigger and stronger. In fact, the stronger he felt, the stronger he *became* within the organization, which, before he took over, was pretty unorganized. As time went on some silent coups took place in which several young "lieutenants," much higher up than he was, disappeared under mysterious circumstances. He took over their jobs. As his influence and power grew, so did his fondness for fine clothes, fine wine, and fine art.

I said, "So he may have been buying forged paintings from Sherry Maughn. Maybe with the help of Ian Maxwell."

"He has an art fetish, so that would fit what I've heard about him," my father said, then went on with his story.

It was after the feds caught Hugh Gardner flying drugs in from Mexico that Ortiz really took power. He was probably the small, dapper man that Gardner met each week at the helipad in the desert. And, oddly enough, the only time he didn't show up for the drop was the day Gardner and the Samoans got busted. (Interesting.) A domino effect ensued and toppled the higher levels of the mob, leaving Ortiz in charge.

"They say he has a beautiful, though well-fortified, hacienda on the beach in La Jolla," Dad said. "He still keeps himself surrounded by muscle, has managed to successfully inoculate himself from the authorities"—I think he meant *insulate*—"probably through bribes of one kind or another, and they say he operates the whole magillah from the beach. He rarely leaves the house, though I heard that he *has* been to Boston a few times in the past year or so."

Kelso and I looked at each other. I said, "Remember Sherry Maughn's phone calls from room 601 at that hotel in Boston, that were charged to her home number?" He nodded. "When you get a chance, find out the dates of those calls and see if you can connect them with any flights Ortiz might have made east around the same time. It would be helpful to find out if Sherry was a guest at the hotel but she probably used an alias."

"That trip may just be a rumor, though, Jackie," Dad said. "His wife, on the other hand, a young Anglo woman from Pasadena, she loves to gad about. She flies off to Hawaii and Italy and Europe, all over the place. She attends all kinds of social events too, like the ballet, the theater, charity balls, and the like, usually with one young stud or another on her arm."

Kelso and I looked at each other.

"Maybe we should take a trip out West?" he said.

"Maybe," I said. "We'll see what develops." To my father, I said, "Good work, Dad. You know, you should have put in for detective years ago. You'd have been darn good at it."

"Eh," he said, embarrassed.

* * *

We got to Boothbay Harbor around eleven and hired a boat to take us out to the middle of Linekin Bay. When we docked at Aunt Zita's, Tipper was there to greet us, barking and shaking her tush. I think she remembered me, because when I got off the boat she spun around in happy circles then jumped up on me and whined a little. I knew what she was whining for (a tennis ball), and I just happened to have a couple in my "safari vest," as Lily Chow had called it. I produced one, showed it to Tipster, and she whirled around again and ran to the end of the dock, turned to face me and barked, urging me to throw it, which I did. She went after it.

"Do all the dogs in Maine love you like this, Jackie?"

"I don't know, Dad. I haven't *met* all the dogs in Maine."

"Just give him time," said Kelso.

Tipper brought the ball to me then backed away, shaking her tush. I smiled, thinking of how fun it was going to be for Jill Krempetz to have a little Tipper dog of her own. I could just imagine her, sitting in a rocking chair, taking it easy with a knit throw across her lap and a wicker basket full of tennis balls within arm's reach. Thinking about this made me feel good and even hopeful for her recovery. Dogs can do that for you sometimes—they can keep you young and healthy, even when the doctors have run out of ideas.

The four of us walked up the steps and past the house with a quick wave from Aunt Zita, who was watching from behind the screen door. She called Tipper but the dog ignored her, as did I. We got to the steps leading down to the beach. Tipper and I went down first, followed by my dad and Kelso.

We got to the gunhole and found Dr. Liu—tall, thin, with long black hair and thick glasses—along with two of his assistants measuring things with a cloth tape.

Jamie was watching them work.

"How's it going?" I said.

"Hi, sweetheart." She came running over, happy to see me; yet her eyes seemed to hold some hidden sadness.

Dr. Liu smiled at me and said, "Ve'y *in*tuhsting! Ve'y *in*tuhsting!" (After spending a little more time listening to him talk and learning to decipher his accent, I realized he'd just said, "Very *in*teresting! Very *in*teresting!")

Then, after Jamie introduced us, he went back to measuring things and muttering under his breath.

I introduced Jamie to Jack, Sr.—which is how I sometimes refer to him—and she wondered out loud what exactly *she* should call him. She couldn't very well call him Jack, she said, since that was what she called me (it *is* the name on my birth certificate), and she was reluctant to call him Jack, Sr., since his given name is actually John (which he's never been called by anyone), so she was a little confused.

My dad helped her out. "Aw, just call me Dad," he said.

She smiled, hugged him, then said, "Okay, Dad. I need to talk to Jack privately for a minute. I hope you don't mind."

"Hey, whatever you gotta do." He shrugged.

"Probably some silly details about the wedding," I joked.

She took me aside. "Jack," she seemed very serious, "I'm afraid I have some bad news about Jill Krempetz."

"Oh, no." I could feel something happening inside me.

"I'm sorry, honey. She passed away peacefully in her sleep last night."

My heart dropped to my knees. Peacefully, I tried to say, that's good, but I couldn't get the words out.

"Her family is flying her ashes back to Michigan on Saturday. That's where they're having the funeral."

I wanted to say something about how much she loved Camden and how her ashes should stay right here in Maine but all I could do was press the heels of my hands as hard as I could against my eyes to try and keep the tears from coming. Strangely enough, it worked, at least momentarily. When I was done, I took my hands down and smiled a sad smile at Jamie.

She took both my hands in hers. "Are you all right?"

"Not really," I said, "I think I need to go up to the backyard and kind of be alone for a while. Do you mind?"

"Not at all," she smiled. "Let me know if you need me."

"I will. Come on, Tipper." The dog followed me up the steps and I found a shady spot, put my back against a tree and sobbed like a baby for a while. Tipper, good little girl that she was, climbed in my lap and let me hold her.

"She was going to get a dog," I told Tipper, petting her. "A little corgi like you. And now she can't. Now she—" I tried to stop crying. "I'll never see her again."

I cried even more. When I was finished I sat for a while feeling bad about feeling bad, knowing that Jill wouldn't like me to cry over her like this. Then, after my breathing got back to normal and I'd stopped sniffling, I sat a bit longer, then went back down to the beach, with Tipper at my heels.

Jamie met me at the bottom step. I smiled and hugged her. "I'm okay now." I sniffed a bit. "Thanks, honey." I looked at Dr. Liu. "So?" I sighed. "What have you found?"

"Ve'y *in*tuhsting! Ve'y *in*tuhsting!"

It puzzled me how he could go through the entire higher educational system in America and still have such an impenetrable accent.

"We find b'ood, yes? I tink maybe it's yoh b'ood."

"My blood?"

"Yes! Up daya on de boosh!" He pointed to the thornbush that I'd scratched my cheek on. "It show up nice and b'ight when we sp'ay it wit' lumino'!" I took this to mean that they found blood on the thornbush when they sprayed it with luminol. "De p'oblem is . . ." he went on.

"Yes? The problem is . . ."

"De p'oblem is, we don't find b'ood on de wocks. None of de wocks *heaya*," he waved his arm, indicating the rocks along the beach, "have any b'ood any*waya*. *I* tink, you see befoah, I tink maybe dis Beeson hit his attackah wit' one of de wocks. Dat woo esplain de b'ood on his han'."

I nodded. "It would explain the blood on his hand. Was that the same as the blood on the cap I found?"

"Dah's wight. It was his *attack*ah's b'ood. Den I tink, maybe he slip on de wet wocks, you know, wet f'om de *ocean*, and maybe his *attackah* hit his head on de *bow*duh." He pointed to the boulder. "But we dohn find any b'ood, any*waya*!"

"Well," I said, "there's been quite a bit of rain. There was a huge thunderstorm the other night."

He nodded. "Yes. It wash de b'ood off de wocks." He said to Jamie, "Doctah Cuttah, you tay him bout oh*top*sy?"

"No," she said. "I haven't told him yet."

"You tay him now?"

She nodded and told me they'd found a microscopic hole in Beeson's forehead, one that had apparently been caused by something like a microlaser that bored through the temporal bone then through the brain, causing a minuscule yet deadly aneurysm. It had then penetrated and passed through the occipital bone, at the back of the skull, where there was another tiny hole along with some burnt hair follicles. It was the burnt hair that caused Dr. Liu to look for this mysterious wound.

"Stuhwaight line." He demonstrated with his hands.

"A straight line?"

"Yes! Just like a lazuh, but ve'y sumoah."

"Like a laser, but very small?" (Uh-oh, Kelso's Zen hologram had just made another entrance.)

"Yes, yes! Eensy-teensy!" He squinted and held his thumb and forefinger together, with just the tiniest space between them. "De size of a singoh mohecue."

"A single molecule?" I said. "That's impossible. A nanolaser wouldn't have enough power to penetrate through bone, would it?"

"Yes! Exac'ly!" He nodded and laughed. "Nanolazuh are used mos'ly fo' fibuh optic, not like a CO_2 lazuh, dat can cut th'ew metal." He shook his head. "Ve'y mystee'yus."

"Maybe it was a particle beam of some kind?"

"Yes!" He laughed giddily. "Shuah! In a big physics labato'y, maybe, but heaya on de beach? I dohn *tink* so!"

I thought it over. "And this eensy-teensy laser, or whatever, that's what caused the radiating skull fracture?"

"Dat's wight. F'ont an' back." He gestured, front and back. "Dees lazuh, oh whatevah, it also cause de ano*wism*."

"And the aneurysm is what killed him?"

"I tink so. Maybe." He shook his head emphatically. "But it would be ve'y hahd to p'oove."

"Unless we find that eensy-teensy laser."

He raised his hands. "If you *find*, I would like to see."

"I would like to see it too," said Jamie, putting a hand on my shoulder. "And I think I know where it's located."

"Yeah, me too." I turned back to the famous criminalist. "Okay, Dr. Liu, thanks. Write up a full report, but don't tell anyone what you've found. Not yet."

"Dohn wohh'y." He shook his head. "I'm not c'azy. I just act *like* it some*time*!"

31

We left Kelso and my dad in Boothbay Harbor with the keys to my Suburban and a DeLorme map of the area. (DeLorme is a *great* map company located in Yarmouth, Maine.) Their job was to canvass all the marinas and try to find the sailboat I'd seen, the one with the orange and turquoise striped sail.

While they were doing this, Jamie called Maxwell and asked if we could come see him. He said he'd already given a statement but would be happy to see her, so we took her father's runabout to Maxwell's private island, out where Penobscot Bay meets the Atlantic Ocean, out where a mad scientist invents things like a ve'y sumoah lazuh.

"Would you stop *imitating* him?" Jamie shouted over the roar of the engine and the splash of the salt spray.

"Sorry," I shouted back. "I didn't realize I was doing it."

"You've been *doing* it since we left Aunt Zita's."

"I'm sowwy, but it's ve'y hab*eet* foh*meeng*."

"Shut up! He's a brilliant man and you should show him moah weespec'. Jack! Now you've got *me* doing it."

We laughed ourselves silly for a while.

Finally, Jamie shouted, "It *is* habit forming, isn't it? But it's still not right. The poor man, he not only has an awful accent but a speech impediment as well."

Now I felt bad. "Well, dah esplain tings."

"Will you please," she was laughing again, "stop it?"

"I'm sorry." I could feel my face get tight and my eyes start to fog up. "I just can't believe I'm never going to see Jill again, and I'm a little nuts about it right now."

"Oh, honey." She took my hand.

"I'm sorry. I'll try to be good." I sighed. "You know, if she'd just gotten a mammogram two or three months earlier." I tried to hold back the tears again. "Promise me, you'll go to the doctor tomorrow and get tested?"

"Jack."

"Promise me."

"Okay, I promise."

"She was so young, you know? Just a few years older than you are."

"I'll make an appointment when we get back, okay?"

"Okay."

It was a long trip, taking us halfway between Monhegan and Matinicus Islands, which gave us plenty of time to turn our attention back to the case and to discuss the possibility that Ian Maxwell had killed Gordon Beeson.

"It's not going to be easy to trap him," I shouted. "He's exceptionally intelligent. We have to be very careful not to tip him off that he's a suspect."

"I know. And there's no *way* he's going to confess, if for no other reason than to do so would reveal the technology behind his latest invention. He's very proprietary and secretive about his contraptions, you know." She sighed. "This is just going to kill my father."

"I know, honey. But Jonas may have some unconscious suspicions of his own about Maxwell's role in the murder."

"What do you mean?"

"Jonas invited him to the party at Aunt Zita's, and he halfway expected the man to come."

"You mean that's how the body ended up on Aunt Zita's beach? Maxwell was on his way to the party?"

"It makes sense." Then I told her about Sherry Maughn's studio, the Samoans and the San Diego connection.

"So Beeson and Sherry Maughn may have been stealing

some of Maxwell's artworks, forging them, and selling the originals to this guy Ortiz?"

"That's one possibility."

She thought about it. "If Maxwell *knew* about it, that would give him a motive to kill Beeson."

"Yes," I said, "but what if Maxwell and Sherry Maughn were in on it and Beeson *wasn't*, but then he found *out*. That might also give Maxwell a motive."

She looked sad. "We seem to be pretty sure that Maxwell killed him."

I shrugged. "Autopsies don't lie."

She nodded. "This is going to devastate my father."

"I know, I'm sorry. What did you think of *my* dad?"

"He's very sweet. He kind of reminds me of you, in a disarming sort of way."

This was a surprise. "How?"

"I don't know." She lowered her voice and imitated my father's laconic brogue: "'Hey, whatever you gotta do.' It sounded exactly like you, Jack. What's wrong?"

"Nothing. I've just tried my whole life to be the exact opposite of him. I guess I failed, huh?"

She laughed and patted my arm. "Don't feel bad. I *like* your dad, and if you recall, I *love* you. Just the way you are."

"Hey, maybe we should have a cookout at my place, and have the two old guys meet each other. What do you think?"

"Jonas and Jack, Sr.? I think that would be wonderful. Will you make your famous brisket?"

"I didn't know it was famous. And some steaks and burgers and hot dogs and potato salad, the whole deal. We'll do it Friday, right after your father gets back from Boston."

"It can be our engagement party. We'll have to invite everybody." She kissed me, then said, "Okay, *now* what is it?"

"I was just thinking, what if Beeson knew what was going on with the forged artwork—if that's even the case, we don't know for sure that there *was* any forgery. But what if he *knew* and told someone in the FBI or the U.S. Marshal's Office?"

"Yeah? What about it?"

"I don't know. I just think maybe we're getting in way over our heads with this thing, and if the grand jury doesn't indict me, we should just let it lie. What's so funny?"

"You really think you're capable of walking away from this? Just like that?"

I chuckled. "Hey, I'm only human. I can engage in a little wishful thinking once in a while, can't I?"

"Sure. That's how we met, remember?" She smiled. "You wished that I would go out with you and I did."

"That's true. And I wished that you would marry me, and you said yes. Actually you said, 'Yes, yes, yes, yes, yes.'"

She hit me. "When did you wish that I would marry you?"

"From the moment I first met you, in the hospital. Remember? When I took you into the stairwell and kissed you?"

"Jack, I keep telling you, that never happened."

"Then you slapped me, remember?"

"Jack—that was just your imagination. Or maybe that's how you met Kristin Downey."

No, I knew Kristin Downey during my grad school days at Columbia. She's now a Broadway set and costume designer. She's designed everything from opera at Lincoln Center to a play directed by Mike Nichols to a brief Broadway stint by the magician Lance Burton. She's married to multimillionaire vitamin tycoon Sonny Vreeland who inherited Sun-Vee Vitamins and Supplements from his mother and father. She's called me in Maine a few times, threatening to come visit, though in typical Kristin Downey fashion, she's never made good on her threats. Which is fine with me. Things tend to get stirred up when she's around. When I knew her, she had a lot of emotional problems. She was a lot of fun sometimes, and just the opposite at others. It was, I suppose, part of my attraction for her at the time. Like my mother, I wanted to cure her of her emotional lows (though I sure loved those highs). I never told Jamie about her illness, since as far as I know she's now taking medication for it. Meanwhile, Jamie is totally jealous of her. (Her and Laura Linney, who I only met a couple of times at the dog run in New York, years ago!)

"No," I said, "as I recall, I first met Kristin Downey at a

falafel place on Broadway and 110th Street after what I thought was a date with her sister."

"Wait. You dated her *and* her sister?"

"Apparently not. The sister didn't think so, anyway. The point is, I didn't meet her and kiss her and have my face slapped by her in the stairwell at Rockland Memorial Hospital. That was *you*, brown eyes. You and only you."

She laughed and kissed me. "Whatever you say, Jack. Whatever you say."

32

It was quite a place, even from a distance. The exterior of the house—all four and a half stories of it—was completely finished. It had apparently been designed by some hotshot modern architect—the kind who doesn't believe in straight lines and right angles. Still, the layout fit in perfectly with the environment: the rocky cliffs, the crashing waves. Jamie said the outer structure had been completed some time ago and that certain sections of the interior—mainly the living quarters, most of the ten bathrooms (all Roman marble), Maxwell's workshop, and the four kitchens—were also finished.

"He has four kitchens?"

"Yep, one on each floor. With a chef for each one."

"Remind me to have that kind of money some day."

"Hey, some *countries* don't even have that kind of money. In fact, did you know that Maxwell once tried—"

"—to secede from the U.S. and declare his island a sovereign nation? Yeah, I heard that rumor. Is it true?"

"Who knows. He *is* kind of crazy."

As we pulled up to the dock, I started counting the cabin cruisers and runabouts tied up there. There were five of each. And that was nothing, apparently, because there was *also* a gargantuan boathouse, which, Jamie said, housed a fifty-foot yacht, a catamaran, and two racing sailboats.

"A fifty-footer? It sounds like it could be the one I saw in

Linekin Bay right after I found the body. Maybe Maxwell really *was* on his way to Aunt Zita's when the murder took place. Only he was on his *yacht*, not in a helicopter."

"Well," she said, switching off the engine, "the evidence does seem to be piling up against him. Hand me that rope."

Far to the right of the dock was a wide, flat stretch of rock, paved over with asphalt. This was the helipad. There were two big choppers "parked" there, with space for a third.

Once we got the boat secured, we walked up the dock to a chain-link gate with an attached buzzer and security camera.

Jamie pressed the buzzer. A moment later a disembodied voice said, "Who's there?"

"It's Dr. Jamie Cutter and Jack Field."

"Come in."

A soft click indicated that the gate was now unlocked. We went through, turned left up a set of blue slate steps into a beautiful Chinese rock garden, then through another gate— this one made of rough cedar—which led to a rose garden. We went through that, up some more slate steps, and then onto the concrete deck of a near Olympic size swimming pool, with a small waterfall pouring into it and several hot tubs nearby, disguised as blue grottos. To the right sat the clay tennis courts—four of them—surrounded by a high, black chain-link fence. Beyond the pool, the diving board, the chaise lounges, and a row of green and white striped canvas cabanas, was the back of the house. Ian Maxwell stood in the doorway, barefoot, wearing sunglasses and a short terry-cloth robe over swim trunks, swirling an iced drink in one hand and clenching a pipe between his teeth. I thought of Hugh Hefner, though Maxwell was actually quite handsome. He had wavy hair (currently wet), worn straight back, with gray streaks at the temples, just like Mr. Fantastic. He was also quite tan.

"He looks like Reed Richards, doesn't he?" I said.

"Who's Reed Richards?"

"Mr. Fantastic? He's the leader of the Fantastic Four."

"What the hell are you talking about?"

"It's a comic book. I'll explain later. By the way," I said from the right side of my mouth, "did you notice that his swimming trunks and his torso and his hair are all wet?"

"Yeah? So what?" she said, giving Maxwell a big fake smile and a wave from across the pool. "He's probably just been swimming."

"Then why aren't his *feet* wet? And why aren't there any footprints coming from the *pool*?"

She checked to see if I was right. "Huh," she said as we came around the shallow end. "Is that important?"

We approached Maxwell's smiling face. I leaned over and whispered in her ear. "That depends. First impressions are everything. Especially if you're trying to fool a couple of crack detectives like us into believing you're innocent."

"Jamie, my dear. So nice to see you again."

He held out his hand and there were introductions and handshakes and air kisses and offers of refreshment, which I declined until Jamie jabbed me in the ribs.

"Yeah, I guess I'll have a small glass of scotch, neat, if you've got any."

"How does Johnnie Walker Blue Label sound?"

"Sounds terrific."

"Nothing for me," Jamie said.

"Fine, fine. It's a shame that we have to meet again under such tragic circumstances, but there you are." He took the pipe from between his slightly chapped lips, turned sideways and pointed toward the back door. "The kitchen and dining room are right inside. I'll join you as soon as I've dried off."

We went through the door. I turned to thank him but he had disappeared into one of the cabanas. I turned back to find an English butler in full regalia, just placing a small glass of scotch, neat, on the dining room table.

"Your scotch, sir," he said.

"But how did you . . . ? That's quick service."

"Yes, sir. Mr. Maxwell likes it that way."

"Me too," I said, coming to the table, picking up the glass and sniffing the amber liquid. I took a careful sip. It was good. It was very good. "Thanks, Jeeves."

Jamie tsked at me.

"The name is Charles, sir. But if you like, you may call me Jeeves instead. I'll answer either way."

"Thanks, Charles."

He nodded a small bow. "If you require anything else, sir, just let me know." He quietly took himself to another part of the room and receded into the shadows.

"Charles?" I said.

He stepped forward. "Yes, sir?"

"Just checking."

Jamie shook her head and sighed.

"Very good, sir." He receded again.

Maxwell rejoined us, wearing a Brooklyn Dodgers baseball cap, natural-colored linen slacks, a brown, factory-faded, over-sized T-shirt—not tucked in—and leather flip-flops. He came over to the table, bringing a bright smile with him.

"How's your drink?" he said.

"Excellent," I opined.

"Good. Let's go into the study to talk. Do you mind?"

"No, not at all," Jamie said, getting up. "In fact, the study would be great. I'd really like to see the study."

Uh-oh. She was acting talkative and girlish.

"Charles?" Maxwell said, but the butler was already standing at the study door, holding it open for us. "Shall we?" Maxwell gestured with his pipe. Then, as we passed the butler, he said, "Have Paul join us."

"Very good, sir."

To me, Maxwell said, "My security chief, Paul Kemp. He can probably answer some of your questions about Gordon better than I can."

"Peachy," I said.

Jamie shot me a look.

We came inside and looked around. There was a lot to look at—among other things, a Pissaro landscape, a Cezanne still life of a bowl of fruit, and a self-portrait by Picasso.

We sat on some very modern and artsy furniture—covered in some kind of soft, cashmerelike gray material. There was track lighting, with half a dozen lights specially trained on the art-work. I sipped some more scotch.

"Nice Cezanne," I said, not able to take my eyes off it.

Maxwell sat and puffed on his pipe. "You like that picture, Jack? May I call you Jack?"

"Feel free. And I like it quite a lot, actually."

"Me too. It's not as valuable as the Picasso—that cost me ten million, but the Cezanne is one of my favorites. I have another upstairs, if you'd care to see it later. Plus a Van Gogh and a Chagall you might like. Ah, here's Paul."

Paul Kemp was fairly tall, with a totally bald—or clean-shaven—head. And though I couldn't be sure, it seemed to me that he was the maverick Navy SEAL who'd tried to kill me and Sherry Maughn at the carnival on Sunday.

"I know you," I said dumbly.

"Yes," said Maxwell, "I believe you two have already met. Have a seat, Paul."

"I'd rather stand, sir."

"Have it your way." He looked at me. "I had thought to put this meeting off awhile. But 'the sooner the better,' that's always been my motto. No sense in wasting time, now, is there?"

"No, there isn't."

"And the two of you have met twice, actually. Once at the carnival, and yesterday when Paul was impersonating U.S. Marshal Rondo Kondolean. Although, I believe he actually *is* a U.S. Marshal, aren't you Paul?"

"Yes, sir. On special assignment."

"So, it was you," I said to Kemp. "You tried to kill me and Sherry at the carnival. And you actually *did* kill her yesterday, didn't you? You shot her with a .22." That didn't seem right to me somehow. Unconsciously I knew that it couldn't have been Kemp who'd killed Sherry Maughn, but it didn't fully register why at the time.

Kemp stood there, saying nothing.

I looked over at Jamie. She just stared at Maxwell, no longer talkative and girlish.

33

Finally, she said, "How did you *know* that we knew?"

Maxwell shrugged. "Parabolic microphones, my dear. Paul has been monitoring your conversations since the two of you docked. He and I had a brief chat out in the cabana, which is when I realized that my ruse about having just been swimming hadn't fooled you into thinking I wasn't wounded." He took off his baseball cap, turned sideways and showed us a bandage on the back of his head. "It was my blood on the yachting cap Jack found at the scene. A man with a gash in his head wouldn't be likely to go for a swim, now would he? Hence, the swim trunks and the wet hair." He looked at me. "I should have actually gotten into the pool, though, shouldn't I?"

I said, "That's past tense. In fact, past perfect. What I want to know is, what are your intentions *now*? To kill us?"

He laughed. "Hardly. *You* I could do without, but I like Jamie. Besides, no matter what kind of evidence you come up with to prove I killed Beeson—and I'm not saying I did, but even if I had, it would have been justified—I won't spend a minute in jail. Paul has seen to that. Haven't you, Paul?"

"Yes, sir. I killed Beeson *and* Sherry Maughn."

Jamie was still dumbstruck.

"And why the hell," I asked politely, "did you do that?"

"They were having an affair," he recited. "I was in love with her. I lost my mind, momentarily."

"You flipped out," I suggested, "went nuts."

"Yes, sir," he said flatly. "I was temporarily insane."

I looked at Maxwell.

He smiled.

I said. "So, why do you think killing Beeson was justifiable?"

"I'm not saying I *did* kill him, you understand. But *if* I did, it would have been a matter of national security."

"National security?"

"Certainly. Everything I *do* is a matter of national security. I'm more important to the government than the President himself, you know. I really am."

The guy was bonkers, and not just temporarily. But I wasn't about to tell *him* that. "Why are you so important?" I said. "Because of your defense contracts?"

"Not just defense contracts. Espionage tools, advanced robotics, superconductors, holographic imaging, you name it."

"How about if you name it?"

He laughed but shook his head no—he wasn't going to tell me his industrial secrets. "Here's what I'm thinking," he said, "I could use some guard dogs for the property. I don't like dogs, personally. In fact, I despise the barking little parasites. But I could put you and your staff at the kennel on permanent retainer. I might even throw in that Cezanne you like so much, as an added incentive."

"You mean a bribe," I suggested.

He puffed his pipe. "Call it a perk."

I got up and went over to the painting. "Is this a genuine Cezanne?" I turned to look at Maxwell. "Because I wouldn't care to own a forged copy."

"I doubt if you'd be able to tell the difference."

"Sherry was that good, huh?" I finished my scotch.

He shrugged. "If I knew what you were talking about, I might be able to respond to that." He puffed his pipe.

"I was just wondering: Why live on an island?" I put down my empty glass. "It seems awfully inconvenient."

"Not at all. I have a full staff. I have my choice of different modes of transportation. And I have my privacy. Besides, the

sea holds many mysteries. You know, the secrets of the deep."
He waggled his eyebrows like Captain Nemo.

"Un-huh. And does Señor Ortiz know you sold him a bunch of forged paintings? How's that for a mystery?"

His face darkened. He shot a look at Kemp. "You had to miss him, didn't you? You're supposed to be a crack shot."

"Sorry, sir. But I was sandbagged by that lush friend of his, that Lou Kelso fellow."

"Like that's an excuse?"

"Boys, boys," I calmed them. "What's done is done."

Maxwell put his pipe down next to an ashtray, turned to me and tried to smile. "I must admit, you've done some excellent detective work, Jack. May I still call you Jack?"

"Sure? May I call *you* Your Evil Highness?"

He nearly doubled over with laughter.

"You *are* evil, Ian," Jamie said. "Don't you *know* that?"

"Am I?" He sighed and stood up. "Paul, would you escort these two to the helipad? I'm afraid I've given them just about all the time I can afford right now." He turned to Jamie. "I hope you don't mind, Jamie. I had your father's runabout refueled, then asked one of my people to take it back to his place in Christmas Cove for you. I've also arranged to have you and your fiancé flown back to the mainland."

"I *do* mind," she said, looking down at his pipe.

I said, "So do I. I'm not comfortable with the idea of having the Coast Guard find our bloated bodies bobbing in the waters of Muscongus Bay two weeks from now."

"Oh, *please*. You said it yourself: 'What's done is done.' Yes, Paul may have tried to *kill* you. But that's all over with—more's the pity." He went to the door, which was immediately opened from the outside by Charles. "We've made arrangements with the government to be done with this whole mess. Part of the agreement was that there be no more dead bodies, especially *yours*. Isn't that right, Paul?"

"Yes, sir."

I said, "And in return, you won't be prosecuted for murder."

Maxwell smiled. "Something like that."

To the butler, I said, "Did you hear all that, Charles?"

"I'm sorry, sir. My hearing isn't what it used to be."

"I doubt that, Charles. I doubt that very much."

"Awfully kind of you to say so, sir."

I looked at Kemp. "So, what was that after-shave you were wearig the other night? When you planted the transponder under my car. Some kind of moose-musk?"

He shook his head. "Cougar urine."

"Lovely," I said.

Maxwell interrupted our repartee. "I believe you may have a chance to meet the *real* Agent Kondolean tonight, Jack, and he'll explain to you the details of our arrangement."

"Is that right? I'd still feel more comfortable going home the way we came. Wouldn't you?" I said to Jamie.

She agreed, so as we walked through the spacious dining room, Maxwell and Kemp got on the two-way with someone named Brian, who was apparently piloting the runabout for us, and asked him to turn around and come back.

At this point we were nearly at the kitchen door, but Charles had somehow gotten there ahead of us and insinuated himself into a position to open it. Jamie said, "You know what I just realized? I left my handbag in the study."

"Allow me, ma'am," Charles said as if to go.

She said, "That's all right. *I* can get it."

"Yes, ma'am, but if you'll just allow me—"

"Hey, Charles." I stopped him, though his eyes followed Jamie. "I think I'd like to have another taste of that good scotch before I go. Would you mind?"

"Not at all, sir. A small glass, neat. Is that right?"

"You know it is, old chap."

"Very good, sir." He smiled, bowed slightly, and went to the bar.

Maxwell finished his radio call and said, "The runabout should be back at the dock by the time you get there. And one other thing, I would advise against talking to Señor Ortiz."

"I hadn't considered it, actually," I lied.

"That's good. The deal I have with certain parties in our government is that you and Jamie are not to be touched. But there was no mention made of what might happen to your father at his little security post at the Coronado Cays."

I stared at him. His smile was full of malevolence.

"At his age?" he leered. "A sudden heart attack? A stroke? These things are hard to predict, yet easily arranged. Just a drop or two of some tasteless, odorless poison, dropped surreptitiously in his coffee when he's not looking, and he's off to his final reward with no one the wiser, except the grieving son."

I shook my head. "You'd have to use something that metabolizes quickly so it can't be traced. Otherwise—"

"Don't worry, I know of several such substances. So, be a good son, Jack, and don't cause trouble for dear old Dad."

"As you wish, Your Evil Highness."

Charles arrived with my scotch. "Your drink, sir."

"Never mind, Charles. Drink it yourself, if you like."

"Very good, sir." He receded to the bar and placed my unimbibed refreshment on top of the polished oak.

Jamie came back with her purse. "Got it," she said, smiling and patting the handbag, which, if I knew anything about my sweetie, now held not only her keys, her checkbook, and her credit cards, but an evidence bag, containing a formerly sterile cotton swab—presently smeared with some of Maxwell's saliva, along with epithelial cells from his chapped lips that she'd just swabbed off the mouthpiece of his pipe.

Good girl.

34

We held off talking until we were well out on the open water, then Jamie shouted, "What are we going to do, Jack?"

I put my finger to my lips and motioned for her to give me her purse. She did. I took out her checkbook and pen and wrote on the back of the checkbook, "The boat is probably bugged. Did you get his DNA?"

She read the note and nodded.

I shouted, "It looks like there's nothing we *can* do. He's really got us over a barrel, this Maxwell."

"I guess you're right," she shouted. "Besides, if the government is involved, it's hopeless."

"At least Kemp is going to jail and not me."

"But Jack! He's getting away with murder!"

I put a finger to my lips and said, "I know, honey. Let's just be thankful we're still alive! And there's my dad to think of."

"You're right. There's nothing we can do." She yawned.

"You look tired," I said. "Did you get any sleep last night?"

"Not much, I'm afraid."

"You want me to take over the wheel?"

"I would, honey, but remember last time?"

She was referring to an incident where she and I went to Monhegan Island to track down a fugitive waiter. Some things happened. I took the runabout without her, almost got lost at sea, and nearly died of hypothermia.

"It's only two o'clock," I shouted. "Just point me in the right direction. You can take a nap."

"Okay."

We switched places. She pointed me to a landmark on the horizon, then to a compass to the right of the wheel. "Just keep this little dealie here pointed west. And keep the nose of the boat pointed toward that lighthouse. Can you see it?"

It was a tiny speck on the horizon, but I could see it.

"Good." She climbed into one of the back seats (there are three), bunched up a blanket for a pillow, got her long chestnut hair out of the way, made herself comfy and cozy, closed her eyes, and in no time she was fast asleep.

Out on the open water, my hands on the wheel, I thought about Ian Maxwell and his strengths and weaknesses.

His strengths were obvious. He had all the money in the world, or so it seemed. He also had friends in high places, willing to keep him out of jail. I was certain that his government allies were looking out for him. I was also certain that Paul Kemp was willing to go to jail in his place, though I doubted that he would ever do any serious time, and would probably find a fat bonus check—with half a dozen zeroes tacked on—when he got out of prison (or the nuthouse, whichever way it went). Maxwell was also highly intelligent and crafty. And, for the most part, he seemed capable of keeping a cool head when things got iffy.

But what were his weaknesses? If I could find them and exploit them, I could him bring him down.

For one thing, he had a huge ego. He didn't think he'd ever be caught doing anything illegal. That could be a wild card in the deck. For another, he really lost his cool when I mentioned Señor Ortiz. He'd even warned me not to talk to him. That might be his biggest Achilles' heel. Now the question was, what did I have to offer Ortiz in exchange for his help in bringing Maxwell down? And how could I get his attention? I'd have to ponder that for a while.

I let my mind go blank, sang a little Bing Crosby softly to myself, as a kind of Zen meditation, and piloted the boat.

The lighthouse got closer and closer, but was still quite a

ways off. After a bit I thought I saw what looked like a lobster boat, off to the right, or the starboard side. As I drew nearer I saw several large objects floating beside it. I remembered Flynn's description of how drugs are smuggled along the Maine coast, and realized that the objects were probably bales of marijuana. As I got closer I recognized a figure on the boat. He was tall and thin and was using a longshoreman's hook to pull one of the bales toward him.

It was Farrell Woods.

I brought the runabout up close and Woods saw me. Jamie was so tired she was still fast asleep.

"So, Farrell," I shouted, "up to your old tricks, huh? And *I* thought you were too sick to get out of bed today."

He didn't seem the least bit embarrassed. He just shrugged and shouted, "Things aren't always what they seem, Jackie boy. Permission to come aboard?"

I pulled the runabout next to the hull. He jumped onto the prow then clambered in next to me. There was a woman on board. I recognized her. It was Cindy Brimhall, the tie-dye lady. She scowled at me.

"Farrell," she shouted, "we don't have *time* for this."

"Just a sec," he told her. Then he explained that he was working with an underground group, buying and supplying marijuana to cancer patients along the coast, at cost. Yes, it was illegal, he said. And yes, he'd lied about being sick. But he never knows until the morning of a drop when he's got to go out and harvest the stuff. And it has to be picked up quickly before the Coast Guard catches on.

"I guess I'm fired, huh?"

I thought it over. "On any other day but today, yeah. I'd fire you in a New York minute."

He smiled. "I thought you never used that expression."

"I'm not proud of using it now, but it seemed the best way, given our history, to get my point across."

"I gotcha."

"No, you don't got me. Jill Krempetz died last night."

He took this in and his eyes welled up with tears. "Ah, man," he said, "I really thought she was gonna make it."

"Me too." I collected myself and said, "So, given that this stuff, illegal as it is, can ease the suffering of people like Jill, I'm going to have to think about whether I should fire your ass or just pretend I never saw you."

Then I told him about her ashes, and how her family was going to fly them back to Michigan for the funeral.

"That ain't right, man. She hated Michigan, and she loved the coast of Maine. We gotta do somethin'."

I told him about an idea I had in mind, not about Jill's ashes, but one that would put a couple of Samoans to sleep for a while. I asked if he could get me the necessary substance.

He said he thought he could, which I thanked him for. I was also thankful that he didn't ask me any questions.

"You're rehired," I said. "Just don't lie to me again."

He promised not to.

"Oh . . ." I told him about the cookout on Friday. "Do you think you could get those friends of yours—you know that little swing band—what are they called?"

"The Blue D'Arts?"

"That's the guys. If they're available, do you think they'll come play for us on Friday?"

He shrugged. "They're kinda pissed off at me since I stopped dealing grass, but I'll have 'em call you."

"Great, thanks. And maybe Tulips could come and sing backup or something."

He smiled. "She'd like that."

"Farrell!" shouted the tie-dye lady, "get your ass back in this boat! Now!"

Jamie woke up. "Jack? Where are we? What's going on?"

"Tell you in a minute." To Woods, I said, "And if you come up with any ideas about how to deal with Jill's ashes, count me in."

Jamie sat up and rubbed her eyes. Woods nodded and shook my hand, then crawled over the windshield onto the prow and got back on board the lobster boat. I gunned the engine and swerved out to the open water.

Jamie said, "Jack? What was that all about?"

"Sorry, sweetheart. I was just getting directions from some drug smugglers, but it's not what you think."

She looked over her shoulder. "Is that Farrell Woods?"

"No," I said, sniffling a little, thinking about Jill again. "A lot of people make that mistake. That was actually Florence Nightingale. Or somebody like her."

35

It was almost dark by the time we got back to the kennel. There were two cars in the parking area—a Lincoln Town Car and a gray Ford sedan. The Feebs and marshals had come to call.

We went inside and Jamie headed straight for the bathroom. I headed straight for the liquor cabinet. Frankie followed me, wagging his tail and showing me a chew toy he'd found near his bed. Good boy!

Kelso was on the sofa, drinking some of my scotch—the Glenmorangie, no doubt—and had apparently been entertaining the feds—Baker and Kuwahara and a tall black man I'd never met.

They stood up. The tall one said, "Mr. Field, can we have a word with you?"

I ignored them, poured myself a little Dewar's, went to the kitchen and checked in with Leon on the intercom. The dogs had all been fed and put to bed, he said, and I owed him such-and-such amount for working overtime. And by the way, he went on, you promised to make chicken tonight and all I had was a bologna sandwich and some jalapeño potato chips.

"Don't worry," I said. "We'll have a big cookout on Friday. I'll make steak and hamburgers and chicken and hot dogs, and potato salad and maybe some grilled oysters. How's that sound?"

"Okay, except the oysters. What about my overtime?"

"You'll get your overtime. How's Magee doing?"

He told me he'd borrowed my copy of *Natural Dog Training* and had started some of the exercises, even though, as near as he could tell, they didn't make any sense.

"Don't worry. They'll make sense to Magee."

I remembered some clients of mine, back when I still lived in New York, who'd found a stray dog in Prospect Park in Brooklyn. They named her Penelope, and I'd given them some of the same exercises that Leon was now using on Magee.

Meanwhile, all the other dog owners in Prospect Park thought they were crazy to be running around, getting Penelope to chase them, to jump up on them, to dance with them, to play tug-of-war, and all the rest of it. "We took Chelsea (or Lucy, or Cody) to a trainer," they would say, "and he never had us do any of the crazy stuff you guys are doing."

A few weeks passed and this couple noticed that whenever these other dog owners called their dogs, nothing happened. But whenever they called Penelope, she would stop whatever she was doing and run like a bullet, as fast as she could, back to them. And she hadn't been like that at all in the beginning—in fact, just the opposite.

Meanwhile the other owners would give the command over and over, like so, "Chelsea, come! Chelsea, come! Chelsea, come! Chelsea, come!" which turned to pleading, "Chelsea, please come, honey? Please? Come to Mommy," which turned to red-faced screaming, "Chelsea, come here, this instant! Goddamnit, Chelsea, I mean it! Come here *now!*" soon followed by, "I have cookies! Who wants a cookie?" and eventually ended with a shrugged explanation, "She thinks she's alpha. What can you do? You guys got lucky with Penelope."

"No, we didn't," they tried to explain. "It's all those ridiculous exercises Jack had us do."

But the other dog owners never did get it.

I got off the phone with Leon, put an ice cube in my scotch, and Kelso yelled—from the living room, "You know, you've got visitors, Jack."

"I noticed," I said loudly, so he could hear me. "I had a few things to take care of first."

Jamie came out of the bathroom, came into the kitchen and said, "I need to go upstairs and call my dad."

"Good luck," I said as she left. Then I poked my head into the living room and said to Kelso, "Where's Jack, Sr.?"

He told me my father was already fast asleep in the guest bedroom, with Hooch at his side. They'd had a hard day— Kelso and my dad—canvassing the marinas, all with no luck.

"Why were you canvassing the marinas?" one of the Feebs asked Kelso. "And why no luck?"

"My dad wants to buy a boat but he has high standards," I said, coming into the living room where the feds all sat in relative discomfort; the air conditioner wasn't running.

Frankie took his toy to his bed and started chewing.

The feds stood up and I came over and we shook hands as if we were great pals and really liked each other a lot and there were no hard feelings between us, even though there were. Baker introduced me to the real Marshal Rondo Kondolean, and I shook his fat, sweaty hand.

I started to sit down but Kuwahara said, "Hang on a second, Field. Do you mind if we check you for a wire?"

Kondolean said, "We've got some sensitive type things need bringing up. We're just being careful."

"Fine." I put my arms in the air and they frisked me. When they were satisfied, I sat next to Kelso and wondered to myself why the air conditioner wasn't turned on. Then I stretched my legs and said, "So. To what do I owe this so-called pleasure?"

"We're, uh, making an announcement on the noon news," said Kondolean, whose face seemed soft and pliable. "The grand jury has reached a decision not to indict you for Gordon Beeson's murder."

"That's good to hear."

"So, we're going to arrest Paul Kemp instead. He's Ian Maxwell's—"

"Yeah, I know who he is. I had a little chat with Maxwell earlier today, so I'm up on the little fantasy you've all cooked up to circumvent the law and let a killer go free. A psychopathic killer, I might add."

Kondolean wiped his brow and looked at Kelso. "I thought you said he would be willing to play ball with us."

"I'm sorry," Kelso said. "I'm a little drunk. I thought you were referring to something else. You see, we're having a soft-ball game on Saturday. So, if any of you guys want to come play ball with *us*—"

I laughed. "Yeah, we still need a shortstop and a third baseman, so if anyone here can handle those positions . . ."

"I'll play," said Baker.

Kuwahara glared at him.

"Shut up," said Kondolean, wiping his brow again. "Hey, Field, don't you believe in air-conditioning?"

I started to get up but Kelso said, "It isn't working."

I looked at him and saw something in his eyes that told me to play along. "Yeah, I've been having trouble with it."

"You ought to get it fixed," said Kuwahara.

"I don't recall inviting you over," I said to him, then looked at Kelso. "Did *you* invite them over?"

"No," he said innocently, "*I* didn't invite them over."

I looked back at the feds. "So, who invited you over?"

Kuwahara said, "That was very clever, by the way. How you got that tape of your conversation with that dead painter intro-duced as evidence before the grand jury."

"Did *I* do that? If so, it *was* clever, wasn't it?"

"Don't act cute. We know you had Sinclair do it for you. We've been keeping tabs on you and your cronies."

"Cronies?" Kelso said. "Jack has no cronies. Other than yours truly Jack is a peculiarly croniless individual."

Kondolean shook his head. "Look, we just want your word that you'll drop this case and let us do our jobs."

"My word? Why would my word mean anything to *you*?"

"I don't follow."

"You took an oath when you joined the marshals, yes?"

"Yeah, so?"

"It was a solemn oath to uphold the law and defend the con-stitution of the United States, am I wrong? So why the hell would someone who betrays his oath on a daily basis put any faith in the word of a dog trainer and ex-cop, whose only purpose is one that you wouldn't even remotely understand?"

"Oh, I wouldn't? Try me."

"Upholding the law and bringing a killer to justice. That's my agenda. What's yours?"

Some hot looks were passed between Kondolean and the Feebs. Jamie came downstairs and sat between me and Kelso.

"What'd I miss?" she said, holding my hand.

Kondolean said, "There's a greater good here."

"A greater good? That's a laugh."

"Jack, what'd I miss?"

"They're telling us to back off so Maxwell can get away with murder." I looked at Kondolean. "That's a greater good? Now you're sounding like the Nazis, like Hermann Goering."

"Now, wait a minute—"

"No, tell me, is there *really* a greater good, or is that just something you tell yourself to salve your conscience? Oh, wait a minute, I'm sorry. You probably don't *have* a conscience, do you?"

Jamie said, "Don't mind him. He's had a long day. Isn't it kind of hot in here?"

"So have we," said Kondolean. "And yes, it is. Apparently your fiancé's A.C. is on the fritz."

"And did you know that Hermann Goering, your favorite Nazi, was also at one time the head of the German Humane Society? It just goes to show that you can't always—"

Jamie interrupted my rant. "Would anyone like a little something to eat? A cold beverage?"

"I pay my taxes," I said. "Let these assholes buy their own food and liquor."

Kondolean sighed. "The thing is, if you don't play along with us, there are a lot of agencies under the federal umbrella—including the IRS—that can make your life miserable."

"Now they're threatening me," I said to Jamie.

"Well, Jack," she said, looking at the air conditioner. "There's your *problem*. It isn't plugged in." She got up and went over to plug it back in.

Kelso stopped her. "Don't do that."

She turned, puzzled. "Why?"

Kelso couldn't think of anything to cover with, so I jumped in: "You'll blow the fuse again. I need to have an electrician come take a look at it."

Still baffled, she came and sat back down. "Well, anyway, Jack," she patted my thigh, "sometimes you just have to take a philosophical attitude about these things."

"I don't think that's the case here, honey."

Kondolean said, "You have a foster son, don't you?"

I could feel my face turning red.

"Jack, darling, just let it go this time."

I said, "Look out for number one, right?"

"Right. Think of Leon." She gave my hand a hidden squeeze to show that she was only trying to get rid of them.

Kelso said, "Let me just get one thing straight here, though, Marshal Kondolean—and this is for you guys too, Agent Kuwahara, Agent Baker: you're saying that the FBI and the U.S. Marshal's Office want us to back off catching the real killer, who is actually this Ian Maxwell character, and let you arrest and prosecute Paul Kemp, who's actually innocent?"

"That's correct. Maxwell is off limits."

"And if Jack doesn't go along with the Bureau and the marshals, he'll be harassed by other government agencies?"

"We'll do everything in our power to make sure that happens, yes. Oh, we'll *deny* it, of course, but—"

"Good. I'm a little drunk right now, and like I said, I just wanted to get it straight in my mind."

Kuwahara and Baker conferred for a moment, then Kuwahara said, "Are you asking this as Field's attorney? Because—"

Kelso waved his glass of Glenmorangie. "No, no, I'm jis axsking as a drunk crony of his. His one and only crony, by the way, or did I already mention that? I forgot." He took a sip of scotch. (Personally, I thought he overplayed it a little, but it seemed to mollify our unwelcome guests.)

To placate them further, I sighed and said, "Okay, fine. I'll back off. I guess I've got no choice. You satisfied now?"

"Yep. That's all we wanted to hear."

"Good. I got some things off my chest." They got up, as did Jamie and I. "You know," I said as we walked them to the door, "I spent a little time in Quantico and I have a lot of respect for the Bureau. But in this case—well, let's just leave it at that."

"One and only crony," mused Kelso, who still sat, drinking. "I should write that one down." Frankie looked up at him and wagged his tail.

We got to the door and Kondolean said, "I guess I can understand your position. I just hope you understand ours."

"Sure I do, sure I do." I walked them out to the porch.

They walked down the steps toward their cars, and I said, "Oh, just one other thing." They turned to look at me, their keys in their hands. I made a Nazi salute. "Sieg heil!"

Jamie started to hit me, but just laughed instead.

36

We went back inside. I went for the liquor cabinet; Jamie went for the fridge. Frankie followed her. (Dogs love it when you open the fridge.)

Kelso went to turn the air conditioner back on.

A strange-looking man, mid-fifties, with black hair, pasty skin, and black/silver eyes came out of the laundry room behind the kitchen. Jamie screamed and dropped a milk carton on the floor. Frankie started barking.

"I'm sorry," shouted Kelso over the barking. "I should have warned you about my friend, Carl. He also goes by the name Dr. Lunch."

"Dr. Lunch?" I said. "Oh, yeah. You told me about him. Frankie, quiet. He's an electronics genius. Frankie, shush."

Frankie stopped barking.

Jamie caught her breath and said, "You scared the life out of me."

"Sorry," said Lunch, blinking.

The A.C was now blasting away. Jamie looked at Kelso. "I thought it wasn't working. And I thought you were drunk."

He shrugged an apology. "I was playacting a little."

She shook her head. "Let me clean this up." She grabbed some paper towels and began sopping up the spilled milk. "Frankie, don't drink that!"

"It's okay," I said. "Let him help clean it up for you."

To Dr. Lunch, Kelso said, "Did you get it?"

"I got it all right." I saw now that Lunch held a tape recorder and a small parabolic microphone. He rewound the tape, stopped it, then played it back. We heard the following:

Kelso's voice: "Let me just get one thing straight here, though, Marshal Kondolean—and this is for you guys too, Agent Kuwahara, Agent Baker: you're saying that the FBI and the U.S. Marshal's Office want us to back off catching the real killer, who is actually this Ian Maxwell character, and let you arrest and prosecute Paul Kemp, who's actually innocent?"

Kondolean's voice: "That's correct. Maxwell's off limits."

Kelso's voice: "And if Jack doesn't go along with the Bureau and the marshals, he'll be harassed by other government agencies?"

Kondolean's voice: "We'll do everything in our power to make sure that happens, yes. Oh, we'll *deny* it, of course, but—"

Kelso's voice: "Good. I'm a little drunk right now, and like I said, I just wanted to get it straight in my mind."

Lunch switched off the machine. Kelso looked at me. "What do you think, Jack? A sound byte for tomorrow's news?"

"Maybe." I sipped my scotch. "It might be too soon for us to show our hand, but it'll make good collateral."

Frankie went back to lie down on his bed by the hearth.

Jamie finished cleaning up and came over to shake hands with Dr. Lunch. "I'm Jamie," she said.

"Nice to meet you," said Lunch. "Sorry I startled you."

She smiled. "That's all right." She looked at me and Kelso. "I guess that's why you boys were playing a little game with the A.C."

Kelso said, "We wanted a clean tape, with no background noise. Plus, the heat made them a little sluggish, mentally."

I waved my scotch at Lunch. "Would you like a drink?"

"No." He made a face. "I don't drink."

"He's a health nut," said Kelso.

Lunch shrugged and said, "I found these on your phones." He dug in his pocket and pulled out several electronic bugs. "They've also got cars watching for when you leave. One's at Perseverance, the other's in Hope." He dug in his other pocket. "Oh, and I found this on your woody." It was a transponder—a twin of the one Kelso found under the Suburban.

"Thanks," I said, taking it and the bugs from him.

"Nice car, by the way. Did you fix it up yourself?"

"No," I said, "I bought it restored like that. And as for the tails, we can always take the dirt road to Payson's Corner, and then drive down Wiley Creek Road to 105."

"I was, um, I was just going to suggest that. In fact, that's how *I'll* be leaving."

"Funny, I didn't see your car out front."

"No, you wouldn't have." He smiled. He turned to Kelso. "I have to go now. I have a class in the morning."

Kelso explained. "He's a high school chemistry teacher in Connecticut, when he's not helping me bug and debug things and hack into files at the Defense Department and such."

Lunch said good-bye, handed Kelso the tape machine and the parabolic mic, and left via the kitchen door.

We just kind of stood there, then I finally said, "Well, let's stock up on snacks and things. We've still got a long night ahead of us. How did your father take the news about Maxwell, by the way?"

"Not very well, I'm afraid." She sighed. "As you can imagine, it came as quite a shock."

"I'm sorry. Did Sinclair call?" I asked Kelso.

"Yeah, he said he arrested the Samoans like you asked."

"Why do you keep calling them Samoans?" Jamie wondered.

"It's just a joke. Plus it's easier to say than Maoris."

Kelso said, "They're in Flynn's jail in Rockland."

"It's not funny, though. Jokes are supposed to be—"

"To me and *Kelso* it is. Right?" I said to Kelso.

"Well, it's not *funny* exactly. It's just kind of *fun*. And it's not a joke. It's more like a riff."

Jamie said, "What's a riff?"

He shrugged. "I don't know, it's kind of a guy thing. You riff on a certain word or phrase until you get tired of it. Like 'jejune upstarts.'"

To Jamie, I said, "Speaking of jokes, you want to hear my new ones?"

"What? You have some new lightbulb jokes?"

I said I did.

Kelso went back to the liquor cabinet.

"Just let me make a sandwich while you tell them to me."

"Fine." I took a sip of scotch. "How many Jack Russell terriers does it take to screw in a lightbulb?"

"How many?" she said, going to the fridge.

"Just me! I can do it! I *know* I can do it. Just one more jump and I'll get up there! Really, just one more *jump*!"

"That's pretty good," she said, getting out the bread and swiss and sliced turkey and mayonnaise and mustard. "Next."

"How many Labrador retrievers does it take to screw in a lightbulb?"

"How many?"

"Did you say ball? Ball? What ball? Where's the ball?"

She laughed. "Next." She took her food to the counter to get a knife, but opened the wrong drawer and found Leon's firecrackers. "Jack, what are these doing here?"

"Leon bought them at school, then decided he'd better hand them over to me. The silverware is in the next drawer over. How many border collies does it take to—"

"How many?" She put the firecrackers back, found a butter knife, and began making her sandwich.

"Just one, but listen, why stop at one lightbulb? I can change every bulb in the house if you want. Come to think of it, I could also rewire the place while I'm at it. In fact, I could rewire every house on the block. Please, can I do it? Please? And when I'm done I could regrout the bathroom tile, shingle the roof, and build a deck in the backyard. How about a swimming pool? A swing set? Anything else you need?"

She laughed. "These just go on and on, don't they?" She finished making her sandwich and got some orange juice from the fridge (in lieu of the spilled milk).

"They're funny to some people."

"Dog lovers, no doubt."

"Yep. Hey, what did you do with those bolt cutters, by the way? The ones we used to break into the salvage yard?"

"The night we found Hooch?" She bit into her sandwich.

"Yep."

"They're in your tool closet in the back of the kennel. Why? Are we planning to ruin somebody else's fence tonight?"

"We sure are."

"Oh, good. That'll be fun."

Jamie ate her sandwich and drank her juice. Kelso came back, holding a fresh glass of my scotch. I gave him his instructions: (1) find out if Kondolean and the Feebs had a valid warrant for the wiretaps on my phones; (2) book the three of us—Kelso, Jamie, and me—on a flight to San Diego in the afternoon; (3) keep the Samoans in jail, but book them on the next flight (after ours) out West; (4) rent a stretch limo and a realistic-looking ambulance from a movie auto-supply company, along with a couple of ambulance attendants from Central Casting; and (5) do a background check on Miguel Ortiz and the layout of his hacienda.

"Aren't you going to write any of this down?" I said.

"I'll remember it. At least until I sober up."

I laughed a sour laugh. "Which could be a while, huh?"

Jamie finished her sandwich and said, "So, tell me what we're doing tonight, exactly."

"We're breaking into the carnival to find a painting."

"You know, I just remembered, I actually left the whole bag in the closet, with everything in it except the Polaroid. We should be fully equipped for another adventure."

"Am I coming?" Kelso asked.

"No, you're too drunk," I said.

"I'm not *that* drunk. I *was* faking it, you know."

"Yeah, but you're drunk enough. Which reminds me, how are you planning to get back to the motel? You can't drive."

"I guess I'll just crash on your couch, if that's okay."

I told him it was, and he stumbled off to the living room. Frankie trotted behind him.

Jamie made a tsking sound, and I said, "Yeah, I know," meaning, Yeah, he's a hopeless drunk. What can I do?

She shook her head and said, "No, *you*, you idiot. I'm upset with *you*." Her phone rang. She looked at the caller ID, opened it and said, "Hi, Mom. Can you hang on a sec?"

"Me?" I said.

"Yes, *you*, Jack. You need to go talk to him." She was very clear. "Just look at your dog! *He* knows Kelso needs comforting even if you *don't*. Now, go in there and talk to him, without being clever and sarcastic and judgmen—"

I huffed. "I don't have time for that."

"Jack, just do it. Okay? He's your friend and he needs you." I just stood there. "Go!" she said.

I put my arms in the air. "Okay."

I went into the living room. Kelso was drinking some more of my scotch and petting Frankie. I poured a splash or two for myself, sat down across from him, and, while Jamie spoke to Laura, we had a conversation about his drinking problem and about Tracy—the girl from his past—and why he felt responsible for her death. I won't go into the details—they're his own personal business—but I finally got a better glimpse into the reasons for his dark, Kelsonian sadness. And we agreed to talk about it some more, once the case cleared.

I came back to the kitchen, where Jamie was now off the phone with Laura. I said, "Okay. We had a talk. It was good. And we agreed to talk about it more, later, too."

"Good." She kissed me and used her thumbs to wipe away the tracks of my tears. "Now, was that so hard?"

"Kind of, a little," I said, still sniffling a bit. "I mean, we're a couple of guys, you *know*? Oh, before I forget—do you have a sexy getup, kind of slutty but upscale?"

"No." She shook her head and gave me a look. "Why?"

"Because when we get to San Diego you'll be impersonating a call girl for our two Samoans. Hey, how many bulldogs does it take to screw in a lightbulb?"

"You've *got* to be kidding me."

"Is that in reference to your impersonating a call girl? Because, oddly enough, that's exactly what the bulldog says."

37

It was a warm, moonless night. I drove the Suburban with the lights off, past a sign that said, CARNIVAL CLOSED FOR REPAIRS, then turned left into the empty parking lot next to Cap'n Salty's Seafood Shack.

Jamie and I got out and went around back, where I grabbed the black nylon bag she'd packed for our previous break-in. I threw it over my left shoulder and we half walked, half ran (crouched over like they do in the movies) until we got to the chain-link fence at the south end of the carnival grounds just behind the lobster pounds. Our point of entry was at roughly the same location where Paul Kemp, the supposed maverick Navy SEAL, had left the grounds after he'd tried to kill me and Sherry Maughn. It was the perfect spot—close to both Artists' Alley *and* our getaway car.

We crouched down next to the fence. I unzipped the bag to get out the bolt cutters. It was full of stuff.

"Wow," I said. "You weren't kidding. Everything's here. The flashlights, the bolt cutters, the wire cutters, the PowerBars, the Gatorade, extra batteries—look! even your tampons."

She hit me.

I said, "Hey, you never know. They might come in handy." I stashed the two flashlights and the extra batteries in my safari vest, then handed her the bolt cutters. "Now, the trick, like I told you last time, is to use your back and leg muscles, not your wrists and elbows."

She handed them back.

I said, "I thought you wanted to learn how to do this."

She shook her head. "It's not my area."

I chuckled. "But, honey, last time you said—"

"I know. So I changed my mind. According to you my area is being a slutty call girl for a couple of Samoans."

"That's just pretend, for tomorrow night. Tonight, you're going to be James Bond, like you've always wanted."

"Well," she took the bolt cutters back, "all right. How do you do it, again?" I coached her, and with a little effort she cut open one of the links in the fence. "Hey! I did it!"

"Yes, you did!"

She smiled and held the bolt cutters out to me. "Okay, now you do the rest."

"Un-uh." I stepped away, my hands in the air.

"Jack! Come on!"

"No. Stop being such a *girl* and do it!"

She huffed. "In case you hadn't noticed, I *am* a—"

"I *had* noticed. And you're *not* a girl. You're a beautiful, exquisite, and extremely powerful woman."

She smiled. "Thanks, but that's not the point."

"What *is* the point?"

"The point is you can do this a lot *better* than I can. And you're just patronizing me by—"

"No, I'm not. And what happens next time if I have a broken arm or a sprained wrist? Huh?"

"Jack, I thought there wasn't going to *be* a next time. I thought this was supposed to be your final case."

"Yeah," I scoffed, "that's what we said the last time, remember? And the time before *that*."

She laughed. "I know, but still—"

"And what happens if I'm taken captive by the bad guys and you have to break into their hidden lair and rescue me?"

"Easy," she laughed then smirked, "I'll put on my hottest hoochie-mama outfit and just 'sex' my way in."

"Fine," I laughed. "But look, we don't have all night to argue about this. Are you going to do it or not?"

"Yeah," she griped, "I'll do it."

She got down to work and in fairly short order had about four feet worth of chain-link severed—enough to crawl through— then she put the bolt cutters back in the bag. I zipped it up, pushed it through the slit, and was about to go through myself when, still on her knees, she stopped me.

"What is it?" I said.

She hugged me as hard as she could in that position, then kissed me just as hard. "Thanks, honey," she said, her eyes glistening.

"You're welcome." I brushed her hair out of her face and kissed her some more.

She said, "I love you."

"And I adore you, brown eyes. Now, let's go."

I squirmed through the slit in the fence, held it open for Jamie, and then we scuttled our way to the back of Artists' Alley. We took a position there for a moment to check for any security guards who might be roaming the grounds.

"They probably have a set schedule," I said. "You know, take a stroll around every couple of hours or so. The rest of the time they'll be back at the security trailer watching Conan O'Brien."

"Who's Conan O'Brien?" (Jamie goes to bed early.)

"Anyway, *your* job, once we get to Sherry's booth, is to keep an eye out and warn me if anybody's coming."

"And what will *you* be doing?"

"Taking down the center pole in her booth, and hopefully finding a forged painting rolled up inside."

"Oh! Very clever, Jack."

"I hope so."

We didn't see any flashlight beams sweeping the grounds, so we scuttled across the alley to Sherry's booth, which was wrapped in yellow tape marked POLICE BARRIER—DO NOT CROSS. We were fearless though; we crossed it anyway and went inside.

We cast our beams carefully around the booth. I showed Jamie how to do it, by placing your fingers over the lens, letting the bare minimum amount of light through to see by. This created strange shadows on the canvas walls of the tent. Everything was still inside the booth, except the cashbox.

"Okay." I switched off and pocketed my flash. "I'm going to lift up the pole so you can take a look inside."

"I hope the whole place doesn't cave in."

"It won't."

"Are you sure?"

"No. But even if it does, it's just made of canvas."

"Explain that to the security guards when they come by and see us flailing around inside a flattened tent."

"Don't worry. This'll only take a second."

I pulled the pole out of the dirt then maneuvered the bottom end toward the back of the booth, at about a thirty degree angle. The ceiling sagged but, luckily, didn't cave in.

"Okay," I told Jamie. "Shine your flashlight inside. See if you can find a rolled-up canvas."

She came around, got down on her side, on one hip, and did as I asked, but couldn't see anything.

"Nope. There's nothing here, Jack."

"Are you positive?" I couldn't believe it. I was sure the missing painting had to have been stashed inside the wide center pole in Sherry's booth. "Here," I said, "come hold this up a minute and let me take a look."

"Jack, what's the point?" she said, still shining her beam inside. "There's nothing in here. I'm *telling* you."

"Just let me check for myself."

"Okay." She got up and dusted herself off. "But we're just wasting time. It's got to be hidden somewhere else."

She held the pole up while I shone my flashlight inside. I looked and said, "You're right. There's nothing here but a little dust and some stale New England climate."

Jamie cracked up. "That's as bad as your Quincy line. How long did it take you to come up with *that* one?"

"Sorry," I said, getting up and taking the weight of the pole and the canvas from her. "I stole it from Kelso. That's how he describes the filing cabinets in his office; only he says 'New York climate.' It sounds better when he says it."

"It would have to."

We got the pole back in place and I was about to start searching the booth when we heard the crackle of a walkie-talkie coming from not far away.

We clicked our flashlights off, hunkered down, and listened. Jamie clutched my arm.

"Base, this is Kendrick. We may have some activity at the crime scene. Come back?"

"Kendrick, this is Base. What crime scene? Come back?"

"The murdered painter's booth, Base. I thought I heard some voices and saw a flash beam. Come back?"

"All right. Wait there until—what the shit?"

We heard what sounded like automatic weapons fire. Jamie dug her fingers deeper into my arm.

"Ow!" I whispered.

She eased up. "Sorry, honey," she whispered back.

"Kendrick," crackled the walkie-talkie. "We've got a situation at the front gate. Come back now. Over."

"I'm on my way. Over."

We heard footsteps running away.

"Okay," I told Jamie, "we don't have much time. The sound of gunfire is probably just a diversion, provided by Kelso and my dad using Leon's firecrackers."

"What? But, how do you—"

"Kelso said something earlier about tailing us out here. Plus, I saw his car behind us. And since he's too drunk to maneuver, I'm guessing he woke up my dad and had *him* drive. Meanwhile, we've got to find that painting."

"But how did he know that the guard was about to—oh, I get it. He used Dr. Lunch's parabolic mic, didn't he?"

"Very good, James. And see, that's the annoying thing about Kelso—even when he's drunk, he's still smart as hell. Now, you check those mailing tubes."

She went over to them. "What are we looking for exactly? I mean I know it's a painting, but what does it look like?"

"You got me. I only know what it *doesn't* look like." I flashed my beam on one of Sherry's Tolkienesque creations. "For instance, it doesn't look like—wait a second."

She turned. "What is it?"

I went over to the painting and put my flash behind it, shining it through. "What do you see, honey?"

"Jack! There's another painting behind it!"

"Yep. And it looks like a Matisse or a Picasso. I'll take it out of the frame. You wipe down the pole and anything else we left our prints on."

"We should've worn gloves."

"I know. My bad."

I used the pliers-like end of the wire cutters to pull out the staples that held the canvas to the wooden frame. When I was done, I tossed the top painting aside, folded up the forged Picasso (it was a copy of the one we'd seen in Maxwell's study earlier), and stashed it in the nylon bag.

The firecrackers had stopped exploding.

We got our stuff together and left the booth just as Hendricks, or whatever his name was, came running toward us, his flashlight shining at the far end of the row of booths.

"Hold it right there," he shouted.

We ran for our lives, across Artists' Alley, past the other booths, and through the underbrush between them and the fence, our flash beams dancing crazily in the dark. It amazed me how fast Jamie could run. I was very proud of her.

The guard came running after us, shining his flashlight and calling home base on his walkie-talkie as he ran.

We got to the fence, with the guard about thirty yards or so behind. I held the slit open for Jamie, she went through, and I pushed the nylon bag after her, then tried to crawl through myself. I got almost all the way there but couldn't make that last foot or so. The guard caught up with me, dove at my leg, and was now hanging on, not about to let go.

I turned sideways, shined my flashlight in his face so he couldn't recognize *mine*, and used my free leg to kick him hard in the shoulder. He grunted in pain but still hung on.

I said, "Look, I don't want to hurt you."

"I'm not letting you get away."

"If I have to break your collarbone, I *will*."

"Forget it. I'm not letting go."

I kicked him again, harder. He rethought his position.

"Good," I said, from the other side of the fence. "Now, just lie there and moan like that for a while. Okay?"

"Bobby Lee! Bobby Lee!" Jamie called from the Suburban, badly imitating a hillbilly accent. "We already stol'ded somebody's nice car. Let's not make it any worse, hon!"

"You're right, Darlene," I said, following her lead. "An' when you're right, girl, you are right!"

I ran over, clicked the doors open with my key chain, threw the nylon bag in the back seat, and we got in and drove away, laughing like a couple of teenagers.

" 'Bobby Lee,' " I laughed. "That was clever thinking."

"Thanks."

"You're welcome. But he'll have a description of the car to give to the State Police. We've got to stash it somewhere. Have you got your cell phone with you?"

"Of course." She pulled it from her purse.

"Good. Call Kelso on *his* cell and have him meet us in East Boothbay. We'll stash the car there and report it stolen in the morning."

She held my hand. "Can't we park somewhere first, and mess around in the back seat for a while?"

I looked at her, surprised. "You really *want* to? Now?"

"Well, *I* don't," she said shyly, "but Dar*lene* does. And she wants to somethin' fierce."

I said, "Yew got it, Darlene," and I pulled over behind a tall stand of pines.

38

Jamie left early the next morning—which was Wednesday—to take care of some things at the hospital and then go to her apartment to pick out a call girl dress. Meanwhile, I got the dogs exercised and fed, then made a phone call to Otis Barnes, getting him out of bed. Otis's paper, the *Camden Herald*, is a weekly. It comes out on Thursdays, and I'd promised to give him some info on the case before he put out his next edition.

"Listen, Otis, the FBI and the U.S. Marshal's Office are making a statement, live for the news at noon."

"Then why call me at seven-thirty?"

"Because you'll want to be there, prepared for their disinformation campaign, so you can shout a couple of questions their way. Listen." I played Dr. Lunch's tape.

"Jesus, Christ, let me grab a pen." I waited. He came back on the line and said, "Can you play that again?"

I said I could and I did.

"Jesus Christ," he kept saying, over and over.

"Are you swearing or praying?" I asked him.

"A little of both. Do you know how huge this is? Ian Maxwell is a murderer? And the FBI knows about it and they're letting him get away with it?"

"Okay, but listen, Otis, play it cool. I don't want Maxwell fleeing the jurisdiction. Set up your questions the way a prosecuting attorney would, and save your rebuttal for tomorrow's *Herald*. Remember, the FBI is backing him."

"I got it." He rehearsed it for me: " 'Kemp is Maxwell's chief of security, does this mean that Maxwell is somehow involved in Gordon Beeson's murder?' Something like that?"

"Perfect. Then they'll make some sort of denial, which you can gently cram down their throats in tomorrow's paper."

I sighed. I hadn't talked to Jonas about this yet, and felt bad that I was going ahead without his prior knowledge or permission. But since I was positioning the whole thing as an unsubstantiated rumor, I did it anyway:

"Oh, and another thing, just kind of as a favor to me, could you call Maxwell's PR people and ask if there's any truth to the rumor that Jonas Cutter is pulling out of the development deal they had going?"

"Okay," he said. "Why?"

"Never mind. Just do it. It'll piss Maxwell off."

He laughed. "Whatever you say. By the way, I heard your car got stolen last night."

I laughed. "Something like that. Oh, that reminds me, Jamie and I are having an engagement party Friday evening out at my place. We've got a band lined up—the Blue D'Arts—and there'll be lots of food. I hope you can make it."

"Sure. I can even put a notice in tomorrow's paper."

"Great. And Otis, make sure you leave my name out of the other thing, and don't quote the tape I played you directly. Not yet."

"You're going to get me a copy, though, right?"

"Yeah, by special messenger this afternoon."

"Thanks, Jack. I owe you."

I hung up and called Donna Devon's cell number. She was out of breath when she answered. "Hello?" (pant, pant).

"Donna? It's Jack Field. Is this a bad time?"

"Not really. I'm at the gym. I'm on the step machine. It's incredibly boring, so I'm glad to have something to think about besides the timer on this damn thing. I must have climbed to the top of the Empire State Building by now, and the timer says I've still got another fifteen minutes to go. So, what's up?" (I think she may be a morning person.)

I told her about the FBI's impending announcement and suggested that she attend the press conference and ask a couple of pertinent questions. "Also, see if you can get the station to give you a live stand-up afterward, and—"

"Jack, I'm a weekend anchor, not a field reporter."

"Yeah, I know. But I have evidence that Ian Maxwell killed Gordon Beeson and that the federal government is covering it up. So, are you a reporter or not?"

"Wow, yeah, sign me up." She was really breathing hard now. "Do I get to know what this evidence *is*?"

"Not until I'm ready. You're going to have to trust me. But when I'm ready, it won't be evidence, it'll be proof."

She paused. "Do you know how turned on I am right now?"

I laughed. "No, but if I see a girl named Darlene later, I'll mention it to her."

"Who's Darlene?"

"Never mind. Maxwell is nuts, by the way. Certifiable. So dig up some of the wacky stuff he's pulled in the past, and use that to close the stand-up."

"Like when he tried to secede from the U.S. and declare his island a sovereign nation?"

"Yeah. And use phrases like 'reclusive billionaire inventor' and 'mad genius' to describe him."

"Okay?" She paused. "Why?"

I sighed. "I need to rattle his cage so he'll slip up and give himself away."

"You have this all figured out?"

"Honestly? No. I'm playing it by ear. But listen, he tried to have me killed, and then, after the feds told him to lay off, he threatened to kill my father."

"Jesus Christ."

"To quote another reporter who's in on this, yes."

"Anything else?"

"Yeah, put a call into Maxwell's PR firm," I told her, and repeated what I'd told Otis.

"Jonas Cutter? That's your fiancée's father."

"I'm aware of that."

"Is he? Pulling out of the project?"

"It's just an unsubstantiated rumor, for now. Or it'll quickly be*come* a rumor once you and a few other reporters have asked the question."

"Oh . . ." There was quite a long pause. "You are a sneaky sonovabitch."

"Well, I may not *like* my dad all that much? But he *is* my dad and I love him. Besides, nobody threatens my family and gets away with it."

She sighed. "That Darlene is a lucky girl."

"Yeah, and by the way? Her real name is Jamie."

"I thought so, but I wasn't going to say anything."

I hung up, then got out the fake Picasso and an art book and went over them with a magnifying glass. Sherry's copy was a nice bit of work, but I knew something interesting about Sherry Maughn. She was proud of her talent and felt she deserved more recognition than she got. There had to be something in the painting which reflected that; something she'd put in it to prove that she was as good or better than Picasso. Yes, I was falling back on my training as a profiler, but I had a hunch I would find something, and I eventually did, in the figure's hair. I held the lens closer, then farther away, until I got the perfect magnification. There it was, just what I'd been looking for. Two strands of hair were actually letters—one was an S, the other an M. She'd "signed" her forgery of Picasso's self-portrait.

Farrell Woods showed up a little while later. I got out my Polaroid and had him shoot a photo of me and the painting, then he gave me the Rhohypnol I'd asked for.

I told him I'd be out of town until Thursday morning and that he and Mrs. Murtaugh would be in charge till then.

"Where you gonna get your paraphernalia?" he asked, after I told him my plan.

"I'm sure there are places in San Diego that sell glass pipes and metal screens," I told him. "It's illegal, but they do it all the time. Anything else you think I'll need?"

"You could buy a couple of butane lighters. Just to make it look real. How are you getting the stuff on the airplane?"

"Jamie's a doctor. She can carry it in her MD's bag."

"She'll love that. Hey, this picture came out great."

Jamie decided on her little black Valentino. It wasn't slutty, but it was upscale and sexy. I think she was actually kind of excited about our upcoming adventure.

Kelso got us first class tickets on a three-thirty flight, which, with the three-hour time difference, gave us plenty of time to set things up, first in Rockland, then in Portland, and finally, once we got there, in San Diego.

Our first stop was the Rockland County Jail. I had one of Flynn's deputies take the Samoans into an interview room so Kelso and Jamie could watch through the two-way mirror.

I came in wearing a suit and carrying a briefcase. I said, "Well, boys, I've been hired by a Mr. Ortiz, on your behalf." I handed them tickets for a flight leaving Portland at five. "I've just secured your release. Mr. Ortiz wanted me to tell you there'll be a limo waiting for you at the airport, with two girls; Lorelei and one of her friends."

They looked at each other and smiled.

"The boss takes good care of us, eh, bro?"

"You got it, bro."

"He also wanted me to tell you to enjoy yourselves. But don't call him. He'll contact you when he wants you."

"We won't, sir."

"You can tell him that for us, sir."

"I will." I turned as if to leave. "Oh, and he said you can stop at Taco Bell on your way home. It's on him."

I gave them two twenties and they high-fived each other.

On the way out Kelso said, "Remember I told you about the Zen hologram? How everything is connected on some level?"

"Yeah?"

"Well, did you know that they use two-way mirrors like the one in that interview room in a laser? That that's how they get the photons all lined up in the same direction?"

"I did not know that. Dah's ve'y *in*tuhsting."

Jamie hit me, then chuckled.

Our next stop was the TV station. I had one of the sound guys speed-dub two copies of Dr. Lunch's tape, one for me and one for Otis Barnes (I didn't trust Donna Devon with it). I kept one copy and messengered the other to Otis at the *Herald*.

When that was done, we went to the bank around the corner, where Kelso and I rented a safe deposit box and left the original tape inside it. We had two keys, so neither one of us could unlock the box without the other one being there.

"Don't you trust each other?" Jamie said.

"It isn't that," Kelso explained. "It's that if one of us loses his key, like if we get kidnapped or—"

This was making Jamie nervous, so I said, "Never mind. It's just an added precaution."

We got to the airport in plenty of time to go through security, which we did without a hitch. Jamie and I were a little worried they might search her bag, but they didn't.

It was a long flight, with a stopover in Salt Lake City. Kelso passed the time by drinking and telling us about the origins of his fascination with, and his unending love for, Dr Pepper, and why he drinks the diet variety. He'd even brought some in a carry-on bag so he could mix up a few Kelso Christmas cocktails (a shot of Irish whisky, a dash of cinnamon schnapps, and Diet Dr Pepper over ice) for the trip.

"The thing is, they don't make real soft drinks anymore. They used to be made with pure cane sugar, but back in the seventies, there was a failure of the sugarcane crop in South America, so all the bottlers switched to corn syrup, which is cheaper but made the sodas taste lousy. This is why Coca-Cola changed their formula, by the way. It didn't taste the same with fructose, so they fooled around with it, trying to get it to match the original flavor. It didn't work."

Jamie said, "But why do you like Dr Pepper so much?"

"Oh, right," Kelso said, taking a sip of his eponymous cocktail. "Well, that goes back to when I was a kid."

"Ah," said Jamie, "it's a comfort food."

"Yes, or a comfort beverage. At any rate, in the summers when I was a kid, we used to go to my grandma's farm in southern Colorado. One of the big treats was a visit to the old-fashioned soda fountain at the Rexall Drugstore. They made this drink there called an Iron-Port and Cherry."

Jamie wanted to know what an Iron-Port and Cherry was. (I'd heard the story before, so I was barely listening.)

"Well, the cherry part is obvious. But I didn't figure out what iron-port was until a few years ago, and I'm still not sure I've got it right. You see there are two types of cream soda—light vanilla and dark vanilla. I think iron-port is just another name for dark vanilla cream soda. So one year we go back to my hometown, which is Columbine—"

"Wow," Jamie said. "I didn't know that."

"Yep. And one day I bought a bottle of Dr Pepper at the local grocery store and it tasted almost exactly like the Iron-Port and Cherry I used to drink at the Rexall soda fountain. That's when I started drinking Dr Pepper. It tasted so good to me, I can't even tell you.

"But when all the bottlers started using corn syrup, I stopped. And that's why now I drink Diet Dr Pepper. It really does taste more like *real* Dr Pepper. And I'm talking about the original "10-2-and-4" variety they used to sell in green glass bottles.

"But I've heard—and I don't know if this is true—that there's a place in Texas, not far from where Dr Pepper was invented, that still makes it with cane syrup. One of my goals is to go there someday and reacquaint my taste buds with the real thing."

With that he fell asleep, or passed out; dreaming, I suppose, of that bottling plant in Texas, or of the Rexall Drugstore in Colorado, or maybe both.

Jamie squeezed my hand then yawned and began looking through the magazines in the pouch in front of her. I opened my paperback copy of *Somebody's Darling*, by Larry McMurtry.

An old guy across the aisle said, "Psst."

We looked over.

"He's right, you know." He pointed to the sleeping Kelso. "I've been to Dublin, Texas. They really *do* make the original Dr Pepper in a little bottling plant there. They even use those old green glass bottles with the '10-2-and 4' logo."

"No kidding," I said.

"Yep. Sure is delicious too."

The flight attendant came by. "Say, Stewardess," the old guy said, "you don't have any Diet Dr Pepper, do you?"

"I'm sorry, sir. All we have is Diet Pepsi."

"Oh. Well, never mind." He sat back and tried to enjoy the rest of his flight.

39

We got in the limo and drove with the windows down, so I could see everything. It was strange being back in town after twenty years. I felt like Rip Van Winkle. Some things were so familiar—the freeways, the palm trees, the muggy salt air, the mariachi music blaring from a '65 Chevy at a stoplight. But there were other things—like the new skyline, with its glossy, angular buildings—that took some getting used to.

We'd told the driver, whose name was Teddy, that we needed rolling papers and a bong, so he drove us to a seedy section of town—not too far away from where I grew up, sad to say—and that's where we bought the glass pipes and bowls and screens to fool our Samoan friends into thinking they were going to be smoking rock cocaine with two hookers in the back of a limo.

We went back to the airport, located the Hollywood ambulance and the two Central Casting attendants, whose names were George Sullivan and Tip Boxell. Sullivan looked like he should be an extra on a cowboy picture. Boxell looked like a Boy Scout, all grown up but gone a little to seed.

Jamie used the ambulance as a dressing room to put on her Valentino gown, black hose, and high heels, and for putting on her call girl makeup and shpritzing her hair.

At one point the door opened slightly, Jamie poked her face out—just her face, mind you—and said, "Jack?"

"Yes, honey?"

"Zipper."

I came over and helped with her dress.

Meanwhile, George and Tip wondered aloud what the "gig" was and when they were getting paid. Kelso said something about double "golden time," which caused them to shut up. Golden time is actor's slang for double overtime, which amounts to three times your usual pay. For movie extras the pay is roughly $150 an hour, so double golden time would be $900 an hour. These guys must have thought they'd died and gone to extras heaven.

Once Jamie got dressed, there was the usual obligatory staring and trying not to stare (I thought I heard George say, under his breath, "Whoa—Cindy Crawford!"). Then we all stood around, some of us waiting for the Samoans to arrive, some mentally counting up their double golden time, all of us occasionally staring at Jamie.

At some point Kelso ran out of booze and asked if he could send Teddy on a run for a pint of Dewar's. I suggested he check the minibar in the back of the limo instead. He did and stocked up.

After about *my* fortieth time staring at Jamie, she said, "What are you lookin' at?" with a kind of Darlene attitude.

"Nothin'," I said, all Bobby Lee–like.

"Oh, yeah?" She came over and jabbed her finger in my chest. "You think you can afford me?"

"I don't know."

"You better *believe* you don't know, fella. It'll cost ya five hundred an hour if you want to be with me." She looked me up and down. "You even *got* that kind of money, cowboy?"

"Maybe. In my other pants."

"Well, you'd better go get your other pants then, sport."

"Will you two knock it off?" Kelso said, after downing a minibottle of Jack Daniel's.

I resisted telling Jamie about his bedmate of the other evening (one half of Eve Arden), not for *his* sake but Jamie's.

Boxell was the first to see the Samoans, and he hadn't even been looking. "Hey, look at *those* guys! They're *huge*!"

It was T'anke and Kong, coming out the front door of the terminal, looking happy to be home. Everybody got ready for action while I reminded them all of their positions.

"Okay," I said to Sullivan and Boxell, "you guys are supposed to be inside the ambulance. And close the door behind you. Teddy, you get into the driver's seat. Jamie, you're in the back. Kelso, you go and meet them, show them the paraphernalia, and bring them back to the limousine."

I got into the front seat with Teddy. Through the windshield I could see Kelso approach the two Samoans. He was wearing his suit and carrying two brown paper bags with the glass pipes and such inside. He looked around, gave them each a bag, invited them to take a look, then showed them the way to the limo. They followed him and got in the back.

Teddy and I listened over the intercom as Jamie said, "Hi, boys! How was your flight?"

"Pretty good," said one.

"Where's Lorelei?" said the other.

"She had to go inside to freshen up. Would you guys like a little champagne before we get going?"

"Yeah, okay, I guess. Who's got the freebase?"

"Lorelei," Jamie said. "Don't worry. She'll be back soon, then you can really get high."

I heard the sound of the popping cork, then bubbly being poured into two glasses.

"Aren't you gonna have some?" said one.

"I'm a working girl. I can't drink on the job."

"Too bad, eh?" said the other.

"Hey, bro," said the first, "what should we toast to?"

"I know! To comin' home."

"Too right, eh."

There was a clinking sound.

"Good champagne, eh? Tastes watered down, though."

"Yeah, but I think I'm already drunk on just one sip."

More was asked for. More was poured. And more was imbibed. Then, in almost no time at all, I heard the sound of two very large bodies slumping off the leather upholstery and onto the floor of the limousine. (Tasteless, odorless, fast-acting Rohypnol—ask for it by name!)

Afterward, Kelso, Sullivan, Boxell, and I pulled their sleeping bodies out of the limo and onto the asphalt. Jamie watched us, bemused—holding her heels in one hand, and leaning her hip against the shiny finish of the black car.

"Look, you guys," Boxell said, grunting, "I didn't sign up to do anything illegal, you know."

"Think of it as guerrilla theater," I said.

"Or performance art," said Kelso.

Sullivan, who was kind of enjoying himself, said, "Just shut up and grab his other leg."

Then, after we got them laid out in the parking lot, we hefted their carcasses up onto the two gurneys, strapped them carefully and securely into place, then groaned them into the back of the ambulance.

Kelso paid everybody in cash—three hours worth of double golden time. (He used Jamie's money.) Teddy offered to give the two extras a ride to the nearest bus stop, or to the nearest saloon, if they wanted to just hang out for a while and spend their loot. They decided on the latter.

Boxell hesitated before leaving, though. "I don't know," he fretted, "maybe we should call the cops."

Sullivan looked like he wanted to belt him one.

"Don't worry," I said, "we're not planning to hurt these guys. I mean it's not like we actually *could*, anyway."

"Besides," said Kelso, "if you went and notified the authorities, you'd just have to give all your hard-earned money back."

"Not to mention *mine*," grumped Sullivan.

Boxell shrugged and got in the back of the limo.

Kelso, Jamie, and I went over to the bus (which is cop talk for an ambulance) and climbed inside. I got behind the wheel and drove us over to Señor Ortiz's home in La Jolla, the San Diego equivalent of Malibu mixed in with a little Beverly Hills. As we drove, Kelso described the layout of the place:

Unlike Ian Maxwell, Miguel Ortiz didn't enjoy the advantages of Penobscot Bay acting as a kind of moat for his mighty castle, even though the back part of his property edges up against the Pacific Ocean. The security measures he'd procured for the place were focused solely on the front and two sides of the property. There was a high, smooth wall surrounding the grounds, with shards of glass from broken bottles, embedded in concrete, all along the top of it.

"That's pretty serious," Jamie said.

Kelso said, "Well, they tried infrared sensor beams, top and bottom, hooked up to an alarm system in the house. The trouble is, whenever a thick fog would creep in late at night or early in the morning, the alarm would go off."

I said, "How do you *know* all this?"

"I checked the work log and bank records of a local security outfit, among other things.

"After the infrared fiasco," he went on, "they tried using trip wires in roughly the same fashion, but the seagulls set *them* off. The glass shards take care of both the birds and the burglars, although it doesn't seem to faze the fog."

" 'It doesn't seem to faze the fog.' " I chuckled and said to James, "Didn't I tell you he should have been a lyricist?"

On that note, Kelso got gloomy, opened another minibottle, and went inside himself again. I remembered that Tracy, the girl he once loved, had been a cabaret singer (among other things), and had even written lyrics for some of the songs in her act. Kelso still had them all, scrawled in her own handwriting, in a folder somewhere in his office. I sometimes imagine him from time to time drinking scotch, getting her lyrics out, and reading them by the light of his Stickley floor lamp. From what he tells me, she was pretty good—no Johnny Mercer or Cole Porter, but at least she could write some clever phrases, using perfect rhymes to boot, something very few people know how to do these days.

"So, what's the *front* of the house like?"

"Well," he shrugged, "there's a big gate with an intercom and a security camera. You can't get in unless you have an appointment or at least a partial DNA match with someone living inside. No accidental pizza deliveries, no vacuum cleaner salesmen dropping by for a free demonstration, no Jehovah's Witnesses offering to help you corner the market on salvation.

"Anyway," he said, "I figure the best plan of attack is to hire a boat, sail around behind the place, and swim ashore. Did I mention that I got the old lady out of the house?"

"No, you didn't. And why bother?"

"Latino men," he said. "They tend to get a little more volatile when they feel their wives are being threatened. Anyway, she's a theater buff; he isn't. So I e-mailed her some free tickets to the latest Sondheim musical, now enjoying an out-of-town try-out at the Globe Theater, and she's absented herself from the hacienda tonight."

When we finally arrived at 10 Manzanita Court the moon was hanging low over the Pacific Ocean, its golden beams glittering down on the multicolored shards of broken glass stuck along the high stone wall. I drove past it and parked down the block and up around the corner.

I sat there thinking. Finally I said, "What do you say we hold off on the frogman stuff and just ring the doorbell?"

"Hey," he shrugged, "it's *your* party."

"Well, I mean, after all, we have three things Ortiz wants: a ten million dollar painting—at least that's what he paid for it—and his two Samoan bodyguards."

"Knock it off," Jamie said, yawning. "They're Maoris."

"I mean, Maori bodyguards." I turned to Kelso. "You ready to do a little Hope and Crosby routine?"

"What the hell," he said, "let's give it a shot."

"Okay. First let's ditch the cargo."

We got out, went around back, wrestled first one gurney out of the bus and then the other. We started to unstrap the boys but I stopped when I noticed their neckwear. They both wore Maori charms made with leather braids, each one wrapped around a whale's tooth, with some sort of carving on it. I took them off their necks and put them in my suit coat pocket. Then we finished unstrapping them and tipped the gurneys sideways, first one, then the other, leaving the boys on the sidewalk like tomorrow morning's trash. I left a note with Kelso's cell phone number on it inside the shirt pocket of one of them, along with the Polaroid of me and Picasso. Then Kelso and I went back to the front of the bus.

"You stay here, brown eyes," I said through the window.

"Jack! Why can't I come?"

"It's too dangerous."

"If it's going to be dangerous then *you* shouldn't go."

"I have to. You just stay here, honey, and think pretty call girl thoughts."

She shook her head and chuckled. "Like what?"

"Like how you're going to start saving your money so you can buy a fashionable boutique in SoHo someday and finally get off drugs and stop hooking, that sort of thing."

Kelso shoved me and said, "Hey!"

I'd forgotten that Tracy had also once been a call girl, and had dreamed of buying a used record store in SoHo.

"Jeez, I'm sorry, man," I told him.

"Ah, forget it," he said. "So, that's my second time today. So what?"

To Jamie, I said, "Anyway, when Kelso calls you on your cell phone, turn on the siren and drive straight to the front gate, but keep the motor running."

"Okay. Are you sure you're going to be all right?"

Kelso said, "God watches over angels, drunks, and fools."

She smiled. "I guess he's had his hands full with you two, then, for quite a while, hasn't he?"

"Yes, he has angel." I laughed, and, laughing, kissed her, then left her alone with nothing to keep her company but her call girl thoughts, her cell phone, and two unconscious Maori warriors, lying peacefully on the sidewalk.

40

It's a simple process, really. You extend your index finger, about chest high, and press it against a square button on the top part of a little black box. Then you wait for a voice to come out of the circle in the middle of the box. The circle has ridges of plastic over it, painted silver. The voice asks you who you are, and you tell it. It's that easy.

"What are you just standing there for?" said Kelso. "You know there's a security camera watching us."

"Yeah, just give me a sec. I need to psych myself up—"

He pushed the button for me.

A voice crackled through the speaker. "Who is it?"

"Uh, my name is Jack Field. I'm a dog trainer. This is Lou Kelso. He's a P.I. We're here to deliver a painting."

"A painting?"

Kelso said, "Yeah. Tell Señor Ortiz we've got his long-lost Picasso! He'll want to see us."

There was a pause. "Wait right there."

"Hurry it up, amigo!" Kelso shouted, a little drunkenly. "We got other customers waiting!"

After a bit some floodlights illuminated the yard, then the carved front door of the house opened and a tall, muscular man, wearing a silk print shirt and creased slacks, came out onto a brick porch and started down a curved terra-cotta tile pathway. The edges of the path were lined with dichondra—three inches high—that led the eye to the immaculate emerald grass, lush and perfectly cut, like an ad for Lawn-Gro.

The man had dark skin and dark hair—combed back and greased down—and walked at an easy, leisurely pace. He didn't smile or make any acknowledgment as he approached the gate.

Kelso whispered, "We probably interrupted his game of hide-the-salami with the downstairs maid."

"You might want to shut up," I laughed, "and let *me* do all the talking. You're amusing the hell out of me right now, but it might not prove fruitful for our overall purposes."

"I will, as you've requested, kindly shut the hell up."

"Thank you." I laughed some more.

The area around the gate was a foot or so lower than the lawn, so there were a couple of steps leading down to a semicircular space, paved with the same terra-cotta tiles as the path. This space allowed the gate to open and close.

The man and his scowl arrived simultaneously. "Who are you and what do you want?" he said through the bars.

I said, "We explained that already."

"Well, explain it again."

"Once is enough. Now let us in." He made no move to open the gate. "Fine. If your boss doesn't want the painting, someone else will." I turned and walked away.

Kelso, somewhat surprised, turned and followed me.

"Wait! Come back here." I kept walking, casually taking the whale's tooth charms out of my pocket as I walked. "Where do you think you are going? Come back."

I heard the gate click open behind me. I turned and saw that he was holding it for us. He was also holding a gun.

I laughed. "You think that scares us?"

Kelso whispered, "It scares *me*."

"Sure I do." He nodded and smirked. "Guns scare people. You are no different." (He's going to start shooting? in this neighborhood? on a quiet Wednesday evening? I don't think so.)

I walked right back up to him, stood toe-to-toe just inside the gate, and placed the two leather necklaces over the barrel of his weapon. "You still think I'm scared of *you*, Junior?" I poked him in the chest. He took a few steps back toward the steps. "You know who these belonged to?"

"That's impossible." He gaped down at the pendants.

This was my opening. I grabbed the barrel of the gun, tilted it up, and simultaneously gave him a quick, hard knee to the co-jones. He doubled over. I took the gun away, then cracked him over the back of the head with it. He went down like a sack of Lawn-Gro, right on top of the steps.

I heard the sound of two hands clapping.

It was Señor Ortiz, standing on the front porch. He was a small, brown man—Tom Cruise height, maybe five-five—yet dapper, with a little silver interwoven into the deep black weft of his hair, and a small, yet not insignificant mustache. Like Tom Cruise, he seemed to occupy more vertical space than his body was actually capable of. In La-La Land they call it star power. I have no idea what they call it in Mexico.

"Excellent, Señor Field. Very good. I am very impressed. Come up," he waved me forward, "let us have a little talk, you and I."

I put the gun in my belt, kicked Junior lightly, then looked up. "I hope he isn't family. If he is, I apologize."

"No need," he shrugged. "He is a son-in-law, a source of much disappointment. Come," he waved at me again, "let us go inside and have a drink."

"Okay by me," I said, not moving, "but you might want to re-consider inviting my friend here. He'll drink you dry."

"Is that right, Mr. Kelso? You are *uno borrachado*?"

"Sí, señor. Yo estoy muy borracho ahora." Then he whispered, "But not drunk enough to trust you, pal."

"You got that right," I said. "Time to call Jamie."

He flipped open his cell phone, then said to Ortiz, "Let me just cancel some other plans I had, do you mind?"

"Claro que no, señor. Of course, be my guest."

He took a few steps forward, smiling and treating us to some more of his personality. He was very smooth, this guy. He could give you the glad hand and the skunk eye at the same time. I wasn't buying it, though; especially not after I saw him make just the glimmer of a sideways glance toward the door. I also saw what looked like the shadows of some men moving around inside. I didn't count them, but there were at least three, maybe four.

Kelso dialed Jamie's number. As he did, the front gate swung shut electronically and locked itself behind us.

Ortiz moved casually out of the way as four men came through the door, holding semiautomatic rifles, looking like they were ready to shoot.

We took cover behind Junior, below the terra-cotta steps leading up to the lawn.

The siren from the ambulance sounded. When it did, the riflemen looked around nervously then scampered back inside.

I twisted sideways, keeping a low profile, aimed Junior's gun at the lock on the front gate and blasted away.

Sparks flew and the lock cracked open. Jamie screeched the ambulance to a stop out front. Kelso and I got up and backed our way over to the gate.

Ortiz saw that the siren wasn't from a police car and called out in Spanish to the boys inside, *"No es policia!"* or something. They came out with their guns again.

"You two! Stop where you are or my men will shoot!"

I turned at the gate, holding Junior's weapon easily at my side. "I don't think so, Ortiz. A shootout in La Jolla? What will the neighbors say?"

"They'll say it's a Mexican standoff," said Kelso.

I chuckled. "Look, I know your men think it's fun to point their guns and try to scare people, but there *is* a rule about such things—don't aim your weapon if you don't intend to shoot. It's just good old-fashioned manners, really."

He motioned for the gunmen to lower their weapons. "You said something earlier about a painting of mine?"

"Yeah, that was before all the hardware appeared and got pointed in my general direction."

He spread his arms wide. "My apologies. In my business one can never be too careful. Come inside, we will talk."

"Yeah, we'll talk, but when I say so; and where. You'll find your two Maori bodyguards around the corner, enjoying a short siesta. There's a Polaroid of your precious Picasso in one of their pockets along with a cell phone number. Use it to call me and I'll let you know where we can meet."

"I'm afraid that is unacceptable, Señor Field."

"Try and get over it. When you do, call me."

Kelso and I backed our way slowly toward the ambulance.

Ortiz motioned for his men to keep their weapons down, then said, "This is not over, Señor Field."

"Who said it *was*?" I ejected the clip, wiped the gun clean of my prints, and threw it in the bushes.

While I was doing this Kelso put his hand up to his ear, using his thumb and little finger to form a make-believe telephone. "Call me! I'll be on my cell."

I laughed and said, *"Hasta la vista, señor."*

We got in the ambulance as Ortiz stood silently steaming on the wide veranda of his lovely Spanish Colonial.

Jamie said to me, "Are you all right?"

"Just drive, honey," I said, closing the door. "Before they change their minds and actually start shooting. And don't worry, we're both fine."

"Speak for yourself," Kelso griped. "I think I just sat on one of my minibottles."

41

It only took five minutes for the phone to ring. By this time Jamie had turned the siren off and we were on the freeway back to San Diego. Kelso handed it to me. I popped it open and said in a Speedy Gonzales accent, *"Sí, señor?"*

"Very funny, Mr. Field. Where is my painting?"

"In case you hadn't noticed, *I'm* holding all the cards here. Now, here's how this is going to—"

"I want that painting."

"Don't interrupt me again." I pressed the end button.

A moment passed. The phone rang again. I let it ring. It kept ringing. I let it keep ringing. After a bit it stopped, then another moment passed and it rang again.

I said, "Have you got it straight yet, Ortiz?"

"Yes, Mr. Field. How much do you want for it?"

"No, you haven't got it straight. When you learn to ask the right question, you will get the right answer."

"And what is the right question?"

"I'll tell you this much, that ain't it."

I pressed end again. This was driving Jamie and Kelso crazy. Good. It was probably driving Ortiz crazy as well.

The phone rang again.

I popped it open but said nothing.

"What exactly would you like me to *do*, Mr. Field?"

"Excellent question, Miguel. Now you're on the right track. Do you mind if I call you Miguel?"

There was an angry pause. "Not at all."

"Good. Very dishonest of you, right in character. Look, here's exactly what I want . . ." I explained that there would be a plane ticket waiting for him at the Delta Airlines ticket counter at San Diego International Airport. The ticket would not be there until ten. If he tried to pick it up before then, the deal was off. If someone else tried to pick it up, the deal was off. If anyone was with him and tried to buy a ticket on the same flight, the deal was off. He was to take that ticket and get on the plane alone. Then, once we were airborne, I would meet him and give him the painting.

"I don't think I can get much cash onto the airplane. Will you take a check?"

"You're pissing me off again, Miguel."

"Very well. So you won't take a check."

"It's not the check, you asshole, it's the fact that you think I want your money. Did I *ask* you for any money?"

There was a pause. "I was assuming you would."

"It's *your* painting, isn't it? You *paid* for it. I'm just trying to hand it over to you without getting my ass shot off. Is that too much to ask?"

Another pause. "I'm not sure I understand."

"I'll explain it to you on the plane. Come alone."

"Yes, you said that."

"Yes, and I repeated it for a reason. You know, for a supposedly smart character, you've got some pretty dumb moves. Don't make any more of them or you might regret it."

"Maybe I'll make *you* regret saying *that*, señor."

"See? This is the kind of thing I'm talking about. Here I am, trying to do you a favor, and you're making threats."

There was a pause. "I do not understand. Why would you want to do *me* any favors?"

"See, now that's an excellent question. Maybe you'll think of an answer to it on your way to the airport."

Another pause. "Perhaps . . . perhaps I should trust you. You know, in my business, you learn to trust no one. Perhaps you are someone I *should* trust."

"Very good, Miguel. You're starting to catch on."

After the seat belt sign went off, Jamie got up and went to the magazine rack in the back of first class. When she was in position, I got up and wandered back to coach. I looked around, caught Ortiz's eye, and motioned with my head for him to follow me. He extricated himself from his seat (and his fellow passengers) and tagged along behind me up the aisle.

I motioned for him to sit in Jamie's seat, opposite me, and he did. As we sat, Jamie went back to coach, found an empty seat and began reading her magazine. Kelso was passed out, or pretending to be, in the seat next to mine.

I said, "Okay, señor, first of all I have some bad news."

He sighed. "You don't have my painting after all."

"Oh, no, I have it. At least I have the painting that Maxwell sold you. You *were* buying paintings from Ian Maxwell, weren't you? As in, more than one?"

He hesitated. The plane hit a little turbulence.

"That's a simple question, Miguel. Yes or no?"

He shrugged and held onto his seat. "Perhaps it is not as simple as you think. Perhaps it is more like, yes *and* no."

"I see." He was being cagey about their working arrangement. Fine. I didn't have time for being cagey so I simply explained to him about the forgeries.

He shook his head. "No, my friend." The turbulence subsided. "I had all my purchases appraised by an expert."

"Who? Someone you met in a hotel room in Boston?"

He was taken aback. "But how did you know this?"

"If Maxwell could have his paintings forged, wouldn't he be able to phony up some professional documents as well?"

"But I checked into this woman's background. She was an art expert." (It's true; Sherry *was* kind of an art expert.)

"Maxwell has all kinds of government contracts, with the FBI, the CIA, the military, you name it. It would be like child's play for him to pull the wool over anyone's eyes."

He shook his head. "I do not believe the paintings that I purchased were forgeries. I simply will not believe it."

"Listen, you run a pretty big criminal outfit, right?"

"Allegedly." He shrugged a smile.

"Fine. The painting I have in the carry-on compartment is a copy of a canvas I saw yesterday in Ian Maxwell's study. Now in my experience, you don't rise to the top of your field, slimy as it may be, by being an idiot. You have to know a thing or two about human nature. So, ask yourself this: Why the hell would I make this up? And why would Maxwell go to all the trouble of making forgeries to hang on his *own wall*? Wouldn't he know they were copies, and wouldn't knowing that drive him nuts, if he's not already nuts, that is?"

He thought it over. "You ask interesting yet irritating questions." He looked me in the eye. "And what is the favor you are asking of me, in return for this worthless Picasso?"

"You mean the worthless Picasso *and* the information I've just given you?" I smiled. "So, Miguel, I guess you finally found the answer to one of my irritating little questions."

"I had time to think about it on the way to the airport. So? What do you want in return?"

I laid it out. "Call your attorney and have him file a lawsuit against Ian Maxwell for fraud."

He shook his head. "To what end?"

"To get your money back for the forged paintings he sold you, for one thing."

"You think he will actually pay?"

"It's irrelevant to me, but yeah, he might settle. Or maybe you can get him to fork over the *real* paintings."

"But that's not your purpose in asking me to do this?"

"Nope."

"Are you planning to tell me what your purpose is?"

I thought it over. Should I tell him or not? I decided not to. There were a couple of reasons for this. One, I was starting to think that Maxwell killed Beeson in order to impress, or influence, Ortiz. I'd been thinking about it a lot, and my previous theory that he'd done it because Beeson found out about the forgery scheme and had threatened to tell the feds didn't add up.

Maxwell thought he could get away with anything, and he was right. If the government was willing to overlook a murder, why would they chap his ass over some little art forgery scheme? No, Maxwell knew about Beeson's previous life as Hugh Gardner from the git-go and then, when this relationship with Ortiz developed, he used that knowledge for leverage.

"Let me ask you something, off the record. I know you wanted Hugh Gardner dead, so let's not pretend otherwise. Wasn't there a time, in your relationship with Maxwell, as a buyer for certain pieces in his impressive art collection, that you got cold feet about it?"

He thought it over. Not whether it happened, but whether he should tell me about it. He decided to tell me.

"Yes. About six months ago I expressed concern over his relations with some of these governmental organizations you mentioned. To calm my fears, he told me that he also had key connections within the U.S. Marshal's Office." (Yeah, I thought, like Marshal Paul Kemp.) "As you probably know, they oversee the witness protection program." He waited a moment to see my reaction. I nodded, just to keep him talking. "He said he could locate the whereabouts of anyone who might have testified against me or any of my people in the past."

"He didn't mention Hugh Gardner by name?"

He shook his head. "No, I was the one who brought that up—but I fear I may be saying too much."

I nodded. "You're probably right. I already know you sent T'anke and Kong to kill Gardner and Sherry Maughn."

He smiled. "And how do you know this?"

"They told me. Not intentionally, but they did."

He knit his brow. "This is, as you say, off the record?"

I shrugged. "I don't like you. I don't like how you make your money. If I were a San Diego cop or a DEA agent, I'd bust your ass in a minute. I would make it my business to bring you down and see that you never saw a day of sunlight in your life where you weren't looking at it through iron bars. You're vicious and brutal and you peddle in human misery. You may believe that heroin and cocaine and prostitution are all victimless crimes, but that ain't the case. And even if it were, you're forgetting all

the violence and gunplay and murder, and all the blood you
have on your hands that will never wash off. But none of that is
my business. My business is solving a murder case back in
Maine, so, yeah—whatever you tell me is off the record and I
won't use it to nail you for any crimes you may have committed
in California.

"There is one thing I'll give you, Ortiz, and that's the fact
that you're up front about being a crook. Not like these guys in
the FBI and the Marshal's Office. You, at least, haven't taken
any oath. You're a slime ball, but you're a kind of honest slime
ball. Still, none of you pricks—you *or* the feds—has anything
like a conscience as far as I can tell, but that's a story for another day."

"Finished?"

"For now."

"May I now tell you what I think of you and your *borracho
amigo,* so pathetically passed out here?"

"Sure, I guess. Tit-for-tat."

"You two are nothing." He spat it out. "Nada. You are what I
wipe off my slippers when my little Chihuahua he misses the
paper and shits on the floor."

I said, "He probably needs more wee-wee pads. You know, a
larger target area? He probably spins around a lot before he
poops and that's why he keeps missing the paper."

He stared at me for a moment then cracked up. "But how did
you know this? You have never even seen my little Paco."

"It's a Chihuahua thing. Try using three or four pads, or, what
do you use, newspapers? The *Chronicle*?"

"The *Wall Street Journal.*"

"So, put two pages of the *Journal* down instead of just one
and Paco will stop making his mess on the floor."

He shook his head in amusement. "A lousy dog trainer, and
you're getting mixed up with Ian Maxwell, Miguel Ortiz, and
the Federal Bureau of Investigation. I am embarrassed to say it,
Señor Field, but I think I have respect for you, if for no other
reason than the way you stood your ground earlier tonight. You
were outmanned and outgunned, I mean by plenty, and it did
not disturb you, not even in the slightest."

"Oh, I was disturbed all right. I just didn't let it show, that's all."

"Well," he threw his arms up, "then I should respect you even more, no? Me? I have always around me my men for my protection. But you, my friend, you are a rare animal."

"Yeah, yeah. I just do what I have to do so I can get back to my dogs, that's all. Look, one thing I'm not clear on. Why did you send T'anke and Kong to kill Sherry Maughn?"

He shrugged. "That was me being a prick without a conscience—as you put it—I'm afraid. I actually just sent them to get the painting, but they tend to do things all the way or not at all, so I may have mentioned that if she didn't give it to them easy, they should convince her to do so, hard. They may have taken that to mean that—"

"—they should kill her. I get it."

"They are very strong, those two. How did you—"

"They might tell you about it someday. I won't."

I got up and reached into the overhead space, got out a briefcase, sat back down and handed it to Ortiz. "You can take it into the bathroom and look it over, if you like."

"Thank you, señor. I will consider the lawsuit."

"You don't even have to actually file it. Just threatening Maxwell with it serves my purpose. Oh, by the way, have you got a magnifying glass at home?"

"I do not think so. Why?"

Just then a flight attendant floated by. "Would you two like anything?" he asked. We told him we were fine, and he nodded and continued floating till he was out of sight.

"When you get back to La Jolla," I told Ortiz, "you might want to get one. Use it to check out the hair of the figure in the portrait. You'll see two strands that aren't in the original. They're in the shape of Sherry Maughn's initials."

His eyes burned as he thought about this. "I think maybe I would like very much to kill this Maxwell fellow."

I shook my head. "Keep your ass in San Diego, Miguel. Just file your lawsuit and let *me* take care of Maxwell."

"And if you don't? Or can't?"

"What? You doubt me, all of a sudden? Didn't my work with the Samoans—sorry, the Maoris—prove anything?"

He laughed and admitted that it did.

"You know *why* I did that, don't you?"

He shrugged. "To impress me? To keep me off guard?"

I shrugged. "I could have done that by killing them too, you know. Just as I could easily kill *you* right now." I leaned forward and put my hand around his throat and held him in place, squeezing just hard enough to make him nervous.

His black eyes kept their cool, but just barely.

I let go and patted his cheek. "You're soft and weak, Miguel. Not all the bodyguards in the world—Maoris *or* Samoans—can save you from someone who *really* wants to kill you."

He let out a long, hot breath. "Maybe I will have to kill *you* someday." His black eyes burned again. "I have some very good friends in Maine, you know."

I shook my head and smiled an easygoing smile. "Neither you nor Eddie Cole worries me in the slightest."

"So, you know about my relationship with Eddie Cole?" I nodded. "It doesn't matter. I have other friends. Anyway, Cole is no longer *in* Maine. At least," he said smoothly, "not as far as I know."

"That interests me not in the least. And why the hell would you want to kill me, Miguel?"

"Because, señor, you are a very dangerous man, I think."

"Didn't I just give you a ten million dollar painting? *And* some valuable information. And this is the thanks I get?"

He nodded and smiled. "Thank you, señor, for the painting *and* the information. I will, as you say, keep my ass in San Diego. Just keep yours in Maine."

"Sounds like we've got ourselves a deal."

"*Sí*. We have a deal." With that he stood up and took the briefcase with him back to coach.

Kelso sat up. "Jesus, what an asshole."

"Yeah," I said. "Did you get all that?"

He smiled and took a pack of Marlboros out of his shirt pocket.

"Are we planning to nail him with this?"

I shook my head. "To quote Bob Dylan, 'To live outside the law you must be honest.' That cuts both ways. I made him a promise and I intend to keep it. On the other hand, he may need a little help remembering his part of the bargain."

He patted his hidden recorder. "And this will help."

"That's right." I stood up. "I'm going to go get Jamie. I have a feeling she may have fallen asleep." I stopped.

"What is it?"

"Something just occurred to me. We think Kemp killed Sherry Maughn, right?"

"A .22 to the head, execution style, yes."

"But she'd been shot *at* the day before, remember? At the carnival. And as far as we know, the shooter was Paul Kemp, who she may have recognized, stocking mask notwithstanding."

"*Whom* she may have recognized."

"Yeah, yeah, 'whom.' So how does Paul Kemp get into her house, sneak into her studio, and come up behind her to shoot her in the back of the head like that?"

"I don't know. He was very quiet and stealthy?"

I shook my head. "Her floorboards creak. It had to have been someone she knew and trusted."

Kelso got it and nodded. "Then we've *got* to nail Maxwell, Jack. And I mean, big-time."

"Oh, we *will*." I walked a few seats back, thought of something, turned and said, "Is it 'will' or 'shall'?"

"Either one's fine," he said.

42

When we got home the sun was just coming up. I was glad Kelso had squandered Jamie's money on first class seats. We actually got some sleep on the flight back.

At any rate, it was Thursday—a day for marinating.

First of all, I put the brisket in a mixture of crushed garlic, vinegar, chili powder, ground cumin, salt, pepper, brown sugar, tomato paste, onion powder, and a bottle of Guinness, and then wrapped it in plastic wrap.

The steaks got a dry rub of garlic, salt, pepper, ground cumin, and a little chili powder; again wrapped in plastic.

The chicken got three varieties of marinade: the breasts were rubbed with cilantro-infused olive oil, fresh rosemary and tarragon, dried parsley, salt, lemon pepper, a squeeze of fresh lemon juice, and a squeeze of fresh lime; for the legs and thighs I used curry powder, regular olive oil, ground coriander seed garlic, ground cumin, turmeric, mixed with some ghee; and I brushed several *whole* birds with a store-bought BBQ sauce mixed with a little ghee, cumin, coriander, and paprika.

For Ian Maxwell the marinade was composed of CNN, MSNBC, Fox News Channel, the broadcast networks, and the local Maine outlets. This was mixed with just a dash of gossip that Jonas Cutter was pulling out of their development deal, a pinch of the salty news that Miguel Ortiz was filing a lawsuit against him for alleged art fraud, all stewing in a flavorful broth of a rumored FBI cover-up of Maxwell's possible involvement in Gordon Beeson's murder.

We'd missed most of the media frenzy—Jamie and Kelso and I—due to our little out-of-town production in La Jolla, California. But here's the chronology of how it played out:

It had started simply and, some had thought, innocently enough, at Wednesday's press conference held by Rondo Kondolean and Myles Kuwahara, announcing the arrest of Paul Kemp for the murder of Gordon Beeson. A couple of reporters—Otis Barnes and Donna Devon—asked if there was any truth to the idea that the FBI and the U.S. Marshal's Office were involved in an attempt to cover up Maxwell's culpability in the murder. They denied it, of course. But the question was asked, twice, on live TV, and the networks were all watching—not to mention the *New York Times*, *Washington Post*, and *Wall Street Journal*. The idea had been put out there.

Donna Devon ended her stand-up after the press conference with the line, "Ian Maxwell, a mad genius? Or just stark raving mad? Back to you in the studio." (Yay, Donna!)

In no time reporters were scrambling for a lead. Calls were made to confidential sources within the government. Former employees of Ian Maxwell were hounded for interviews. One of Maine's congressmen—who just happened to be facing a hard-fought reelection bid—stood up on the floor of the house, in the middle of a debate on housing legislation (live on C-Span, of course), and called for an investigation into Maxwell's finances as well as an immediate moratorium on all government contracts with Maxwell Industries.

This was followed (on the cable news outlets) by the obligatory speculation and "talking heads" bullshit from so-called pundits whose sole job is to try to look intelligent while engaging in incredibly mindless, meaningless—not to mention totally moot—hypothetical fantasies as a way not to shed any light on the situation, or—heaven forefend!—to actually report the news but to kill time between commercials for beer, personal hygiene products, and the latest wonder drug from a major pharmaceutical company: "Side effects are mostly mild and may include acne, vomiting, diarrhea, edema, muscle spasms,

colon cancer, loss of bladder control, ulcers, unexplained
bleeding, mild hallucinations, cardiac arrest, irreversible coma-
like symptoms, occasional stomach upset, and a painful
screaming death while foaming at the mouth. Ask your doctor if
Gonzilactin is right for *your* heartburn!"

Dr. Reiner, meanwhile, was also being roasted, basted, and
broiled. Jamie and I had had our sous chef, Dr. Liu, leak his
preliminary findings to the media (without any mention of the
ve'y sumoah lazuh—I didn't want Maxwell knowing we knew
about the murder weapon). It was quite apparent that Reiner
had jumped the gun in his autopsy. It didn't hurt that every time
the media showed a clip of him claiming that his job was simply to determine the cause and manner of death, not to track
down suspects or tell the police who (or whom) to arrest, they
always followed it with a clip of Detective Sinclair (my new
best friend) saying, "Dr. Reiner specifically told me, on the
night of the murder, that Jack Field was the killer and that I
should arrest him as soon as possible."

By Wednesday night the Governor had made a formal request for Dr. Reiner's resignation. (I made a mental note to vote
for him in the next election. Twice, if possible.)

These were good things. There *were* some drawbacks, however. When we got home there were a lot of reporters and camera crews traipsing around the grounds, crushing the grass,
tying up the phone lines, and generally intruding on the quiet
country atmosphere generally regarded as part of the rustic
charm of Dog Hill Kennel.

We were lucky. We had Flynn on our side. He sent over a
couple of deputies. They chased the reporters off and then used
their radio cars to block the entrance to my property.

Then when the *Camden Herald* hit the stands later that morning—with Otis specifically accusing the feds of lying, saying
that there were three anonymous sources, and an audiotape that
would verify this fact—the story took off and clips of the press
conference, Dr. Reiner, Detective Sinclair, et alia, were shown
over and over and over, ad nauseum.

This was covered big on the morning news-and-chat shows,
along with the "breaking story" that Miguel Ortiz, a reputed

San Diego drug lord, was filing a lawsuit against Ian Maxwell for art fraud, claiming that the inventor had sold him forged paintings to the tune of over fifty million dollars.

The story was out there. And it was huge.

Lily Chow and the crew came out around noon to get some shots of me and Leon training Magee. In the middle of our session I got a call on my cell phone from someone at the FBI in Washington, wanting to know how the story about the cover-up had leaked to the press. I said, "Hang on a sec," went inside the house and played them Dr. Lunch's tape.

"We'll get back to you," they said (after a long pause).

The next development, which took place a couple of hours later, was the report that agents Baker and Kuwahara were the subjects of an internal FBI probe and had been suspended from active duty. The same was true for Marshal Kondolean. (The poor jejune upstarts! They had only been following orders!)

Then Blair Theobald, a young, blonde DHS case worker, came to the kennel, making angry noise about taking Leon away from me, claiming that she'd received negative reports about my treatment of the "child," as she called him, from sources high in the federal government. I played the tape for *her*, and she actually started to cry when she heard Kondolean's threats.

"How can they *do* that?" she said. "Don't they know they're playing with children's *lives*?" She became extremely bitter and furious, and the next thing I knew, *she* was on TV, making accusations against the feds.

So by later that afternoon, as the meat was marinating in the back of my fridge, Jamie, Kelso, and I were entertaining ourselves by lolling around the living room, clicking around the dial, and watching Ian Maxwell being marinated in the press. Frankie and Hooch, meanwhile, were oblivious to the frenzy. They just lay by the hearth, Hooch snoring loudly, Frankie gnawing on a rawhide. My dad couldn't join us. He was still out combing the marinas for that elusive sailboat. That's my dad. He's like a pit bull when he's on a case—totally obsessed in his dogged pursuit of justice.

"See?" Jamie said. "This is another nice quality you've inherited from your father, Jack. You're very persistent."

"Yeah," Kelso said, "you mean pigheaded."

Meanwhile, Ian Maxwell, ever the reclusive, mad genius, refused to make a statement to the press. He was hiding out on his private island. This tactic backfired when the network news anchors all ended their broadcasts on Thursday evening by asking the burning question, "Most Americans are now asking themselves, what exactly does Ian Maxwell have to hide?"

That's when my cell phone rang. It was him.

"I warned you about this, Jack. Remember?"

"No. Remind me."

"I said if you spoke to Ortiz I'd have your father killed."

I cracked up. "You're telling me this on a cell phone, you idiot?" I couldn't stop laughing. "What if some smart reporter has figured out the bandwidth on this number and is listening to this conversation right now? What if they're taping it? What if I'm taping it my*self*, you maroon?"

"Your father will still be dead, asshole."

"Well, he'll be here all week. In fact, we're having a little cookout tomorrow. You can come kill him then, if you like. Of course, you haven't got the guts or the know-how to kill a man in public like that and get away with it, do you?"

"It's time you took this a little more seriously."

"Oh, and bring Charles with you. We're having a band. I'd like to see if he can dance. Just don't bring any high-tech criminal devices, nanolasers, and such? We may have to search you before we let you sit down to eat with us."

"Your father's a dead man." He hung up.

That's when I started to worry a little about the old man. It's also when I knew I had Maxwell hooked. Or *thought* I did. The phone rang again, right away.

"Yes, Your Evil Highness? *Now* what is it?"

"Jack?" It was a woman's voice. In fact, it was a very familiar-sounding woman's voice.

"Sorry," I mumbled an apology. "I thought you were . . . I was just talking to . . . wait, who *is* this?"

"It's Kristin," she giggled. "Kristin Downey."

I cupped my hand over the phone and said to Jamie, "It's Kristin Downey, of all people."

She held her hand out. "Here, I want to talk to her."

I laughed and held the phone away. "No, honey, I'm not going to let you talk to her until you stop acting jealous."

"I'm not jealous, I just want to talk to her."

"Jack? I'm in Maine, in Waterville. Hello, Jack?"

"*I'll* talk to her," said Kelso, grabbing the phone. "Hi. My name's Lou Kelso." There was a pause. "No, I'm a friend of his. They're having a discussion." Another pause. "He and his fiancée." Another pause. "Didn't he *tell* you?"

Jamie hit me. "You didn't *tell* her about me?"

Kelso said, "Oh, I get it." He cupped his hand over the phone and said to Jamie, "She knows who you are, she just hasn't spoken to Jack since you two got engaged."

"Give me the phone!" She reached across my lap to grab it. I held her wrists. Kelso got up and walked away. Jamie wriggled around and tried to kick me but I twisted sideways, still wrestling with her. "Ow!" she said, kicking me.

"I don't know," Kelso said, "I think October fifteenth." He looked over at us. We stopped wrestling and both nodded.

"Oh, I'm sure you'll get one," he went on. "I don't think they've mailed *any* of them out yet. They just decided on the date a few days ago." Another pause. "Yeah, it is kind of last minute." Jamie got her hands free and hit me. "Sure, I can do that. Let me find a pen first." He looked at me, and I jerked a thumb at the end table. He picked up a pen and parked his hip on the arm of the sofa. "By the way, Jack's hosting an outdoor soiree tomorrow, around five."

"Oh, no! Don't invite her to the cookout!"

"Yes, tell her to come! I want to meet her."

I hung my head. "This is a nightmare."

To Kristin, Kelso said, "Jamie says to come. She wants to meet you." He cupped his hand over the phone and said to Jamie, "She wants to meet you too."

"Good." She smiled.

He listened and wrote something down. "Okay. See you tomorrow." He clicked the cell phone shut and tossed it to me, then sat back down and handed me the scrap of paper.

Jamie snatched them both out of my hands, jumped up, hit

"last call" and "autodial," pocketed Kristin's number and address, and in no time at all was talking and pacing. "Hi, Kristin? This is Jamie Cutter, Jack's fiancée? I'm *so* glad to talk to you. I've been dying to meet you." A pause. "I know! There's so much I want to ask you *too*!"

"I'm screwed," I told Kelso.

"Eh. It's chicks—what are you gonna do? You gotta let 'em palaver like this till they get it outta their systems."

Jamie glared at us and took the phone into the kitchen. The last thing I heard was, "He did?" A pause. "I know, he does that with me *too*! The exact same *thing*! All the time!"

Just then the front door opened. Frankie and Hooch jumped up and barked, but it was merely my dad, so they wagged their tails at him and wiggled their way over to say hello.

He kicked off his shoes and came over to the sofa, looking tired as hell. He sat next to me. I tried to wave the foot odor away. Kelso got up and sat in the armchair.

Hooch, meanwhile, was sniffing my dad's discarded brogans; he *liked* the smell. Frankie went back to his bed.

Dad tossed a miniature videotape in my lap. "I got you your tape," he said. "So, when's supper?"

"Help yourself to whatever's in the fridge, Dad. Did you take a look at what's on it?"

"No, but the young couple—a nice pair of kids, Dan and Shannon—say they remember seeing something strange going on in the background. I could have looked at it, I suppose, but I wanted to bring it back as soon as possible." He patted me on the knee and said, "I'll think I'll go hit the head."

"Good," I said as he went toward the bathroom. "I got you some Gold Bond foot powder. It's on top of the toilet. I know you've been on your feet a lot. And thanks for finding the tape. We'll have the technical crew at the TV station look at it tonight." Then I got up and went to the kitchen, taking the tape with me.

I snatched the phone away from Jamie.

"Jack, what are you—"

"Wait," I said, then, "Hey, Kristin, what's goin' on?"

"Hello, Jack," she giggled, "I like your girlfriend."

"You mean my fiancée," I corrected her, "and, yeah, so do I. She's great, isn't she?" I smiled at Jamie. "Listen, I may need your expertise as a set designer tomorrow."

She laughed. "You want me to decorate your party?"

"Well, that would be nice, but—"

She kept laughing. "So what do you want, a luau theme with tiki lamps, or maybe a Texas barbecue motif?"

"Neither. I want you to help me collar a killer."

"Really? That sounds fabulous," she said. "What time do I show up? And what do I do with my stepdaughter? We're in Waterville. She's starting college here in the fall."

"Bring her along. I'll look forward to seeing you both. And come around noon. Here's Jamie." I gave her the phone.

She cupped her hand and said, "Bring *who* along?"

"Ask her yourself." I grabbed my keys.

"Jack, where are you going?"

"To take this videotape to the TV station," I said on my way to the door. "And then to go get Tipper. She's going to help us trap Maxwell. If he shows up tomorrow."

"Okay, but come back here first." She spoke into the phone, "Kristin, can you hang on a sec? Good."

I came back over to her. "What is it?"

"Just this." She put the phone down and grabbed me and kissed me, long and deep and hard and strong, with passion and tenderness, and hunger and surrender, and with what felt like a bit of eternity mixed in as well. I'd never been kissed like that before—by anyone—although until that moment I would have sworn that I *had* been. I would have also sworn that I'd kissed *her* like that, many times, but I guess I was wrong. I had never even come close, though I was eager now to relaunch my education in that area as soon—and on as many occasions—as possible. And, as she kissed me like that, I knew, suddenly, that I would be owned by that kiss—and owned by *her*—forever.

"Okay," she said lightly, almost casually, when she was through. Then she cradled my face for a moment with her right hand, looked deep in my eyes, and ran her thumb softly across my lower lip. "Don't be too long, honey. Okay?"

I stood there, trying to absorb what had just happened, then said, "You'll *be* here when I get back, though, right?"

"Oh, *yeah*," she smiled, "I'm not going *any*where." Then she gave me a light pat on the check, picked up the phone, and went back to her gabfest with my ex-girlfriend.

I don't think I'll ever understand women, I thought as I went out to the car. I got in, closed the door, and just sat there for the longest time, thinking about it. After a while I started the engine, but just sat some more, wondering if my lips would ever stop tingling, kind of hoping that they wouldn't.

43

I got up early to get the smoker going. I put the brisket in, then Tipper and I spent the morning running around, trying to get everything together, not just for the cookout but for trapping Ian Maxwell as well. After picking up groceries, renting folding chairs and tables, and all the rest, I rushed to get back to the kennel by noon to meet Kristin Downey. She wasn't there when I arrived, so I mopped some more marinade on the brisket, then began setting up the tables and chairs. I was also on the phone nonstop with the brass at the TV station, trying to get them to go along with my plan. It wasn't easy convincing them, and with good reason; it meant putting my father's life in danger, and maybe my own, plus it would be expensive, and there was no guarantee that Maxwell would take the bait.

In the middle of all this I was training Tipper to bark whenever I pulled a tennis ball out of my vest. The plan was to annoy the hell out of Maxwell and keep him off balance. She followed me wherever I went, and so I would stop occasionally, pull out a tennis ball, bark at her until she barked back, then throw the ball for her to chase. Pretty soon all I had to do was reach into one of my pockets in a certain way and she would immediately start barking. (Aunt Zita was going to *kill* me.)

Jamie, meanwhile, had work piling up at the hospital, so she'd spent the morning there, but got a call from the Governor around ten. He said he wanted to meet with her at one-thirty, if she could make it, so she stopped by my place for a pep talk and a quick bite to eat before driving up to Augusta.

"He's going to offer you Dr. Reiner's job," I said as I walked her to her car, with Tipper nipping at our heels.

"No, he isn't."

"Yes, he is. You'll be the next Chief Medical Examiner."

She shook her head. "Well, maybe acting chief, since Dr. Feeney is reaching retirement age, but—"

"You'll have to get new business cards printed up."

She laughed. "Jack, that's not going to happen. I'm far too young for the job."

"We'll see."

She clicked her doors open and I kissed her for luck, watched her drive away, then Tipper and I got back to work, me setting up the party, she barking at my pockets.

Dorianne Elliot came over around one. She owns a construction company in West Rockport and had volunteered to help with the "set decoration" that was to be designed by Kristin—if she ever showed up, that is, which she finally did around two-thirty, driving a silver 450SL. Dorianne was in the house at the time, helping Laura with some of the side dishes.

As Kristin got out of the car I noticed that she hadn't changed much in twenty years. Five-foot-five, blond hair and pretty brown eyes with long, light lashes (all hidden now behind Italian sunglasses), she had a rectangular face, quite lovely to look at, a high forehead, a small, straight nose, flat cheekbones, and a lush lower lip accentuated by a slight overbite and the fact that one of her front teeth crossed slightly on top of the other. She wore an above-the-knee floral print dress, which showed off her legs and had a nice southward dip in the bodice, treating me to the sight of a spray of freckles I'd been on intimate terms with years ago. I had the feeling she was wearing it to make me remember, fondly, her legs and her freckles.

We hugged and kissed hello (on the cheek), all this as her stepdaughter got out of the car. Then we spent a little time trying to get over how long it'd been since we'd seen each other and the like. To test Tipper, I reached in my pocket while we were talking, and she immediately started barking.

"What's her problem?" said Kristin.

"Oh, nothing," I said. "She's just a corgi."

She shrugged, shook her head, and then introduced me to her stepdaughter, Jennifer Vreeland, or "Jen," as she called her, a tall, mopey-looking girl of seventeen or eighteen. She had dirty blond hair, made even less pretty by the addition of pink and green hair coloring. She wore grubby jeans, a ripped T-shirt promoting some band or a bar or some type of product I was unfamiliar with, and big, black biker boots, with chrome clasps instead of laces. Her jewelry consisted of two huge silver rings, one in the shape of a skull, the other with a Celtic knot and cross motif, and earrings which involved more metal stuck through more holes in the skin than the human ear should be asked to put up with.

"Hey, where are all the dogs?" she said, smiling suddenly through her mopiness, and through a big wad of chewing gum. "Or do you just have this one little barkaholic?"

I liked her immediately—mopiness and all—and pointed her to the kennel building. "There's some more dogs inside."

Shyly, she said, "Okay if I go say hello to them?"

"Be my guest."

"Cool," she nodded. Then to Kristin, she said, "Later, Kris," and went over to the kennel.

"That's my stepdaughter," she sighed. "She misses her puppies. We've got three Dalmatians at home."

"Three Dalmatians? What, are you crazy?"

"No," she giggled, "but my husband is." (I liked *him* immediately too.) "So, Jack," she put a hand on my arm, "what kind of decorations did you have in mind, exactly?" I explained what I wanted, and she said, in a scolding, though not unpleasant tone, "It would've been nice to have a little more notice for a job like this, you know."

"Hey, I asked you to come at noon."

She crinkled her nose and gave me a look over the rims of her Fiorucci sunglasses. "I didn't mean two *hours* more, Jack," she said as if speaking to a child, "I meant something more like two *weeks*."

Dorianne came out of the house. Introductions were made and Kristin started pacing around the area between the house and the kennel building, looking the place over.

I noticed that the dogs didn't bark when Jen went into the kennel. Kristin noticed my lack of attention and said, "What is it?"

"Nothing. It's just that the dogs usually bark when strangers come inside the kennel."

She shook her head. "That girl has a special way with animals. It's uncanny. At any rate, I think we'll want to put the table center stage, here. And then over there, stage left . . ." She pointed to the back of the kennel, which was actually on her right. "I don't want to get too fancy here, but did that used to be a barn?"

"Yes it did."

"Good. We'll need some bales of hay and maybe some rusted farm implements scattered around. It wouldn't hurt to have some of that burlap netting they use for landscaping, to hide the camera crew. Plus we'll want a large mirror standing right next to the camera slot between the bales of hay. It would be nice if we could have a floodlight or two shining on it. I learned that trick from Lance Burton. Magic—it's all about where the audience's attention *isn't*." Then she pointed to the carriage house. "And then upstage, behind that window in the front door. No camouflage necessary. Notice how the light reflects back at you from this angle? No one can see inside." Then she pointed to the second story bathroom, on her left. "And stage right, up there, behind that window. It's high enough to be out of sight. And it wouldn't hurt to have a small camera planted directly overhead in a branch of the oak tree. Where are you putting the helicopter and satellite van?"

"The van will be behind the carriage house. They're going to land the chopper in Mrs. Murtaugh's driveway. She runs my grooming salon. I'll show you where it is."

"It doesn't matter..But we'll need more netting to hide them." She turned to Dorianne and said, "Are you just standing there for a reason?" Dorianne stared at her. There was a frozen moment. Finally, Kristin made an apologetic face and said, "I'm sorry. I'm used to dealing with lazy New York union slobs. I didn't mean to offen—"

"That's all right," Dorianne lied. "I just need to talk to Jack a minute before I go."

"Fine. But please hurry. We don't have much time."

Dorianne took me aside and told me she'd need some money for a couple of truck drivers, the bales of hay, the burlap nets, the mirror, and two or three workmen. I asked her how much she needed, and she told me and we went into the kennel building so I could write her a check. Jen was just leaving.

"Cool dogs," she said, cracking her gum.

"Yeah? How many dogs were there?"

"What?" she said defensively. "You think I stole one?"

"No," I laughed, "it's an innocent question. I just want to see if you were paying attention."

"Oh." She shrugged, thought about it, counting them in her head. "Twelve, I guess."

"Good. Can you tell me what breeds they are?"

"Probably. All except that silvery, Maltese-looking dog. I've never seen one of those before. Is she a mix?"

"No. She's a Löwchen. It's an unusual breed. What about the others?"

She told me the breeds of all the dogs inside the kennel and got them all right except for Cassie—whom she called an "amateur schnauzer" instead of a *mini*ature schnauzer, but I think she was just "riffing" when she said that.

"That's very good," I said, impressed.

"Cool. Do I get a prize?"

"No," I laughed, "but you've got a job if you want one. Your mom says you're starting college near here in the fall."

"She's my *step*-mom," she pointed out emphatically, then an amazed smile crept across her face. "You mean, you'd actually *pay* me to *work* here?"

"If you promise not to crack your gum when I'm around."

256 LEE CHARLES KELLEY

"I could do that." She took the gum out and threw it in the trash. "And I'd work here for *free*, you know."

"Yeah, I kind of figured. Anyway, I'm serious about the job, but only if your parents will let you work off-campus."

"I'll handle my parents. When can I start?"

I gave her a card. "Call me when you get settled in and know your class schedule and everything. If you want, you can work here nights. There isn't much to do then so you can just hang out with the dogs and do your homework."

"Wow, that's really great," she said, stuffing my card in the pocket of her jeans. "I'll call you in September."

After she left I sat down and wrote Dorianne a check.

She looked at it. "How long have you known me, Jack?"

"I don't know. A couple of years? Why?"

She waved her check at me. "Because my name is spelled with one n, not two!"

"Oh, sorry," I said, a little taken aback by her anger. "Do you want me to write you a new one?"

"No. Just spell it right the next time. Okay?" She went to the door, stopped, sighed, and turned to look at me. "I'm sorry. I just don't like your ex-girlfriend very much."

"Yeah, I don't know what that was all about."

"Oh, I do," she said. Then she went on to ask me a bunch of silly questions about my relationship with Kristin, when did we break up, who broke it off, why have we kept in touch over the years, does she know that I'm about to get married, has she met Jamie, is she on friendly terms with her, why did I offer her stepdaughter a job, and so on.

I kept answering, somewhat patiently, but finally said, "Doriane, what's with all these questions?"

She shrugged. "Look, this woman giggles when you *talk*, she touches your arm when she talks to *you*, she's showing off by bossing me around, she's pretending to like Jamie—it all adds up to one thing. She doesn't want you to get married."

I cracked up. "You've got to be kidding."

"Trust me. She probably isn't even aware of it herself. And it's not like she wants you back or anything. She just doesn't want Jamie to have you."

Just then Kristin walked in. The dogs started barking. Tipper ran back toward the kennels and joined the noise.

"Still here?" she said to Doriane.

There was another of those long frozen moments. I interrupted it by saying, "Um, Kristin, could you kind of watch your tone a little? Doriane is a very good friend of mine and you've been behaving like a real—"

"That's okay," Doriane said, "I was just leaving." She gave me a pointed look, walked out, and slammed the door.

I called Tipper and told the dogs to be quiet. They did. I was still at my desk. Kristin came behind the front counter and sat on top of it, right in front of me

I said, "I offered Jen a job, if that's okay with you."

She crossed her legs and watched my eyes as she did so. "She gets enough money from her father, but she's eighteen, so she's free to do whatever she wants. Within reason."

"Un-huh."

"What's that supposed to mean?"

"Nothing." I stood up.

She got off the desk, lost her balance briefly, or seemed to, which made her fall against me. As she did she put her arms around mine, looked me in the eyes, then kissed me, soft and warm on the lips.

Me? I just stood there.

She tried a little harder, then, when I still didn't respond, she said, "What's wrong with you?"

"What's wrong with *you*?"

"What? It's just a little kiss for old times' sake."

"No it isn't. I'm getting married. You're al*ready* married. *And* you're supposedly my fiancée's new best friend."

"Oh, face it, Jack. All men stray sooner or later."

"Not me."

"Especially you. You're not a hundred percent committed to Jamie, I can tell. I've got the radar for it."

"Well, your radar is off. Way off."

"No it's not. I'm telling you, sooner or later, Jack—"

"Fine. Can we do it later, then? Because—"

"I might not be around later." She gave me a look.

"Aw, shucks. I guess I'll miss out." I went to the door, turned back to look at her. "Did you really think . . . ?"

Doriane had been right. And I'd been right last night, after Jamie kissed me. I'll never understand women. Here I am, in a battle for my life, or at least a battle for my father's life, and I have to deal with *this* now? *Please!*

She tried to look dejected

I put my hand on the door.

She just stood there.

I said, "Are you coming or what?"

"Okay, fine. I'm coming." She came to the door.

"And don't try to pull anything else later on, okay?"

"Why would I try to pull anything?"

"What did you just do? *Not* try to pull something? Look, I hate to ask you this, but are you off your meds?"

She stared daggers at me. "Screw you."

"I just want to know how to handle the situation."

She put her hands up. "I made a mistake, okay? That's all. I apologize. Now are you satisfied?"

"Not really," I said, then held the door for her, tried to paste a smile on my face, and also tried not to notice how my hand was trembling as I held the door open.

Just then Lily Chow came up the steps. We backed up so as to not get run over. "Jack!" she said. "You've got to take a look at this videotape your father found!" She stopped and looked at us. "I'm sorry. Did I interrupt something?"

"No, but I'm glad you did."

She nodded, then did a kind of double take and shook her head. "Wait, that doesn't make any sense."

"I know. That's why I said it."

Then Kristin went off somewhere to stew and to find her stepdaughter. Lily and I went to the news van to look at the tape. We ran into Kelso on the way over.

"Hey, Jack," he said, "I couldn't get any info on where Maxwell was the day Sherry Maughn was murdered. But security logs showed that Paul Kemp was on the island all day."

"It's not enough. Maxwell's defense team will argue that Kemp doctored the records. And with Kemp's confession—"

"Wait," said Lily, "you guys think Maxwell killed the painter as well as her boyfriend?"

"That's our theory, yes."

"This is huge. Wait till you see the tape." The four of us (including Tipper) went up the hill to the van, which was parked on the county road above my property. Lily said, "I don't know if you've heard, but the DA has offered Maxwell a plea of Involuntary Manslaughter and he's agreed to take it but he hasn't allocuted yet. Once the DA sees this tape—"

"—he'll have to withdraw the plea offer?"

She nodded.

"By the way," I told Kelso, "I've got a little bit of a problem with my ex-girlfriend. She just tried to make out with me inside the kennel."

Kelso laughed. "It's the dogs," he said. "They're like babe magnets."

"It's not funny. And the worst part is, I don't know how I'm going to tell Jamie about this."

"Are you nuts?"

Lily said, "Are you crazy? You can't tell her."

"I have to."

"No, Jack," they both told me, almost in unison. "You can't tell her."

"Well, we'll see."

"Don't do it, Jack," Kelso said. "Just let it go."

We got up the hill. Lily opened the van door and we got inside with Jaime Gonzalves, who was manning the video recorder. I sat on a canvas folding stool. Tipper jumped up in my lap. (I guess she wanted to see herself on TV.)

"It's all cued up," Gonzalves said. He pressed a button, said, "The image has been digitally enhanced because most of what you see actually took place in the background. Now watch."

We saw Beeson swimming ashore, even though his wrists and ankles were bound with ropes. (Those Navy SEALs are good!) He took the ropes off, then Maxwell's boat appeared in frame. Maxwell could be seen near the railing with a mechanical device of some sort; fairly large yet handheld. He aimed it and there was a sudden flash of reddish-yellow light coming from the device. Beeson stumbled on the rocks, but got up. He was woozy, though, teetering and looking ready to fall over. Maxwell jumped over the side of his yacht and waded ashore. Beeson picked up a rock. There was a struggle. Beeson cracked Maxwell on the head and then fell down, face first. Maxwell leaned over the body and his yachting cap fell off. Just then the tennis ball rolled into frame. Maxwell looked up at the stairs leading to the backyard, picked up the tennis ball and put it in the dead man's hand, then waded back to the boat. Tipper appeared in the frame and started barking at him.

These weren't the best images, mind you. They had been cut together, between moments when Dan and Shannon—as my dad had called them—were videotaping each other, so there was kind of a herky-jerky quality to the editing. And Maxwell's face wasn't clear. He had his back to the camera until he began wading back to the boat. That moment was only captured on tape for less than a second.

"Can you run it back and freeze that shot?" I asked.

"It's already done. Let me find it." While he was doing that he said, "By the way, we enhanced that shot of Eddie Cole you wanted blown up."

"Yeah? And?"

He shook his head. "We sent it to the State Police Crime Lab. They have face recognition software? They couldn't get a conclusive match. It might be him, it might not."

Mostly to myself, I said, "He was probably on his way to the airport, to catch a plane to San Diego."

Gonzalves said, "Wait. Here it is."

The freeze-frame came on. It was still inconclusive. A good defense team could raise reasonable doubt that it wasn't Maxwell. But we had the hat and we had the DNA from his pipe. It was enough, I thought, to tie the two together.

Kelso disagreed. He'd been a prosecutor, and he thought it could be argued that the laser went off accidentally and that Maxwell only went ashore to help Beeson. Then, after he was hit on the head, he wasn't thinking clearly and that's why he planted the tennis ball and went back to the boat.

"You're right," I said, then told Jaime Gonzalves and Lily

Chow. "It looks like we still have to get him to confess to killing Sherry Maughn."

"And to get him to try and kill your father on camera," Kelso said.

44

"Two parties in one week, Jack," said Jamie, licking the barbecue sauce off her fingers, "I'm impressed. It seems like you're finally getting over your misanthropic tendencies. And I'm also impressed with this barbecued chicken of yours."

"Thanks, honey," I said, looking around for Kristin. "Your mother's been a big help. So have Jonas and my dad."

It was about five-thirty. I was in my apron, tending the grill, which was just in front of the carriage house. I'd put the charcoal in a bed of sand (for reasons that will become clear later). Dad and Jonas were over by the smoker, off to the left and back toward the hill that leads to the county road, chatting and keeping an eye on the brisket.

One of my reasons for hosting the bash was to get Jonas and my dad together, but they had little in common; or so it seemed until Dad brought up the subject of trout fishing in Maine, and Jonas lit up. They had now become inseparable.

Meanwhile, the place was fairly crowded. I'd set up folding chairs and card tables in the yard between the house and the kennel. There was a long wooden table near the grill, covered with butcher's paper, on top of which sat bowls of potato salad, corn on the cob, Laura's homemade biscuits, fresh butter, some chips and dips, along with some disposable cups, paper plates, plastic tableware, buns and condiments for the burgers and hot dogs, paper napkins, paper towels, and so on. There were also half a dozen plastic coolers littering the yard, full of bottles and cans of soda and beer.

The cars were parked in the driveway, the kennel parking area, and some on the rough grass between the gravel drive and the play yard. Latecomers had to park up on the county road and pass inspection by Deputies Quentin Peck and Mike de-Spain before being allowed entrée into the party.

I'd told Leon he could invite some of his friends over—as long as they didn't shoot off any firecrackers—so five or six high school kids showed up; a mix of boys and girls. I set up a special table for them on the other side of the carriage house— far away from the band (they had their own boom box and a bunch of hot new CDs)—and I stayed out of their way.

The rest of the guest list included some people from Aunt Zita's party—including Jonas, Laurie, and Tipper—a few of my clients, Jamie's friends and family, my kennel staff, and some colleagues from the TV station (including Lily Chow, Brianne O'Leary, Mike Brooks, Donna Devon, and three hidden camera crews), plus Kristin Downey and her stepdaughter, Jen. Kristin was around somewhere looking to cause trouble, I just knew it. Jen was hanging out with Leon and his crew. I'd also invited Dr. Liu but he was already busy working on another case.

I'd even tracked down my jailhouse roommate, Gavin, and had invited him and his girlfriend Darcy. I guess I felt guilty about impersonating an "angel of the Lord" while he was still drunk and susceptible to suggestion. He kind of shyly shook my hand and apologized for his behavior. I apologized for mine. Then he told me he and Darcy were getting married in Christ, whatever that meant, and I lied to him some more, I'm afraid, and told him I was very happy for the two of them and that I was sure it would be a marriage made in heaven, all the time secretly wondering how many months it would be before they were screaming at each other on the Jerry Springer show.

Otis Barnes and Lou Kelso were also enjoying the festivities and celebrating the fact that, at sixty years old, Otis had been getting job offers from most of the major networks and from *Time* magazine. Kelso had no personal reason for celebrating, but he doesn't need one.

Tipper was still at my heels the whole time, just as she'd been since I'd picked her up at Aunt Zita's the night before. I was still teasing her with hidden tennis balls, practicing. Frankie and Hooch, meanwhile, were in "barbecue quarantine" inside the house. They were trained not to beg, but I didn't trust my party guests not to offer them bits of food when my back was turned.

Mixed in with the rest of the partygoers were a dozen state troopers and Rockland County Sheriff's deputies, all dressed in plainclothes, all eating barbecued chicken, and all keeping a careful and watchful eye on my old man. Most of them had little or no experience with an operation of this kind, so it wasn't too hard to catch them from time to time talking into their sleeves or pressing two fingers a little too tightly against an earpiece.

Farrell Woods showed up sans Tulips. The poor girl didn't feel steady enough yet in her recovery, he told me, to be around people who were getting high on alcohol. Plus she had some crazy project she was working on, trying to prove that the canine pack is a self-emergent system.

"Probably your idea, huh, Jackie boy? And what the hell is tensor calculus?"

I told him I had no idea. That's why I needed her help.

The Blue D'Arts were set up on the side porch, stage right of the kitchen door (which means they were on the left). They were composed of bass, drums, keyboards, and a guitarist who also doubled on chromatic harmonica, fiddle, and mandolin. They played a kind of folk/swing music. (Kelso loved them—they knew everything from Joe Venuti to Townes Van Zandt.) They were singing an original number, "Everybody's Havin' Fun but Me," which was appropriate, because I was going nuts trying to juggle Kristin, the TV people, and the food.

"Have you heard from Sheriff Flynn?" I asked Jamie.

"Nothing so far. Sinclair has some State Police boats watching his island. Are you sure he'll come?"

I laughed. "Who knows? I played him as best I could but I ain't no Heifetz. Hell, I ain't even no Dennis McGregor."

"Who's Dennis McGregor?" asked Brianne O'Leary, coming over with an empty plate.

I tilted my head toward the fiddle player with the band. "He's the tall, bald guy in the band."

"They're probably *all* bald under those hats."

I laughed. "Okay, well, he's the fiddle player. Anyway, I was just saying; I'm not a Jascha Heifetz or a Dennis Mc—"

"Being modest again? I told you it's not like you. And he'd *better* come or we've wasted a lot of money here today."

"I know. It's nerve-wracking."

"Ah, poor little doodle," Jamie said, stroking my arm. "Are your nerves wracked?"

"Yeah, they're pretty wracked."

She leaned close and whispered in my ear, "I can unwrack them for you later, if you want."

"Yeah?"

"Oh, yeah. I'll pour you a little wine, then let you ply your wiles on me. That should do it."

"It usually does."

"Look," Brianne said, "can I get some chicken?"

Just then Jamie's cell phone did its Mozart prelude; she flipped it open and said, "Yes? Okay, I'll tell him." She flipped it shut and smiled at me. "Ian Maxwell has just left his island in one of his choppers. He's flying solo, headed in this direction. He should be here in about an hour."

"Good. Can you watch the grill while I make a last minute check on everything? And in case I didn't congratulate you yet on the job offer from the Governor, congratulations."

"Thanks. For the fourteenth time. And I told you, I still don't know if I'm going to take it."

I handed her my apron and gave her a kiss. "I told you he'd make you the new Chief ME. And whatever you decide is fine with me." I started to go.

"Let me come with you, Jack," said Kristin, appearing out of nowhere and taking my arm. "I haven't had a minute alone with you this whole time."

"I know," I said pointedly, "there's a *reason* for that."

"Oh, knock it off, Jack," Jamie said. "I keep telling you, I'm not jealous. Besides, Kristin and I are good friends now."

"Is that right," I said skeptically. "In that case, why don't the two of you watch the grill together and let me take care of some things on my own?"

"Jack," said Jamie, "what's the matter with you?"

"Nothing. It's just crunch time, that's all."

I gave her a kiss then I went over to see my dad, alone. Laura had joined him and Jonas by the smoker. I gave Dad his hearing aid and said, "You need to start wearing this, Dad."

"Oh, that's right." He tried to put it in his ear but couldn't get it to go in properly.

Laura said, "Let me help you, John." He gave her the hearing aid, while I gave her a look. She shrugged as she helped him put it in. "I can't very well call him Jack, can I?"

"I *like* her calling me John," said my dad.

"Okay," I said, with a cavalier shrug. "It just sounds weird to me, that's all."

Laura got the hearing aid in. "There, that's just fine."

Jonas laughed and patted Dad on the back. "I guess we're getting to be a couple of old codgers."

"Did you say you're rooting for a couple of Dodgers?"

"No," shouted Jonas, "Codgers. I'm a Red Sox fan."

An hour later Ian Maxwell arrived by helicopter.

45

The blades and the rotor cut the air to shreds. Dust flew. I closed the cover on the grill. The cups and napkins blew everywhere. Paper plates corkscrewed in the air and zoomed around like crazy, fledgling Frisbees. People shielded their eyes. Some cursed in anger, some laughed in amazement. Shooting gravel cracked a windshield or two. It was not an event that was easily ignored.

The young kids ran toward the play yard, shouting and laughing and pointing up in the air. Tipper and I came running over with them. Tipper was barking like crazy.

Then the chopper got closer to the ground and hovered for a moment, for just that one magic, unbelievable snapshot in time when you see a huge hunk of metal and glass suspended just a few feet off the ground and you wonder—if you've never seen it happen before, and maybe even if you *have*—how the hell does something that heavy just float in the air like that? And then it slowly touches down, bounces once or twice, the engines are cut off, and the roar and the buzz subside.

Lily Chow and her crew were shooting this, at my request. We all heard the sound of a loudspeaker coming from the chopper, but nobody could understand what was being said. Finally, when the blades stopped buzzing, we heard a voice saying, "Turn off those cameras!" It was Maxwell. "I mean it! Turn off those cameras now!"

Lily looked at me. I made a show of shrugging and nodding. She told the crew to put down their equipment, and they did, then stepped away. Tipper barked at the chopper.

As Maxwell got out, Peck and deSpain came down, dressed in their uniforms. Maxwell was wearing cargo shorts, running shoes, a Hawaiian shirt, and a baseball cap. The two deputies and Tipper and I met him at the gate.

"Good," he said easily to the deputies. "You want to frisk me? Go right ahead. You won't find anything."

He was right. They found nothing except his keys, his wallet, some folding money and a little pocket change. Not even a ballpoint pen, which would have been my first guess as to how he had planned to sneak the poison into the party.

I was stumped. Maybe he wasn't going to try anything today. Maybe he'd wait until it was safe, like six months from now, after he'd done his time in a federal country club on the Involuntary Manslaughter charge. I didn't think so but I couldn't be sure. So where was the poison hidden? It had to be poison, right? He had no technogadgets on him. He'd already bragged to me that that's how he was going to do it—a colorless, odorless toxin. So where was it? Had he planted it somewhere on the premises the night before, planning to casually and surreptitiously pluck it from the bushes or the play yard fence? Maybe he had a strip of celluloid hidden in his shoelaces and tipped with curare. He was in cahoots with the CIA, maybe he had a hollow tooth. Maybe I was being overly cautious. He wouldn't try anything with all these people around. He'd wait, bide his time, do it later.

Relaxed now, I reached into my pocket as if grabbing a tennis ball. Tipper barked and I said, "So, Your Evil Highness, you decided to grace us with your presence."

"What's with that dog?" he said.

"Tipper? I don't think she likes you."

He shook his head. "I told you I don't like dogs," he said, and began walking up the hill.

We waded through the crowd that had gathered around the gate, mostly kids, though a few grown-ups had come to gawk as well. Maxwell was on his best behavior, smiling warmly and exuding charm. He didn't have a care in the world, though he was annoyed that Tipper wouldn't stop barking at him.

I gave a nod to Dennis McGregor and the band stopped playing. I wanted a clear recording on the hidden mic.

My dad was waiting at our prearranged table. I offered Maxwell a seat across from the old man. He took it and I sat on the other side.

"I'm glad you changed your mind about killing my dad," I said, just loud enough for the mic to pick it up.

"Who said I changed my mind?" He smiled his evil smile.

"Well, at least I know you won't try anything here with all these people around. Tipper, quiet." She shushed.

"That sounds like a challenge."

"Well, I sure *hope* you don't kill me," says my dad. "It may not be much, but it's my *life*."

"Don't blame *me*," Maxwell said, like a true narcissist. (They're never to blame for anything—if things go wrong, it's always someone else's fault.) "I warned sonny boy here not to talk to Ortiz, but he went ahead anyway. If you die—or I should say, *when* you die—it'll be no one's fault but his."

Laura Cutter came over with three bottles of beer and three plastic cups. She popped the top on one of the beers and began pouring it into a cup, saying, "The brisket turned out just perfect, Jack. We're letting it rest a bit, though, before serving it."

"That's not necessary. It's slow smoked, not roasted. You can serve it right away."

"Good, we will, then. Three orders here?" I looked at my dining companions. They both nodded. "Three it is," said Laura, opening another beer.

My dad said, "No cup for me, Laura. I'll drink mine right out of the bottle, if you don't mind." He gave Maxwell a look. "I don't trust this guy."

"Dad, he's not going to poison your beer."

"What? I didn't hear you."

"Turn up your hearing aid."

"What?"

To Maxwell, I said, "His battery's a little low. In more ways than one." To Laura, I said, "We'll drink ours from the bottle, thanks."

"Fine. I'll get your food," she said, and left.

My cell phone, which was sitting on the table, rang. I reached for it, knocked it off, and it fell on the grass. My father and I both reached down for it, bumping heads.

"Ow! Dad, let me get it."

"What? What did you say?"

I finally got ahold of the phone, we both sat up, I answered it and said, "No, you've got the wrong number," then looked at Maxwell. "I inherited someone's old cell phone number. I get these kinds of calls all the time. I probably shouldn't have even brought it to the party, you know?"

He just shrugged and smiled his evil smile.

Over his shoulder I saw Kelso. He nodded casually, then walked drunkenly over to us, sloshing his Kentucky lemonade as he walked. "Hey, aren't you Ian Maxwell, the murder-rer?"

Maxwell didn't turn to look. He kept his eyes glued on mine and said, "Could you tell your, um, drunk friend to leave me alone?"

"Hey, I'm talking to you," Kelso said, tapping him on the shoulder. "I'm right here." He stumbled, and spilled his drink all over Maxwell's shirt and onto his lap.

I reached in my pocket. Tipper barked.

Maxwell looked down at the mess then stood up and shook his head. He was steamed.

"I'm sorry," I said, standing up. I handed him some napkins while reaching into my vest pocket again. Tipper barked again. To Kelso, I said, "Could you go somewhere else, where you're not such a menace?"

"Fine," he said, grumbling and stumbling away. "I'm such a menace I should disappear. It's what I'm good at."

I shrugged an apology at Maxwell then told Tipper to be quiet and she shushed.

My dad sipped his beer.

I sat back down and said, "Just one thing puzzles me, still. Why did you kill Sherry Maughn?"

"Me?" he said, sitting back down and watching my dad drink. "I didn't. Paul Kemp did. He's even confessed."

"Paul Kemp was on the island all day. You weren't."

"Wasn't I?"

"No, you were out that morning. Someone saw you getting on a boat in Rockport Harbor, just after the murder took place." (This was a lie—we had no eyewitness.)

"A case of mistaken identity, I'm sure."

I raised my hand and motioned to Brianne O'Leary. "And then there's the videotape of Beeson's murder."

"Videotape? You must be kidding me."

"No, a young couple were videotaping themselves just a stone's throw from the island. They caught you and Beeson in the background of their shots." Brianne brought over a camcorder, the kind with a viewing screen, set it down in front of Maxwell, and pressed play.

He watched it.

"That doesn't look like involuntary manslaughter to me," I said, when it was over.

Maxwell shook his head. "Fine. If the DA wants to take it to trial, we'll see what a jury says. I'll get a not guilty verdict. You can't even be sure it's me on the tape."

"We can, though. We have your DNA on the yachting cap. And my industrious fiancée has a sample to test it against."

"That's impossible. I never gave her permission to take my DNA."

"She doesn't need it. She was acting as a private citizen. She got it from a pipe you were smoking the other day."

Jamie walked over with a file folder, came around behind Maxwell and laid the folder on the table in front of him. "I had the lab run both samples—using a DNA testing machine you invented, by the way—and they're a perfect match." Then she took his hat off, showing the bandage on his head. "And then, there's this wound on your head. Exactly where Beeson struck you with a rock. I think a jury will be convinced that it's you on the videotape."

"If it was," he smiled, taking the hat from her and putting it back on, "I don't remember it. I guess I must have sustained a concussion when I was attacked."

"Yeah, that makes sense," I said. "Thanks, Dr. Cutter." She took her file folder and walked away. "But I was noticing how you threw that rock in the water. It's odd."

"I don't know why you say it's odd. Perhaps I was disoriented from the blow to my head."

"You were feeling a little loopy." I reached for my pocket again. Tipper barked again.

"Perhaps. I don't know. I don't remember, you see, so I couldn't possibly tell you why I did that."

"Yeah, I'm not interested in *why* you threw the rock, though. I'm interested in *how* you threw it. And where."

"I'm not following you." He looked down at the dog. "She's really starting to annoy me."

"That's because she saw you kill Gordon Beeson."

"Oh, that's just ridiculous."

"I wouldn't be so sure." I told Tipper to shush and she did. "Dogs can be very sensitive to things like that. And as for the rock, it's the trajectory of the throw that interests me. You probably threw the .22 you killed Sherry Maughn with in just about the same way."

"Is that right?" He laughed.

"The ocean hides many mysteries. You said so yourself. So the State Police have got some divers down looking for that gun now in Rockport Harbor. They're looking at the way you threw that rock on the videotape to determine the possible trajectory of the murder weapon. And when they find it, I'm betting they'll find your fingerprints all over it."

"How do you know I didn't toss it off the cabin cruiser I was supposedly seen on?"

"Did I say it was a cabin cruiser?"

"I'm pretty sure you did."

"No, I just said it was a boat, not a cabin cruiser."

"It doesn't matter. It wasn't me."

"Besides, you wouldn't have taken the gun with you to the boat. The sooner the better—isn't that your motto? You like to get things over with. You'd have tossed it right away."

"You seem to think you know a lot about my personality."

I shrugged. "I used to do a little profiling. I guess old habits die hard."

He shook his head. "Anyway, even if they *do* find the gun, it won't have *any* fingerprints on it because of the saltwater. It will have washed them off. The ocean hides many mysteries, remember?"

"Oh, they'll find your prints all right. They may be hard to trace, but they'll be found. They use a technique nowadays called VMD."

"I think I've heard of it."

"Yeah, it stands for Vacuum Metal Deposition. It's used on items that have been submerged in water. So, don't worry, they'll find them. Just as soon as they find that gun."

He shook his head and sighed patiently. "You know, now that I think about it, I, um, sort of recall Paul Kemp showing me a small caliber handgun sometime last week. I may have handled it while I looked at it. So, if they find a gun in Rockport Harbor with my fingerprints, it doesn't necessarily mean that I shot anyone with it, now does it?"

"You've got an answer for everything, don't you?"

"Well, I'd love to stay and sample your cooking, but I really should go home and change out of these bourbon-soaked clothes." He stood up. "I don't suppose you'll invite me to the funeral, will you?"

"Whose funeral is that?" I said dumbly.

"Your father's. His time has just about come." He even looked at his watch, the bastard.

"Don't tell me you're still thinking of killing him."

"Oh, I already have." He grinned. "And you'll never be able to prove it. Just like you'll never be able to prove—"

Jack Sr. grabbed his throat. Something was happening in his eyes. He looked at me, then at Maxwell. "You sonovabitch," he said to Maxwell, then fell out of his chair onto the grass and lay motionless.

I stood there with my mouth hanging open then said weakly, "A doctor. We need a doctor." I got my voice back and yelled, "I need a doctor over here, *now*!"

"It's too late for that," said Maxwell, grinning.

Jamie came running over. "Jack, what is it?"

I pointed to Jack, Sr., lying in the grass, then to Maxwell. "He killed my father."

"Oh, Jack, no!" She knelt next to my father.

"Don't look at me," Maxwell said, all innocent. "I was searched when I got here, remember? How could *I* have killed him?"

Quentin Peck and Mike deSpain came over. "What's going on?" Quent said.

Jamie looked up and said, "It's a false alarm. He's fine." She helped my father to his feet.

"That was kind of fun," Dad said.

Jamie took a handkerchief and a plastic evidence bottle from her pocketbook. (She calls it a pocketbook, I call it a shoulder bag.) She picked up *my* bottle, then poured the beer into the evidence bottle.

Maxwell was nonplussed. "What . . . what are you doing?"

"Oh," I said, "we switched bottles when you weren't looking. Remember? When my friend spilled his drink on you? My father switched my beer bottle with the one you tampered with. So the bottle Jamie is collecting as evidence has the poison, or whatever you used to try to kill my father, still inside, mixed with the beer. And you, Your Evil Highness, have been caught on camera administering said substance in said bottle. In fact, you've been caught on *four* cameras."

I pointed to the camera up in the branches of the oak tree, the one in the upstairs bathroom, the one in the carriage house, and the one Kristin had hidden artfully behind the bales of hay by the kennel.

"You sonovabitch." His eyes were blazing. He had the face of a murderer. I hoped the cameras were getting a good shot of that look. "You recorded all this?"

"Even better," I said. "It's being broadcast live. There's a satellite truck hidden behind the carriage house. You're on network TV. Come to think of it, you're probably being seen all over the world—CNN, Al Jazeera, who knows?"

Quentin Peck came forward with a pair of handcuffs. "Ian

Maxwell, you're under arrest for the murders of Hugh Gardner and Sherry Maughn, and the attempted murder of John Field."

In total shock, Maxwell glared at me for a moment, and then, before they could put the cuffs on him, he ran for it.

Peck and deSpain drew their weapons and shouted, "Halt! Stop or I'll shoot!" and the like, but he ran as hard as he could toward the play yard and his chopper. Meanwhile they *couldn't* shoot because some of the kids were still down there gaping at the fascinating machine, poking the toes of their tennis shoes into the chain link to get higher up for a better angle for gawking.

When Peck and deSpain saw this, they gave chase on foot, but Maxwell was too fast. He got there well ahead of them.

Brianne O'Leary, though, was already on her handheld radio talking to Mike Brooks, so before Maxwell even got the door closed on his copter we heard the sound of rotors and whirling blades coming from Mrs. Murtaugh's house.

Maxwell's chopper lifted into the air. Quent, on the other side of the fence now, got a couple of rounds off, one of them cracking the side window, another putting a hole in a fuel tank.

Maxwell kept rising up, but his gasoline (or whatever kind of fuel they use) was dripping all over the place. Then, when he got high enough over the trees and the power lines, he took off to the southeast.

Mike Brooks banked his chopper to the right and went after him in hot pursuit.

Everyone was standing, craning their necks, trying to see what was happening. And then behind me, from the porch, a guy grabbed one of the Blue D'Arts' microphones and said, "It's on TV!" There was a squeal of feedback as he said this. We all turned to look. The feedback kept squealing, but he kept talking. "They're showing the whole thing live! You've gotta come see this!"

Suddenly, everyone at the party went into phase transition and ran inside the house.

Me? I sat back down, put my hand on my dad's knee and said, "Nice work, Dad."

"What's that, sonny? I can't hear you."

I laughed. "You can take your hearing aid out now."

"Ah, I was just having fun. I can't believe he actually tried to kill me." He gave me a broad grin and put his hand on my shoulder. "But you had his every move covered, didn't ya, Jackie boy? And him a dangerous killer."

I shook my head. "I once worked with a Chihuahua named Tiki who was a lot more dangerous than Ian Maxwell."

Jamie came over. "Jack, aren't you coming?"

"Where?"

"Inside to watch the helicopter chase!"

I looked down at the watch I wasn't wearing and said, "You know, I would, honey, but it's almost seven o'clock."

She looked at the watch she actually *was* wearing. "Okay. What happens at seven?"

"That's when the dogs get exercised and fed."

"You mean, you don't care what happens next?"

"Me? Not particularly. I already did my part."

"But what if he gets away?"

I stood up. "It doesn't matter. He's already cooked. In fact, I'd say he's been fricasseed, whatever that is."

She shook her head at me like I was crazy. "Well, I don't know about you, but I want to find out what happens."

"That's fine, honey. You can go ahead." I turned toward the kennel. "But I've got dogs to take care of."

"Jack!" She sighed and turned to go up to the house.

Leon and Jen came over, with Magee following them. Leon was kind of following Jen, a bit like a puppy dog himself.

Jen said, "Can we come with you and play with the doggies?"

"Don't you want to watch the helicopter chase?"

Jen wrinkled her nose and said, "No, that's so bogus."

Leon said, "Two white men in helicopters? Nah, I don't think so." He didn't mean it, and Jen and I both knew it. He looked back toward the carriage house, where his own TV sat waiting for him. We caught him looking and he said, "Well, yeah, you know, unless one of 'em blows up or something."

"You have got so much to learn," Jen said, as if she had just appointed herself his teacher.

He kind of shrugged shyly. He had such a hard teenage crush on her.

"Jack!" Jamie called from the porch, letting Frankie and Hooch out in the process. "Come inside! They're flying over Rockport Harbor now!"

Tipper raced up to the house to meet the bigger dogs.

"That's fine, honey. Let me know how it all turns out!"

She shook her head at me and went inside.

Then Leon, Jen, and I (along with Tipper, Frankie, and Hooch) all went to the kennel to get the rest of the dogs.

A little while later, while the animals were all running around the play yard, nipping and feinting and play biting and such, we heard some loud gasps of amazement and then some horrified screams coming from inside the house.

We all stopped what we were doing—the dogs included—but then the moment passed and we all went back to playing again.

Epilogue

After the party was over and most of the guests had gone home, Farrell Woods and I collected the leftover sand and ashes from the grill, broke into the funeral home where Jill's cremated body was being held, waiting for her relatives to come from Michigan to pick it up, and traded them for Jill's remains—ashes for ashes, sand for sand. (To the untrained eye cremated human remains look like a mixture of sand and ashes, which is why, at the cookout, I'd put the charcoal in a bed of sand.) We felt a little bad about the fact that her family would be keeping the residue from my barbecue in an urn on the mantel while Jill would actually be resting peacefully in the waters of Camden Harbor, but we knew she would've wanted it this way.

We drove down to the docks, and stood around, kind of dumbly, wondering what to do.

Woods said, "I guess we just throw 'em in the water?"

"Yeah. Maybe I should quote the Twenty-third Psalm."

He gave me a surprised look.

"Catholic school," I explained.

So I spoke the words of the psalm and we scattered her ashes on the saltwater of Camden Harbor and bid our last farewell.

As for Ian Maxwell and the famous helicopter chase, by now nearly everyone in the world has seen the footage at least a dozen times, so I shouldn't even mention it except to say that it was a good thing the carnival was still closed for repairs that evening, because when Maxwell ran out of fuel, eventually lost control, and then crashed into the Ferris wheel, well, a lot of people could have been hurt otherwise. As it was, the only one injured was Maxwell himself, who, sad to say (or maybe *not* so sad), didn't survive the crash.

If it had been a movie, there would have been a huge fireball a second after the impact. But since Maxwell's fuel tanks were empty, there was no explosion, just a lot of tangled metal. And of course, the impact knocked the Ferris wheel over, sending it crashing onto the other rides in a kind of slow motion chain reaction. Oh, it made a spectacular scene, no question. And they replayed it on the news over and over and over. In *super* slow-mo, digitally enhanced, the whole deal.

Leon liked it, even without the explosions.

There was also videotape of Maxwell playing with the bill of his baseball cap, like a spitball pitcher, and then a moment later reaching his hand over my father's beer bottle while Dad and I were fumbling for the cell phone I'd dropped "accidentally." When the tape was enhanced and played in slow motion, you could see him dropping a tiny pellet into the beer.

My dad and Jonas and I took off up north the next day, and spent the weekend trout fishing—just the three of us. When we got back there were dozens of calls waiting for me on my office answering machine; people were asking me to do TV interviews, offering me job opportunities in broadcasting, and even some publishing deals. Those were the only calls I returned, but since they wanted me to write about the Maxwell case, and I wanted to write about dogs, I turned them down.

I took Dad to the airport and saw him off, then stopped at the TV station to help out with the editing on Leon's television debut. Him and Magee. It turned out great. Magee now had a killer recall. He would turn on a dime while running full speed and then come running back even faster than he'd been running before. Now, *that's* great TV.

As for Kelso, after the cookout he got a call from Dr. Lunch. There was a big break in the Sebastian Video case, the one that had got him a jail sentence. Kelso now had the chance to completely vindicate himself and bring closure to that chapter in his life. He flew back to New York that night to check out the lead, with a promise to me that he'd also check himself into a rehab clinic in Connecticut when he was done. (He tells this story better than I do, so I'll just go on:)

Detective Sinclair called during the week to tell me that the State Police had followed several leads regarding Eddie Cole and the idea I'd given them earlier that he might be hiding out in Portland, but none of them panned out. Cole was still at large. I suggested that he contact the authorities in San Diego; that Cole might be hiding out there.

For some reason, Kristin Downey stayed in Waterville that whole week. I didn't realize it took so much time and money to get a kid enrolled in college these days. But it wasn't just the tuition and books, apparently; there was housing to consider (campus or off-campus), plus a telephone hookup, an AOL account, cable TV, some new clothes, and Kristin wanted to buy Jen a car—something nice, like a Thunderbird convertible. The girl opted for a used, rust-red International Harvester pickup, which made me like her even more than I already did.

She spent her spare time at the kennel, hanging out with Leon and the dogs. Frankie was her favorite, and he was totally enamored of her. Speaking of which, Leon was always starry-eyed around her, too, which she seemed to find both amusing and endearing. As for myself, I was looking forward to having her come to work for me once school started.

A week after the cookout and the helicopter chase, Jamie and I were on the roof, listening to Tierney Sutton's *Blue in Green*, eating homemade ice cream and getting buzzed—but not bit, thanks to insect repellent—by dozens of mosquitoes. We were also discussing whether we should move the wedding back to February now that she was both Chief State Medical Examiner and the head of pathology at Rockland Memorial Hospital.

I still hadn't told her about that kiss in the kennel. In fact, I was just working up to it as we sat on the roof, discussing our wedding plans.

"It's nice sitting up here," Jamie said. "And this music is as delicious as your homemade ice cream."

"Isn't it? Hey, we should have Doriane build a terrace so we can be more comfortable when we hang out like this."

"You know what I was thinking? What if we were to expand the master bedroom and bathroom?" She looked at me. "Or am I not supposed to talk about that with you?"

"No, that's fine, honey. I think it's a great idea."

"But you said guys don't like to talk about—"

"No, it's re*decorat*ing we don't like to talk about. We *love* to talk about re*model*ing."

She shook her head. "I don't think I'll ever understand you, you know that? Not completely, anyway."

"I hope not. Just like I hope I never understand you completely." She asked me to explain, and I did. "Because if I did, then things would get boring. No, I'm hoping to spend the rest of my life getting to know you, sweetheart."

"Ah, Jack," she said, and kissed me.

"And I'll tell you something *else* I hope."

"What?"

"That this whole Ian Maxwell debacle is the last murder case I ever have to solve. It was a doozy."

Jamie's eyes twinkled as she said, "Is that more wishful thinking on your part, Jack, or do you really mean it?"

"That's not fair. It isn't like I didn't mean it the last time and the time before that. It's just that things always seem to come up, and you and I are the only people around with enough sense to set them right."

She sighed. "That's true."

We finished our ice cream and I was about to tell her about Kristin's kiss when Kristin herself drove up in her silver Mercedes. She jumped out of the car and ran toward the front door, frantic and all wound up about something.

"Kristin," I called, "we're up here."

She craned her neck to look up at us. "Oh, there you are." She sighed. "Thank god, Jack. I need your help."

"What is it?"

"It's Jen," she said. "She's gone. I'm worried she may have been kidnapped. You've *got* to help me *find* her."

I looked at Jamie. She smiled and shook her head knowingly. "Go, *go!*" she said.

I kissed her and said to Kristin, "I'll be right down!"

When I got to the window, Jamie said, "Jack?" and I turned to her. "Maybe solving crimes is just your area."

"No, it's not," I said, a little peeved. "Dogs are my area." I climbed through the window and thought of Jen—that funny, mopey girl I really liked, who was now God-knows-where. I turned back and smiled at Jamie. "Well," I said, "I guess it's possible to have more than one area."

She laughed and nodded.

"Are you coming?" I said.

"You go. I'll be down in a minute." She looked around, trying to imagine how the terrace was going to look once we got it built. "I just need a little more time to figure out where I'm going to put all the sconces."

Author's Note

As always, the dog training techniques and philosophies Jack espouses are not just my own, but are based in large part (in fact, almost exclusively) on the ideas of Kevin Behan, found most notably in his book *Natural Dog Training*, which, as of this writing, is available online from Ex Libris. Other ideas come from a number of articles on Kevin's Web site: NaturalDogTraining.com, and from private conversations Kevin and I have had about dogs and training over the years.

I've read quite a library full of books, worked with trainers from different fields, and tested a lot of different methods and techniques. I've found that none of them works as well as *Natural Dog Training*, pure and simple. It is the best and most complete dog training system there is.

However, the idea that the pack is a self-emergent system is, as far as I know, mine and mine alone (at least so far).

The idea that the pack becomes a coherent system (like the light waves in a laser) when hunting large prey is also, as far as I know, mine exclusively, although Kevin has expressed to me the idea that when canines hunt they're "in phase." And in *Natural Dog Training* he tells his readers to tune into "the dog's wavelength." Both these ideas suggest a state of coherence, and both were instrumental in my hypothesis that dogs are capable of entering a coherent state, emotionally.

At the time I finished writing this book (September, 2003),

Jack's idea about finding "the binary code to unlock the secrets of all canine behavior" was just a whimsical sidelight to the main action, and was, in my mind, just a novelistic fantasy. However, since then I've discovered that research is currently being done at Yale with "feral robotic dogs," who've been programmed to "sniff out" environmental toxins by working together as a "pack."

The focus and intent of the research is not to mimic or recreate the complexity of actual pack behavior, but early results show promise that a comprehensive computer model of canine behavior *can* eventually be achieved.

Other researchers, in the fields of complexity, systems dynamics, chaos theory, and emergence, have also been experimenting with complex social dynamics, and more data about how the pack *really* operates may well be on its way. This suggests that the imminent downfall of the alpha theory and that Jack's fantasy about finding "the binary code to all canine behavior" may one day become a scientific reality!

You can tell me I'm nuts, tell me I'm brilliant, or just plain e-mail me at: kelleymethod@aol.com, or you can log on to my Web site at: LeeCharlesKelley.com.

Lou Kelso would like to hear from anyone who knows the origins of iron port. You can contact him at: LouisKelso@aol.com.

(Oh, yeah, and the Blue D'Arts are a real band. They're from Sisters, Oregon!)

Thanks for reading my book! See ya next time!

Recommended Reading

Natural Dog Training by Kevin Behan. Originally published by William Morrow and Co. (1993). Now available from Ex Libris. The best book ever written about dogs.

Dogs: A New Understanding of Canine Origin, Behavior, and Evolution by Raymond and Lorna Coppinger, University of Chicago Press (Trade, October 2002). Ray Coppinger believes, as Jack and I do, that the alpha theory is illogical and that training practices based on it can be harmful to dogs.

Play Training Your Dog by Patricia Gail Burnham, St. Martin's Press (1986). Shows the importance of playing tug-of-war and teaching a dog to jump up on command.

Dogs that Know when Their Owners Are Coming Home: And Other Unexplained Powers of Animals by Rupert Sheldrake, Three Rivers Press (2000). Posits the idea that dogs may be telepathic.

Shutzhund Theory and Training Methods by Susan Barwig and Stewart Hilliard, John Wiley and Sons (1991). The basic principles of shutzhund, as laid down by Max von Stephanitz roughly a hundred years ago, long before the dog training world was infected by the myth of alpha, still hold true.

The following books are not about dogs or canine behavior, per se, but reflect a paradigm shift in scientific thinking that may soon have a strong impact and reshape our current understanding about how dogs and wolves think and operate.

Emergence by Steven Johnson, Scribners's (2001). This book has nothing to do with dogs but may provide thoughtful readers a new way of looking at pack behavior.

Swarm Intelligence by Russell Eberhart, Yuhui Shi, and James Kennedy, Morgan Kaufmann (2001). Describes a new model of social intelligence and learning adaptability, which may help create a new mindset about canine behavior and pack social dynamics in many thoughtful dog owners.

The Evolution of Cooperation by Robert Axelrod, Basic Books; Reprint edition (1985). Shows how cooperation, the fundamental aspect of the canine pack instinct, is necessary and valuable in the natural world.

Coming soon!

Eye of the Needle: For the first time in trade paperback, comes one of legendary suspense author **Ken Follett's** most compelling classics.
0-06-074815-X • On Sale January 2005

More Than They Could Chew: Rob Roberge tells the story of Nick Ray, a man whose addictions (alcohol, kinky sex, questionable friends) might only be cured by weaning him from oxygen.
0-06-074280-1 • On Sale February 2005

Men from Boys: A short story collection featuring some of the true masters of crime fiction, including Dennis Lehane, Lawrence Block, and Michael Connelly. These stories examine what it means to be a man amid cardsharks, revolvers, and shallow graves.
0-06-076285-3 • On Sale April 2005

Now Available:

Kinki Lullaby: The latest suspenseful, rapid-fire installment of **Isaac Adamson's** Billy Chaka series finds Billy in Osaka, investigating a murder and the career of a young puppetry prodigy. 0-06-051624-0

First Cut: Award-winning author **Peter Robinson** probes the darkest regions of the human mind and soul in this clever, twisting tale of crime and revenge. 0-06-073535-X

Night Visions: A young lawyer's shocking dreams become terribly real in this chilling, beautifully written debut thriller by **Thomas Fahy.** 0-06-059462-4

Get Shorty: **Elmore Leonard** takes a mobster to Hollywood—where the women are gorgeous, the men are corrupt, and making it big isn't all that different from making your bones. 0-06-077709-5

Be Cool: **Elmore Leonard** takes Chili Palmer into the world of rock stars, pop divas, and hip-hop gangsters—all the stuff that makes big box office.
0-06-077706-0

Available wherever books are sold, or call 1-800-331-3761.

Don't miss the next book by your favorite author.
Sign up now for AuthorTracker by visiting
www.AuthorTracker.com

PERENNIAL

An Imprint of HarperCollinsPublishers
www.harpercollins.com

DKA 1104